The
OREGON
VARIATIONS

STORIES

William L. Sullivan

Navillus Press
Eugene, Oregon

For Alison Lurie,
who believes in grandfathers

♭

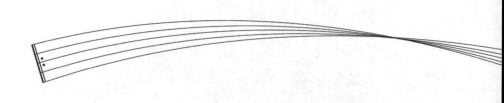

Our stories
Are trees
Inside out –
Stroll in a door
And leave

Published by the Navillus Press
1958 Onyx Street
Eugene, Oregon 97403

www.oregonhiking.com

Printed in Oregon, USA. All rights reserved. ISBN 9781939312044

Some of these stories have appeared previously elsewhere: "Quadvertising,"
"Mice," "The Secret Place," and "The Twins" in *Author's Bazaar;* and "The
Old Sea Lion and the Fisherman" in *Groundwaters.*

Cover: Steens Mountain above the Alvord Desert, and *Allow Me*, downtown
Portland's 1983 "Umbrella Man" sculpture by John Seward Johnson II.
Frontispiece: Drawing of the author's log cabin by Janell Sorensen.
Page 335: View from the log cabin kitchen by Janell Sorensen.

CONTENTS

ARIA FOR TENDERFEET

Jack limped out to the porch to check the road from Fossil again. If this was God's country, why was it so damned lonely?

Like an old backache, the solitude twinged every six months or so — usually when his son was coming, and always when he was late. This time Alan had promised to bring the grandkids in the early afternoon, and already twilight was filling up the John Day River canyon like syrup.

March evenings were a piece of magic in the Oregon desert, when the world balanced between seasons, and Jack was sorry his two young grandsons were missing it. A red stripe of sun flared a rimrock banner a mile uphill, where the Dobson Ranch ended and the sky began. Cliff swallows spiraled across that border from red to blue. The river muttered in the sagebrush shadows about distant snowmelt. A single cricket chirped. And the great dark coolness of the night, sweet with the tang of alfalfa and sage, slithered up around the ranch house like a ghost.

Five generations of Dobsons had held this ground since the 1860s, when the Indian lands of Eastern Oregon opened to settlement. Ezekiel Dobson, returning empty handed from the gold fields of John Day, strayed from The Dalles Military Wagon Road at a ford, followed the bank downstream, and fell in love with this riverbend. Jack's grandfather defied the Depression here, paying taxes with Merino sheep and sawing his own boards to build a house of dreams. Where was the Dobson, Jack wondered, to take up that legacy?

The big white eye of Canis Major was staring over the canyon when the headlights of Alan's imported hybrid finally shivered down the washboard gravel. The tires thrummed across the cattle guard, bounced in the pothole everyone else avoided, and dusted to a stop in front of the porch steps. Alan opened the door, lighting up the car like a bulb. The back seat was so jumbled with bags that Jack couldn't even see the kids at first.

"Sorry it got to be so late," Alan said, popping the trunk without even looking up. Although he had the high forehead and the trademark axe-blade nose of a Dobson, his tie and his rimless spectacles practically shouted that he was a librarian. Alan spent his days fielding online reference questions at a State Library computer in Salem.

"I understand," Jack lied, limping down the stairs, favoring as always his toeless left foot. He had never understood why his only son showed so little interest in the ranch. The day Alan graduated from Fossil High School he had driven across the mountains to Salem to start a summer job as an intern in the State Capitol. Instead of coming home that fall, he had gotten a scholarship at Willamette University. After his junior year abroad in Osaka, he had married Mari.

"Mari's still in the hospital, so I had to pack everything by myself. Then we had to stop in The Dalles to buy the kids ranch clothes, and by then they were so hungry we got tacos in Condon."

Jack stooped to look in the back seat window. He was always astonished to see how Misha and Tosh were changing as they grew, and to realize, despite their round faces and narrow eyes, that they were Dobsons. This time, asleep in a web of straps, the five and seven year olds seemed even more foreign. They were both wearing little cowboy hats, pearl-buttoned cowboy shirts, brand-new Levis, and little, pointy-toed cowboy boots.

Misha and Tosh — what kind of names were those for cowboys, Jack wondered? Alan had told him the names weren't even Japanese. If they ever came to Wheeler County for good, they'd be teased in school and laughed out of the rodeo grounds. When Alan and Mari had announced they were expecting another boy, Jack had lobbied hard for Ezekiel. They'd finally settled on Zeke, which was even better.

Alan set down a suitcase and put his hand on his father's shoulder. "This is for you, Dad, as a thank you."

"A thank you?"

Alan sighed. "I know how much the ranch means to you. So I've talked it up to them. They're all excited about being cowboys with Grampa. I can't tell you how grateful we are, taking them for two weeks on such short notice."

Jack looked at him, puzzled. "But we already talked about this. With the new baby, you and Mari are going to need some time alone to get things settled down."

Alan looked down and tightened his lips. "I couldn't tell you on the phone, Dad. There isn't going to be a new baby."

"What?"

"Zeke was blue, Dad. He never took a breath."

"My God. How is Mari?"

"She's going to be all right, but—" Alan's voice caught.

"But what?"

Alan nodded toward the back seat. "These are the only two grandchildren you're going to get."

Jack and Alan unloaded the car in silence. When only the sleeping boys were left, Jack whispered, "I'll take them straight to bed."

Alan shook his head. "They'd never forgive me. We'll have to wake them so I can say goodbye."

"Goodbye? Now?" Jack slowly closed the door until the dome light went out. Then he faced his son in the dark. "You can't drive back to Salem tonight. You wouldn't get there till four a.m., and you'd probably fall asleep and kill yourself first. What makes you so damned afraid to spend a night in your old room?"

Alan's voice was steady. "Mari's hurt, Dad. She needs me. And as for visiting, you know perfectly well I bring the family here twice a year. But what about you? You've never come to see the guest room I built for you in Salem. Not once."

Jack's shoulders sagged. Just a few years ago he had been right about everything. It had been Alan's job to listen and learn. But now that Jack lived alone and Alan had a family, the roles were reversed. How had that happened? Now it was Alan's turn to be right about everything, and the old man was supposed to listen and learn. It was no use explaining that a ranch was as demanding as a wife. Here he dealt with difficult births every week. He had sick steers to tend and calves to feed. How on earth could he go sit in a guest room in Salem?

Alan opened the car door. "Wake up, boys." He unbuckled Misha's seat belt and shook his arm. "Come on."

The older boy squinted against the light, squirming. His cowboy hat tipped loose and rolled into the foot well. Alan walked around the car, opened the other door, unbuckled Tosh, and lifted him out of his booster seat. "Let's all go inside now so Papa can say goodbye."

Jack picked up the fallen hat and led Misha by the hand to the porch.

"Where are we?" Misha whined.

"You're at the ranch, cowboy."

"Grampa? Did you get a puppy like you said?"

Another sore point. Jack's sixteen-year-old Australian shepherd, Beulah, had passed away in the winter. She had simply gone out to the hill overlooking the cattle pen, laid her head on her paws as if to keep watch, and died. He'd told the grandkids over the phone that he was going to get a puppy. But when it came right down to it, he didn't have the heart to replace Beulah. She had been the smartest dog ever.

"Not exactly," he told Misha. "Instead I decided to tame the barn cat. I call him Mr. Jones."

"A cat? I wanted a puppy."

The floorboards creaked and the screen door banged behind them. Then they were in the parlor with the dusty maroon sofa, the juniper burl coffee table, the threadbare fake Persian rug, the reed organ that hadn't worked for forty years, and the familiar mingled scents of old magazines, pine woodsmoke, and mice.

Alan faced the boys at arm's length. "OK, all your things are set up in the bunkroom. Misha, you're in charge of Tosh. Both of you, behave yourself and do whatever Grampa tells you. Understand?"

Misha nodded bravely, but Tosh began to cry. He buried his face in Alan's crotch. "Papa! Don't go away!"

"I'll be back in a week or two, depending on how fast Mama gets well. You can call my cell phone whenever you want, OK?"

Alan peeled Tosh loose and gave the boy's hand to Jack. "I have to take care of Mama now. You two be good, OK?" Then he turned and opened the screen door.

Tosh jerked at the end of Jack's arm like a leashed dog after a squirrel. "No, Papa! Don't go!" The boy tugged Jack out onto the porch.

Jack had seen this tearful farewell coming. Was it really what Alan wanted? To put on a show? To prove the boys loved him?

Alan pressed a button on the car's dash, starting the engine's faint hybrid hum. Then his window whirred down. "G'bye! Love you both!"

By now Tosh was bouncing up and down, crying, "No! No! No!" Even Misha had tears and a quivering frown.

The red taillights gradually shrank to a single dot, climbing the canyon. When the dot finally disappeared among the stars, Jack suggested, "How about we make some cocoa before heading to bed?"

Tosh clutched the porch post with a defiant grunt. "Uhhn!"

Misha started to wipe his eyes, but then he suddenly ducked. "What was that?"

"What?"

"A giant black thing!" Misha looked up at the dark corners of the porch. A shadow fluttered. "There!"

"That's just a bat," Jack explained. "They catch the moths that come to the porch light in the evening."

Tosh sounded interested. "A bat?"

"Bats eat bugs. They don't hurt people, they help."

For a while the boys stared, watching for movement. Then a yip from across the river made Misha turn. "That sounded like Beulah! You said she's dead."

Tosh clutched the porch post tighter. "Do dogs have ghosts?"

"Well, I don't know," Jack admitted. If any dog did, it would have been his clever Australian shepherd. "But I can tell you that wasn't a dog. It was a coyote."

A pack answered from a much closer field, definitely on this side of the John Day. Between the yips sailed the eerie, half-insane howl of the alpha. Even Jack, who had heard this song a thousand times, felt the hair rise up on the back of his neck.

By now both boys were clinging to their grandfather. Tosh asked, "What do coyotes eat?"

"Mice, mostly. Jackrabbits, if they can catch them."

"Grampa!" Misha gasped, pointing down the stairs. A pair of green eyes gleamed from the dead grass.

"It's all right." Jack put his arms around the boys. "That's just Mr. Jones, coming for dinner."

The black, short-haired cat slunk from step to step, his ears perked, watching the boys suspiciously.

"Mr. Jones?" Tosh asked. "What does he eat?"

"Come on, I'll show you." Jack opened the screen door. The cat shot through at an angle. Jack followed across the parlor to the kitchen, where an enamel coffeepot boiled at the back of a massive woodstove. Jack's mother had installed an electric range when the powerline arrived in the 60s, but Jack still preferred the cast iron version, shiny with nickel-plated vents, claw feet, and curlicues. The electric range was just a machine you turned on, but the woodstove was a companion you fed with care.

"Reow?" The black cat rubbed a shoulder against the refrigerator door, his tail a big question mark over his back.

"All right, already." Jack opened the refrigerator and took out a black plastic container. "This is how I tamed Mr. Jones. He grew up in a barn. Half wild, with no manners at all. But he became a house cat the day I taught him about chicken."

Jack set the plastic container on the table and removed the dome, revealing the bony carcass of what had once been a whole barbecued bird. "I drive into town every Friday for supplies. The grocery has a display right up front with these cooked chickens under heat lamps. One is enough for a whole weekend for me. But what am I supposed to do with the bones and skin? Tame cats, I say." Jack tore off a chunk and handed it to Misha. "Here, try with a wing."

Mr. Jones stood up, put his front paws on Misha's hip, and sniffed. When Misha set the wing on the floor Mr. Jones went to work, biting and shaking his head. Misha petted him. The cat purred as he ate.

"He's soft," Misha said.

"Let me try!" Tosh took an entire fatty tail from the container. Soon he too was petting the cat.

"I like him," Tosh said. "Why do you call him Mr. Jones?"

Jack had to think a moment. "I guess there was an old TV show about a detective named Barnaby Jones. The cat reminded me of that detective, always snooping around like he was trying to solve mysteries."

"But aren't black cats bad luck?" Misha asked.

"Maybe, but Mr. Jones isn't entirely black. See? One of his front paws is white."

The boys examined the paw with interest. Tosh asked, "How did that happen, that Mr. Jones got one white paw?"

Jack sat back in a kitchen chair. This was no time to lecture about genetics. "I guess I could tell you the story my grampa told me."

The boys looked up at him like puppies.

"Well, my grampa used to say black cats get white paws if they step in a pan of milk on a lucky day."

"Weird," Misha said.

"Only on lucky days?" Tosh knit his brow. "Is today a lucky day?"

Jack's first reaction was no. So far this day had been anything but lucky. First he had learned that his grandson Zeke had been born dead. Then his son Alan had fled the home ranch, leaving nothing but tears. If anyone was going to turn the awful luck of this day, it would have to be Jack himself. But how? He felt like a lonely old cowhand, trying to turn a frightened herd from the cliffs ahead.

"Yes," he heard himself say. "Yes, it is a lucky day."

"Why?"

"Because," Jack ran his hand over his jaw, trying to come up with something, anything. "Because it's the equinox."

"The what?" Tosh asked.

But Misha was already waving his hand, as if wanting to be called on next. "I know! I know! The equinox is March twenty-first. Grampa's right. My teacher said it really is like magic, because everywhere on earth is the same today, half night and half day."

Tosh thought about this a moment. "If today's a magic day, maybe we could make Mr. Jones' other paws turn white. Grampa, do you have a pan of milk?"

Jack cleared his throat. "Uh, sure." He had bought an extra gallon of milk, knowing the kids were coming. He had also planned a slew of activities — hiking and riding and eating — in the hopes that he might teach his grandkids to love this ranch as much as he did. Why not start by dipping a farm cat's feet in milk?

And so they spent the rest of the evening chasing Mr. Jones around the house. The cat had already eaten his chicken dinner, and without food as bait he was still a half-wild barn animal. The boys laughed, spooking the cat and spilling milk. Eventually Mr. Jones escaped outside by throwing himself against the screen door. Jack and the boys stood on the porch, staring out into the darkness where a black cat had merged with the night.

"It's time you boys went to bed," Jack said.

"But Grampa! We haven't caught Mr. Jones yet. And tonight's the magic night."

"He'll come back. He likes to sleep behind the stove. Look, we'll leave the pan of milk here in front of the door. Then when I let him in later, he'll step in it."

The boys were skeptical, but there didn't seem to be another plan. They walked back to the bunkroom and sat on the beds while Jack pulled the pointy little cowboy boots off their feet. Then they dressed in their pajamas and crawled in.

As Jack tucked them in Misha said, "That was fun, Grampa."

Tosh added sleepily, "Don't forget, will you? About Mr. Jones?"

"Get some sleep now. Tomorrow's going to be a busy day for Dobson Ranch cowboys."

Jack left a night light in the bunkroom, closed the door, went to the kitchen, and poured himself a shot of Monarch Canadian. He usually undressed in front of the stove. In winter it was the only warm place. Tonight he needed some inner warmth as well.

He pulled off his boots and stared at his mismatched feet. Perhaps it was taking off the boys' silly little boots and seeing their perfect toes that had made him think about his own accident. He had been about their age, running to go to his first day of school. He had been so proud that he didn't have to wear cowboy boots. He was going to school in new, store-bought Converse basketball shoes. He was going to be a basketball star and travel the world. He was so excited that he broke one of his parents' rules. A neighbor was going to pick him up at the paved road, two miles up the canyon. To save a few seconds, Jack had taken the forbidden shortcut behind the hen house. On the way he had stepped in a camouflaged coyote trap. The high-top shoes really were good for jumping, so he had nearly cleared the zigzag of the leg-hold's teeth. But the canvas had offered little protection when the teeth snapped shut on his toes.

Now as he looked down at the scarred club of his left foot, he wondered what a hospital in Salem might have done. Even then a skilled surgeon might have been able to sew toes back on. But the part-time GP in Fossil concentrated on his other job, as a large animal veterinarian. Jack had never been able to play basketball. He had never run again. He had been tied to a lonely ranch.

Jack finished his whisky, closed the stove vent, and switched off the lights. He was about to limp to his bedroom when he heard the familiar twang of cat claws on the screen. He'd let the damned cat in and out so many times since Beulah died that he could do it in his sleep. So he stumped across the dark parlor, opened the door, and pushed out the screen.

No cat. What the hell was the matter with Mr. Jones now?

Jack stepped out to look. And he felt his left foot splash into something cold.

Jack swore as he danced on one foot, trying to wipe the milk off his toeless stump. And of course that was when Mr. Jones saw his chance and dashed inside through Jack's legs, tripping him up so he fell backwards on his butt.

As Jack sat there on the floor, in the dark, he started to laugh. Bowled on his ass by a cat, tricked by an ancestor who'd never breathed, beset by midget Japanese cowboys in his own house — the whole day had been too crazy to be real. Maybe he'd fallen asleep in the porch swing that afternoon and was still napping. Maybe there was magic afoot after all. Shaking his head, he got up, closed the front door, and walked across the parlor to his bedroom.

The next morning, when Jacob Dobson awoke from uneasy dreams, he felt as if he had somehow been transformed in his bed. He looked at the clock and realized he had overslept. How was he going to inspire his grandchildren with the Dobson Ranch ethic if he didn't get up until nine? He threw the blanket aside, swung his legs to the cool wooden floor, sat up, and stared down in disbelief.

He had ten toes.

Not five, as he had had every morning for fifty years, but ten. Somehow in the night his disfigured left foot appeared to have re-grown. At first he assumed this was some kind of optical illusion, a visual trick that made his left foot mirror his right. To test this theory, he tried to move the imaginary new toes. They wiggled in response. But the sight was so odd, and the feeling so alien, that he might as well have been watching the wriggling legs of an up-turned beetle.

"Grampa! Grampa!" Misha and Tosh banged open his bedroom door. The smaller of the two boys clutched a sleepy black cat like a bag of beans. "It didn't work! Mr. Jones splashed milk all over the porch, but he still only has one white foot."

Jack looked at them open mouthed, suddenly remembering the cat, the story, and the milk.

"The magic didn't work!" Tosh said.

"Maybe it wasn't for the cat." Jack pointed to his toes. "Look at this."

The boys looked. "So what?"

"I seem to have ten toes," Jack explained.

The boys looked again at their grandfather. Then they exchanged a worried glance. Misha said, "Everyone has ten toes, Grampa."

Jack blinked. "Haven't you ever noticed that I limp when I walk?"

Tosh shrugged. "I don't know. Why?"

Had he never told them about his accident? Jack leaned down and felt his left foot. The toes seemed real. There were tiny hairs on the knuckle of the big toe. The middle toenail had a jagged edge that would snag socks. He stood up and shifted his weight from side to side. There was no pain, and no sense of imbalance.

Quickly Jack ran though the reasonable possibilities.

Perhaps he was still asleep. How could he check? He'd read in a magazine that clocks don't work in dreams. But the second hand on his bedside alarm clock was ticking along just fine. So this couldn't be a dream.

Perhaps the last fifty years had been a dream, and he was only now waking up to the real life he'd been living all along. But then how had he told time all those years without clocks? That didn't make sense either. The magazine article must have been crazy.

Crazy? Perhaps he was insane, and the whole world was a carousel of his own delusions.

Or could this all be part of a hypnotic trance? Once he'd ordered tapes from a cable TV channel and tried to teach himself hypnosis. He'd woken up a few times a little confused, but that was years ago.

Perhaps —

"Grampa?" A small worried voice brought him back to the ranch house. "What's for breakfast?"

Here was a question he could answer. To hell with toes. Even if he was dreaming or crazy, hungry grandsons came first. "We'll have a cowboy breakfast, boys — bacon and eggs."

"Bacon!" Misha looked hurt. "Have you forgotten? Tosh and I don't eat meat."

Jack had in fact blanked on this, probably because it didn't seem to fit with reality either. How could anyone be a vegetarian on a cattle ranch?

"Then we'll go with eggs and pancakes. Just give me a minute to get organized here. You two get dressed and I'll light the stove."

Jack put on a fresh pair of jeans and a blue work shirt. When he pulled on his cowboy boots, however, the left one jammed. He'd always kept a sock wadded up in the toe of that boot so his foot wouldn't slide around. Now he simply took out the padding and the boot fit fine.

With a day's worth of ranch chores ahead, he really didn't have time for any more nonsense. He quickly lit a fire in the woodstove, whipped up a batch of pancake batter, and soon was directing the whole breakfast square dance—the sizzle of eggs in butter, the strut of steaming hot cocoa, and the dos-i-dos of flapjacks on the griddle.

Misha and Tosh packed it away with the appetite of a hay crew. "What's next, Grampa?" Tosh asked.

"Next comes breakfast for everyone else on the ranch. First up, the bummer calf. Come on, you'll need sticks."

They needed the sticks not for the calf, but rather for its mother, a range cow that had gotten mastitis. Although she couldn't produce milk, she insisted on hanging around the ranch house to be near her calf. Eventually she had learned to lift the gate latch with a horn so she could graze the green circle of front lawn. She was big and had a frightening, crooked horn, but she was so skittish that she shied at the wave of a twig. Delighted when they discovered the power of their sticks, the boys were soon bopping her backwards towards the gate. She lifted her tail and spurted frantic green blobs of poop like grenades.

Jack laughed so hard at this rodeo clown act that he forgot to limp. Meanwhile the calf was bawling at him from the shed. Jack took the boys inside and showed them how to mix milk powder and water in a bucket. The calf wobbled up on unsteady legs, stared at the boys with wide brown eyes, and jerked back. Jack had to let the calf suck his finger to trick it into tasting the milk. Then it found the bucket and slurped it empty while the boys held on. Finally the calf looked up in alarm, its whiskers white.

"Where's its Papa?" Tosh asked.

"He's with the rest of the herd, two miles up Painted Canyon. We'll take the truck to feed them next."

Misha said, "Then the bummer calf is like us."

That made Jack pause. "How so?"

Misha looked embarrassed. "Well, his mother's sick and his father's gone, but at least you're taking care of him."

Jacked rinsed out the bucket without reply. He didn't like this comparison. Bummer calves were too tame and weak to use for breeding stock. Usually he sent them to slaughter in the fall.

"Let's go back to the house," he said.

At the gate Tosh said, "Race you, Grampa!"

Jack winced. They should know he couldn't—or wait. He eyed the porch, a hundred yards ahead.

"Ready, set," Misha said. "Go!"

The boys took off like foals. Jack pushed forward with his right foot and marveled when his left responded. Right, left—could he really remember this after fifty years? The boys' hands flailed like whirligigs as they ran, but Jack pumped his arms like pistons. Impossible! Halfway to the house he actually passed Tosh. Gaining fast on the older boy, Jack realized he didn't want to get there first. He slowed and gasped, although he was far too exhilarated to be tired.

Just ahead him Tosh triumphantly tagged the porch railing. "Beat you, Grampa! We won!"

Jack bent over with his hands on his knees to catch his breath. His head was spinning, but not from exhaustion. He had run! For the first time in years, he had run. And although he had tried to let the boys win, the truth was just the opposite. He was the winner. By some miracle, these children had let him run.

"Let's go feed the rest of the cows," Misha said.

"Hold your horses, cowboy. First I've got to pack us some lunch." Jack went into the kitchen, fixed cheese sandwiches, and stowed them in a backpack along with three cans of soda. Then he loaded the kids in his Chevy—an old yellow pickup that didn't hum like Alan's hybrid. It pinged so loud you knew it had a heart. A big old star in the windshield sent out spidery cracks like a road map. A missing fender turned the front right tire into a gap tooth. A rusty coathanger served as antenna, although the only reception in the canyon was a Spanish language station in Yakima, and then only at night.

Jack brushed straw off the front seat, fished up three sets of seat belts, and buckled everyone in. Then he drove half a mile to a pole shed surrounded by metal dinosaurs—a century of Dobson swathers, balers, hay rakes, and tractors. He backed up to an Aztec pyramid of compressed alfalfa.

"We need six bales," he told the boys as they got out.

They clambered up the stair-stepped side of the stack. Jack slapped hay hooks into either end of a fifty-pound bale, yanked it loose, and set it in front of them. "Roll it off the edge into the truck. Try not to hit the hood, and whatever you do, don't fall."

The boys had to work hard to tip the square bale at all. Their feet slipped on the straw and got caught in cracks. But eventually they thumped it forward to the edge of the stack. Tosh held back, afraid of the brink. Misha pushed the bale with his foot. It fell fifteen feet, glanced off the tailgate, arched its back like an angry cat, popped its orange twine, and spewed alfalfa across the barn floor.

Jack nodded. "Try again."

Misha lined up the next bale six feet to the left.

Tosh dared to peer over the edge. "You're gonna hit the roof."

Misha pushed the bale. It hit the roof with a bong. Alfalfa sprayed out sideways, mostly into the bed.

For the next four bales the boys worked together, arguing about spin and trajectory. Three bales actually landed intact, and the last one hit so squarely that the truck bed bounced, squeaking like a rusty box mattress.

Taking the bales out of the truck was not so much fun. The feed lot in Painted Canyon was a wasteland of dust, cow pies, and flies. Bulls with pitchfork horns and buffalo shoulders eyed them suspiciously, as if the boys might be coyotes that needed trampling. Mud and manure had clogged the spring that supplied the watering trough, so Jack had to spend most of an hour shoveling muck. When he finally washed off he found the boys in the pickup, slumped on the seat with boredom.

"Why do you think this place is called Painted Canyon?" Jack asked.

"I don't know," Misha said. His voice announced that he didn't care.

"Because of paint?" Tosh suggested.

"That's right, because of paint. Indian paintings thousands of years old. Not many people have ever seen them. Want to?"

Misha stuck with his bored-to-death voice. "Are they hard to see?"

"Yes, because they're in a cave." Jack put on the backpack with the lunch. "You coming?"

"OK." Tosh jumped down from the truck.

Misha rolled his eyes. "It's better than waiting here."

"First let's fix your pants." Jack reached down, yanked the pant legs out of Misha's boots, and pulled them down on the outside.

"Hey!" Misha complained. "That way covers up my boots."

"Only a tenderfoot wears boots over his pants."

The trail scrambled along red scree high above a green crescent of riverbend. The last time Jack had been to the cave he had gone with a ranger from the John Day Fossil Beds, the National Monument that bordered the Dobson Ranch to the south. Jack had struggled then, limping as the ranger told him about a Nature Conservancy offer to buy ranchland along the river. He'd been so angry about wasting ranchland for wilderness that he'd stumbled. Now the climb seemed easy.

They crawled up into the cave's opening, a red mouth in a long wall of black cliffs. Swallows screamed overhead like ricocheting bullets. The overhang wasn't deep, and barely tall enough for Jack to stand up. The boys explored the entire cavern in two minutes. When their eyes had grown used to the murk, they found the red figures painted on the black ceiling: two spirals connected by a branching loop.

"Weird," Misha said. "Looks like a psycho beetle."

"Yeah. A bug," Tosh added.

Jack had always thought the petroglyph resembled a lizard, but he said nothing. He unpacked lunch on a flat rock. The boys went straight for the pop, thirsty from the hike in the desert.

Eventually Misha asked, "Why would someone paint a beetle in a cave?"

"This was a vision quest site," Jack said. "When Indian boys turned thirteen they'd come to a place like this and sit here for days, without eating or drinking."

"They'd just sit?" Misha asked.

"That's right. If they stayed long enough, eventually they'd see a vision of a spirit. Maybe it would be the spirit of Owl or Coyote or Blue Jay. Whatever it was, it would guide them for the rest of their lives."

"I guess here they saw a bug," Tosh said, his mouth full of cheese sandwich.

Misha, however, set down his sandwich and looked silently out the cave entrance at the canyons below.

That night Jack built a bonfire in front of the ranch house so the boys could roast marshmallows for s'mores. It had been a good day—a miraculous day, really. Sparks from the fire shivered up to join the stars of the desert night. The coyote pack from the night before had moved downriver, a distant choir.

Jack showed the boys how to whittle points on willow sticks with a jackknife. Then he demonstrated browning a marshmallow over coals. Tosh's marshmallow caught fire, but Jack blew it out fast enough to salvage it. In fact, wedged between graham crackers with a square of chocolate, the crunchy, burnt marshmallow was surprisingly delicious. Soon they were all burning marshmallows and laughing. Misha tried to put out a flame by whipping his stick and accidentally launched a fiery marshmallow overhead. The comet arced upward, paused, and then blazed back toward them. Whoops!

When the marshmallows were gone the boys sprawled sleepily

on a blanket and poked the dying fire with their sticks, sending more sparks to the stars.

"Tell us a story, Grampa," Misha said. "About when you were our age."

Jack leaned back into the shadows. When he was their age, he had stepped in a leg-hold trap. Instead of going to the first grade, he had gone to a doctor who had sewn up his stump like a football. After that, school had been a nightmare. Kids had laughed at him, mimicked his limp, and called him "Crip." In high school he had watched from the sidelines as the other boys played basketball. Once, at the Jefferson County Fair in Madras, he'd stopped by the Navy recruiter's booth, just for curious. The crewcut officer in dress whites there had told him that yes, Vietnam was a tropical paradise, but no, they didn't need disabled men, even as ship's cooks. Finally he had found his peace with Marabel, a girl who had contracted polio from a sugar cube in the third grade. She fought shortness of breath for twenty years at the Dobson Ranch until the air finally gave out. This was not a story he wanted the boys to hear.

"Grampa?" Misha asked.

"Beulah," Jack said. "You remember her?"

"Sure," Misha said.

Tosh nodded uncertainly. For a five year old, a dead dog is a dim ghost.

"When I was your age, an Australian sheep shearer named Dave Vaughn brought a shepherd dog to the ranch. Sparky was a long-haired Australian dog, motley as an Appaloosa and smart as a whip. He could run on the backs of cows, change direction when you whistled, and nip bulls till they stayed in line. We'd never seen anything like it. Sparky's granddaughter was Beulah."

"Did Beulah ever have puppies?" Misha asked.

"I'm afraid not." Jack stared into the fire. "And Vaughn was here just the one summer. He said everything is backwards in Australia. The man in the moon frowns upside down. Orion stands on its head. People drive on the left-hand side. Summer is winter."

"Did he take Sparky back to Australia?"

"He took Sparky with him, but I don't think they went to

Australia. He said they were on a walkabout. It's like a vision quest, I guess, but instead of sitting in one place to find your spirit, you keep moving around. Vaughn said he was planning to go all the way around the world, if he had to."

Tosh said, "I've been around the world."

Jack looked at the five year old with surprise. Then he realized it was true. "You went to Japan to see your other grandparents."

"Yeah." Tosh yawned. "It's more fun here."

"Didn't you like Japan?"

Tosh just yawned again.

Misha said, "It was kind of lonely. People stared at us. Kids pointed. They said we talk like babies and have big noses."

Jack tightened his lips, embarrassed that he had assumed his grandsons would fit in among the Japanese. Now when he looked at them he recognized the Dobson nose. The family's trademark axe blade lay buried in their faces like a tomahawk.

Tosh nodded forward, his eyes closed. It had been a long day on the ranch.

"Time for bed, cowboys," Jack said. He wrapped Tosh in the blanket and carried him to the house.

Misha followed a step behind. "Grampa? Am I a tenderfoot?"

Jack stopped. "No," he said. "You're not."

After putting the boys to bed Jack wandered back into the yard, suddenly afraid to sleep. He stared into the embers of the dying fire and shivered. That morning he had woken up whole, mysteriously released from a trap that held him since he was six.

The glow of a hidden moon lit the silhouettes of junipers on the canyon rim to the east. A breath of cold night air reddened the coals at his feet. Jack loved the spirits of the Dobson Ranch. But he had never before been able to run away from them.

The moon sailed clear of the rimrock, painting the ranch house with what looked like milk. And a silver cat paced before the screen door, waiting.

THE EASTBANK ELEGIES

(OVERHEARD ON THE PORTLAND ESPLANADE)

But I had it done and he was like
A residue of something
Collected at the golf show
How does he keep a straight face?
I'm glad I'm out of that relationship

All the kids were in the house
Like chillin' right there
Once a techno-development comes out
Now who bothers to grow
Eleven things

Ever since the device came to China
Nobody could be just, you know
Omigod, do you get any days off?
Like wholly unstructured relaxing time
A half life

So it's going to be happening at my house
Unless you checked that off your list
Let's just say he doesn't like her either

Look who's laughing now
I love my job. Not

Very mushy brains, I've got
A scene with Jane Fonda
Next you're talking to the dog
Ick!
I'm ready to jump

THE SECRET PLACE

For Rick and Laura's third date they joined a Friday night art walk in downtown Eugene. Then they slipped off to dinner at Cafe Xerxes, precariously near to Rick's apartment. Laura toyed with the graham crust of their shared chocolate decadence torte, buying time.

"I read in this magazine," she began, already wishing she hadn't admitted it was from a magazine. Somehow that sounded too supermarket-hausfrau. "If you're going to be soul mates, you shouldn't have secrets."

"I don't have secrets," Rick said. "Certainly not from you."

Laura looked up at him. She had powerful blue eyes, even without makeup, and she could see him reel. That she still had this effect on men gladdened her more than any compliment he could have offered.

"It's not just about sharing secrets," Laura went on. "It's about secret places."

"Secret places?"

"Everyone has a secret place. Somewhere you retreat when times get tough. A place where you're safe from the troubles of the world. Don't you have a place like that?"

He thought a moment. "I do. But I'm not sure you want to go there. It's not the first thing you'd choose to share, no matter how brave you are."

Now it was Laura's turn to ponder. Would he laugh if she told him about her own secret place? He'd think she was living in the past, which wasn't true at all. It was so easy to make the wrong impression.

Suddenly she feared that she had spoiled the evening. Only crumbs remained of the decadent dessert. In another minute Rick would ask for the bill, and they would argue over who should pay, and she would ride the bus home alone. Then she would be where she began, a forty-year-old Springfield mother with two troubling teenagers and a merciless alarm clock. When it jumped up jangling Monday morning she would put on green scrubs and drive to her job as a CAT scan technician. Some things you cannot change.

"I'd like some decaf," she said firmly, as if she were announcing a decision to join the Marines.

Rick raised a finger to signal a waiter.

"It's so expensive here," Laura said, looking down. "Can't you make us something at your apartment?"

By the time they had climbed the stairs to his garret room on Ferry Street her natural shyness had returned. In movies the actors tore off their clothes before they were even inside the door. Laura found herself unable to take off her coat.

The chill of his bachelor studio didn't help. Rick had been married twice, but you wouldn't know it by looking around. The rims and spokes of half-built bicycle wheels cluttered a drafting table in the middle of the living room. Against one wall stood an exercise bicycle with a big tool box. A couch hunkered against another wall. A brick-and-board bookshelf offered nothing but outdoor guidebooks. When she peered through the kitchen doorway she saw a counter with empty beer bottles from obscure craft breweries.

The warmest spot in his cave was the refrigerator, where magnets supported crayon drawings signed with endearing clumsiness by Evan, his five-year-old son. The boy also grinned from half a dozen soccer team photos. But even this domestic collage left Laura uneasy. Several of the photos featured a beautiful blond woman with her hands on the boy and her brown eyes on Rick.

Suddenly Laura wanted out. She looked toward the door, her escape route blocked by more than just an exercise bicycle.

"I know what you're thinking," Rick said. He walked to the kitchen and turned on a coffee machine.

"You do?"

"You're wondering why a guy who bicycles so much has an exercise machine in his living room."

This was so far from her thoughts that she blinked. What did she really know about Rick? They had been introduced by a mutual friend at a party where a local guidebook author was showing travel videos. Rick was single and had a steady job in a bike shop. They had agreed to take a Saturday bike ride together to prowl the antique shops of Coburg. On that trip they had laughed at retro Barbies and shared an Oakshire IPA in their sweaty Lycra bike clothes and it had been fun. They had parted with a lovely little kiss. But in retrospect, they had learned little about each other, outside of the mandatory scorecard of exes and children. Laura had one ex and two kids. For Rick, the tally was two and one. Judging from his apartment, she could guess why he had trouble staying married.

"Things aren't what they seem," Rick said.

"No?"

"No." Rick walked to the exercise bicycle and opened the tool box mounted on the handlebars. Inside were several dozen glass bowls, nested inside each other on their sides, arranged by size. Together they looked like a gigantic glass pine cone — or maybe an insulator for a power station.

"What is it?" she asked, afraid that the device might be dangerous, or that he might be bonkers, or both.

"A glass harmonica. Benjamin Franklin invented them. I could —"

The coffee maker interrupted from the kitchen with an orgasmic gasp and a long, steamy sigh.

"Do you like Irish coffee?" Rick asked. He went back to the kitchen and took two glass mugs from a cabinet.

"Yes, but —" Laura pointed to the glass contraption. "You play music with a bicycle?"

He laughed, pouring a finger of Bailey's into each mug. "All the bicycle does is turn the glass bells. To play you have to touch them with your fingers."

"A glass harmonica," she repeated. "How did you get it?"

Rick poured a layer of cream onto the Irish coffees. "The story starts when my first wife died."

"I thought you were divorced."

"From Katherine? No." He gave her a mug of coffee. Then he lifted his own cup, took a sip, and licked a mustache of cream from his upper lip. "Katherine thought she had beaten her cancer before we got married. Still, that's why we didn't have children. She struggled twelve years, and then — well, then that was it."

"I'm sorry."

"I wanted a fresh start, but all I knew was bicycling. So I decided to bicycle somewhere crazy. I'd follow the longest river in North America from its start to its end."

Laura was still standing in the kitchen with her coat on, but the spiked coffee and the story had reduced her urge to run. "You biked the Mississippi?"

"Actually I started at Yellowstone, which is longer than just following the main Mississippi stem. But yeah, I ended up in New Orleans. I dreamed I'd find my new beginning at the end of the river."

"What did you find?"

"My second wife, Rita." Rick frowned.

Laura swirled her coffee. "I thought you were going to tell me about a glass harmonica."

"I am. You see, as soon as Evan was born, Rita stopped noticing that I exist. It turned out that she'd already reconnected with her old high school boyfriend. Anyway, when she finally demanded a divorce I decided to go bicycle the Danube."

"Another very long river."

"Too long. I only had enough vacation time to do the German-speaking part. I started in the Black Forest, rode down through Ulm, and ended up in Vienna, imagining I'd find my pot of gold there."

"Another wife?" Laura hadn't wanted this to sound so brutal. By way of apology she took off her coat.

Rick finished his coffee. "I didn't find anything at first. Nobody would talk to me. I went to museums. Finally I heard a demonstration of a glass harmonica and thought, that's it. I'll make one of those."

Laura went back to the living room for a closer look at the array of nesting glass bowls. If he had really built this instrument, he must have learned a lot about glassblowing. "How does it work?"

Rick sat on the bicycle and began pedaling. A loop of chain below the tool box made the row of bowls start spinning. The glass rims glistened, wetted by a reservoir of water in the bottom of the box.

When he touched his finger to the rim of a bowl an unearthly tone swelled across the room. To Laura, it sounded like the singing of an angel from a world beyond the grave.

"Mozart was so taken with the glass harmonica that he wrote a piece for it," Rick said. "This one I made up." When he touched the bowls again, two angels began singing a wordless harmony.

Laura had never heard such intoxicating tones from glass. Certainly not on those Christmas Eves as a child when her Danish uncle Holger had tuned three crystal goblets by drinking beer from them until he could play a boozy version of "Mary Had a Little Lamb" on the rims with his thumb. Nor in college, when her roommate's Hawaiian boyfriend had filled their dorm room with a marijuana haze before rubbing a Tibetan singing bowl into an om-like drone.

She sat on the sofa and closed her eyes, swimming in the melody as if it were a long, exotic river. When the last of the vitreous tones died away she opened her eyes to find that Rick was sitting beside her on the sofa.

"Amazing music," she said. "Somehow it explains a lot."

"I told you my story," he replied. "Your turn."

She looked down. "It's not much. I'm not musical. I married right out of Thurston High School."

"And? Come on, tell me about him."

Laura sighed. "Jerold was a welder who spent a lot of time watching sports on TV. To jinx teams during big football games he'd make me wear a yellow T-shirt inside out, braless."

Rick nodded. "Sounds interesting. What went wrong?"

"Well, all the times he said he was at sports bars he was really watching dancers at Wiggles. When I confronted him, he agreed it was time to move out. That left me with Matthew and Wendy. Now Matt's trying to be a heavy metal guitarist. Wendy's a moody fourteen-year-old who gives me snarky advice about clothes and hair."

"But you listen to her."

Laura smiled. "Is it that obvious?"

"You're a vision. I don't know who is smarter, your daughter or you."

Rick leaned in to kiss her, and to Laura's own astonishment, this now seemed like a good idea.

An hour later, lying beside him in his bedroom, she felt as if she were one of the glass bells, ringing all over. She knew she would have to catch the bus to Springfield, but she wasn't ready to go home quite yet. Rick was a man of many layers.

She put her head on his chest. "I'm feeling brave. Tell me about your secret place."

Rick gave a sigh that lifted her head. "It's a lake."

"A lake? Where?"

He sighed again. "When my brother Nicholas and I were kids our father got a job installing wiring at Army bases in Germany. I learned German. Nick learned to love the military. When we got back to Oregon Nick graduated from high school and signed up with the Army. Just before he left for boot camp, Nick and I took a backpacking trip to the loneliest place we could imagine. We'd studied a map of the Mt. Washington Wilderness and found a nameless lake. It's insanely remote, on a lava island."

"What's a lava island?" Laura worried already that she might end up trekking to this insanely remote outpost. She didn't care much for camping, even at regular car campgrounds.

"A patch of forest that got left in the middle of an old lava flow. To get there we had to scramble two miles through a desert of jagged black rock. But then there was this lake where no one had ever been. No campfire rings, no footprints. A deer with big antlers walked up and stared at us, completely unafraid. We swam naked, set up our tent, and watched the stars come out over Mt. Washington."

She rolled aside to rest her head on the pillow. "Do you and your brother go to this secret lake a lot?"

Rick's voice was flat. "Nick died later that summer in a helicopter crash."

"Oh! I wouldn't have asked if —"

"No, no," Rick interrupted. "No secrets. That's what you said, and you're right. I told you about my secret place. Now you've got to tell me about yours."

Laura squirmed to look at the bedside clock. She swung her legs to the floor. "If I'm not back by midnight, Wendy's going to turn into a pumpkin."

"Sorry, my love." Rick wagged his finger. "First you have to tell where your secret place is."

She stepped into her panties, pulled them up, and sat back on the bed. "It's not a where, it's a when."

"A when? How does that work?"

"My favorite place is my thirteenth birthday." From his gaze she could tell he was distracted by her lack of a shirt. She picked her bra off the floor. "When I turned thirteen my parents let me take my best friend Pam with us to a beach cabin in Pacific City. It turned out the Anderson brothers from Marcola High School were staying in the cabin next door. Mike and Mark were fifteen and sixteen. Normally they wouldn't have noticed us. I mean, that was the first summer we could wear two-piece bathing suits with a purpose."

"You've grown up a lot," Rick said.

She shot him a warning glance, clipping her bra strap behind her back. "The Anderson boys taught us how to ride skim boards on the water as a wave goes out. They built a bonfire for us on the beach, roasted marshmallows, and gave us each our first real kiss."

Laura felt her face redden — as much at the memory of Mark Anderson as at the fact that she was pulling on her pants in Rick's bedroom. She continued, "Anyway, when we got back to the cabin, my parents had a birthday party all set up, with mint chocolate cake and presents. Pam gave me half of a broken-heart charm, engraved 'Best Friends Forever.' Then we stayed up late, playing Ouija by candlelight."

"What did the Ouija board predict?" Rick asked.

"Alluring fates with the Anderson boys." She smiled at him over her shoulder as she buttoned up her blouse.

He scooted over on the bed, put his hands on her shoulders, and kissed the back of her neck. "Do you really wish you were thirteen again?"

The nuzzling tickled, and she laughed. "There's a lot of my thirteenth year I wouldn't want to do over. But when things go wrong, I think about how happy I was that day."

"Your secret place is tricky," Rick mused. "I can't go to the past with you. I suppose I could rent us a beach cabin in Pacific City."

"And maybe I could backpack across the lava to your secret lake." She kissed him on the cheek. "But right now I have to go home."

He followed her to the door with a bath towel wrapped around his waist. They agreed to meet at Cafe Yumm for lunch on Wednesday. Then they thanked each other for the evening, kissed again, and wished each other sweet dreams.

But their dreams that night were not sweet.

In her dream Laura discovered that the boys in the beach cabin next door were not the Andersons, but rather a sixteen-year-old Rick and his eighteen-year-old brother Nick. Gangly and pimpled, Rick laughed at Laura's formless swimsuit. Worse, Nick surprised Pam on a path in the dunes and kissed her by force. That night, Pam viciously allowed the Ouija board to predict that Laura would end up marrying Rick. Laura retaliated by having the board say Nick would die in the Army. They both went off to bed in tears.

Alone in his Eugene apartment, Rick dreamed that he was climbing across a lava field. Halfway to his secret lake he found a deflated happy-face balloon. Trash like that could have blown in from Eugene, he told himself. But then he noticed a Budweiser can in the cinders. He heard the voices long before he reached the lake — six men at a bonfire on the shore. Behind them, hanging from a pole they had spiked between two pines, was the antlered deer.

On Wednesday, when Rick was pedaling along the Willamette River bike path to meet Laura, he was so busy watching the reflections of the water through the cottonwood trees that he missed the turnoff to the cafe. The rush of the river riffles seemed to be playing a counterpoint to the hum of his spinning spokes.

He pulled over on the riverbank and watched the whitewater. He would turn back to meet Laura, of course.

But what would happen, he wondered, if he could keep going upstream? Rivers have only one mouth, but they have countless sources. Perhaps he'd been going about his relationships backwards all his life. Perhaps, instead of looking for the right ending, he should have been bicycling against the current, searching for the secret place where the river begins.

When Rick arrived at the cafe, Laura wasn't yet there. And when she did show up, five minutes later, the look in her face told him it was only to say goodbye.

Roller Girls

"Let the uncivil war begin!"

The announcer's voice echoed across the Oaks Park skating rink. The crowd's roar, a tide of adrenalin and lust, leaked through the locker room doors to Lady Nightshade and her team.

Nightshade straightened her nun's robes nervously. Fans loved it that Portland's two women's roller derby leagues were so evenly matched. But Nightshade found it disturbing. In last year's bout the Vampirates had anticipated too many of their strategies. She had sensed betrayal. And now Mutiny was skating on the other side.

Nightshade put the palms of her hands together. "Let us go slaughter the undead."

"A-women," the thirteen nuns beside her replied.

Nightshade rammed the door open with her shoulder and led the team, their black-and-white gowns fluttering like moths, into the glare of spotlights.

"Direct from Beaver Town," the announcer's voice rose above the clamor, "The stars of Oregon's first roller derby league, please give it up for the Filthy Habits."

A pipe organ rumbled from hidden speakers while the nuns skated twice around the rink, as pious and orderly as schoolgirls in a Madeline children's book. Then the organ crashed into a cacophonous chord. Shrieking guitar riffs launched an electric beat. In unison the nuns ripped off their habits, revealing gold lamé hot pants, spiked black halter tops, black knee pads, and constellations of tattoos.

"Captain of the Filthy Habits, number Sweet Sixteen, she's a micro lightning bolt of unholy speed, here's Ratty Iron Thighs."

Ratty gave a shy wave. Impish, tiny, with a mouse-brown ponytail, she had always gone by the nickname Ratty, even before she quit the Olympic ice skating team and became a software engineer for Intel in Hillsboro.

She was the second fastest skater in the state, so she almost had to be captain, even if applause gave her hives.

"Leading the pack, it's the hot Goth Vice Captain, number F-17, Lady Nightshade."

Nightshade pumped both fists in the air. She loved attention, and as her mother always said, if she couldn't get good attention, she went for the bad. Why else, her father said, would she have pierced her beautiful child-like face seventeen times with studs and rings, tattooed her rosy cheeks with batwings, tortured her light brown hair into red and blue ridges, and painted her doe eyes with the black sockets of a corpse? Why else, her mother asked, would she have thrown away a potentially promising career in laptop repair to become manager of Tickles, the Beaverton franchise of a sex shop chain?

Why indeed.

Nightshade's parents were not among the cheering fans in the bleachers of the old roller rink hall that night. She knew this without squinting. But she could also feel the electric proximity of Mutiny.

And as so often when she thought of Mutiny, Nightshade remembered the look on her parents' faces when she came home from the first day of school and asked if they would buy her a Barbie doll.

"A Barbie?" Her father set down the skateboard he had been airbrushing. In those early years he still wore his Humboldt County ponytail, and he hadn't yet traded his hemp culottes for Dockers.

"Barbies are anatomical monstrosities. They're consumer shit from a television's anus."

"Hush, Shawn," her mother said. "I'm sure it's just something she heard about from a new friend at school. We want her to make friends."

"We should never have come to Oregon."

Nightshade's mother shook back her long black hair, the way she did when she wanted to change the subject, or draw attention to herself, or both. Then she steered Nightshade by the shoulder toward the kitchen. "Let's make fruit smoothies and you can tell me all about school."

But it was too late. The doe-eyed, rosy-cheeked love child had discovered the first of many magic buttons that could juice her hippie parents. It was even more satisfying than Osterizing celery into green mush. The only toy she begged for that Christmas was Malibu Barbie. After her bedtime she overheard long discussions about the freedom to make mistakes and explore even the darkest corners of one's inner self.

When she opened the pink box on Christmas morning, her heart was beating like a pepper-pepper-pepperpot skip rope. By then she had seen the commercials on a friend's TV, and although she hated the singsong hype and the beaming child actors, the doll itself had moaned to her.

Beside their living Yule tree, with its garlands of popcorn and cranberries, the long-legged surfer babe in high-heeled flipflops had seemed like an alien scout from a dangerous planet. Nightshade unwound the twist-ties that chained Barbie to her pink prison. And then, even though her parents were watching — or maybe because — she slowly removed the striped coverup and the little sparkly bikini.

"Hot on the shiny gold tail of our deadly Nightshade," the announcer continued, "Say hello to some of Beaver Town's baddest blockers, Rhonda Roadkill, Quarter Pound Her, Pain Mixer, Scare Bear, Thunderpuss . . ."

That night, after Nightshade's parents had eggnogged themselves to sleep on the futon in front of the open wood stove, she took Barbie out the back door into a night of frozen stars and crunchy grass. She unlocked the workshop where her dad built custom skateboards — the business he had brought from California.

Nightshade flipped on the light, walked to the workbench, and turned on the disk sander. Her father had taught her to sand wooden dowels into knitting needles. Now the wheel hummed menacingly. She held Naked Barbie, feeling the slender legs, the apricot buttocks, the bug-eyed breasts. Then she turned Barbie's chest toward the spinning sander.

The tits touched with a surprised squeak. But then the doll relaxed and the breasts began grinding away.

Nightshade stopped to look, curious, excited, afraid. Malibu Barbie had a little round hole in each boob, as if her plastic chest were encrusted with barnacles, and not breasts.

Nightshade put an index finger into one of the holes and twisted slowly. Her eyes were damp when she held the doll to her own flat chest and kissed it on the head.

"And now the new girls on the block, Rip City's devastating, darling demons, the Vampirates."

On the bench of the Filthy Habits, Nightshade felt Ratty clutch her hand.

Fourteen women with red bustiers, red mini-skirts, red fishnet stockings, red helmets, and red lipstick skated out into the rink's spotlights. The Vampirates had white fangs attached to their mouthguards and little white swooshes on their butts. Nike paid for their uniforms — another of Nightshade's peeves. Her Beaverton league refused corporate sponsorship on principle.

"Leading the Vamps is the Rip City captain, number K9, Bloody Laces. Hot on her heels, and hot on her wheels, is the Olympic speed skater Paula Nono, number five foot zero. Next up, a recent arrival from Beaver Town, the long and lovely Mutiny, number 666."

The first time Nightshade had seen Mutiny, rollerblading on the Fanno Creek bike path, she had chased her breathlessly for a mile, dumbfounded that the Barbie of her childhood could come to life. A long blond ponytail swished from the back of her pink baseball cap. Her stilt legs seemed even longer atop rollerblades. She had pouty little lips, creamy skin, and breasts that jutted out from her jersey like elbows.

The long-legged girl on rollerblades made Nightshade dangerously curious. Nightshade had not seen her Barbie doll undressed since the sanding incident. Even her parents had failed to discover that the doll's bikini bra was stuffed with Kleenex.

Nightshade caught up with the girl at the Albertson's parking lot. She was sitting on a picnic table, folding her legs to untie her laces.

"You skate pretty fast," Nightshade ventured, suddenly blushing. The two of them looked so different—the Malibu beauty and the Goth beast.

The girl smiled. "It's how I run away from relationships. I'm hell on wheels."

Was she talking about boyfriends? Nightshade plowed ahead. "Have you ever thought of trying out for a roller derby team?"

They never did use each other's real names, even after Mutiny began spending nights at Nightshade's apartment. When you join Fresh Meat, the training program for Beaver Town wannabes, you have to pick a derby name and stick with it. So Mutiny was Mutiny.

Nightshade coached three nights a week, trying to teach her the rules:

A game lasts an hour and is called a bout. A bout is divided into jams, racing battles that can last up to two minutes apiece. Although each team has fourteen members, only five play at a time—four blockers and one jammer. Jammers score points by lapping the other team's blockers. Blockers can't score points, but they can disrupt things by bashing other players. You can't use your hands or elbows. You can't hit someone from behind. You can't trip people. But all other blows are allowed.

Thunderpuss trained the blockers—big girls with hips and boobs that could do damage. Nightshade dealt with jammers—

fast, sneaky girls. Mutiny excelled at both without trying, and without noticing rules.

A referee in a black-and-red harlequin clown suit blew his whistle to start the first jam of the bout. Eight blockers — four red and four black — skated out warily. Thunderpuss kept the Filthy Habits in line.

A second whistle blew, and the jammers were off, kicking skates, Mutiny for the Vampirates and Ratty for the Habits. They wore big stars on their helmets so everyone could see they were the only ones who could score points.

Ratty swung wide, trying to outflank the blockers on the curve, but a Vamp hip sent her spinning into the spectators. Mutiny shot through on the inside and found open track.

The ref whistled and pointed at her: lead jammer, the only player with the power to call off the jam before the two-minute limit.

Vamp fans chanted, "Mutiny! Mutiny!"

She pouted — her mouth seemed made to moue — as she sailed around the oval.

But Ratty had scrambled back to her feet, focused now so keenly on Mutiny that she no longer heard the crowd. Low to the ground, one arm behind her back, she kicked up speed, sailed through the pack, and burned around the track. By the time Mutiny saw what was happening and tapped her hips to signal the end of the jam, they had each passed three opposing skaters. The scoreboard lit up, "3 - 3".

Back on the Habit sidelines, Nightshade and the bench coach agreed: A wall. They needed the blockers to form a wall to stop Mutiny.

But when the Vampirates skated into position for the next jam, Mutiny was not among them. Instead they had brought out their top jammer, the fastest Portlander on wheels, Paula Nono.

Ratty looked back to the Habits' bench, uncertain, obviously hoping to be replaced. Instead they cheered her on. "Kill her, Iron Thighs."

First whistle: The Habits skated out, practically holding hands, a wall of giant oscillating butts spanning the track.

Second whistle: Ratty and Paula set out, swinging their hands to accelerate. Thunderpuss opened a gap to let Ratty through, but Paula beat her to it. Paula ricocheted off Scare Bear's shoulder, spun 180, skated backwards a sec, hopped about, and was off to the races.

Most of Beaver Town's league meeting had been spent debating Paul Brown—aka Paula Nono. Spirits ran high at the Bridgeport Brewery over pints of hyper-hopped ale.

"He should be disqualified," Pain Mixer said. Pain Mixer had to drink colas, and it made her even more aggressive. She painted houses for a living—hard work that had given her a hard body, a hard heart, and a thirst for hard liquor. Skating with the Filthy Habits helped her keep clean.

Pain Mixer thumped her cola on the table. "A man with a sex change operation should be just as illegal as a woman who takes male hormones."

Nightshade shook her head. "We can't discriminate against transgendered people."

"Oh? Let's ask Ratty."

Poor Ratty squirmed. Everyone knew she had married Paul after the Atlanta Olympics. But Ratty was so quiet that no one knew exactly what she felt.

"Don't call her him," she muttered.

"We've got to collar him, Ratty," Mixer objected. "Nono's killing us."

"You can collar her, but don't call her him."

The table fell silent as people parsed her words. Thunderpuss burped. "Say what?"

Ratty drew a pentagram in spilled beer with her fingertip. "Till-death-do-us-part. Paula hasn't really changed. I have. At least I'm trying to."

Near the end of the second half the Filthy Habits trailed 49 to 62.

"We need defense," Nightshade told Ranga Tang, the bench

wench. "The wall isn't working."

Ranga was a gangly, fortyish housewife who lived for her nights out. She had torn a knee ligament in a bout and now coached from the sidelines.

"Whack a mole?" Ranga suggested.

Nightshade nodded. It wasn't a team strategy at all. It was a one-on-one defense that bared each player's strengths and weaknesses.

When the blockers lined up for the whistle they didn't have to be told which opponent to cover. Everyone knew her nemesis by now.

The Vampirates responded by skating out in a tight cluster, but the Habits took them apart one by one. When the second whistle blew and the jammers set off—Ratty and her sex-switched ex, Paula Nono—the rink ahead of them was clogged with stumbling, battling women. For a full minute neither of the jammers could get through the chaos. Then Margarita, a Vamp blocker who furtively loaded up on beer during halftimes, appeared to lose her balance. Flailing, she "accidentally" threw an elbow into Pain Mixer's stomach. Fans for both teams howled in outrage.

The ref whistled Margarita out for a major, sidelining her for the rest of the jam. Shaken by the blow to her stomach, Pain Mixer skated on like a zombie, leaving a hole the size of a freeway ramp. Ratty got through first, but Paula followed in her slipstream. Then it was just a question of speed.

Paula had lost muscle mass by taking female hormones, but she still did not fill her vampire outfit well. The red bustier had little to push up. The red miniskirt hung over thighs that looked like posts. Nor had the sex change operation been able to soften her unlovely, square-boned jaw. And she still had the reckless aggression that had won her a bronze medal as a man. With the fans stomping in the bleachers, "Go! Go!" she laid down two of the fastest laps the rink had ever seen, caught Ratty, and added three points to the Vampirate lead.

"I'm out of ideas," Ranga admitted to Lady Nightshade on the sidelines. Time was short, and the Filthy Habits were behind by sixteen points. "We can't stop Nono."

Nightshade glanced over to the Vampirate bench. Mutiny wasn't even bothering to skate anymore. Instead she had taken over as bench wench, prepping their players with the secrets she had learned as a member of the Filthy Habits.

"Put me in for Pain Mixer," Nightshade said grimly.

"What? As a blocker?" Ranga stared at her, astonished.

Nightshade nodded. "I've got a strategy they won't guess."

Her last big fight with Mutiny had been on the evening she took Mutiny to meet her parents. Of course Mutiny had always been a high maintenance lover. Nightshade expected that. Barbie had been demanding too, looking at her with those big eyes, saying, "I need a convertible for summer. And an evening dress for the prom."

Nightshade had been needling her parents for weeks, warning them to be polite to her new partner, no matter how shocked they might be.

To Nightshade's horror, her parents loved Mutiny. Her father couldn't take his eyes off her — the opulent curves, the wide eyes, the sassy walk. Her mother cornered Mutiny in the kitchen, offered her sherry, and asked about the secret of her silky hair. Treachery!

Nightshade huddled together with the team, keeping her voice low. "I'm going in for Pain Mixer as a blocker."

Pain Mixer looked down. "Was I that bad?"

"No. It's a trick. After a lap, I'll do a star pass with Ratty and become the jammer."

The team thought about this a moment. "How will that help?" Ratty asked. "You can't catch Paula either."

Nightshade replied, "I can if you dish her."

Dishing was a suicide move. Not exactly illegal, but dangerous. Ratty tightened her lips.

"You have to face your fear," Nightshade said. "You have to stop Paula."

Driving home from her parents' house, Nightshade had been

furious. Mutiny had pandered to her parents like a call girl. But before Nightshade could tell her off, Mutiny launched an attack of her own.

"You're not really a rebel," Mutiny said, idly winding her long blond hair around her wrist. "Honestly, you're just like your parents."

Nightshade almost ran a red light. She braked hard, turned to Mutiny, and said, "What are you talking about? Look at me!"

Mutiny cast her a look through long lashes. "All that Goth shit is just make up. Your parents told me their stories. The crazy thing is, they think they're rebels too."

This stopped Nightshade cold. She had come to the same conclusion about her parents long ago. Her father had rebelled against his father — a woodworker who made fake Amish furniture in Philadelphia — by running away to become a woodworker with a skateboard shop. Her mother had refused to take over her parents' coffee shop in Florida. But was selling herbal tea in Oregon all that different? Their long hair and hippie clothes had been nothing but make up.

The car behind Nightshade honked: the light was green. She drove on in a daze. Mutiny had been the real rebel all along — like Barbie, ditching jobs and people without a care. Only dimly did she hear Mutiny saying, "The Vampirates seem like a great bunch. And don't bother bringing me my things. Keep them or sell them or whatever. Paula Nono says she'll buy me everything new."

By the time the ref blew his whistle for the final two-minute jam, many of the fans had already left, convinced the game was over. The announcer did his best to raise enthusiasm. "Well! Here's Lady Nightshade trying her hand as a blocker. Watch out, little F-17, you're trapped in a squadron of big bombers now!"

With the second whistle, Ratty and Paula set out as jammers, looking for holes in the pack ahead. Meanwhile a heavyweight Vamp girl bashed Nightshade so hard with a shoulder that Nightshade spun around and fell hard on her kneepads. Nightshade had hardly gotten back on her feet when a hip knocked her out of the rink altogether. The Vampirates were having such fun pummeling Nightshade that Ratty slipped through the pack. Sixteen points ahead, the Vamps didn't even seem to care.

But then Ratty simply stopped. She stood there like an angry statue, her arms crossed. After the puzzled pack had passed her by, she took the cover off her helmet — a cloth with the white star marking the jammer — and furtively traded it to Lady Nightshade for the striped cap of the lead blocker.

Paula Nono had noticed none of this, still stuck behind the pack.

Ratty took a deep breath, focusing on her prey. Then she crouched low, picked up speed, and cut along the inside of the track like a missile. The instant she hit Paula, Ratty threw back her arms, smashing her boobs painfully into Paula's shoulder. Both of them flew off the rink, crashing headlong into chairs and spectators.

In the melee that followed, Paula took a swing at Ratty, knocking off her helmet. Fans pulled them apart, but not before Ratty had called Paula a son of a bitch and Paula had responded by throwing her mouth guard at her, vampire fangs and all. Refs promptly expelled them both for the rest of the evening.

Meanwhile Lady Nightshade had put on the jammer's star. Sixty-five seconds remained in the game. Her opponents had no jammer, so they could score no points. And although four big Vamp blockers still stood in Nightshade's way, she was ready for revenge — to show them what a fighter jet at full throttle could do to a squadron of bombers.

Nightshade danced through the pack and found clear track before they even realized she was no longer a blocker. On the second lap she feinted right, and then left, and then shot through a hole in the middle. By the third lap the Habits' blockers had managed to stagger the opposition. Light on her feet, Nightshade wove past the Vampirates like a skier through slalom gates. On the fourth lap the Vamp blockers were trying so hard to watch for her over their shoulders that their heaviest girl lost her balance. She took down all the others as she fell, barricading the entire width of the track with bodies. Rather than plow into this train wreck, Nightshade jumped. She flew over the pack with her knees tucked and landed hard on the far side as the final buzzer sounded.

"And that ends the bout!" the announcer exclaimed. "Or wait. The refs are consulting."

Someone in the stands began stamping her feet impatiently. Soon everyone was stamping. The bleachers thundered.

"We have a tie!" the announcer shouted over the din. "With sixteen points in the final jam, the Habits have evened the score. But there's no such thing as a tie in roller derby, so we'll be going into a sudden death overtime—a duel between the team's top remaining jammers."

Nightshade had always known it would come to this. Mutiny waved to the crowd, flashing her wide Barbie smile as she skated up to the line. She shook back her long blond hair and strapped on the jammer's star helmet.

Nightshade skated solemnly to the line, ignoring Mutiny and ignoring the crowd. This wasn't a duel.

It had never really been about rebellion.

THE REALITY SHOW

I remembered the dream so clearly!

I had driven to Portland to apply for a spot on Jerry Menola's reality TV show. He's such a huge star, and I'm such an unknown, that I knew my odds were slim. By the time I checked into a hotel near the studio I felt self-conscious enough that I gave the clerk a fictitious name—Ron Taylor. The clerk swiped my credit card without looking at it. He handed it back to me and said, "Have a nice stay, Mr. Taylor. You're in 105."

For some reason he'd given me a colossal suite with two queen beds, each in a separate room. The second room had a glass door that opened onto a patio. Beyond was an atrium pub where a grunge band was playing loud music.

I went back to the inner room to watch TV. Every channel was playing the same Jerry Menola rerun—the episode where a fifty-year-old bank manager discovers that the make-up artist assigned to prepare him for the show is his high school girlfriend.

The next morning I awoke to voices. The people sounded suspiciously close, as if they might be in the other room of my hotel suite. Cautiously, I opened the door. Four long-haired, half-dressed young men lay sprawled on my other queen bed. Electric guitars leaned against the walls. The glass door to the patio stood half open. Apparently the grunge band had broken in and made themselves at home.

"Ooh, man, where are we?" One of the gangly kids squinted up at me. He wore a blue goatee that hung to one side — a badly glued fake.

"You're in my room," I told him.

"Really, man? We did some evil stuff last night."

I picked up the phone. "Desk? I have an intruder here in Room 105."

Obviously I was still in a dream, because a manager in a smart suit immediately appeared. He sized us up and asked, "Which one of you is Ron Taylor?"

I hesitated, but Dangling Goatee raised his hand. "My name's Ron Taylor."

"No, no," I objected. "I'm the one who rented this room."

The manager said, "Could I see some ID, please?"

The kid pulled out an Oregon driver's license with "RONALD REAGAN TAYLOR" in giant letters. Apparently his parents had named him for a president from Hollywood.

I protested, "But my credit card paid for this room. You can check."

The manager shook his head. "We block the names on credit cards for confidentiality." He turned to the young band member. "I'm sorry for the disturbance, Mr. Taylor."

Then the manager took me brusquely by the arm. "If you'd come with me, please."

Could things get any worse? As we were leaving I heard a click from the armoire. The faux mahogany door was ajar. I shook myself loose from the manager and pulled the closet open.

And there, of course, was Jerry Menola, sniggering among the bathrobes with a television camera in his hand.

It made perfect sense. In my dreams, things always go from bad to worse. This was just the kind of joke I could retell at dinner parties for years.

The problem was that when I actually opened my eyes — eager to write down the tale before it slipped away — I found myself in a room I did not recognize. Lying beside me was a woman I did not know.

Suddenly I realized I was in the wrong episode.

My head hurt.

This was the lousy rerun where, after twenty-seven years of marriage, I had lost Saundra.

I got up carefully, so as not to disturb the sleeping woman. Outside it was dawn—or dusk? A Dennys beside an empty freeway off-ramp blinked "24 Hours".

I tapped about the room, naked, searching for my clothes. All I could find was the television remote. I held it in my hand a long time, pondering the hieroglyphic buttons. Please, I thought, let one of them work.

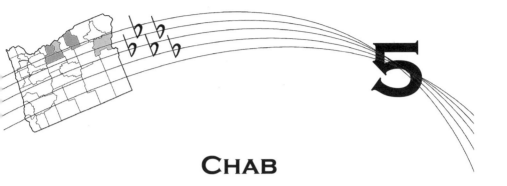

CHAB

Anne lived for haywire connections. She had worked as a Google matchmaker for years—ever since the data center opened in The Dalles. Why did improbable odds make love burn so brightly?

One shy data coder had wanted to propose to a staff librarian on the Eiffel Tower. Anne had managed to book them to the same Paris conference. She didn't arrange for him to catch a stomach bug at a sidewalk cafe, but it would have been a touch of genius. When he finally lured the librarian up the tower by moonlight he nearly fainted in the elevator and then fumbled so badly that he dropped the ring forty stories. It's a story they would tell their grandchildren years later, laughing.

Anne loved her work. But she was not so keen on the voicemail message labeled *Vera Pelham* that showed up on her professional cell phone that morning.

"Anne, sweetheart?" Her mother's voice crackled distantly, as if from another planet. "I know you don't like it when I call you at work, but this is *about* work! I need your expertise, honey. I'm just not used to living alone. I'm certainly not interested in moving to some nursing home where old women play dominoes. I miss male companionship, and I'm thinking you've got prospects in your files. Now it's only an hour's drive to Boardman. I'll make your favorite monsterone stew. Why don't you come by on Sunday and we'll talk?"

Chab would rather have been stationed on the Moon, but he had been assigned to the Boardman relay outpost years ago, and he'd grown fond of the place. Chab had a knack for picking up frequencies others missed. The young guys at the station chuckled when he built a haywire antenna with castoff equipment, fishing for improbable connections during the long, empty hours of his retirement.

Chab no longer asked to be flown home. He understood that it wouldn't pay at his age. Besides, no one was waiting for him there anymore. This was his home now, a world of vast spaces and stark beauty. In the mornings he'd stand with his arms outstretched, casting a long shadow across the desert as he let the sunlight recharge his body.

He thrilled when storms raked the horizon. In fact, it was during one of Boardman's most dangerous storms that he first made contact with The Voice.

Soaring humidity and a fully overcast sky had sent the rest of the outpost staff underground for safety. Only Chab had stayed above, sealing the control room as best he could. This was his chance to dabble in mission work. With no one to laugh at him, he diverted the station's power arrays to his makeshift antenna. Then he closed his eyes and waited.

For hours there was only static, a formless blur in his head. But why would there be static if this frequency was supposed to carry nothing at all? Perhaps if he concentrated, even this noise might become decipherable.

Night had fallen and Chab had begun to drift toward sleep when The Voice separated itself faintly from the blur.

"Is—someone—there?—Yes—No—"

Vera regretted the voicemail she had left on her daughter's office phone. She wasn't that desperate, not really, and Anne couldn't be expected to understand. A daughter will always be her parents' child. Even if the daughter runs a dating service—even if her father has been dead for almost a year—she can't be expected to imagine other partners for her own mother.

For the first few months after George's heart stopped Vera had walked down to the library almost every day. Boardman is a small town with more tumbleweeds than people, so she rarely made it out the gate of her white picket fence before someone hailed her, telling her how sorry they were for her loss. Eventually she read every uplifting life story in the little library's biography section, and she still felt depressed. She needed someone to take care of. She was used to that role. On the way home she stopped by Ray's Food Place to pick up a carton of milk or a cantaloupe, hoping for a little gossip. Maybe there was a man as lonely as herself. But she knew everyone in town already. When she got back to the crooked screen door of her white clapboard house the only one to take care of was herself.

An angry artistic phase followed. Vera checked out an Impressionist art book from the library, dug her acrylics out of the closet, and started painting a full-size replica of Munch's *The Scream*. She ran out of red paint halfway through. Rather than buy more she flipped through the book for something that would use her tubes of black and Prussian blue. The next day, when Munch's bloody sunset was dry, she started painting over *The Scream* with *Starry Night*.

She preferred Van Gogh right away. The Dutchman was also troubled, but he saw behind the simple terror of loneliness to powerful, dark truths. Above a sleeping village on a cloudless night, the sky boiled with danger. Giant yellow stars glared out like eyes. Blue-black whirlpools churned through the Milky Way.

Vera went to the store for another cantaloupe. Already a dozen were sitting on her kitchen counter, a row of dumb bald heads. You could slice them all open and they still wouldn't talk.

That's when she called her daughter Anne. Many hours later Anne finally called back. Yes, she did have files about eligible men, but because she ran a Google workplace service, most of the men were pimply video gamers in their early twenties. No, she couldn't get away this weekend, but perhaps at the end of the month? Yes, she'd look forward to monsterone then. And by the way, have you seen that new British series on PBS? It's really quite entertaining.

Vera hung up the phone, her hand shaking. She considered throwing the cantaloupes into the street, just to watch them crack open. She glanced at the cupboard where George had kept his whisky. But she knew it tasted awful, and it wouldn't help. Finally, biting back her frustration, she did as her daughter suggested and turned on the television.

A pregnant noblewoman was lying on a canopy bed in a high-ceilinged room with a fireplace, complaining to her chamber-maid, "But if the Earl doesn't have a male heir, Reginald will take everything."

"They's wise of knowin', milady," the maid suggested darkly.

"What ways? Tell."

"Fust, tike off yer weddin' ring, milady. A ring is the gitewye of spirits."

The noblewoman drew in her breath, covering her ring finger with her other hand.

The maid held out a piece of string. "Toy yer ring to this, milady, an' swing it over yer belly." She lowered her voice. "If it swings strite, you've a boy. If yer ring suckles, it's a gull."

Vera turned off the television. This was rubbish. But it was too early for bed. She stared at her Starry Night painting. Had Van Gogh based it on real constellations, she wondered, or was it rubbish too? She went out the back door to see if she could recognize anything, but storm clouds had moved in. It was a rare night in Boardman when you couldn't see any stars at all. The air smelled tinny, like rain.

She rubbed her hands together, standing there in the dark. She had taken her wedding ring off after the funeral to let the world know she was alone. Her left hand still felt naked. What if a ring really was a gateway to another world?

Drawn by an emptiness even she could not explain, she went inside, turned on the bedroom light, and took the jewelry box out of its hiding place in the cedar chest. The ring George had given her seemed so frail, its gold thinned by forty-eight years of wear. But it was the other ring—the secret ring—she searched for now. She rummaged down past the costume necklaces and paste earrings. At the very bottom, tangled in the chain of her high school choir pin, she found it: a simple silver band, tarnished almost to black, with a tiny diamond.

She had never told George about her first engagement, and she certainly wasn't going to tell Anne. In fact, even Vera's parents had never learned about Willis Spalding, the Baker City combine mechanic she met at a dance. Each summer he followed the wheat harvest from Utah to British Columbia, repairing engines and replacing pulleys. He'd spent most of August in Boardman that year. They had rendezvoused for evening walks through the newly mown fields.

Vera rubbed the old ring with a polishing cloth, remembering. Willis had given her a free ticket to the rodeo. He wasn't famous, but he had won a reputation as a cow rider. The cow-riding contests served as a warm-up to the main events. Anyone could sign up to ride a cow, and a lot of young men did, thinking it would be an easy way to show off for the girls. But the wild, long-horned range cows at the rodeo were nearly as mean as bulls. Eight seconds was a long ride. Willis averaged twenty-five, and usually walked away with a small cash prize. Once he had walked away without a finger. A year before coming to Boardman he had ridden a shifty white-faced Hereford in Wenatchee. He tied his hand extra tight to the animal's big, shivering back, hoping to add a few seconds. When he was finally thrown loose the rope coiled around his ring finger and yanked it off.

Vera held the ring up to the light. The silver was shiny again. She remembered the Sunday afternoon Willis dropped to his knee in the stubble, looked up with a goofy grin, and said, "Maybe I can't wear a wedding ring, but I sure want you to. I love you, Vera. I've never met a woman like you. Please tell me you'll be my wife."

She had said yes. They had kissed and talked about all kinds of crazy futures. Then night fell and she had to hurry home.

She never saw Willis again. Days later she heard about a fleet of combines in Moro that had needed emergency repair. Why didn't he call, or at least write? That winter the Vietnam war deepened, and a whole swath of young men vanished like wheat before a mower. She waited a year, wondering.

Then there was George, with his draft deferral as an electrical engineer for the McNary Dam. He wasn't nearly as good looking, but he had all his fingers and earned enough to drive an Oldsmobile. He talked in monosyllables — except, of course, for the word "marry".

After Anne was born George got a job at the Fivemile Wind Farm, closer to Boardman, and they bought the white clapboard house in town. She remembered the time she pressured George to let her see the Fivemile windmills up close. She hadn't realized they were hollow. A door at the base opened onto a little control room full of meters and blinking lights. From there a spiral staircase wound up a dizzying steel shaft, seemingly forever, to a tiny lookout window beside an enormous white hub. Great white blades slowly swept shadows across the sky. Far below, the fields she had known all her life spread out like a map. From that frightening aerie George's windmills looked like an army of giant robots. In that moment she had seen them as power-hungry aliens, striding out from the Columbia River dams to conquer the world. She never asked to be taken to the windmills again.

Vera brought both rings with her to the kitchen, although she already knew which she would use. She took a paper plate down from the cupboard. With a pencil she wrote two words on the plate: YES at twelve o'clock and NO to the right, at three o'clock. Then she tied her silver ring to a string and dangled it over the middle of the plate.

"Is someone there?" she asked.

A distant roll of thunder made her flinch. The ring swayed forwards to YES, but she had flinched in that direction, so it didn't count.

"Is someone there?" she repeated.

Rain began to patter on the roof. The storm was closing in.

The ring swayed front to back, over YES.

"Is it George?" she asked.

The ring circled a moment and then slowly swayed the other way, to NO.

She had expected this. She knew expectations are what matter in such games. Still she asked, "Is it Willis?"

She wanted it to be Willis. That would make the game more fun. She even wiggled her finger a little, from front to back.

But the ring ignored her hint. It swung as steadily as a grandfather clock's pendulum, side to side, over NO.

Outside, a gust of wind blew a can clattering down the street.

Vera set down the ring. She thought for a moment, her lips pursed. Then she took another paper plate from the cupboard. This time she wrote the letters from A to Z around the rim. Then she held up the string again, dangling the silver ring over the middle.

"All right," she said, "Then who are you?"

The ring simply hung there for a while, spinning slowly in place. Gradually it began wobbling back and forth—an erratic swing, not like a pendulum at all. With every other swing it pointed to a different letter: C, H, A, and B.

Then the ring slowed and stopped.

The hair on the back of Vera's neck stood on end. "Chab?" she asked. For the first time in ages, she had the feeling she was not alone, and it gave her chills.

Anne walked straight to the kitchen, lifted the pot's lid, and took a deep breath, savoring the mingled scents of olive oil, garlic, and tomatoes. She closed her eyes and exhaled, a long, satisfied sigh. "I love your monsterone, Mom."

As a child, Anne had begged her mother to make larger and larger batches of minestrone soup. Eventually it had become a monsterone stew, full of black beans, tortellini, and half a garden of vegetables.

"Promise you'll take a few quarts home," Vera said. "It would take years for me to eat this much all by myself."

The words "all by myself" hung in the air. Anne took a bottle of shiraz from her shoulder bag. Her mother didn't drink but Anne did, and she wanted a glass now. As she twisted the corkscrew she said, "You know, Mom, the population I deal with at work simply doesn't include retirees. I'm sorry I can't help. I miss Dad as much as you do, and I know how lonely it can be out here, but — "

"It's all right," Vera interrupted, putting her hand on Anne's arm. The simple confidence in her mother's tone made Anne stop.

"Honestly, sweetheart," Vera said, "I'm fine."

Anne poured herself a glass. "Mrs. Haskins at the library called to tell me you were painting *The Scream*."

Vera laughed. "That was weeks ago. I'm better now. I've moved on."

"Really?" Anne took a drink.

"Really. I've been painting other things. See for yourself." She held her hand out toward the living room.

Anne took her glass with her. On the living room buffet she found a clumsy copy of Van Gogh's *Starry Night*. However, a far more interesting painting stood on an easel by the window. The unfinished work was an expressionistic version of the same night sky, miraculously transformed by radiating beams of light.

A sudden suspicion made Anne glance around the room. Something had changed. The usual biographies had vanished from the coffee table. Instead there was a book about space by Stephen Hawking and a treatise on enlightenment by the Dalai Lama.

"You've been seeing someone, haven't you?" Anne demanded.

"Well no, not seeing. We haven't actually met. We just chat."

"You've been *chatting?*" Anne almost dropped her glass.

"Who I talk to is my own business."

"Mom! I warned you about Internet chat rooms for seniors. They're not some kind of harmless lonely hearts club. Tell me the truth: Has he asked you for money yet?"

"No!" Vera drew back, shocked.

"That's what these cyber Casanovas are after. Before long he'll want your account number. Or he'll suggest a bank transfer for what seems like a good reason. He only wants your money."

Anne had used the words *your money* instead of *my inheritance*, but Vera heard both versions.

"You don't understand. Chab isn't like that at all."

"Chab? What kind of name is that?"

"It's hard to explain."

"You're chatting with a man who calls himself *Chab?*"

They glared at each other for a moment. Then Vera waved the whole issue aside. "You'll feel better once you've eaten. Come on, help me set the table."

Anne did as she was told.

The dinner went surprisingly well. Vera changed the subject, relaying the news she'd heard at the supermarket check-out line. Stan Delaney, the owner of the Horseshoe Tavern, had put off repairing the place for so long that his wife Maeve ran a bath in their upstairs apartment and fell through, tub and all, into the billiard room. Rita Wellesley, a waitress at the R&L truck stop on I-84, had announced her bid for mayor while wearing her old Hooters uniform. And Seth Orr, the irrigator at Seven Goats Alfalfa, had reversed all the sprinkler heads so his mile-wide circular field could "unwind."

Vera was serving tiramisu when Anne apologized. "I'm sorry I blew up about Chab."

Vera handed her a dessert plate. "Oh, that's all right. It's been stressful for both of us since your father passed away."

"No, really. This is what I'm supposed to do for a living, and I messed up. I'm willing to listen now." Anne dipped a spoon into the tiramisu. "So what's he like?"

"You mean Chab?"

"Of course." Anne took a bite. "Mmm, this is good."

"Well," Vera began cautiously. "He's very understanding. And more communicative than your father ever was."

"How old is he?"

Vera bit her lip. "Older than me."

"Really?" Anne raised her eyebrows. Men in chat rooms usually lied that they were younger. "Where's he from?"

"I'm not sure exactly."

Anne held back a knowing smile. "Well, where does he say he is now?"

"He says he's here in Boardman."

This caught Anne off guard. "But you haven't seen him?"

"No." Vera took a large bite of tiramisu, as if keeping her mouth full might save her from answering more questions.

"Boardman's not that big. Is he new in town?"

Vera shook her head silently. Somehow she felt uneasy reporting that Chab had been in Boardman for five hundred years.

"Wait," Anne said. "You didn't meet this man on the Internet, did you?"

Vera shook her head again.

"Then how? By dialing a wrong number?"

Vera swallowed. "Sort of."

Anne waited for an explanation.

"Promise me you'll keep an open mind?"

"All right," Anne said slowly. Her mother seemed happier than she'd been all year. The town's librarian had taken the unusual step of alerting Anne to her mother's depression. But now *The Scream* was gone, replaced by a painting full of light. Whoever Chab was, if he inspired her to read Stephen Hawking and the Dalai Lama, he couldn't be all bad.

"You really promise?" Vera asked.

"Yes. I'm listening."

"It might work better if I show you," Vera said, switching to a matter-of-fact tone. "Take off your ring."

"My ring?" Anne had been married three times. She told people that marriage was a professional hazard for people in her line of work. The ring she wore now was relatively new, a token from the high school graduation of her son in Nyssa.

"I know it's Adrian's ring. I'll give it back." Vera took out the paper plate marked YES and NO. Then she tied the ring to a piece of string and held it over the plate.

"What on earth are you doing?" Anne asked.

"Just hold the string still and ask a question."

Anne held the string. "What kind of question?"

"Not that kind. Something about love. Ask if you'll get married again."

Anne stared at her mother. "Mom, this is the kind of game I played at sleepovers when I was ten. It doesn't work for grownups."

Vera frowned. "It works better when there's clouds. Chab says they focus the signal."

"Mom?" Anne set down the string. "Don't tell me this is how you've been talking to Chab."

"You promised to keep an open mind."

"Well yes, but—"

"But what? What do you know about it? What does any of us know?"

Anne took a deep breath. "All right. I think you'd better tell me everything about Chab."

When Chab saw how brightly his supervisor was glowing, he knew he was in for a grilling. Word must have leaked about The Voice.

Tall, square-shouldered, and nearly opaque, N'nahoj had been in charge of the Boardman relay station for only a hundred and forty years. Despite his youth he was known as a cautious administrator—and a brilliant strategist at Venusian chess. Even now he was restacking the blue and green glass cubes on his desk, as if preparing for a tournament.

"Come in, Chab. Have a seat." N'nahoj waved him to a chair. "I hear you've become a fan of storms?"

"Well, I—"

"Playing with poison is a dangerous game." N'nahoj tapped a row of three blue cubes, toppling a green cube at the end. "I've also heard that you've been diverting power from the station's arrays."

"The arrays aren't used during storms. I've done no harm."

"But you no longer have that kind of authorization, Chab."

Chab looked down. "I know, commander."

"N'nahoj studied him. "Are you using our equipment to chat with family?"

"No!" Chab looked down again. "I have no family."

N'nahoj frowned. He should have known this, but the files didn't go back that far. The earliest report he had for Chab was when he had requested an assignment on the Moon. That's where the interesting mission work was, of course, smoothing out misunderstandings among seventeen irascible species. But Chab had a gift as an electrical engineer, so he had been sent to the Earth instead. The larger planet was a more efficient location for a communication relay, but it was an otherwise uninhabited world with seas of poisonous dihydrogen oxide. Deadly rainstorms were just one reason no one requested Boardman.

"Then with whom are you attempting to communicate?" N'nahoj asked. "You're an engineer. You must know that the antenna you've built is little more than a toy. Without access to our power arrays, it couldn't carry a signal across the canyon."

"I don't need a long-range device to communicate, commander."

N'nahoj hit the desk. "Communicate with whom?"

Chab was silent for a long time. Finally he said, "I believe I have established contact with a new race."

"Really?" N'nahoj spoke as evenly as he could, but it was hard to hide his skepticism. "Using your antenna?"

"At first I used the antenna. I needed more power to amplify the signal. Rain clouds seem to help focus it as well."

"And what kind of signal was this?"

"Static at first, commander." Chab sat up taller, more comfortable now that he had begun to share his findings. "The noise felt like a blur in my head. When I learned to discern the signal, however, it grew stronger and clearer. Letters, words, emotions — the language of Vera."

"Vera?" N'nahoj couldn't help but smile. "What kind of a name is that?"

Chab shrugged. "That's what my contact calls itself. Vera uses a silver ring as a microphone.

N'nahoj stopped smiling as he considered this. Everyone knew silver had the power to reflect communication. Perhaps Chab was onto something after all. "Still, I don't see how you could be picking up a signal from another planet."

"I'm not."

"What?"

Chab held up his hands. "I don't even need the antenna anymore. My mental connection with Vera has become so strong that we can hear each other talking in our heads."

N'nahoj laughed. Talking in aliens' heads was easy, but only if the aliens were close by. "Impossible. This Vera you're talking with would have to be here in Boardman."

"Vera *is* in Boardman."

"Your contact lives here?"

"Yes. The whole Vera race lives on Earth." Once Chab had gone this far, there was no turning back. "Seven billion of them live here. This planet has been inhabited all along. We just can't see them because they're living in some kind of alternative dimension."

"Really?" The commander had been unsure from the first whether Chab might be mentally ill. Now it was obvious that the retired engineer was suffering from hallucinations. The loneliness of a remote outpost could be damaging, and Chab had been on Earth longer than anyone. The commander played for time while he decided what to do.

"So tell me, Chab, does the Vera race look like us?"

"No, they don't," Chab said. "They're composed mostly of water."

"They're made of poison instead of light?"

"Exactly. They actually have to drink dihydrogen oxide every day. And unless they cover up their bodies they burn in the sunlight."

"Fascinating." N'nahoj was growing more troubled by the minute. Chab was contradicting himself. Aliens made of water couldn't possibly burn. And if they avoided sun, where did they get energy?

"I've been thinking in terms of our mission," Chab went on. "With a population of seven billion, I figured there might be rival clans that need our mediation. And I was right. Misunderstandings between clans have led to years of warfare."

"I see. And how many clans have you identified?"

"There seem to be only two. Vera belongs to a clan called Women. The beings named George and Willis are in the clan of Men.

But George is dead and Willis is in hiding." Chab leaned forward. "I might be able to mediate a reconciliation, but I'm going to need more power. Reaching out among a population of seven billion requires a vastly amplified signal."

"N'nahoj ran a hand over his face. Chab needed treatment for his delusions at a medical center, but space travel was out of the question. Not only was their budget too tight, but Chab was too old. Already his body was speckled with dark spots where the glow of life had waned. He might only survive a few more decades. No, Chab would have to stay on Earth, and N'nahoj would ask for medical advice to be sent by relay. Here Chab would be a manageable risk. If his hallucinations provided him with solace in his old age, perhaps they were a blessing in disguise.

"Chab?" N'nahoj said.

"Yes, commander?"

N'nahoj set blue squares in the corners of the five-tiered game board on his desk. "Do you play Venusian chess?"

"A little."

"Then you know that the most beautiful strategies are the ones no one sees."

Chab nodded. The goal of chess was peace. The greatest masters seemed not to play at all.

"I want you to keep working on your project with the Vera beings, but I don't want you to talk about it with anyone but me."

"All right." Chab didn't trust the commander's calm tone. "Will you authorize my use of the station's power?"

N'nahoj sighed. He shook his head.

"Tell me the truth," Chab said. "You don't believe anything I've said, do you?"

N'nahoj did not like to lie. He wasn't good at it, and this elderly engineer deserved better. "It's hard, Chab. It's hard for me to believe."

Chab placed a green cube in the center of the game board, where it invisibly connected all of the corner pieces. "It's hard for me to believe too, commander. But what does any of us know?"

After helping with the dinner dishes, Anne packed up two quarts of monsterone, hugged her mother good-bye, and drove back to The Dalles.

Vera sat alone at the dining room table, put her hands over her face, and cried. Her daughter had treated her like a child. Perhaps she deserved it, sliding into the foolishness of a second childhood. Chab sounded like one of those dreams where you come up with a brilliant idea for a recipe pairing asparagus and marshmallows. In the morning, you realize it was laughable nonsense.

Vera tried to read. She tried to paint. She even tried watching TV. Finally she tried to sleep, but she just lay there in bed, thinking darker and darker thoughts. Anne hadn't even attempted to send her to a psychiatrist. Instead her daughter had merely patted her hand and said, "Chab sounds like a nice person—or being, or whatever. If talking with him makes you happy, I'm all for it. But I want you to promise that you'll keep Chab as our little secret, OK? You know what we say in the dating business: You're more likely to get struck by lightning than to find a good man after forty."

Sometime after midnight, when the full moon cast long shadows across her bedroom, Vera sat on the edge of her bed and put on the silver ring. She didn't know what scared her more—that the voice would still be in her head, or that it would be gone.

"Chab?" she asked. "Are you there?"

Time ticked like a pendulum: YES NO YES NO

Eventually a weary voice in her head answered, "Yes."

"Are you real, Chab?"

Another pause. "Are you real, Vera?"

Tick. Tick.

"I think so, Chab, but I might be insane. I told my daughter about you today. She said I shouldn't tell anyone else."

"I told my commander about you. He said the same thing."

"My daughter thinks I'm a crazy old woman."

"My commander thinks I'm a crazy old engineer."

Tick. Tick.

"I'm looking at the full moon. It just came up."

"I'm looking at it too. It's beautiful tonight."

Tick. Tick.

"Chab? Do you think there's a way I could come to your world? Maybe through the ring?"

He sighed. "I wish you could, Vera. But I don't think you can exist here. The rocks and the sky and the moon are the same, but all the other things you describe — trees, birds, flowers — we don't have those. You are water. I am light. Our Earths are not the same."

She had known this, of course. Still she turned the silver ring around and around on her finger, its tiny diamond an orbiting moon.

"I'm fading, Vera," Chab said.

"Fading?"

"I've developed age spots. Each day when I stand in the sun there is less and less to recharge."

"Chab! Can't you do anything about it?"

"No. I thought I should tell you. I have less than a century to live."

Vera laughed.

"Is death funny on your Earth?"

"No, it's just that everyone on my Earth has less than a century to live. I'm sixty-eight and my daughter thinks I'm as old as the hills."

"I see. Then we will have to work faster."

"Work faster on what?"

"Finding Willis. My commander doesn't want me to use the station's power array, and he's watching more closely. It will be hard for me to gain access to the control room."

"Oh, don't worry about Willis too much," Vera said. Perhaps because the ring had been the key to their contact, Chab seemed to think that her broken engagement loomed large in human history. Vera had been slow to correct this impression.

"Every misunderstanding is important, Vera. Mediating peace is my purpose. But I don't have enough power to contact seven billion beings. Can you help me narrow the search?"

"I'm not sure." Vera had never really looked for Willis Spalding. As an eighteen-year-old girl she had been shy and a little ashamed about her secret engagement to a traveling mechanic. She had not dared to ask anyone in Boardman where Willis had gone. She had simply hoped that he would eventually call. After marrying George, she had been glad that the call never came.

Chab asked, "Would it help if I describe how to build a search antenna?"

She shook her head. "I've got a search antenna. On my Earth, we call it the Internet."

Mrs. Haskins thought Vera Pelham's sudden interest in history was a good sign. The librarian often helped elderly Boardman residents use the computer for genealogical research. Mrs. Haskins was discreet enough to show them the program and then leave the library's computer room so they could track down their high school sweethearts in secret.

Vera ran into trouble with her Internet search right away. The world was full of Willis Spaldings, but none of them was the Baker City combine mechanic who had proposed to her in a Boardman wheat field in 1966. In fact, no one by the name of Spalding had ever appeared in Baker County's birth, graduation, marriage, or death records. Why would Willis have lied about his home town? And what else might he have invented?

Employment records proved to be another dead end. Combine mechanics work as independent hired hands. They earn cash and rarely file tax returns. Finally Vera looked up the newspaper reports of rodeo results. The articles listed bronco busters and calf ropers, but they didn't bother to name cow riders.

After three hours Mrs. Haskins told Vera that grade schoolers were waiting to use the computers for homework. Vera quickly wrote down the phone numbers of a wheat rancher in Moro and a rodeo manager in Wenatchee. Then she walked home from the library in a daze. It seemed as if Willis Spalding had never existed. Was she the only one who had been able to see him? They had talked, they had kissed — or had she only dreamed these things?

Suddenly Chab seemed more real to her than the man she had pledged to marry. She took the silver ring out of her pocket. It was plain and cheap, the sort of ring you might find for ten bucks at a flea market.

Back home she called the wheat rancher in Moro. Yes, the man told her, he had hired many a mechanic in his day. He even remembered an emergency back in the fall of '66 when a fleet of ten combines had run over the same wire fence, snarling the machinery something awful. He had called in a mechanic from Boardman, but that's all he recalled. Willis Spalding? Nope, name didn't ring a bell.

When Vera dialed the Wenatchee rodeo manager a little boy answered. She nearly hung up, but then decided to soldier on. "Um — I'm trying to reach a Marvin Henner? With a question about the rodeo?"

"Grandpa!" The boy shouted so loud Vera had to hold the phone away. "Some lady wants to talk rodeo!"

The phone clunked. A door slammed. Slow footsteps creaked closer — the uneven footsteps of a man who limps.

"Aiyup?" a gravelly voice bellowed.

"Mr. Henner?"

"Aiyup."

Vera feared this noise might be the man's entire vocabulary. "I'm a historian here in — in Hermiston. I understand you managed the Wenatchee Rodeo back in the 1960s?"

"Aiyup. Booked 'em, ran 'em, announced 'em. Kind of a one-man show."

Vera's hopes rose. "I'm doing a retrospective on forgotten rodeo stars. I wonder if you happen to remember a cow rider by the name of Willis Spalding."

"Willis Spalding?"

"Yes."

"Never heard of him. And I'd remember too. I never forget a rider."

Vera's throat grew tight. "He was —" She wiped her eyes before she could continue. "I'm sorry. He was missing the ring finger on his left hand. I thought he might have lost it in an accident in Wenatchee."

A weird rumbling from the phone slowly jerked its way up the scale. Finally it burst out as a deep-throated laugh. "Oh, you mean Jake!"

"Jake?"

"Aiyup! Damn fine rider. Good mechanic too. He used a different name in every town, but here we always called him Jake."

"Why would he change his name?" Vera hesitated, and then added, "Was he in trouble with the law?"

"No, no. Jake was a straight shooter. He just didn't like leavin' tracks. Some guys are born to move on. Hooey, that man had a way with women, though. Whenever he hit a town they practically lined up to take turns."

Vera flushed red. "Is that why he kept moving on? To run away from broken promises?"

"Ma'am, I don't know what kind of historian you are, but I've got an idea. You're not the first woman to call looking for Jake. But you're the first to doubt his word. I said he was a straight shooter and I meant it. He didn't need to promise women anything more than they got. The man was a cow rider by profession. Twenty-five seconds with Jake was a damn fine ride. The day a Hereford tore off his finger he looked at that gap in his hand where a wedding ring would go and said, "Ain't met a girl yet that could tie me down.""

And Vera thought: A year later, he met me. But apparently he hadn't treated her the way he treated other women. He had gone for walks with her, talking about the future. He hadn't tried to lure her into a hayloft. Until he gave her the ring, he had not even kissed her. In the summer of 1966, when Jake became Willis, he had briefly been a different man. She had known him as a shy, happy gentleman. Perhaps that had been the person he wished he could be.

"Ma'am?" the gravelly voice asked. "Anything else I can help you with?"

She breathed the words, "Where is he now?"

The laugh boomed again. "That's what they all finally ask. I guess Jake served a while on an aircraft carrier off the coast of

'Nam. Then I heard he started jobbing around the world as an aircraft mechanic — always changin' his name, movin' on, never workin' for the big airlines. But hell, it's been twenty years since his trail went cold. Like I say, Jake don't leave tracks."

The rodeo manager coughed a minute before he could continue. Then his voice seemed smaller. "I'm sorry about your history project, ma'am. But there ain't nobody on God's green Earth gonna find that cow rider of yours now."

The only good thing about fading, Chab decided, was that it made hiding easier. He had not been able to recharge in the sun that morning anyway. The clouds of a massive storm had moved in overnight, blocking the usual frequencies and casting a gloom over Boardman. When rainstorm sirens sent the relay station staff scurrying to the safety of the basement shelters, Chab slipped into a corner of the control room. He closed his eyes, cleared his mind, and let his body grow dim. Distantly he heard voices calling his name, but the calls stopped once thunder began rumbling outside.

When Chab opened his eyes he was so weak he could hardly stand. The muggy air reeked of poison. He sank into a chair at the main control board and looked out the window. A gigantic cumulonimbus thunderhead had reared up twenty thousand feet above the desert. Flashes of lightning crackled from the dark cloud, seeking out anything that dared to rise above the plain.

For the first time in centuries, Chab felt genuine terror. Was he doing the right thing, risking so much, disobeying a direct order? Fear briefly relit his glow — although by now Chab's body was little more than a sieve of light, riddled with the holes of age.

Then Chab remembered Vera, and his eyes narrowed with renewed determination. He threw the switches, shifting the station's power array to his makeshift antenna. Soon thousands of voices were echoing in his head, a Babel from a world only he could hear. He needed more power!

Flashes on the horizon lit an ominous slanting blur of poison rain. The approaching thunderhead kept strengthening the signal. Tens of thousands — No! Hundreds of thousands of voices roared through his mind at once. So many people! And they weren't all like Vera. Her Earth was more complicated than he had thought possible. How could he reach one voice in that cacophonous multitude? He needed more power!

Jagged bolts of lightning forked down into the desert. Thunder boomed three seconds behind each flash, and then two, and then one. When a bolt finally hit the power array, the crash boomed nearly at the same moment as a blinding flash. Bluish arcs of electricity snaked from panel to panel, converging on the control room.

Chab sat up with a gasp, his spirit fired with unbelievable life. Billions of voices! Billions! And they were not just from two clans, but thousands upon thousands. So much war! So many misunderstandings! Vera's world was a firestorm of hate and sorrow and loneliness. How could anyone untangle so many wrongs?

The next lightning bolt hit the control building itself, blasting the window to shards. The explosion knocked Chab against his chair. Raindrops blew in the open window like bullets, piercing his chest and arms. Intense beams of light shot out from each of the rain holes.

Chab had time for one last thought before his spirit drained into the power array. Then the gap that had been his body imploded, destroying what remained of the control room.

A lonely cry for love echoed across worlds.

Vera worried when she didn't hear from Chab in the weeks following the Great Storm. There had been a moment, after the lights went out and the rain was beating on the roof, when her heart had lurched with sudden anguish. Perhaps a message?

Scientists were now saying that a solar flare had disrupted the Earth's magnetic field. Around the world, power grids had faltered or failed. Televisions had gone dead for days. Radio stations had come back on the air more quickly, but with heavy static. The astronauts on the International Space Station were still out of touch. Across the planet, auroras had lit the night skies with a bluish glow.

Commentators were saying that everyone on Earth had learned the importance of communication. We had seen for a moment that we were a single clan, living together on a small, fragile world.

At first Vera wore the silver ring day and night, hoping to reestablish contact with Chab. But after a few weeks she set the ring on her bedside table. She had to admit that it felt good not to hear voices in her head. For once she could hear herself think. Even her husband George, who hadn't talked much out loud, had filled her head with unspoken demands.

She had taken care of other people all her life. Vera was beginning to realize she was tired of it.

When her daughter Anne called from The Dalles to say she couldn't make it to Boardman that weekend, Vera replied, "That's all right, sweetheart."

"Really? You're not upset?"

"No," Vera said. "I've decided to take the bus into The Dalles on Sunday."

"But I'm busy. I've got a conference at Google with — "

"I said it's all right," Vera interrupted. "I can take care of myself. There's a free brunch at the Klickitat Retirement Village. It's sort of an open house, and I'm thinking I'll go take a look."

"A retirement village?"

Vera was glad that she could still surprise her daughter.

On Sunday Vera got up early to get ready for the bus trip to The Dalles. She had had trouble sleeping anyway, what with all the traffic noise. Boardman wasn't usually loud, but on weekends gangs of motorcyclists gunned their motors through town, touring the sunny backroads of a route the Chamber of Commerce advertised as the Zoomatilla Loop.

Rather than wear a dress, which would require panty hose, Vera chose a practical traveling outfit of slacks and a jacket. She put everything she needed for the day in a large bag that she could carry over her shoulder.

A strange thought struck her as she closed the bag. What would happen if she didn't come back? She might like Klickitat Village.

She had all her essentials in the bag. She looked around the living room critically. Her house in Boardman felt like an empty shell. The memories here were not all good.

Vera bit her lip. On an impulse she went into the bedroom and put on the silver ring.

"Chab?" she asked.

Nothing. It was just as well. She was getting used to independence. Childhood sweethearts and dream men from chat rooms always turn out to be boors in real life. She had outgrown such games.

Vera sighed, slung the bag over her shoulder, and walked back through the house.

Another impulse: She took out her house key and set it on the living room table. Why not leave it there for the day, as if she were walking out of a motel room? Perhaps the past forty-eight years had been nothing more than a stopover on a different journey.

When she finally pushed open the crooked screen door she was irritated to see one of the bikers revving his engine in the street. Orange flames had been painted on the gas tank of his big black Harley-Davidson. The man wore a black leather jacket. His helmet and dark glasses exposed little but a grizzled beard.

The bike growled again. This time Vera noticed the motorcyclist's hand on the throttle.

Vera opened her mouth, but couldn't speak. She walked unsteadily down the porch steps.

The biker's left hand was missing the ring finger.

"Willis?"

The man shrugged. He had the broad shoulders of a cow rider.

"But how did you—" Vera searched for words. "I mean, after all these years?"

He shrugged again.

"Have you been hearing voices in your head?" Vera demanded.

The man tipped up his dark glasses, exposing blue eyes she hadn't seen for almost half a century.

"It's called a conscience," Willis said.

An extra helmet sat on the back seat.

Vera covered the silver ring on her finger, but Willis had already noticed.

"Give you a lift somewhere?" he asked.

THE OLD SEA LION
AND THE FISHERMAN

One week the most popular video on the Internet featured a talking sea lion.

It started out as an ordinary tourist movie from the Newport bayfront, probably taken with a cell phone. Sea gulls screech atop pilings. Tourists in shorts and sunglasses point at half a dozen huge, blubbery sea lions lolling on an abandoned dock. The animals are so fat the old dock is half underwater. Their fur is wet, scarred, and mangy. A big bull arches his neck and barks to scare away a young sea lion trying to find a place on the dock.

"RaaaaAAA! Urg! Urg!"

The younger sea lion falls back into the bay and swims under the dock, looking for another spot. The tourists laugh.

Then the mangy old sea lion looks straight into the camera and says, "You think we're fat and lazy, don't you? I know, that's all most people see—obese sea lions hanging around the docks, snapping at each other, grunting, picking fights. If we're not at the docks then you see us out on sand bars, sleeping it off. Or maybe you see us on Saturdays, fishing where they've just stocked a river, or below a dam where the fish pool up and it's easy pickings. You think: What a bunch of fat, lazy bastards!"

The sea lion beside him scootches up on the dock to get out of the water, his fur rippling as he gallumphs closer. The old sea lion turns and bares his teeth, "RaaaaAAA! Urg! Urg!"

Then the old sea lion looks back at the camera. "What you don't see is the truth. We get up every morning before dawn and swim thirty miles out to sea in all kinds of weather. Then we dive four hundred feet deep, over and over, hour after hour, down to the edge of the Continental Shelf. We get the tough fish down there, the ones fishermen don't want. No salmon—they're too fast. It's hard work, and dangerous as hell. When we get back to shore, exhausted, that's what you see. Of course we're tired and cranky. And to tell the truth, we don't give a damn what you think."

The old sea lion jerks his head back and barks, "RaaaaAAA! Urg! Urg!"

The next week there was a new video on the Internet, showing an old fisherman drinking beer at the dimly lit counter of Snug Harbor, a bar by the docks on the Newport bayfront. He has a grizzled white beard, a scar on the back of his hand, and blurry tattoos poking out from his tank-top shirt. You hear the click of pool balls in the background. A younger guy with a backwards baseball cap and a T-shirt bulging over a beer belly squeezes up to the bar. He taps a Camel out of a cigarette pack.

The old fisherman belches at him menacingly.

"Hey," the bartender says. "No smoking inside."

The younger guy grunts, takes his cigarette, and moves on.

Then the old fisherman looks straight into the camera and says, "The tourists who drive down the Oregon Coast mostly see women in the shops. Bookstores, coffee shops, bed & breakfasts—they're all run by women out here. If you're looking for the men, you'll find us hanging around the docks, down in the bayfront bars, snapping at each other, grunting and picking fights. Or maybe you'll see us on Saturdays, fishing where they've just stocked a river, or below a dam where the fish pool up and it's easy pickings. I know what you're thinking: What a bunch of fat, lazy bastards."

The old fisherman finishes his beer and waves the mug at the bartender to signal a refill.

Then the old fisherman looks back at the camera. "What you

don't see is the truth. We get up every morning before dawn and sail thirty miles out to sea, in all kinds of weather. Then we troll for hours, out of sight of land, pitching in the swells, baiting hooks, hauling lines, trying to keep our balance in rubber boots and slickers as waves slosh the decks. It's hard work, and dangerous as hell. If we're lucky and survive, we get back to shore in the early afternoon, exhausted. That's what you see. Of course we're tired and cranky."

The bartender trades the empty mug for a full one. The old fisherman takes a drink too fast, so the foam runs down his beard and drips onto the bar. He wipes his mouth with the back of his scarred hand.

"And to tell the truth, we don't give a damn what you think."

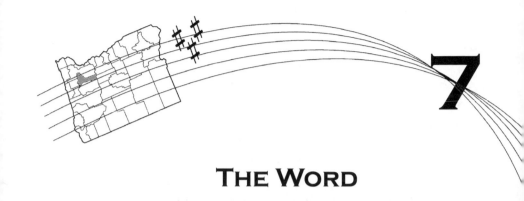

THE WORD

Telephone to glory, O what joy divine!
I can feel the current moving on the line;
Built by God the Father for His loved and own
We may talk to Jesus thro' this royal telephone.

> —"The Royal Telephone" by F.M. Lehman, in *The Radio Hymnal* (Shenandoah, Iowa: Henry Field Seed Company, 1927)

The Mount Cavalry Church of the Holy Revival had fallen on hard times, and not just because of its name. Each service seemed lonelier than the last. Some blamed the young Latino families who were buying up southeast Salem homes and driving into town to attend mass at St. Joseph's. Others blamed the Enchanted Forest billboard. Right next to the church, the theme park advertisement showed happy children emerging from the mouth of a giant witch. If you were taking a carload of kids out the freeway on a Sunday morning, it would be hard not to drive one more exit to "Guaranteed Family Fun!"

Some Sundays the seven elders of the Church Board had the place pretty much to themselves. The roof leaked in the nave, weeping over a neglected Jesus. The part-time pastor had departed to greener pastures. And now the power company was threatening to not even let there be light.

The elders posted advertisements for a minister who could gather stray sheep. On a Sunday afternoon in March they interviewed three candidates.

The first was a retired minister from Winnemucca, Nevada. He wore a saucer-sized belt buckle and apparently had trouble shaving the white stubble from the badlands of his wrinkled throat. He smelled of cigarette smoke, beer, and gambling debts.

The second candidate, Sandy Gorman, was harder to refuse. The forty-year-old daughter of one of the elders, Sandy had earned her divinity degree through years of correspondence courses, replaying the videotaped lessons over and over.

"Heaven is in your heart," she told the elders. "Heaven is in your heart."

All of the elders except Angela Gorman looked down, embarrassed. Sermons needed to be longer than a single sentence, and Sandy, born with Down's Syndrome, could rarely manage more.

The final candidate started with two strikes against him.

"Dexter Morales," the elder Mrs. Gorman read from his resume. "That's an unusual name."

The young, black-haired man sat on the edge of his chair, as if he were hoping to be picked for a high school team. But his voice was deep and his gaze steady.

"My father is a legal immigrant from Oaxaca, Mexico. He manages a crew at Santiam Vineyards. He met my mother doing Forest Service trail work. She's Anglo, a fifth-generation Oregonian."

"I didn't mean—" Mrs. Gorman stopped, because race had been exactly what she had meant.

Mr. Hickley, the grass seed farmer, suggested, "A background in two cultures might help build our congregation. Southeast Salem is changing."

"Perhaps," Mrs. Gorman said.

For a moment no one looked at Dexter. Then Mr. Hamilton, eldest of the elders, pitched the other strike. "Am I to understand that you are just twenty-two years old, and that this would be your first job?"

Dexter smiled, something he did well. "I'm young, but not

inexperienced. I studied theology at Corban University for four years. I paid tuition by working evenings, weekends, and summers. I've had jobs fixing computers, driving a truck for a food kitchen, and selling radio ads. Since graduation last June I've filled in as a substitute minister at churches in Aumsville and Jefferson."

Roger Mires, a hawk-nosed businessman with a Shell station and a tow truck, asked, "If we hired you, Dexter, what would you do different?"

"We're already doing a lot that's right. Uplifting, scripture-based sermons with testimonials from the congregation — that will remain our core message."

Mr. Hickley nodded. He liked that the young reverend used the words "we" and "will" rather than "I" and "would".

Mr. Mires was less impressed. "If we don't do something different we might as well sell the building."

Dexter knit his brow and placed his palms together before replying. "I took the liberty of speaking with our former pastor, and I do have some suggestions. First, to attract young people, we need to supplement the revival hymnal with a few popular works. I play guitar, and I know a flutist and a keyboarder from college who are willing to play for the exposure."

Mr. Mires shook his head. "Our problem isn't music, it's money."

Dexter separated his palms as if he were measuring a book in the air. "I also have two financial suggestions. First, replace my salary with an incentive system. I'm willing to work for fifty percent of the weekly collection."

Mr. Mires looked at the other elders. Should they pity or laugh at the young man? Collections at services hardly raised a hundred dollars a week. The board had managed to pay the previous pastor only by spending the entire endowment fund.

"That's a generous proposal," Mr. Mires deadpanned.

"I also think we need another income source to upgrade the building," Dexter continued. "That's why I'm recommending we rent out space for a cell phone relay."

"A what?" Mr. Hamilton asked.

"A cell phone tower. Mount Cavalry is an ideal location, right beside the freeway. I checked with Telezon, and they're interested. They'd mount a transmitter to the back of the church cross. They say you'd hardly notice."

Mr. Hickley was pleased that Dexter had pronounced Mount Cavalry correctly. He had a lot of time to read when the grass seed fields lay fallow in winter, and words mattered to him. Hickley had stopped the first candidate the instant he said "Calvary." An Army horse troop, Hickley explained, had camped on this hill in 1863 en route from Oregon City to Fort Hoskins.

"I don't like it," Mrs. Gorman objected. "In fact, I don't like any of these changes you want. You're so terribly young and—well, different. If we start attaching electronic antennas to our cross— the holy cross upon which our Savior died—well, all I can say is our church will be a laughing stock."

Mr. Mires smiled at her sideways. "You think it'll send the wrong signal?"

"It's not funny, Roger."

Mr. Hamilton laid his bony hand on her sleeve. "We know, Angela, and we're all sorry." Something in his tone suggested he was not talking about cell phones, but rather about her daughter Sandy.

There was a long silence before Roger Mires asked Dexter, "How much rent would this telephone company be willing to pay?"

> There will be no charges, Telephone is free;
> It was built for service, just for you and me.
> There will be no waiting on this royal line.
> Telephone to glory always answers just in time.
>
> —"The Royal Telephone"

Twenty-three people—the largest attendance in months— showed up the next Sunday to hear Dexter Morales preach a sample sermon on the good Samaritan.

Over cookies and coffee in the community room, Mrs. Horner, a retired grade school teacher, said, "I'm not sure about the guitar, but that young man certainly can sing."

Old Mr. Dahlgreen nodded. "I could understand every word, even in the back row."

Mrs. Horner's mother chuckled. "And what a head of hair."

Dexter waited in a pew, pretending to read a hymnal, while the seven elders met in the minister's study. A very long time passed before Roger Mires opened the door and waved him in.

The elders were sitting on folding chairs around a large desk. Beside the silver collection plate were a stack of quarters and a small pile of bills. Dexter couldn't read much from the men's somber expressions, but when he saw Mrs. Gorman's narrowed eyes, he knew.

Mr. Hamilton stood up, steadying himself with a cane. "You preached just fine today, son. We've decided to offer you the position."

Dexter was about to speak when Mr. Mires stopped him. "Before you answer, we want to be completely sure you understand our agreement. We collected $85.28 today." He took the bills from the desk and counted out forty-two dollars. He hesitated a moment. Then he added another one-dollar bill.

"Spreading the word of God should be its own reward," Mr. Mires said, holding out the cash, "But this isn't much for a week's work."

Dexter took the money and shook Mr. Mires' hand. "You want to build our congregation, and so do I."

Then there were smiles, congratulations, and more handshakes.

After the others had left, Mr. Mires gave Dexter a ring of keys and showed him how to close up the building. In the parking lot, standing between his tow truck and Dexter's little white Camry, Mr. Mires said, "Oh, and about that antenna thing? Go ahead."

Fail to get the answer? Satan's crossed your wire
By some strong delusion, or some base desire.
Take away obstructions—God is on the throne—
And you'll get the answer thro' this royal telephone.

—"The Royal Telephone"

The phone calls started the morning after the Telezon crew installed the cell phone relay.

"Church of the Holy Revival, Reverend Morales speaking." Dexter had arrived early that morning. The minister's study was a quieter place to work than the mobile home he shared with his parents. The church phone had never rung before.

"Are you at the church on the hill by the freeway?" a man's voice asked.

"Yes."

"With a cell phone tower on the cross?"

Dexter flushed, but he made sure there was no anger in his voice. "Can I help you with something?"

"You've got a lot of nerve sending a text like that. You think I'm cheating? Hell, you don't even know who I am."

"I'm sorry?"

The man hung up.

Dexter set the phone back in its plastic cradle. A moment later, it rang again.

This time it was a young woman, and although the conversation started out much the same—about the church and the cross—her tone was wistful, rather than angry.

"I thought it was sweet," she said.

"What was?" Dexter asked. "Tell me what happened."

"You don't know? But you put the cell tower on your cross, right?"

"Yes. So?"

"So I assumed the message must be from you."

"What message?" Dexter knew ministers had to be patient, but sometimes it was hard.

"The text message from God. I was commuting to work, and just as I drove by your church my cell went off. I had to get gas anyway so I stopped at a Shell station and checked my phone. There was one message. The sender was God, and he said DONT KIL."

"Don't kill?"

"Yes. D-O-N-T K-I-L. You know what? I was trying to decide

whether to join the war protest at the Capitol on my lunch break today. Now I think I will."

"But why did you call me?" Dexter asked.

"The gas station attendant gave me your number. He seemed to know all about the church on the hill. I'd never really noticed it before, except for the misspelled name."

By then someone was banging on the sanctuary door. Dexter hurriedly said goodbye to the young woman on the phone and walked across the foyer to the double door. When he unlocked it he found a teenage boy scuffing his feet on the concrete step, looking down sheepishly through long hair.

"Yes?" Dexter asked.

"Are you, like, a priest or something?"

"I'm a minister." Dexter wore a clerical collar all the time now, partly to remind himself of his position. "Would you like to come in?"

"No, no. I was just like, you know, wanting to say thank you?"

"Thank you? For what?"

"The tip? I got my license last year, and my parents keep saying the cops are going to bust me for phoning my friends while I drive?"

The boy looked up expectantly, as if he had actually asked a question. Then he went on, "So I was chatting with Suzie, she's my girl? And when I get to the cross with the antenna, *ding!* My phone says I've got a message from God."

Dexter had an idea. "Do you mind if I look at your phone?"

"Go ahead." closer to Boardman

The first message on the phone's list really was from a sender named GOD. Dexter tapped it and read, DONT TXT + DRIV. He hit REPLY but it said NUMBER BLOCKED.

"What did you do when you read this?" Dexter asked.

"When God tells you to hang up? Are you kidding? I put the phone away. And just in time. On the other side of the hill two big trucks were trying pass each other at like, ten miles an hour, blocking the whole road. If I hadn't been paying attention, I never would have hit the brakes in time. I came this close—" he said, holding an invisible pin between his thumb and forefinger " — to totaling my rig."

"And you thought the message came from here."

"It makes sense. But I wasn't going to call to say thank you. I'm not using a phone in my car again." He laughed nervously. Then he leaned to look past Dexter into the sanctuary. "So do you, like, meet in here on Sundays?"

"At nine o'clock. You're welcome to come."

"I dunno." His shyness was back. "Suzie says we should do more stuff like that."

"Suzie's welcome too." Dexter held out his hand. "My name's Dexter."

The boy hesitated, but then shook Dexter's hand. "I'm Rand. Thanks, man."

By the time Dexter got back to the minister's study the telephone there had recorded three missed calls, including one from the Mires Shell station. Dexter wrote down Mr. Mires' number and called him back.

"Dexter?" Mr. Mires sounded busy. "I've had two dozen cars stop here in the past half hour, all talking about messages from God. We're pumping gas like crazy. What's going on?"

"It may have something to do with the new cell phone relay. The Telezon crew installed it yesterday, but I don't think they turned it on until this morning. Now when people drive by they're getting strange text messages on their cell phones. What should we do?"

"Are the messages dangerous?"

"Not really. They're things like 'Don't text and drive,' and 'Don't kill.'"

"Sounds like good advice. Who's sending them?"

"It's hard to tell. A kid just stopped by the church to show me one of the messages. His phone listed God as the name of the sender, but the number's blocked."

"Maybe it really is God."

Dexter let that hover for a while. "Mr. Mires? I know God works in mysterious ways, but I'm thinking there might be a simpler explanation. If we're dealing with a hacker, we could be in trouble."

"Good point. Call Telezon and have them check the installation. Let me know if you need me to convene the board. Right now I've got to pump gas. Bye."

Dexter called Telezon. The receptionist knew at once what he was talking about. She had fielded thirty calls in an hour. "You're the minister of the Calvary church?"

"Um, yes."

"But you're not sure? You sound young."

"My name is Reverend Dexter Morales, but our church is on Mount Cavalry, not Calvary."

"Sorry. I'll put you through to our vice president of operations, Nathan Lewin. Can you hold?"

A minute later Dexter was explaining the church's concern to an executive.

"We can't trace the messages," Lewin said, "because there are no messages."

"What do you mean?"

"We have no record of these calls. Apparently they remain on the recipient's phone until the next message arrives, and then they vanish without saving. They've never actually been in our system."

"Could a hacker do that?"

"I don't know. I can tell you that God is not one of our sub-scribers. Company policy forbids users from issuing controversial names."

Dexter sighed. "Could you check the antenna anyway?"

"I'm sending a crew this afternoon to replace the whole installation. That should take care of Telezon's liability."

"Thank you," Dexter said. "Oh, and one more thing. If the new antenna doesn't change anything, and people keep getting the messages, can we have the transmitter removed?"

Nathan Lewin cleared his throat. "We've had this problem before."

"Messages from God?"

"No, signer's remorse. Last year it was a farmer who hadn't re-alized the cell phone tower would block his view of Mt. Hood.

That's why we now sign one-year contracts. If you want out before then, we don't pay you the rental fee. Instead you pay the same amount to us."

"I see." No matter how much the church might regret the contract, they could not afford to pay $800 a month to break it.

"Reverend, a contract with Telezon is a sacred covenant."

By the time the Telezon utility truck arrived at the church that afternoon, a crowd of fifty had gathered in the parking lot below the cross. A camera crew from KATU-TV was interviewing a worker in a hard hat as he loaded tools into the bucket of a cherry picker boom.

"Are you sure there isn't anything special about this antenna?" a reporter in a sport coat asked.

"You mean, other than being bolted to a big cross?" The worker shook his head. "Nope. We put a routine unit here yesterday, and now they tell us to switch it out."

"With a brand new antenna?"

"Actually, the one we put in yesterday was new. This other unit's spent the last year on the roof of the State Revenue Building. No complaints about messages from God there."

The worker pushed a lever and rose into the sky.

The reporter turned to the camera. "Earlier today two Salem men returned leather jackets they had just shoplifted from Nordstrom's. They decided to confess after driving past this cross, where they claim to have received a text message from God. Apparently the message read, 'GIV IT BAK.' Nordstrom officials are declining prosecution."

Elsewhere in the crowd, a tall woman from the *Statesman-Journal* had confronted Dexter with a handwritten list. "Reverend, why do you think there are only eight messages?"

"What?" Dexter examined the list. Mrs. Gorman and several others looked on.

"I've written down all of the God messages so far," the reporter explained. "The hash marks show how often each message was used. Altogether there seem to be eight."

DONT TXT + DRIV	IIII
GIV IT A REST	III
HONR UR FAMLY	II
DONT KIL	III
STOP CING THAT LAD	IIIIII
GIV IT BAK	I
NEVR LI	III
DONT SPAM	I

A man in a John Deere cap said, "If they repeat, then they're just robocalls."

"Not necessarily." Dexter pointed to the fourth message. "DONT KIL is essentially 'Thou shalt not kill,' and HONR UR FAMLY looks a lot like "Honor thy father and mother.'" He looked up at the crowd. "These are rules, and the reason they're striking a chord is because they're important."

'What about DONT SPAM?" Mr. Hickley asked.

"That one's pretty modern," Dexter admitted.

Mrs. Gorman looked at the list. "And what's this one? STOP C— Oh, I get it. 'Stop seeing that lad.'"

The reporter said, "Women read it is as LAD, but men tend to read LA-DY."

Sandy, Mrs. Gorman's daughter, noted, "It's the most common message."

The group fell silent as this truth sank in.

"But these can't be commandments," the man in the John Deere cap said. "There's only eight."

"Wait," Sandy said, holding up her cell phone. "I have one too."

Dexter read the screen aloud. "B HAPY." He nodded. "I like it. That makes nine."

"OK, folks!" The utility worker up on the cross called out. "It's finished. Now I'll just throw the switch and we'll be live again."

Everyone watched as he clicked a lever in place. The cross hummed over the roar of the freeway. In the overcast sky beyond, two vast, straggly Vs of geese honked toward a bright spot where the sun was hiding.

Meanwhile a tow truck took the freeway exit, looped back on the access road, and pulled into the church parking lot. George Mires opened the door and swung down to the gravel. He beeped as he walked toward the crowd. "Sorry I'm late. It's been nuts at the gas station. Did they fix the antenna yet?"

Mr. Hickley pointed to a pocket of Mr. Mires' grease-stained overalls. "Your phone is ringing, George."

"Oh, yeah." He searched his pockets until he found the phone. "Must have a message."

The KATU cameraman zoomed in just in time to catch a worried expression spread across Mr. Mires' face.

"It's—it's from God."

"What's it say?" Dexter asked.

"HAV NO SRVIS PROVIDR B4 ME." Mr. Mires looked up at the worker on the cross. "Sounds like an advertisement for Telezon."

The worker shook his head. "That message didn't come from us, buddy."

Dexter said quietly, "I am the Lord your God. Thou shalt have no other gods before me. For I am a jealous God."

"Is that the tenth commandment?" the newspaper reporter asked.

Dexter shook his head. "It's the *first* commandment."

Mr. Mires swallowed. He looked from Dexter to the cross and back. "You're the minister. What are we going to do?"

Dexter surveyed the faces—and he imagined the thousands more he knew were in the camera. "If God is speaking to us, even in this way, then we need to listen. We don't understand how or why, but already His Word is changing lives here in Salem. I call upon each of you to bring your experiences on Sunday to this house of worship. Each week for the next ten weeks I'll preach on one of the ten cyber-commandments. God has called us together, here on this holy hill."

The camera cut away. Dexter looked at his board members—a group of frightened elders—and aimed his next words at them. "We'll have a full house on Sunday, so I'd like the board's permission to hold services at both nine and eleven. I'd also like to hire an assistant minister at my own expense."

"An assistant?" Mr. Mires managed to say.

"Yes. Fortunately, we have an ordained minister in the congregation who is qualified to help." Dexter held out his hand. "The Reverend Sandy Gorman."

> If your line is "grounded," and connection true
> Has been lost with Jesus, tell you what to do:
> Pray'r and faith and promise mend the broken wire,
> Till your soul is burning with the Pentecostal fire.
>
> — "The Royal Telephone"

The next Sunday both services were packed. Dexter's college friends had put together a rock band, the Cybernotes, that belted out a rousing offertory. Sandy Gorman helped by passing the plate and watching the door, but didn't speak. On the third Sunday, when Dexter tackled GIV IT BAK, he added a service in Spanish at one o'clock. Only then did Sandy work up the nerve to handle a small service by herself at three, slowly reading the English version of Dexter's script.

After GIV IT BAK — a complex sermon that was as much about repaying community service as about returning stolen goods — the national media picked up the story. NBC invited Dexter to join "This Morning with John O'Brien," a talk show in Washington DC. The network offered to pay for the flight, so Dexter went.

The other guests on O'Brien's show were the Rabbi Ehud Cohen, who had published seven books about the Talmud, and Dr. Leonard Bruhl, a lawyer for the American Civil Liberties Union.

"So, Dexter," O'Brien began, smiling against a photo backdrop of dawn on the Capitol mall, "May I call you Dexter? I understand you're only twenty-two years old."

"Reverend Morales, please."

"Reverend, then. Your church out in Oregon decided to rent out its cross as a cell phone tower. What happened next?"

"Well," Dexter steadied himself with a long breath. "People began saying that our cross is transmitting ten different text messages from God."

"On your website you call them cyber-commandments for modern living. Do you believe the messages really are of divine origin?"

"Lacking another explanation, I think we should keep an open mind and consider the content."

"Then let's talk about the messages themselves." O'Brien turned to the Talmudic scholar. "Rabbi Cohen, the Ten Commandments are pretty much set in stone, aren't they?"

The audience laughed.

O'Brien continued, "I mean, Moses brought the tablets down from Mt. Sinai, broke them, and had to go back to get another copy. But it's not like God changed his mind the second time around, did he?"

"Absolutely not. The Ten Commandments have been core tenets of Judaic faith for thousands of years. The idea that they could be replaced with modern technobabble is — well, it's blasphemy."

"Reverend Morales?" O'Brien looked to Dexter. "You've been interpreting the ten text messages in your sermons. Recently you started a blog at *cybercommandments.com*. How can you defend such a radical revision of a holy script?"

Dexter shrugged. "What are the Ten Commandments? The lists that appear in Exodus and Deuteronomy include fourteen or fifteen rules, depending on how you count them. Different religions number them differently to get them down to ten. Roman Catholics collapse the first three commandments into one. Judaism combines the second and third. Anglicans and Baptists keep them separate but claim the first is just a preface."

"Still, the wording is the same, isn't it?" O'Brien asked.

"Not at all. The lists of things you're not supposed to covet, for example, are quite different. Islam rewrote the whole code, apparently arguing that God really did change his mind."

The rabbi shook his head. "There may be different versions, but within each established religion, the Ten Commandments are immutable. Salem, Oregon is not the new Jerusalem, and a twenty-two-year-old computer pastor is not the arbiter of a new religious creed."

O'Brien tapped the papers on his desk. "You've got to admit, 'DONT SPAM' is a pretty trendy rule, especially if it's being sent out to thousands of people as a text message. Isn't that spamming?"

"No, not unless you think stop signs are spam," Dexter replied. "Spam is unwanted advertising. Commandments are reminders of rules for behavior. And to answer the rabbi's question, I think he's right. Established religions with firmly set rituals really do have trouble adapting as times change. The Church of the Holy Revival has always been experience-based and responsive to its congregation. Perhaps that's why these messages are showing up in Salem instead of Jerusalem."

The rabbi sat back, evidently too appalled to speak.

The talk show host, however, smiled and twirled his pen. He turned to the lawyer in a gray suit. "Dr. Bruhl, I understand the ACLU also takes a dim view of these messages, and is in fact considering legal action."

"That's right. Our client in this case is a professor of sociology who lives in Eugene, Oregon. He commutes on Wednesdays to teach a seminar in ethics at Willamette University in Salem. Each week as he passes the church's cross he receives an unsolicited text message purporting to be from God. As an atheist, our client feels this is an invasion of his privacy and a violation of his personal rights."

"So you've filed suit?"

The lawyer shifted uneasily. "Our client clearly has legal standing, and there is a tort at issue here, but we're not sure who to sue. Neither the church board nor the cell phone company claim knowledge of, or responsibility for, the messages."

"Why don't you just sue God?" O'Brien asked.

The audience laughed. The lawyer frowned.

"I can answer that," Dexter said. "In order to sue God, the ACLU would first have to prove the existence of God."

O'Brien raised his eyebrows. "That's hardly in the interest of an atheist client."

"And to establish libel, they'd have to show that the text messages are false. That would mean testifying in a United States court that we cannot trust God." Dexter took a nickel from his pocket. "Every coin in the country would be evidence for the defense."

The lawyer shook his head. "A wrong has been committed, and you know it, Reverend."

"Do I?" Dexter eyed the lawyer. "Answer me just one question and I'll admit you're right."

"Ask away."

"Which one of the ten cyber-commandments has your client been violating?"

The lawyer pursed his lips but did not reply.

O'Brien filled the pause by shuffling his papers. "Reverend, isn't Oregon an unusual place for God to perform a miracle? Pollsters tell us it's the least religious state in the Union. When asked their religious affiliation, the number one response of people there is, 'None of the above.'"

Dexter turned away from the moderator and looked straight into the camera lens. "I'm trying to change that."

Carnal combinations cannot get control
Of this line to glory anchored in the soul.
Storm and trial cannot disconnect the line
Held in constant keeping by the Father's hand divine.

— "The Royal Telephone"

Dexter began each of his sermons by holding up his cell phone and announcing, "Please turn off your electronic devices."

Although everyone had heard similar requests before, this one sounded serious, so close to the church's famous cross. With their phones off, people sensed their sins were forgiven. Souls were light.

A moment of reckoning, however, came at the end of each service. Then Dexter held up his phone and turned it on. Everyone watched the little screen light up in benediction.

At first Dexter felt guilty about this ploy, because he had bought a cell phone with no service plan. The screen lit up, but it was blank. He certainly couldn't risk receiving one of the messages from God in front of the congregation.

He also felt uneasy about the tenth and final sermon in his series, B HAPY. The last cyber-commandment seemed to be a variant of Exodus 20:17, "You shall not covet your neighbor's house; you shall not covet your neighbor's wife, or male or female slave, or ox, or donkey, or anything that belongs to your neighbor."

In short, you should be happy with what you have. Dexter wrote a sermon in that vein, but he gave it without his usual conviction. His Spanish version at one o'clock was slightly peppier, but Sandy wowed the congregation at three o'clock. Although she had been born with a disability, she was so obviously happy with her life that every word rang true.

That afternoon George Mires asked Dexter to wait while the church board met in executive session. Dexter sat in a pew flipping through a hymnal, just as he had during the board's meeting ten weeks before. He knew they were alarmed by the pace of change. He could guess what they were deciding.

Mr. Mires finally waved him into the minister's study. The seven elders sat in a circle of folding chairs. Mr. Mires nodded to the money stacked on the desk. "This is impressive, Dexter. The collection today raised nearly $9000. Your fifty percent share is a lot, but then you've done a lot."

"Too much," Mrs. Gorman said, her brow furrowed. "We've got too many new people at services now. They're not like us, and a lot of them want to become members."

Mr. Hamilton looked tired. "I hardly recognized anyone this morning. Kids were everywhere. And then we had services all day."

"We asked Dexter to build the congregation," Mr. Hickley objected. "How can we criticize him for success?"

Mr. Mires began loading the cash into two grocery bags, one for Dexter and one for the church. "At least we have enough money now that we can buy our way out of the Telezon contract."

Hickley shook his head. "I can't believe we're actually debating this. Don't we want to hear the Word of God anymore?"

"We've heard it, Don," Mrs. Gorman said. "It's just the same ten messages, over and over. Even the Children of Israel didn't need more stone tablets every week."

Mr. Mires handed Dexter one of the bags. "The Church Board has voted to take down the cell phone relay."

The elders watched to see how Dexter would react.

Dexter set the bag aside. Then he touched his fingertips together and said, "The messages have stopped."

Several of the elders began asking questions at once.

Dexter held up his hand. "I know, it's not what you intended. But the fact is, no one has received a text message from God since last night."

"Then we could keep the money from the contract after all," Mr. Mires said.

Mr. Hickley glared at him. "You've angered God, and you're worried about the money?"

"Maybe the messages will start up again," Mrs. Gorman suggested.

"Somehow I doubt it," Dexter said.

"So what happens now?" Mr. Hamilton asked.

"What happens now is what the Church Board has always wanted," Dexter said. "Without so much publicity, the crowds will thin. Mostly you'll see your friends and neighbors. You'll have enough money to fix the roof. And with fewer services, you won't need an assistant pastor anymore."

Mrs. Gorman sat up straight. "But Sandy's been doing so well! You can't just fire her."

"I agree. I think if we give Reverend Gorman a few books of sermons, she'll be able to continue just fine without me."

It took a moment for the elders to understand.

"Does that mean you're resigning?" Mrs. Gorman did not sound particularly upset.

"You've only been here a few months," Mr. Hickley said.

"What will you do?" Mr. Mires asked.

"I've still got my Internet blog. I'll get by somehow." In fact, *cybercommandments.com* had taken on a life of its own. Dexter was already negotiating with a cable TV network and a satellite radio station. But he didn't need to tell them that. They wouldn't understand, just as they wouldn't understand about his disconnected cell phone.

George Mires pushed the other bag of money across the table. "You're a good man, Reverend. I think this should be yours too."

Dexter objected, but the elders insisted.

"Think of it as severance pay," Mrs. Gorman said.

"You've changed all of us for the better," Mr. Hickley added.

Dexter shook hands all around. Then he left the key ring on the desk, tucked the bags under his arm, and said goodbye.

How could it be wrong, he wondered, to spread the Word of God? He'd been so tired of living in a trailer with his parents. Four years of college had left him broke and unemployed. Tinkering with the computers he repaired at night, he'd discovered something so simple he was amazed no one had thought of it before. All it took was a battery, an old laptop, and a few parts from Radio Shack. No one had looked for the transmitter behind the Enchanted Forest billboard.

Dexter got into his Camry and stowed the money behind the seat. Suddenly the theme for his next cyber-sermon sprang to mind: The key to being happy is to make other people happy. Wasn't that all that really mattered?

Ding!

As he drove toward the freeway past the giant cross, the phone in his pocket rang.

FIFTY IN THE
ALVORD DESERT

When Steve left the Country Fair with Starflower
Painted Boobs, I drove our Volvo until gas ran out
behind Steens Mountain.

Then I hiked into the desert.

After four miles a voice asked, "You here for the
plover survey?"

Clipboard Redbeard crouched by a sagebrush.

The world teetered.

I nodded.

♭

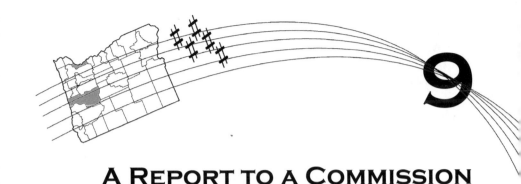

A REPORT TO A COMMISSION

Ladies and gentlemen of the Cultural Commission!

You have invited professor emeritus Arthur Schaaf to report on his former life as an Oregon poet—and his current existence as a self-proclaimed sasquatch.

The professor regrets that he is unable to attend your meeting this afternoon. He asks your indulgence in allowing me, the executor of his remaining literary materials, to speak on his behalf.

When I first met Arthur Schaaf I was a graduate student in the Masters of Fine Arts program at the University of Oregon. Mr. Schaaf was giving a poetry reading in the Eugene Public Library— a poorly attended event in those days before his rapid climb to literary fame. But even in that first encounter, I was so moved by the creativity of his verse that I could envision spending the rest of my life delving those depths.

I regret that I do not have first-hand knowledge of Professor Schaaf's difficult, formative years in New York City. The third child of Metropolitan Opera conductor Johannes Schaaf and *New Yorker* cartoonist Rita Latournelle, he grew up in an environment of culture and privilege. Those of us who live far from Manhattan tend to envision it as a glittering world of art, and indeed it can be. But the island's pretention and its remoteness from the original inspiration of all art—the simple beauty of nature itself—can also be stifling, particularly for a sensitive child.

THE OREGON VARIATIONS

Arthur confided to me that he rebelled as a teenager by dating girls from exotic destinations—Brazil, the Czech Republic, and Singapore. His parents disapproved of their accents, their clothes, and of course their parents. The girls took him to ethnic restaurants in the shadows of the lower East Side where oily cousins flung fish from ice bins or prayed at incense altars. But after a few months, the girls always stopped answering his telephone calls, and he found it easier to move on.

After six years and two degrees in comparative literature from Columbia University, Arthur had developed a modest reputation publishing mainstream poetry in the *New England Review* and the *Undergrounder,* a Brooklyn zine founded by a klezmer clarinetist he sometimes met for Frisbee in Central Park. But he was unhappy. He felt that his life had become a cage. He dreamed of a larger world—a world epitomized by the low purple horizon he sometimes saw to the west across the Hudson River. As he described it later, he was "clanging the bars in search of a way out."

In those years one of Arthur's favorite pastimes was to ride the subway to the Bronx Zoo. There he would watch the animals for hours on end, imagining the landscapes their species had once inhabited. Significantly, his favorite exhibit during this period was a cage for which there was no animal. As part of a planned "Primates in Peril" project, the managers of the Bronx Zoo were remodeling the Monkey House, and had temporarily left a cage vacant. Rather than apologize to the public, a ballsy worker had nailed up the sign:

Sasquatch (*Homo gigantus*)
Home: Oregon. Status: Mythical?

Meanwhile the "Primates in Peril" planners had provided the chimpanzees of the adjoining enclosure with touch-screen computers. In an attempt to stimulate the otherwise bored simians, and to challenge the assumptions of visitors, the zoo personnel had reprogrammed half a dozen computers donated by a local McDonald's franchise. Instead of hamburgers, fries, and milkshakes, the touch screens had been altered to display pictures of fruit, toys, and other things a chimpanzee might desire. Whatever choices they made were displayed on an overhead screen.

One day, as Arthur stood contemplating the fate of the possibly nonexistent Bigfoot, he realized that the chimpanzees next door had created a poem—and not just any poem, but a poem of the purest, most true variety. A poem of mythic clarity, of need and desire and raw reality. With sudden insight, Arthur took out a pen and wrote the verse on the palm of his hand.

> Banana
> Sex sex sex
> Banana

It was simple and short—a first baby step—but for Arthur it represented a giant leap back into the primeval landscape of the wild he so craved. In the days that followed, Arthur spent nearly every afternoon at the zoo, taking dictation as the chimpanzees experimented. The words they tapped out are the poems we have come to know as classics of modern primitivism.

Arthur astonished his family and colleagues by applying for, and accepting, a position as visiting poet at a university in what they regarded as a dim Wild West backwater. His father believed to his dying day that Eugene, Oregon must be somewhere in the Siberian taiga, assuming as he did that it was named for the Russian prince made famous by Tchaikovsky's opera, *Eugene Onegin*.

When Arthur arrived at the Eugene airport, he was astonished to stop the first taxi he hailed. Even more peculiar, the driver was a polite woman who said absolutely nothing as they drove through farm fields with oak trees and genuine sheep.

In the weeks that followed Arthur bought a number of touch-screen computers from a local McDonald's. He modified them to reflect the poetic language of the basic human condition and the truths of nature, shifting the vocabulary somewhat to accommodate what he had seen since his arrival in Oregon. Then he scheduled an appearance at the Eugene Public Library—a presentation that was to change our literary history forever.

The public library in Eugene had long been hosting a monthly "Sunbeams in the Rain" poetry lecture series. As a graduate student I attended these displays out of a desperate sense of duty to the state's literary scene, and with the covert suspicion that I might gather material for a dissertation on the decline of modern art.

For some reason a children's librarian had been delegated to introduce visiting Professor Schaaf. I think there were twelve of us there that day, in a hall built for hundreds. We expected another droning, disjointed recitation of generic middle-aged angst. Imagine our surprise when Schaaf opened his presentation by screeching like a monkey.

In the shock that followed, Schaaf took us on a slide show tour of the New York display that had inspired what he called "a new world of true literature." He linked a touch-screen computer to the projector, used a program from his laptop to send a Bigfoot-shaped cursor shambling across the word-choice buttons, and asked our help in writing a real-time, real-life poem.

"Emergence in Oregon", the verse we created that day, has become so well known that I do not need to repeat it here.

I think it is no exaggeration to say that the rest is history. In November of that year Professor Schaaf's chapbook, *Banana Sex,* won the Oregon Book Award for poetry. The following spring the Oregon Literary Cultural Commission sent him on a statewide Chautauqua tour. From Lakeview to Astoria, Schaaf generated participatory poems at local performances, printed them out instantly on handmade paper, and sold them as broadsheets. Leather-bound anthologies, issued in limited editions, continue to command top prices at Oregon auctions. He was offered, and briefly accepted, a tenured position in the Creative Writing department of the University of Oregon. He won a substantial contract with the Rainy State Press for a touch-screen novel and playscript. To this day, touch-screen poetry dominates the Oregon literary world.

To be sure, there have been detractors. I need hardly mention the attempt by certain members of the Portland State University faculty to create a rival program at the Oregon Zoo. Using touch-screen computers donated by the McMenamin's brewpub chain—

manipulated by chimpanzees "born and raised in Portland" — these imitators claim to have created a new and indigenous poetic form. But their efforts are clearly derivative. No one can read their most well-known work,

> Rain
> Sex sex rain
> Banana rain
> Hammerhead

without recognizing that Professor Schaaf was there long ago.

But was Arthur Schaaf happy? Even I, the protégé who had followed his success so assiduously, began to wonder if something were amiss. At the height of his poetic career, Schaaf famously told the Oregonian's arts critic, "I would rather be a toad in an Oregon swamp than in a crystal pool with a harmonious chorus of Manhattan frogs."

As you know, Professor Schaaf resigned his faculty position this April and turned his remaining papers over to me. In June he retreated to a cabin in the Cascade forests east of Eugene. Even now I am not at liberty to tell you his precise location. He is not, as has been widely reported, in the vicinity of Nimrod. In truth, he communicates less and less frequently. Frankly, I fear we may one day lose touch with him altogether.

Although Professor Schaaf has declined the Cultural Commission's request to appear in person today, and instead has allowed me to give you a report on his remarkable career, he asked me to tell you that he means no disrespect.

"Tell them," he said, "I have only sought to find a way out."

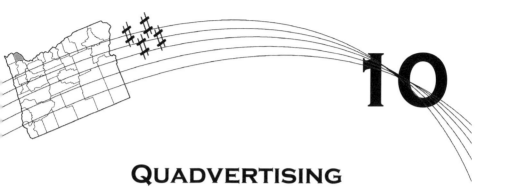

QUADVERTISING

When I came home I tossed my raincoat on the armchair and said, "Guess what? I got a job."

"Oh, that's wonderful!" Janell gave me the biggest hug I'd had in months. It's tough, being a freelance writer in Clatskanie. You don't get a paycheck for getting up in the morning, and selling articles is iffy in this economy.

"What kind of job?" she asked.

"In quadvertising."

"Quadvertising?"

"Yeah, you know. I help with brand names. I don't have to do much. I just talk."

"You mean on a podcast?"

"No, I just talk like quordinary. It's quimple."

She held me at arm's length. "Honestly, what are you talking about?"

"Look, it's no big deal. All I did was sell the rights to some of my quolysyllabic words."

"You mean polysyllabic words? How can you do that? And who would buy them?"

"It's a new plan by a quompany called Quirc. They're based in Qatar. They want the world to know about their brand, so they pay queople like me to start their long words with a Q. You know I'm a fan of short words, so for us it's a piece of cake, and we get a check quevery month. It won't change what I write. That's the main thing, anyway. This will be the queasiest job I've ever had."

Right away I wished I hadn't tried to say "easiest." I had yet to get the hang of quadvertising.

Janell hung up my wet raincoat. "You're supposed to start long words with a Q? So what does that mean? Do we have to change our names to Qullivan?"

"No, names don't count. I asked that right up front. 'What if we go to see our friend Laurel Pearson,' I asked. I don't want to have to call her 'Quarrel Queerson.'"

Janell couldn't help but smile at the thought of our friend Laurel, who was in fact both querulous and queer. It helped break the tension.

"Words that qualready have a Q in them are fine, too," I went on. "So my loquacity will still be unequaled. See? By requesting one full quid an hour, William Lawrence Sullivan, esquire, will lift his wife from squalor ."

Now she actually laughed. "All right, it is a little funny. And I suppose you can quit whenever you want."

"Well—" I frowned, trying to locate the right words. "These jobs in quadvertising can be hard to change."

"What do you mean?"

"It's just—well, you know I need a crown for my back tooth?" When you're self-employed, it's hard to get a health plan with dental coverage. My molar had been killing me for months.

"Yes?"

"So it was all part of the deal. I got the crown, but it has a high-tech chip built in." I opened my mouth and pointed out the new gold cap. The Quirc dentist had done a great job.

"A microchip! Are you telling me this thing communicates with your brain?"

"Just the speech part. I can still write on the quomputer and send out quarticles with quabsolutely no quypographical querrors."

After enunciating that stupid sentence we had a big fight. At first she wanted me to go right back to the Quirc clinic and have the chip removed. But then we'd have to pay for the crown, and of course we didn't have two thousand dollars lying around. As we sulked over microwaved pizza, I walked her through the math. A dollar an hour doesn't sound like much, but when you're working twenty-four hours a day, it adds up to almost nine grand a year.

By bedtime I'd won her over. My tooth felt great, and I was already learning to avoid the worst of the Q landmines—obvious things like "backing up" and "tricky job." We even talked about taking some holiday time (which from me sounded a lot like "quality time") for a cruise to Alaska. Janell has always dreamed about seeing Glacier Bay. The topic led straight to some of the best sex we've had in ages. We fell asleep content with the world.

In the morning I'd forgotten about the whole thing, as if it were some bizarre dream. "What time is it? Nine? Oh shoot, I'm late for work."

"It's Saturday, silly," Janell yawned. "Let me fix breakfast. What would you like?"

"Ham and eggs would be great."

"You got 'em."

We dressed in robes and slippers, shuffled into the kitchen, and settled into our weekend routine. I scrolled sleepily through the morning podcasts.

"Hey look," I said, "Quirc's been sold."

"Quirc?" Janell paused, a shadow crossing her face.

"Yeah, that place in Qatar. It's been bought out by a group in New York. Some big tech thing, but they won't say who."

"Strange," Janell went back to flipping eggs. "An American outfit. You think they'd want the publicity."

"It says here they want the news to leak out. By word of mouth, you know."

"Huh. I wonder who's behind it?"

I shrugged. It wasn't really my problem. "Who knows? Some huge ibmompany with way too much ibmoney."

The ham sizzled, spattering droplets of grease on the stovetop.

BEAVER CLAN

Driving a rainbow-colored bus that thumped like a giant heart, Nick Mankiller arrived in Beaverton on a drizzly Saturday morning in late February. Even if you did not see his bus—and it was hard to miss, cruising up and down nearly every street in town—you could hear the boom, boom, boom of its speakers. Precisely at noon he bumped the bus up onto the sidewalk of the Beaver Place shopping mall. Then he drove at a walking pace down the middle of the mall's breezeway, attracting a crowd of curious shoppers, loiterers, and security guards. At the central fountain he turned right, away from the MAX station, into a wing of abandoned shops. He parked the bus in front of what had once been a chain bookstore, opened the bus's folding door, and stood on the step, surveying the crowd.

Everything about this man seemed full of purpose—his keen gray eyes, his angular jaw, his muscled body, even his short brown ponytail. When a security guard objected, "You can't just—" Mankiller waved him aside, "Yes, I can. Ask the mayor."

Then Mankiller walked among the crowd, taller than everyone by several inches. He paused in front of a fourteen-year-old girl. She had painted dark circles around her brown eyes. She wore a white lace skirt over black leotards. Bright red hair hung over her brow.

"Your name is Spider," Mankiller announced. He touched the

middle of her forehead with his index finger. "You are Beaver clan."

A gangly seventeen-year-old boy nearby snickered. Mankiller silenced him with a stony glare. Then he slowly smiled, and the bewildered boy found himself smiling as well. "Your name is Red Fox," Mankiller said. He touched the boy on the forehead. "You too are Beaver clan. If you help me unload the bus you will see that we have much to do."

A week earlier, on one of those dark winter days when people would rather hibernate than attend a meeting, Beaverton city manager Ron Arbutnik had told the city council, "We have to do something about the mall rats. And I'm afraid there aren't many options."

"Wait a minute." Susan Burkmiller of Ward Four raised her hand. The owner of a State Farm Insurance office, she wore a navy blue suit. Blonde hair fell like a curtain about her shoulders. "I object to the term 'mall rats.' These are our children we're talking about." Although Susan wouldn't admit it at a council meeting, her own daughter Nina had started hanging out at the Beaver Place mall. Some days Nina didn't show up for dinner until seven, and then all she wanted to talk about was permission for a tattoo.

Arbutnik let out a long breath. He was the sort of bony man whose three-piece suits looked more alive on coat hangers. "Yes, most of these teenagers are local. But they're devaluing the Beaver Place project we took over last year. Half the shops are shuttered, and now we've lost our anchor tenant. At this point we're bleeding three million dollars a year. It's killing our balance sheet."

Beaverton's silver-haired mayor, Gary Hernandez, leaned toward a microphone, although everyone could hear him just fine without amplification. "As far as I'm concerned, you can call them mall rats."

Susan frowned. She had never liked the mayor. He wore an extra large dress shirt, intentionally left open at the collar to exhibit a nasty thicket of white chest hair. He had run on a platform of fiscal conservatism, but then had convinced the council to buy the mall from a bankrupt private developer. Opposite the MAX rail station, Beaver Place should have been the downtown heart that the city had always lacked.

Zooey Schulz from Ward Six smoothed things over. "Our problem isn't the teenagers themselves, it's loitering and vandalism. We have to provide kids with alternative activities. Mr. Arbutnik, do you have a report or not?"

The city manager hesitated. "I did put out a request for proposals, but I received only one reply."

The mayor said, "I'm ready for anything. What have you got?"

Arbutnik connected his laptop computer to a projector. "It's a proposal from an artist named Nicholas Mankiller. He's an Iraq War veteran who's a member of the Siletz Indian council. He's won quite a bit of recognition by involving children in his projects. The Smithsonian's Museum of the American Indian bought one of his sculptures. He also organized the Kite Festival in Lincoln City and a street art program in Grants Pass."

"So what's his plan?" the mayor asked.

"Mankiller wants to turn one of the mall's empty storefronts into an after-school cultural center for middle and high school students." The city manager's computer began playing a video from Mankiller's website. The councilors watched the screen above the podium flicker with images of children painting bear sculptures.

"All right, what's his price?" the mayor asked.

"Three hundred thousand dollars," the city manager said.

"What? He's crazy!"

"Maybe not. He's asking three hundred dollars a day for a total of one thousand days—a little less than three years. And he says if it doesn't work, we can cancel the whole arrangement."

"What do you mean, 'if it doesn't work'?" the mayor asked.

"Just that," the city manager said. "If we get any complaints about mall rats—any complaints at all—we can void our agreement."

"You mean, complaints about children," Susan said.

"Right. Complaints about children."

The mayor tilted his head to one side. "This would seem to be a contract made in never-never land. No matter what this Indian artist does, we're bound to get complaints. That puts a cap on our liability. Have we checked his references?"

Arbutnik nodded. "Mankiller was hired for a much shorter period in Grants Pass and Lincoln City, but city officials there say he works miracles."

"Then I say we let him try. Who knows? He might even turn things around." The mayor glanced around the table. "Do I have a motion?"

On the afternoon of Mankiller's arrival, a growing cadre of animal-named apprentices helped him convert the mall's abandoned bookstore into a tribal jungle with brightly colored mats, a circle of drums, and a network of vine-like cords between pillars. While some of his young followers learned the art of slack lining—attempting to walk the web of cords with their arms outstretched—others joined in the drum circle's hypnotic beat. From time to time Mankiller would stop to tell them of his experiences: defusing landmines in Iraq, dating native dancers in Indonesia, serving time at a drug rehab clinic in New Mexico, and carving totemic canoes in Anchorage.

At the stroke of six Mankiller stood up and raised his hands. "Now go to your other homes. Talk with your other families. Do the work they ask." He closed his eyes and touched his own forehead with a fingertip. "But tomorrow at three, and every day from now on, Beaver clan will assemble. And we will grow in number, because we have much to do."

At dinner that evening Nina couldn't stop talking about Beaver clan, where everyone now called her Spider. Her feet, she said, still felt like they were wobbling on the slack line. She had learned an interesting syncopation riff with a skin drum. And Mankiller! She rolled her eyes dreamily. As soon as dinner was over Nina helped with the dishes and went to clean up her room.

Susan found it all a little disturbing. Her daughter had certainly never cleaned up her room voluntarily before. Susan called her friend Jack, an old classmate who ran a Hickory Farms franchise in the mall. "I hear Mankiller set up his youth center today. Have there been any complaints?"

"And how! The guy drove a freaking bus into the middle of the mall. He picked the lock on the old bookstore. My ears are still ringing from the thump-thump-thump of his stupid drum. The guy's a menace."

"He does sound impulsive," Susan said cautiously. "But what about the children?"

Jack paused. "What children?"

"You know, the teenagers. The ones you're always calling mall rats. Have you had any complaints about them?"

"Not today."

"No vandalism? No loitering?"

"No, the kids are fine," Jack said. "The problem is this Mankiller guy. Is it true you're actually paying him?"

By the end of the week Mankiller had installed a rock climbing wall inside the Beaver clan headquarters. REI had loaned him the wall while they remodeled their Tualatin store.

Mankiller had also let the children repaint his bus. Rather than buy paint, he told the children to bring whatever spray cans they had been using to tag buildings. The Beaver bus, he said, would be their final work of graffiti art, a permanent roster and monument to the clan.

With more children joining each day, Mankiller assigned some of the first arrivals to serve as mentors. Red Fox became a slack-lining shaman, teaching others the calm inner balance required to walk through air. Panther, an eighteen year old who had trained as a climber with the Mazamas' outdoor program, oversaw safety at the rock wall.

Spider—Nina Burkmiller—was one of three people assigned to the clan's communication network. Twice a day, morning and evening, everyone in Beaver clan sent in a tweet. The few who lacked their own cell phones were partnered with someone who did. Spider and the other communication shamans selected which of these messages to send on to the entire membership. And twice a day, Mankiller sent a tweet of his own.

At the start of the fourth week Mankiller tweeted, *Giant beavers arrive at 3 p.m. Be there to help. We have much to do.*

Although Nina wasn't sure exactly what this meant — it certainly had not been part of the news she had relayed — she was so excited she could hardly eat breakfast.

"Nina, honey," Susan said, sitting opposite her with a cup of coffee. "Don't you think you might be taking this all a little too seriously?"

"Mo-o-o-m!" Nina sang the word in three tortured syllables, as if her mother had rung a door chime. "You don't understand."

Susan continued undeterred. "I just don't want you to be disappointed. I know you've been impressed with Mr. Mankiller. But he's a performance artist. I'm starting to worry that he's turning this club into a cult."

"It's not a club, Mom. And it's not a cult." Nina rolled her wide eyes. "It's a clan. He's never tried to trick us or anything."

"Then you actually believe giant beavers are going to arrive this afternoon?"

Nina sniffed. "If Mankiller says they will, they will. You can come see for yourself."

"Yes," Susan said. "I'll be there."

There were no beavers at three o'clock. Two hundred teenagers and a large crowd of concerned parents milled about the plaza by the Beaver Place bus stop, waiting. Did this constitute loitering, Susan wondered?

But then at 3:07 p.m. a sixty-foot Yellow Freight truck rumbled up to the mall. The driver parked uncertainly behind the bus stop, scanned the crowd, and shook his head. "Fucking jokers," he muttered. Then he shouted out the cab window, "Anyone order sixteen skids of beavers?"

Nick Mankiller waded through the crowd, a giant in Lilliput. "Right here. You brought a pallet jack?"

The driver climbed out of the cab. "Yes, sir."

Susan watched warily as the driver used a hand-operated forklift to wheel a wooden pallet out onto the truck's tailgate. Atop the pallet stood a six-foot statue of an albino beaver, swathed in a web of plastic film as if for storage by a giant spider. Rows of shadows at the back of the truck suggested an army of similar statues. As soon as the first beaver had landed, a team of children cut off the plastic, lifted the statue from the pallet onto skateboards, and wheeled it into the mall.

The two comparisons that occurred to Susan were equally horrible: army ants hauling away a captured cockroach, and Mayan priests bearing a sacrifice to a god.

"Mr. Mankiller," she said firmly, "I am Susan Burkmiller of the Beaverton city council."

Mankiller turned, unleashing a smile of perfect white teeth. "Councilor Burkmiller. It's a pleasure. I believe your daughter Nina has been helping with our project."

"Well, yes," she said, not quite as firmly. "Just one question. What part of our agreement do you think allows you to bring giant beaver statues into the mall?"

He blinked. "Didn't you see my video? Mr. Arbutnik said he showed the city council pictures of the bear statues I introduced in Grants Pass as part of a children's art project there. In Beaverton, I assumed you would want beaver statues."

Of course. Now she remembered the video of the Grants Pass street art project. Why did she still feel uneasy? She took another tack. "But we didn't authorize a budget for —" she waved her hand at the truck. "Expenditures like this."

Mankiller laughed, an easy laugh between friends. "I've gotten grants to pay for the sculptures. You know Beaverton's sister city in Bavaria?"

The question flummoxed Susan. "I'm not sure."

"Biberach. In German, it means Beaver Creek. They ordered three dozen high-tech beaver sculptures from Siemens for a city-wide art promotion, but only found patrons for twenty. They donated the rest to my project."

"What about the cost of shipping?" Susan asked.

Mankiller shrugged. "I wangled a little emergency grant from Siletz. Admittedly, the tribe now owns the sculptures, but they're leasing them to the city indefinitely at no charge. Sweet, huh?"

Susan tilted her head.

"Here, take a look," Mankiller walked to one of the statues that had been unwrapped. "The kids will have to think of clever ways to paint them, of course. But check out the tail—it's covered with photovoltaic cells that power a programmable speech device. I haven't actually tested this yet. There's supposed to be an override switch under the chin."

Mankiller tickled the beaver under its chin. A stiff German accent behind the blank eyes responded, "Ve are Beafer clan. Bum. Bum. Bum."

The children laughed and took pictures with their cell phones.

"What do you think?" Mankiller asked Susan.

Susan thought it was creepy, but she hesitated to say so. She had caught sight of Nina in the crowd, giving her the squinty look that shouted, *Mom! Please don't embarrass me in front of my friends!*

Susan fell back on her role as a politician. "You've shown a lot of creativity and initiative, Mr. Mankiller, but if these sculptures are going to be displayed in public they'll need the approval of the city's art advisory board."

"Of course." Mankiller gave her a nod, which Susan took as a thank-you-and-goodbye. She turned to leave. But he called after her, "Councilor?"

"Yes?"

"Would this be a good time to submit my first invoice?"

"Accounting handles payroll," she replied, thinking fast. At three hundred dollars a day, Mankiller's invoice for just three weeks would already amount to thousands. Beaverton had recently been forced to lay off library staff. Had the city really received no complaints about kids at the mall?

Suddenly she recalled a city regulation. "Actually, I think the council reviews long-term contracts after ninety days."

"Ninety days," he repeated.

"Yes, there's a compliance check after ninety days."

March brought an Oregon winter that would not end, with cold rain every day. The citizens of Beaverton huddled indoors, watched the news, or shopped at the mall. In fact, much of the local news was about the mall. Traffic counts at Beaver Place had increased so sharply that Nordstrom's had agreed to sign on as a new anchor store. Meanwhile, Nick Mankiller's project had landed in-kind grants from Nike and Tektronix.

Nina told her mother about it while helping set the table for dinner. "So the Nike grant?" she said, clattering the plates in place, "It's, like, two dozen Segways?"

"Two dozen what?" Susan asked from the kitchen, stirring chicken stew.

"Segways. You know, those stand-up scooter things? Anyway, Phil Knight bought them for the Nike campus because it's so big, but then his people were riding them around instead of wearing out shoes, so he gave them to us."

Susan set the stew to simmer. "Why do you want Segways?"

"For the beavers. Tektronix gave us some old GPS hardware. If we put it all together right, the statues won't just talk. They'll be able to move around."

"That sounds—" Susan searched for the right word. Dangerous? Weird? "That sounds complicated."

"Oh, it is. One group of geeks is getting advice from a Tektronix engineer. Other kids are deciding what style to paint them— realistic, graffiti, baroque, or whatever. Communication shamans like me are writing scripts—you know, where the beavers should go and what they should say."

Susan poured the stew into a tureen and brought it to the table. While her husband Darryl was overseas with the Air Force, it was a wonder that they still held regular mealtimes, instead of just snacking. Susan fought hard for sit-down dinners, believing that they were healthier.

As she served the stew, Susan asked, "Are you checking these scripts with the city arts board?"

"They're the ones who come up with the best ideas." Nina slurped a spoonful of broth. It was so hot that she waved a hand in front of her mouth.

"Such as?"

"Mom! This is performance art. You'll have to wait and see."

Throughout April, Mankiller rolled out two new "Robobeaver" statues each week—always on a Tuesday afternoon, just in time for the evening TV news. One of the first statues was painted to resemble a Catholic schoolboy from the old St. Mary's Academy, with a natty cardigan and tie. The schoolboy beaver rolled around City Hall's courtyard, confronting passersby with questions about Beaverton's history.

"Hi! I'm Beaver clan. Do you think the Sawyer's company in Beaverton was the first in the world to sell 3-D photos?" The voice sounded like a shy, freckled thirteen-year-old boy. "Press my right paw for yes. Press my left for no."

If you pressed the right paw the beaver's eyes flashed green. "Right you are! Stereoscopes were known in fancy drawing rooms as far back as 1838. In 1939, however, Sawyer's View-Master toys made 3-D pictures popular for everyone, including me."

Another statue, painted with the bright colors and wide eyes of a manga cartoon girl, gave Japanese lessons as it rolled back and forth in front of Uwajimaya, the huge Asian grocery store on the Beaverton-Hillsdale Highway. "Hi, I'm Beaver clan. Shake my left paw if you think *edamame* is the Japanese word for soybean. Shake my right paw if you think it's an animation technique from the horror movie, *Godzilla Meets the Mummy.*"

At the Nike campus, a "Beaver Woods" statue in a golf outfit gave visitors a narrated tour of the trail around the lake, pointing out buildings and asking trivia questions about athletes.

Many of the remaining statues served as bellhops at the Washington Square and Beaver Place malls. Painted with tuxedoes or maid aprons, they would carry bags to the door of any shop a visitor chose.

Near the end of May, the rains relented. People emerged from their homes as if from a long sleep, squinting at the bright blue sky. Robins, back from their winter in the south, hopped along the sidewalks, waiting for the lawns to be mowed.

Susan's hay fever also returned, as it did every May. Even when she took allergy pills she felt as if her head were swimming in a soup of pollen. She drove her Kia to the city council's lunch meeting with the windows up and the air conditioner on, but nothing could stop the green sexual explosion of weed flowers and grass blooms from seeping in to redden her eyes and tighten her throat.

The night before, Susan had been worried that Nina was developing allergies too. The girl had sneezed and sniffed through dinner, and had gone to bed early. That morning Susan had taken Nina's temperature and had determined that her daughter had merely caught a cold, no doubt from the toddlers she babysat on weekends. So Nina was spending the day in bed. The girl seemed glad to be missing an English test about Macbeth, but she worried that she might also miss Beaver clan at three.

Susan hadn't told Nina that this was the ninetieth day of Mankiller's project. In fact, Susan would otherwise have stayed home to tend to her feverish daughter, but she felt a curious urgency about participating in the council's review.

Susan parked on the street and took her usual shortcut to the council chambers through the courtyard. The schoolboy Robobeaver swiveled after her asking, "What day of the week is the historic Fanno Farmhouse open for tours? Press my left paw . . ."

Susan hurried past. Reporters never bothered to show up for these lunchtime council work meetings. Other than staff and council, the only people in the hall were Mr. Meier — a retiree who hadn't missed a meeting in a decade — and Nick Mankiller. The big Native American leaned in a chair against the back wall, his bare arms crossed. Staff had set up a table by the door with agendas, deli sandwiches, bottles of water, and cans of pop. After everyone on the council had taken what they wanted, there were still several sandwiches left.

"Join us for lunch," the mayor invited, smiling toward Mankiller. "We've got plenty."

A housefly circled the windowless room, buzzing — the only sign that this was May, and the world outside was waking up.

Mankiller's gray eyes scanned the councilors' faces.

The mayor shrugged, sat down, and opened a can of Sprite. He frowned at the agenda. "First up for today's meeting is a budget request from the library, but in deference to our visitor, I suggest we move the Beaver Place review to the top of the agenda. Any objections?"

Heads wagged around the table. "All right," the mayor said, his mouth full of sandwich, "Ron, what's the status on the mall?"

"Financially, we're in much better shape," Arbutnik said, passing out budget spreadsheets. "The economy has picked up statewide this spring, improving tenancy rates at projects like Beaver Place. In fact, I think we could be at full occupancy by mid-summer—except, of course, that the largest available space, the old bookstore, is currently being used as a cultural center."

The councilors considered this a moment in silence. Susan bit back a comment that the state's economy had not improved much in the past three months. Without Beaver clan, most of the storefronts might still be empty.

Zooey from Ward Six offered, "I think the cultural center has been an interesting experiment."

The mayor took a pickle out of his sandwich and laid it aside. "An experiment that I suspected would become a liability, and it has."

A liability? Susan could no longer contain herself. "You said Mankiller might turn the mall around."

"That's all water under the bridge," the mayor replied. "The reality now is that we're passing up ten thousand dollars of income every month by letting him use the old bookstore for free. I say it's time to pull the plug on this art club and move on."

Susan shook her head. "My daughter Nina has had only good things to say about the cultural center. It's not just about art. There's physical exercise, music, writing, and camaraderie. The children involved in the project are doing better in school, and they're better behaved at home. Besides, we can't just close Beaver clan. We have a contract."

The mayor frowned at her. "Are you telling us that your

daughter is a mall rat?"

"Nina's a healthy, well-adjusted fourteen-year-old girl!" Susan looked about the table. None of the other councilors would meet her eye.

The housefly landed on the remaining crust of the mayor's sandwich. He waved it away and asked the city manager, "So what are the terms of our contract with Mr. Mankiller?"

"Actually, we don't have a contract per se," Arbutnik replied. "Council passed the measure as a resolution, which is a little more flexible."

"All right, and what were the terms of our resolution?"

The city manager flipped through a ring binder. "You authorized up to three hundred thousand dollars, at the rate of three hundred dollars a day, on the condition that there were no complaints about children at Beaver Place."

Zooey asked, "Have there been complaints?"

Around the table the councilors shrugged, shook their heads, or simply looked at each other.

Zooey turned to the city manager. "Is this true? No one has complained about graffiti, panhandling, or anything?"

Arbutnik held up his palms. "Not officially, at least."

"Well, I have a complaint." The mayor put his empty pop can into the white deli box with the crust of his sandwich. When he closed the lid the fly buzzed up.

"You have a complaint about children at the mall?" Susan asked, surprised. She hadn't seen him at the mall since the day the city bought it.

"Yes, I do." The mayor opened his mouth, as if he were about to speak, but wasn't yet sure exactly what he was going to say.

To Susan's astonishment, the fly flew straight into the mayor's mouth. And then time stopped.

Actually, time didn't stop so much as hiccup. A moment later, when the mayor started talking again, Susan noticed that everyone else in the room seemed to be staring into space.

"The truth is," the mayor said in a strange low voice, as if he were revealing an inner secret, "I don't like children very much under any circumstances. The most painful part of my political career has been reading Dr. Seuss to squirming kindergarten classes. As far as I'm concerned, children are insane, non-voting dwarves."

The fly buzzed out of the mayor's mouth, and time resumed in a more normal fashion. Susan found herself too bewildered to speak. Had she really heard the mayor say these horrible things? No one else seemed alarmed. Perhaps, Susan thought, she might have slipped temporarily into a daydream. Certainly she had lost a lot of sleep the night before, worrying about Nina.

The city manager was the next to speak. "Even this kind of non-specific complaint would suffice to void the resolution as written."

"In that case we're free to terminate our agreement." The mayor's voice returned to its usual drone. "Legally, we owe Mr. Mankiller nothing. Still, I feel he should be rewarded for his time. Three hundred thousand dollars, of course—" the mayor spread his hands and chuckled. "That's not just fanciful, it's ludicrous. My understanding is that the project incurred virtually no out-of-pocket expenses. In addition to three months of free rent, Mankiller has received grants from Nike, Tektronix, the Siletz tribe, and our German sister city. In short, I think we could repay his initiative generously with—I'm thinking big here—a one-time settlement of perhaps as much as ten thousand dollars."

One of the councilors whistled softly.

At the back of the room, Nick Mankiller didn't move.

Susan, however, rose to her feet. She had not come to this meeting expecting to defend Beaver clan. She still had concerns about Nina's infatuation with the group. But she had not imagined an injustice of this scale.

"Correct me if I'm wrong," Susan began, struggling to keep her voice steady, "But as recently as February we were losing three million dollars a year at Beaver Place. We offered Mr. Mankiller just one-tenth of that amount if he could rescue our investment. By any objective standard, he has succeeded. As a result we now have more than enough of a budget surplus to continue funding his cultural center at the agreed rate. If we renege on our commitment we will lose more than an art project that has kept our children out of trouble. We will diminish the reputation of this council and of the entire city."

Susan glanced to the silent figure in the back row, and thought: Nor would this be the first time a Native American had seen an Oregon treaty broken.

The fly circled Zooey's head like a buzzing halo. She raised her hand and said, "I move that we offer a ten thousand dollar settlement to Mr Mankiller on the condition that he vacate Beaver Place within forty-eight hours."

"Second." Two other councilors chimed in almost simultaneously.

"We have a motion and a second," the mayor said. "Those in favor say 'aye'."

A chorus repeated, "Aye."

"Those opposed?"

"No!" Still standing, Susan slammed her hand on the table. At the back of the room, Nick Mankiller stood up and walked out the door.

"Your objection is noted, Ms. Burkmiller." The mayor looked back at this agenda. "Now about the library—"

"Excuse me." Susan picked up her purse. She hurried after Mankiller, thinking that she should apologize—or perhaps try to make amends. If they landed a grant quickly enough from the Oregon Cultural Trust, he might be able to continue his project in a grange hall or a church basement.

When Susan reached the courtyard of city hall, however, Mankiller was nowhere to be seen. Instead the schoolboy Robobeaver stood there, flashing its big eyes red. And instead of asking questions about city history, it chanted, "Ve are Beafer clan. Bum. Bum. Bum."

Susan hurried out to the street, but Mankiller wasn't there either. The giant beaver followed her at a walking pace. Then it rolled down the sidewalk and headed north along Hall Street, still chanting, "Bum. Bum. Bum."

Now Susan's worries about Nina returned in force. Her daughter could be volatile at the best of times. Battling a fever, she might react badly to the news that Beaver clan was being disbanded.

Susan got in her Kia and headed for her home in the West Hills. Along the way she noticed the manga Robobeaver from the Uwajimaya grocery rolling along a sidewalk on 107th Avenue, a full block from its usual station. Although it still wore a sailor blouse and a white miniskirt—both of which looked odd on such a fat statue—the manga eyes were flashing red. Susan sped up.

Her husband Darryl had insisted that they buy a ranch-style house on a big lot because he wanted their home surrounded by lawn. But then he'd been sent on an six-month tour of duty to Germany, piloting drones from an air base. Susan didn't have time to deal with the yard. Warm weather and long days had made the grass bulge out into meadow-like tufts. Shrubs around the house had sprouted ragged green arms that writhed past the eaves toward the sky.

Susan opened the front door and found Nina staggering across the living room in her nightshirt, her mouth open, her face flushed.

"Nina! You should be in bed."

Nina held up her cell phone. "I've got a hundred tweets already. Beaver clan needs me at the mall."

"No way. You can hardly stand up. And I'm not going to have you spreading the flu to your friends. This house is quarantined."

"Mom! You can't—"

Susan cut her short. "Yes I can." She crossed her arms, standing between Nina and the front door.

"Bitch." The girl had lowered her voice to an eerie, ominous pitch.

Susan stared at the monster before her—a wraith with black rings around red eyes filled with defiance. Had this once been her baby? Susan swung her arm so fast it surprised even herself. Before Nina could retreat, her mother had caught her by the wrist and wrenched free the cell phone. In another second Susan had opened the phone and pushed speed-dial for the number nine.

Before Darryl had left for Germany, the family had agreed that nine was the "nuclear option."

Nina grabbed for the phone, but Susan jerked it away.

"Lieutenant Major Burkmiller," a small, tinny male voice

announced. "Nina, is that really you?"

Almost at once, the fourteen year old's soul seemed to return to her fevered body. Her shoulders slumped.

"Is something wrong?" the voice asked. "It's the middle of the night here in Ramstein. I've got a mission in the air."

Susan held up the phone between them, but kept it firmly in her grip. "Hi, Love. Our daughter has a question for you."

"Um, Dad?" Nina swallowed. "I need to go to the mall. It's really important."

For a moment there was silence from the phone. Then the lieutenant major's voice asked, "What does your mother say?"

Susan tilted the phone closer. "Nina's running a fever. She's got the flu."

"But Dad!" Nina broke in. "Everyone's at the mall right now. They need me. It's super important!"

"Sorry, Nina. Sounds like you don't have flight clearance. Until you're well, I'm afraid you're grounded." The voice was commanding, but with an undertone of worry, regret, — and perhaps just a little amusement. "Love you both. Over and out."

Susan snapped the phone closed. Then she tucked it into a pocket on the butt of her suit pants. "No calls for twenty-four hours. Go to your room and get back to bed."

"Can I at least watch TV?" The monster had fled, leaving the shell of a sick child.

Susan nodded, relieved. "I'll bring you tea and soup."

Beaver Woods was the first of the robotic statues to catch the attention of the media. KPDV reporter Marcus Hampton had been returning from a three-car accident on Walker Road — the sort of ugly story that cries out for an upbeat counterweight — when he spotted a giant beaver in a golf costume, blinking its eye to signal a left turn onto Hall Street.

Marcus nudged the cameraman at the wheel beside him. "Follow that beaver."

Two months ago, Marcus had reported on the unveiling of this particular statue at Nike headquarters. He had even managed to round out the story by getting a sister station in Atlanta to do a parallel interview with the real Tiger Woods. If the robot was now running amok on the streets of Beaverton, it was news. Marcus flipped open his phone and called his producer, Rick Abolt.

It was a slow news day, and Rick pounced. "Don't let the robot out of your sight. Who's the artist in charge of the project?"

"A guy named Mankiller," Marcus replied. "He runs a youth center at Beaver Place mall."

"I'll send Angela Flint to check it out. She's at the zoo, but the pregnant elephant there is boring us to tears. The damned things gestate for twenty-two months."

For the next half hour, Marcus slowly tailed Beaver Woods as it rolled through town. Once when it stopped at an intersection for a light, Marcus had enough time to jump out of the KPDV van with a hand-held camera.

"Excuse me? Mr. Woods?" Marcus wasn't sure how to address a statue.

"Ve are Beafer clan," the robot replied in a clipped German accent. Its eyes flashed red.

"Where are you headed, Mr. Woods? Shouldn't you be back at Nike?"

"Bum. Bum. Bum." The traffic light turned green, and the robot rolled on.

Meanwhile, Angela Flint had found Nick Mankiller amid a somber crowd of teenagers, hauling gear from the Beaver Place cultural center to a brightly painted bus. With a cameraman beside her and a cordless mike in her hand, she asked, "Mr. Mankiller? I'm from KPDV. Am I interrupting something?"

Mankiller walked by, carrying a rolled-up mat on his shoulder. "Just moving out."

"Moving out? Why?"

He set down the mat and looked at her. "You're supposed to know the news. The Beaverton city council canceled my funding. They gave me forty-eight hours to clear out. With the kids helping, I'll have things cleaned up pretty quick. Except for the climbing wall. REI is supposed to come by tomorrow for that."

"Why did the city council cut your funding?" Angela gave him an innocent look. Did he not yet know about Beaver Woods?

He shrugged. "Art's an iffy business. Guess I'm glad they paid as much as they did." He hefted the mat onto his shoulder and carried it up the steps into the bus. When he reemerged a minute later, he seemed surprised that Angela was still there.

"Mr. Mankiller?" she asked, suspecting already that this would be the sound bite used for the six o'clock news. "Do you know where your beavers are?"

He frowned. "Why?"

"Because I'm told Beaver Woods is crossing the freeway overpass at Highway 217. At least five other statues are moving that way. Can you tell us where they're going?"

Mankiller ran his hand over his face. "Look, I don't know anything about this. The local arts board helped the kids program the statues. Some retired guy from Tektronix installed the GPS devices. All I do is write grants and tell stories. The city council threw me out, so whatever happens to the kids' art is their problem."

Angela was about to ask another question, but Mankiller turned away and raised his voice to the crowd of children. "All right, the only stuff left is the drums. You kids can have them, OK?"

"Really?" Several teenagers looked at him in disbelief.

"Yeah, everything has to go. Last one out, close the door."

Red Fox, the seventeen year old who had taught slack lining, stood tall and proudly touched his own forehead. "We are Beaver clan."

Mankiller shook his head sadly, wagging his black ponytail. "Sorry, guys, but you're on your own now. You'll always be Beaver clan, but you don't need a leader anymore." He climbed the steps of his bus, sat in the driver's seat, and turned on the engine.

Angela managed to get her foot in the folding door before he could close it. She held up the microphone. "You don't know where the beavers are going, but what about yourself? What's next for you, Mr. Mankiller?"

He moved the gearshift knob forward. "I'm heading to Alaska."

"Alaska? Is that home for you?"

"This bus is my home."

"Then why Alaska?"

Mankiller shrugged. "Everyone goes to Alaska in May, if they can."

When Susan and her daughter Nina watched the six o'clock news that evening, the story had been edited down to a human-interest feature. After the usual news about Mideast violence, Congressional sex scandals, and a particularly gory three-car pileup, Marcus Hampton's face brightened. "On a lighter note, giant beavers are on the loose. That's right—sixteen robotic art statues took to the streets this afternoon, turning heads and stopping traffic in downtown Beaverton."

The screen cut to a clip of a six-foot beaver with plaid golf pants and a white Nike golf cap waiting at a red light. A voice off-screen asked, "Excuse me? Mr. Woods?" The statue replied, "Ve are Beafer clan." The off-screen voice asked, "Where are you headed, Mr. Woods? Shouldn't you be back at Nike?' The statue flashed its eyes red. It said, "Bum. Bum. Bum," and rolled on through the intersection.

Marcus looked up from KPDV news desk and smiled. "The fun began as part of a performance art project that some say may have slipped off the rails. Native American artist and Siletz tribal council member Nicholas Mankiller oversaw creation of the statues at a cultural center for troubled teens he opened at a Beaverton mall in February."

Mankiller whirled up onto the screen, shrugged, and said, "Art's an iffy business."

Marcus continued, "After the Beaverton city council canceled the project's funding earlier today, Mankiller closed the center and drove off in his rainbow-colored bus, leaving the beavers behind."

"The city council threw me out," Mankiller said, whirling back for a moment, "So whatever happens to the kids' art is their problem."

The screen cut to six beaver statues painted with tuxedoes, French maid aprons, and a manga sailor skirt. In a voice-over

Marcus said, "The art projects were definitely a surprise for commuters on Highway 217. Fortunately, these beavers have been on their best behavior."

The six giant beavers slowly queued up behind a "One Vehicle Per Green" sign, where a traffic light limits freeway access during rush hour. Each time the light turned green, another beaver rolled out along the freeway shoulder.

Next came a clip of a patrol officer in a short-sleeved uniform and a round-brimmed hat. A banner across the bottom identified him as John DeClancy, Oregon State Police. "I almost pulled over the one that's dressed like a school kid. He looked underage." The patrolman winked. "But we're not supposed to profile."

Marcus reappeared. "At this point it's unclear who, if anyone, is controlling the roving rodents. Mankiller has apparently washed his hands of the project. The children involved declined our requests for interviews and went home for dinner."

Nina stood up from the sofa, swaying from fever, her face flushed. "The clan is tweeting. I know it. Give me my phone, Mom.

Susan crossed her arms and shook her head. "No way, girl."

On the television, Marcus Hampton said, "For a live report, let's go now to Angela Flint in Beaverton. Angela, are you there?"

"Yes, Marcus." An inset of a reporter with bright red lipstick and short blond hair slid in from the right. "All afternoon we've been wondering where the sixteen robotic beavers were going. Now that shadows are lengthening for a beautiful May evening, they've gathered here, in a field behind Beaverton's Sunset Transfer Station."

The camera zoomed over her shoulder to a circle of statues in a meadow behind a parking lot. The microphone picked up the chirp of crickets, as well as the faint "Bum Bum Bum" chorus of the beavers.

Marcus asked, "Isn't that the Tri Met park-and-ride lot?"

Angela nodded. "Beaverton police and Tri Met security are both on hand, but it appears neither of them has jurisdiction to evict the beavers. The statues rolled past the station to a wetlands preserve owned by the state Fish and Wildlife Department."

"Sounds like a good habitat for beavers," Marcus chuckled. "Why not let them stay?"

"For now, that's what authorities are doing, in part because we've just learned the statues are property of the Siletz tribe—technically, a sovereign nation." Angela raised an eyebrow. "People here are saying they'll sort it all out in the morning. Until then, I'm Angela Flint, reporting from Beaverton."

Nina sank back onto the sofa. Susan put her hand on her daughter's forehead; it was warm and a little damp, but no longer hot. Could the fever have finally broken?

"Nina, honey, let me get you some aspirin." When she came back a few minutes later with aspirin and chamomile tea, she found Nina curled up on the sofa, fast asleep.

Susan bit her lip. Nina's chest rose and fell softly beneath the nightshirt. Without the usual makeup, the girl's closed eyes looked like a baby's. Adolescence was such a scary stage, teetering on the edge of the nest.

Susan set the tray on the coffee table. Then she fetched a blanket from the bedroom and tucked Nina in.

Crows flew across the city that evening—great black birds, cawing so raucously that you could hear them over the sounds of teenagers clattering plates to clear dinner tables. After that, there were a thousand different excuses, all of them accepted with a nod or an absent shrug: *James wants me to go help with his homework. Megan and I are meeting at Starbucks for a frappacino. I'm just going out for a walk, OK?*

In the spectral light of the long, late May evening, thousands of teenagers ventured out into the streets of Beaverton, checking their cell phones and watching the sky. Some of the older children drove, stopping to pick up friends along the way. Some took the bus or caught the blue-line MAX. Everywhere the crows squawked from telephone poles and roof ridges, weaving a spell of oblivion among the others—the adults and the younger children left behind.

By eight o'clock, when the last rays of the sun were slanting across the distant hills of the Coast Range, igniting great streamers of pink clouds overhead, more than nine thousand teenagers had gathered in the field behind the Sunset Transfer Station. The circle of beavers still flashed their eyes and chanted, but more slowly now that the fading day had dimmed the charge of their photovoltaic tails. Surrounding them, the vast throng of teenagers beat drums and clapped their hands to the slowing rhythm, "Bum . . . Bum . . . Bum . . . ."

A faint white mist crept across the wetlands. Tiny insects on lace wings flitted up from the grass. Redwing blackbirds on cattails sang for all they were worth.

And then the sun shrank to a fiery bead on a far mountain. The light hung there for a moment of rapture, and went out.

The beavers fell silent. The red lights in their eyes blinked weakly one last time, and died.

Slowly, the chill winds of night gathered from across the Tualatin Plains. The children set down their drums. They raised their arms toward the wildly invigorating night breeze. What joy — what impossible freedom! All those thousands of hands in the air, straining, yearning for a different life.

The children nearest the beavers were the first to change. Their hands grew longer and thinner. Then their fingers suddenly bloomed into feathers. Speechless with wonder, the children fanned their beautiful new wings, marveling at the pull of the air. They gave a few trial flaps while their bodies completed the change. Then, with a step of their webbed feet, they were off, flapping into the sky.

When the MAX train from Portland pulled into the Sunset Transfer Station at 8:57 p.m., hauling another load of adults to the suburbs, no one bothered to remark on the spectacle of nine thousand dusky Canada geese, swirling up from the wetlands into an apocalyptic red sky.

The Burkmillers' phone began ringing at dawn. Groggy from a night of fitful sleep, Susan pushed back the covers and swung her feet to the hardwood floor. The phone was in the hall, but the light was already on out there, and she could hear water running in the bathroom. A shower at six in the morning? Nina really must be feeling better. And now Susan needed to go to the bathroom too. She'd have to use the john in the basement, despite the steep stairs and the cold concrete floor.

By the time Susan had found her slippers and put on a bathrobe, the phone had stopped ringing. She trudged downstairs anyway. As soon as she sat on the toilet, of course, the phone started ringing again. Probably a robocall. She finished up, washed her hands, and plodded back upstairs. Incredibly, the phone was still ringing. She picked it up.

"Hello?"

"Susan?"

She frowned. Did she recognize this male voice? With a flush of horror, she realized it might be the military, calling to say there had been an attack on her husband's air base."Who is this?"

"Gary."

"Gary who?" He didn't sound like a soldier.

"Gary Hernandez. Did I wake you up?"

"What do you think?" Why on earth was Beaverton's mayor calling her at six a.m.? It was bad enough hearing his voice in broad daylight.

"Sorry, but we've got a situation. I'm at City Hall with the police chief. We're getting missing persons reports, Susan."

"Missing persons reports? So what? I'm a city councilor, not a detective."

The mayor dropped his voice half a note, as he often did to stress seriousness. "Two hundred kids are missing so far, all between the ages of thirteen and eighteen. More reports are coming in all the time. We're assuming they're runaways. The only thing they seem to have in common is that they were involved with that cultural center. Since you objected so strongly to the vote yesterday, Susan, I wondered—"

But she had already stopped listening, struck by a different worry. "Nina!" She hurried to the bathroom door. "Nina? Are you in there?"

The shower blasted white noise. Susan tried the door, but it was locked from inside. She shouted, "Nina? Are you OK, honey?"

Nina shouted back, her voice muffled, "Jeez, Mom. Leave me alone. And stop calling me 'honey'."

Relieved, Susan turned back to the telephone. The mayor was still going on in his somber tone, " —not suggesting anything, I'm just curious if you've heard anything from Mankiller, or if you know something about their plans."

"Gary, give it a rest." Susan wasn't usually this curt, but it was too early in the morning to be polite. "Whatever situation you've got isn't my fault. I'm sorry if some kids have run away. After what you did to them, shutting down their center without warning, I can't say I'm entirely surprised."

"Then you suspected something?"

"No." She sighed. "All I know about Beaver clan is what I heard from my daughter Nina."

"Your daughter Nina," the mayor repeated. Then he added, with what sounded like genuine concern, "Is she all right?"

"Yeah, she's getting over a cold, but she's still here."

"Can I talk to her?"

Susan frowned at the phone. The last thing she wanted was for Beaverton's creepy old mayor to talk to Nina while she was in the shower. "No! Look, I'm going back to bed. I hope they find the other kids. I'm sure they're fine. Just don't blame me, OK?"

Susan hung up and went back to bed, but she couldn't sleep. The shower kept running. Susan knew how good it felt to take a long shower after recovering from a cold. It was like washing off the old germs. But Nina seemed headed for a marathon record.

The bedroom window kept getting brighter. And then the phone started ringing again.

At first they were calls from the parents of Nina's friends, asking if the friends might have spent the night at Nina's house.

"Nina!" Susan shouted, trying the bathroom door yet again.

"Leave me alone!" Nina called back, over the whine of a hair dryer. "I'm changing."

Changing?

Then Susan got a puzzling call from her brother-in-law, the one who drove a school bus. The grade school run, he said, had gone just like usual, but he'd finished the runs to the middle school and high school with the bus still empty. All of the buses had been empty.

"Nina!" Susan pounded on the bathroom door.

"Go away!" Nina shouted back. "I'm not ready yet."

Finally the media started calling. Marcus Hampton, the reporter she had seen on TV the night before, called in person to tell her that at least four thousand Beaverton children had been reported missing so far. Middle and high school classrooms were deserted. No teenager had been seen in the city that morning — with the possible exception of her daughter, Nina Burkmiller.

"Do you have any idea why that might be?" Marcus asked gently.

Susan shook her head. "No," she whispered — and then stopped.

The bathroom doorknob was turning.

"Ms. Burkmiller?" the voice on the phone continued. "Thousands of children don't just disappear. Could you perhaps speculate — "

As the bathroom door opened, Susan set the phone aside. Nina had cocooned herself in the bathroom for more than two hours, and her metamorphosis could not have been more complete. Instead of black boots, she wore practical Nike sport shoes. Her trademark white lace miniskirt had been replaced by blue jeans that made her legs look longer. A pink, long-sleeved blouse puckered smartly, suggesting that she was wearing a bra. A light touch of blue eye shadow proved what Susan had always believed — that Nina's eyes did not need widening. And although her hair was still hennaed, it had been tied back in a ponytail so it no longer hung in her face.

Susan stood there, stunned. Her daughter was beautiful.

Nina breezed past to the kitchen, as if Susan did not exist. She poured herself a cup of coffee and fixed a bowl of yogurt with granola.

Susan sat opposite her at the breakfast table, her hands shaking. "Nina, honey — "

"Mother." Nina closed her eyes and drew in her breath. "I asked you not to call me 'honey'."

"Yes, but Nina." Susan clenched her hands to keep them still. "Children are missing. Thousands of them."

"I know." Nina stirred the granola into her yogurt.

"You do?" Susan asked. "Where have they gone?"

"To the Copper River delta," Nina replied.

Susan's eyes darted about, as if somewhere in the room — perhaps behind this beautiful young woman — she would find something that made sense.

"Where is that?" Susan asked, at a loss.

"Alaska." Nina stood up. She walked to the kitchen window and gazed at the overcast sky outside, resting her hands on the granite rim of the sink. A scraggly V of geese was disappearing to the north, faintly honking.

"Everyone leaves for Alaska in May, if they can."

THE OREGON VARIATIONS

SEASONING

ACROSS

1 Death notice, for short
5 _____ ski, in the Alpes
10 Former *Tonight Show* host Jack
14 Savory salad herb
19 Hebrew letter used as an abbreviation for rabbi
20 Started a card game
21 Women's magazine with a French name
22 Licorice herb
23 Word before street or money
24 First shot off a tee, usually
25 Advanced math subj.
26 Cousin to bingo or keno
27 Seasoning with ambition?
31 Pay attention to
32 Anagram for rose
33 Open, to a poet
34 Fabulous Greek author (var.)
38 W. hemisphere alliance
40 _____ facto
41 Thicket
43 Communications co. with more than $100 billion in sales

44 Ia. neighbor
47 Sunfish, and an anagram for "loam"
49 Amateur pickling herb?
52 Native nursemaid in India
53 Drug addict
54 US women's patriotic org.
55 Turkey pan
56 Fencing tools
58 British WWII submachine gun
60 Airport code for Berlin
61 Prefix for dynamic
62 Spicy but disappointed salad herb?
64 Tribulation
66 Female
67 Moray
68 The A in IPA
69 Mid pt.
71 Kind of parking or sucker
74 Viennese tobacco pipes
79 Algerian city of Camus' "The Plague"
82 NYSE code for Unisys Corp.
83 Texan town on the Brazos
84 Norwegian port SW of Oslo

85 Lake in Madison, Wisconsin
87 Actress West
88 Marceau act
90 Prefix for liter
91 Informative spices?
93 Kings' toppers, in poker
94 Western author Harte
95 Slavic girl's name meaning "God is gracious"
96 Uncompromising
97 Phoenician city
99 Anita's aunt
101 Vassal
103 Anger
104 The summoner in "World of Warcraft"
105 The sun, for one
108 An herb with moral integrity?
114 Jewish scholar
117 Berne's river
118 Striped, poisonous Indian snake
119 Early garden site
121 Pacific island reef
122 Glance over
123 Roof overhangs
124 Go by camel
125 Religious principle
126 Scrabble word that's an anagram for then
127 _____ board, a flexible file
128 Cellist Ma

DOWN

1 Alt. form for OR
2 Strand
3 Send out, as a notice
4 What the retired chef had?
5 Cousin of div. or mult.
6 Andean land
7 Scottish rope
8 Rock star garnish for Chapter 17?
9 Shorthand secs.
10 Fish, in France
11 Winglike part of a plant
12 Words on a sweater label
13 Plated once again
14 Gala dance party
15 Negative terminal
16 Perch
17 Believer (suffix)
18 Regulus' zodiac constellation
28 Neighbor of Ore.
29 Trampled
30 Fix, as an antique
35 A votre _____
36 River or ocean mammal
37 Prefix for dactyl or saur
39 Blue cartoon dwarf
40 Paris dept., ___-de-France
41 Weather rpt.
42 Abbrev. on an airport monitor
44 Cleopatra's lover Antony
45 Eighth month of the Jewish year
46 Back part of necks
48 Greek mountain of the Olympus Range
50 Bond author Fleming
51 Physical attack charged to a seasoned criminal?
57 Donkey, in Dresden
59 _____ Aviv
60 Rabbit made famous by Joel Chandler Harris
63 Meadows, in England
64 Ersatz butter herb?
65 Dull pain
68 Nuclear regulator agcy. 1946-1974
70 Less polite
72 Roman name for Paris
73 Infant inflammation
74 Arturo Toscanini or Leonard Bernstein, for example
75 Alike
76 Shield emblem
77 Spiked club
78 Cut, as a throat
79 All, to Ovid
80 King's bailiff
81 Assassinated Egyptian president Sadat
83 _____ and Peace
86 Operations, in military speak
87 Sign outside a restroom
89 Vonnegut's ___-nine
92 Before the starting gun
98 Type of doodle dandy
100 Neighbor of Leb. and Syr.
102 Kind of story told by 34 across
104 Secret _____ or literary _____
106 Partner of video
107 Oboe tonal quality
109 Pinball error message
110 Irish islands in Galway Bay
111 Slang for favorite
112 Four, to Friedrich
113 _____ bitsy (small)
114 Blab
115 Ingested
116 French lead-in for marché or mot
120 Recent (comb. form)

(Solution on page 337)

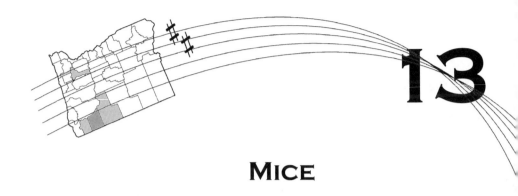

MICE

There were new faces each week at the Barnett Road Coffee Club, but Richard knew everyone would end up talking about his problems with mice.

Even when he was still waiting to order his fifty-cent cup of bottomless black coffee an attractive elderly woman ahead of him turned and exclaimed, "You must be Richard Gruebler! You look so well! Have you heard anything new about the mice?"

Richard wore a short white beard that hid the wrinkles on his neck. An Ashland Parks Department baseball cap hid his thin hair. You might have thought he was sixty-three, instead of eighty-three, except that he had begun to shuffle when he walked and mutter when he was alone.

Richard had founded the coffee club shortly after moving into the Medford Retirement Tower, a glass box that stood on a butte by the freeway like an unplugged television on an end table. Early every Wednesday morning the club's recorder left a photographic roster of new members in the office lobby. Richard tucked it under his arm without looking. Then he shuffled down the butte's spiral path to the world of young people and cars and fast food restaurants with so many empty booths that the waitresses are willing to refill coffee cups all morning.

Richard silenced the elderly woman in the line by raising his index finger to his lips. She was new and hadn't yet learned the first rule of Coffee Club: You don't talk about Coffee Club outside the booth. Even then you don't talk about health.

Richard paid his fifty cents and filled a tray with a coffee cup, four napkins, half a dozen packets of sugar and cream, and some silverware. Then he led the woman to the big circular booth in the back. Two other men and a woman were already waiting there, as curious and uncertain as volunteers at a magic show.

"Welcome, one and all," Richard said. He set down his tray and spread out the roster on the table.

"So you're this Richard Gruebler guy?" An overweight, crewcut man in his sixties humphed. "Listen, I don't even know why I'm here. I don't like clubs."

A long-haired woman in a slender blue muu-muu spoke up, her accent faintly British. "Well, I think it's brilliant. When you get to be our age it's hard to meet new friends. I'd like to thank our host for dreaming it up."

The crewcut man still grumbled.

"Honestly," the long-haired woman said. "It's fifty cents well spent."

"Amen." A bald man with a broad face and a sharp white shirt lifted his cup. "Here's to endless refills."

Richard lifted his cup as well, and for a moment the circle of five silently sipped the rich, dark stimulant from sunny lands far away.

Richard put down his cup and picked up the roster. "By tradition I introduce new members alphabetically, so let's start with—"

He paused to unfold a pair of bifocals from his shirt pocket. "Marie Beer Broughton, born March 14, 1931 in Bismarck, North Dakota."

The black-and-white photo in the roster showed a beautiful girl with bobbed hair, dimpled cheeks, and wide eyes—unmistakably the woman he had met in line. Richard scanned the biography in the roster. "A stenographer, no children. It's unclear from this if you have a husband."

"I've had two," Marie admitted, batting artificially long eyelashes. "With a maiden name like Beer, you marry early."

The bald man raised his eyebrows. "Isn't Beer a German name?"

"Yes, it means 'berry', not 'beer'. Still, I got hitched at seventeen. The next summer my husband got himself chopped up by a baling machine. I moved to Seattle and married an aircraft engineer from Boeing. He built pneumatic struts or some such nonsense. A lovely man, but impotent, so I survived forty years on affairs. Finally I suppose I killed him."

"Whoa! Really?" The grumpy, overweight man perked up.

"Sort of." Marie fiddled with the white collar of her blouse. "If a man is suffering from terminal bone cancer, isn't it a loving wife's duty to slip him a triple dose of his pain medication?"

Coffee cups rose as the five club members considered this silently.

At length Marie dimpled her cheek with a grin. "But we're here to talk about Richard, aren't we? About the mice."

Heads nodded in agreement.

Marie poked Richard playfully in the ribs. "Come on, Mr. Gruebler. You already know about us from the roster, but we're dying to find out about you, the mysterious president-for-life."

Richard held up his hands in protest.

"No, really," Marie said, more seriously now. "When did you first notice the mice?"

Richard stirred his coffee. "I was three, and the world was perfect."

He had lost many memories since his stroke, but certain early scenes remained so startlingly vivid that he could close his eyes and walk around his childhood home, exploring one room after another until he found his mother. Inevitably she would be in the kitchen, stirring a bowl of cookie dough, with sunlight from the kitchen window haloing her auburn hair.

His father, Richard Gruebler Sr., taught drama at Southern Oregon University, which meant that Richard Junior often had the house and his mother to himself. Ashland's madrone and pine woods began just up the hill from his home, but his neighborhood was full of light, the trees freshly cleared to make way for modest two-bedroom cottages with tidy lawns and driveways.

At first he was excited when workmen arrived to tear out the back wall and pour concrete foundations for a new room. But that afternoon when his father came home he learned the truth.

"Rickie," his father said, crouching low. "You're going to be a big brother!"

The house addition was not a new playroom for him, but rather a nursery. His mother was not fat from the cookies she baked, but rather with a younger rival. Already his parents seemed to love it more than him.

At dinner he threw his food. Then he stomped out to the backyard and peed on the fresh concrete. His father spanked him with a slipper and shut him in his bedroom.

Crying, alone, afraid, with the walls of his once-perfect home torn open to the night, he heard the demons for the first time.

"I didn't yet realize they were mice," Richard told the coffee club, staring into his empty cup. "Later I learned they were gnawing the insulation to build nests. But the wall amplified the noise like a sounding board. I thought they must be huge ogres, chewing to get in and eat me."

"Didn't you tell your parents?" Marie asked.

Richard gave a sad laugh. "I did, the next day. But no one believes a kid who says there are monsters in the wall."

The bald-headed man nodded thoughtfully. "And yet there really were monsters. And they didn't go away."

"No, they got worse." Richard tightened his lips. "Once mice get into the walls, it's hard to clear them out."

A waitress with a white cap and a yellow uniform walked by with a glass pot. "Everything all right here? More coffee?"

"Yes, please," Richard mumbled.

She poured his cup full. "Anything else?

"Maybe an egg muffin." Richard counted out the money on the table. He added an extra quarter.

The waitress collected the money. "We'll have that up in a minute."

Richard closed his eyes. When he opened them the waitress was gone and all five coffee cups were full. He sighed and looked again at the roster on the table.

"Alphabetically, then," he said, "our next new member would be Gary Varner Dykeson, born November 23, 1947 in Klamath Falls."

"Yeah, but I'm not joining." Gary scowled, exposing yellowed teeth. Although he sat at the back of the booth, his tattooed arms were muscular enough that he might shove his way free.

"I'm not sure we have a choice," the bald man mused. "People forget so quickly. There's not much of a life waiting for us outside those doors."

Richard picked up the roster. "Let's see. Gary's a divorced log truck driver."

"Until I got diabetes, diarrhea, dia-every-goddam-thing."

"Stop!" Richard held up his hand. "Coffee Club doesn't allow organ recitals."

"Damn rules," Gary sighed, straining the T-shirt on his belly. "When the feds disbanded the Klamath tribe back in '54 we had thirty-two years of good times, no rules at all. Logged the hell out of the old reservation. I drove five truckloads a day at fifty bucks a pop. I'd get so drunk fishing Klamath Lake on Sundays I damn near fell out of the boat."

"Good times," the woman in the blue muu-muu repeated somberly, her eyebrows lowered.

"But then the weenies reinstated the tribe, locked up the National Forest, and gave the lake's water rights to some scum-sucking trash fish. No wonder I got sick and—"

"Last warning," Richard interrupted.

"Go ahead. Kick me out." Gary crossed his arms.

Richard folded the roster below the truck driver's mug shot. "Next we have—"

"No, wait!" Gary frowned, obviously uneasy with whatever might be waiting for him outside. "The mice. I want to hear about when you actually saw the mice. If you still remember."

Everyone watched Richard.

He took a sip of coffee, considering. Then he slowly unfolded the roster. "I was seven. It was a day I am unable to forget."

His little sister Louise had conquered the house with her baby doll eyes and her whining demands. Richard had never asked for treats, but Louise would brazenly open the refrigerator door and ask, "What am I hungry for?"

Richard learned to make up for the lack of attention at home by spending his days exploring the nearby forest. Although his father had strictly forbidden him to cross Park Drive, Richard discovered a three-foot-tall concrete culvert that led beneath the road to the forest beyond. In Richard's mind, crawling through that pipe was not exactly the same as crossing the road. He told his mother he was playing at Jimmy's house, and she was so busy coddling Louise that she never checked.

For most of the long, hot summer between Richard's first and second grade, he spent his days climbing trees, collecting bugs, and chasing lizards. But he dreamed of finding his way through the woods to the Granite Creek Reservoir in Lithia Park. For a quarter, kids could swim in the reservoir's cool water and play ball on the park's shady lawns.

Finally, one scorching Saturday in August, he stole a quarter from his mother's purse, stuffed his swimsuit into a backpack, sneaked a hand towel from the bathroom, and slipped out through the culvert. His heart raced with the thrill of adventure. He was an explorer setting out for the source of the Nile. Jays squawked at him in astonishment. Squirrels scrambled to watch him pass. Sweaty but determined, he climbed to a five-way trail junction in a ridgetop pass. Confusing signs with names he did not recognize pointed in three of the directions. He wished he had brought water, or at least an apple — but then he remembered there would be drinking fountains at the reservoir. It must be downhill in the next canyon. More confident now, he ran down the canyon trail.

But the trail led to a gravel road with no signs at all. And when he turned back he couldn't even find the five-way junction again. A group of hikers passed, but instead of asking direction he hid behind a tree, ashamed. Hour after hour he grew thirstier and more frightened. He missed lunch, and then dinner. The sun was low when he stumbled out of the woods to a city street he had never seen before. Exhausted and frightened, he collapsed on a lawn, buried his head in his hands, and cried.

A woman came out from a porch to see what was wrong. Through his tears he told her his name and address.

"Oh my!" the woman exclaimed. "You really are lost. Come sit on the porch while we figure out what to do."

She brought a miraculous tall glass of iced lemonade, but she also brought her husband. When Richard couldn't remember his own telephone number without mixing things up, the man insisted on calling the police.

In a few minutes a police car with flashing lights pulled up in the street. Richard nearly ran back into the woods, but an officer with a uniform and a gun put him in the backseat and drove him home. Richard knew the spanking of his life was waiting.

Richard set down his coffee. "And you know what?" he told the club, "I think I would have preferred a spanking. I actually felt I deserved to die. I was so embarrassed."

Gary frowned. "Your old man didn't whip you?"

"No. He hugged me and cried. Then he ordered pizza to celebrate. We had never called out for pizza before."

The bald man nodded. "So you lacked catharsis."

Richard looked at him uncertainly. "I guess that's right."

"Guilt is an insidious venom," the bald man said. "You had built up a lot of guilt, stealing money, breaking rules, and getting lost. Without punishment it all remained bottled up inside you."

"But what about the mice?" Marie objected, raising her hand like a schoolgirl with a question. "I don't understand what this has to do with the mice."

The bald man smiled and leaned back with his coffee.

Richard sighed. "That night the mice got into my room. They'd been gnawing in the wall for years. Finally they chewed a hole somewhere. They kept me awake all night, scurrying around. In the morning they'd left damp brown droppings on my dresser."

The woman with the British accent said, "At least then you could prove to your parents that the mice were real."

"That's true," Richard admitted.

Gary asked, "Did they decide to trap 'em or poison 'em?"

"Neither. My baby sister loved animals, and my mother didn't want to upset her. So my father bought live traps and took the mice into the woods."

"But I bet they came back," Marie said.

"Egg muffin!" a girl's voice called from the counter.

Richard stood up. He looked to the group. "Anyone want anything?"

The four new club members shook their heads. Gary muttered, "Endless coffee."

When Richard came back he ate the poached egg off his muffin. Then he turned once again to the roster.

"Our next new member is Jasmine 'Jo' Tyler Jameson. Born June 3, 1946 in London, England." He looked up at the long-haired woman in the blue muu-muu. "According to this you sell tea. Is that part of your British background, or just because your name is Jasmine?"

Jo pulled her hair behind her ear with a fluid motion, exposing an iridescent abalone earring. "Neither, really. My father was a bookmaker by trade. I was twelve years old before I realized he didn't actually make books. His gambling office provided us with lots of money, but very little respect. Father bought me a horse so I could learn to ride like a lady. Instead I rode like a jockey. I became junior jumping champion for our district. Then he bought me a spot in a fancy women's school where everyone was supposed to wear uniforms."

The bald man raised an eyebrow. "Supposed to?"

Jo broke into a mischievous smile. "It was 1967. The headmistress threw me out because I insisted on wearing their uniform without a bra."

Gary sputtered his coffee.

Jo ignored him. "I bought a plane ticket to San Francisco where everyone was hanging out in the parks, the girls without bras, wearing flowers in their hair, singing peace songs. At the end of summer someone told me I could get a job in Humboldt County, running a legitimate business for an illegal marijuana grower. Back then every pot operation needed a bead store or an antique shop—

something to explain why they were making so much money. So I got a job selling organic tea for a year. Then I bought the tea business, expanded, and ended up doing quite well."

Richard scanned down the roster. "You have three children, but no husband?"

"Not technically, I suppose. I moved in with a grower in Takilma who raised marijuana for medicinal purposes. A druidic priest performed a wedding for us in a redwood grove." She sighed and looked out the window, past the cars waiting for the drive-up. "Of course that was forty years ago."

"And it's not really why we're here," Marie added.

Jo rubbed her temples, as if she were developing a migraine. "No, we're here to ask if Mr. Gruebler's mice came back."

Richard sat back. "You don't want to know?"

Jo waved a hand vaguely, as if to dispel a puff of smoke. "Oh yes, of course we do." She managed a small smile. "Did the mice come back?"

"Not for years," Richard said. "Even I was surprised that my father's live trap worked so well."

Gary grunted. "I bet instead of letting 'em go your old man was drowning 'em."

Marie drew in her breath.

Richard took a sip of coffee. "It's possible. I never asked. After a few months I hardly thought about the mice anymore. Until the seventh grade."

The bald man frowned, cradling his coffee cup. "Adolescence is a difficult stage."

"What happened in the seventh grade?" Jo asked.

"My father became artistic director of Ashland's Shakespearean Festival. It was a big honor for him, but kind of awkward for me. My English teacher had him come to class to talk about the plays. We all had to read *The Taming of the Shrew*, which was fine, but then everyone started calling me Richard the Second."

Jo smiled. "Well you are, aren't you?"

"No, I'm Richard Gruebler Jr."

"Still, Richard the Second isn't such a bad nickname."

This was true, but the nickname got worse. One day Richard's junior high school cafeteria had served tacos, which he disliked because they were messy and gave him gas. He had sat alone, and then spilled his tray with a clatter that made everyone watch. Ten minutes before the fifth period bell he had rushed to the boys' restroom, feeling sick and pressured. He bolted himself in a stall, but the bathroom soon filled up with so many boys that all the other stalls were occupied and a line formed.

Jimmy, the school's loudmouth joker, rattled the stall's latch. "Hey, hurry up in there! Jeez, what a stink!"

Richard said nothing, trying to hurry. The latch rattled even louder. Finally Jimmy's head peered under the door. "Hey, it's Richard! Smells like you're performing Act Number Two."

A dozen boys laughed.

Mortified, Richard finished up and flushed. But the residue in the toilet bowl had been so infused with gas that it swirled like a cork. He flushed again, wishing it away.

"The scene's over, Richard," Jimmy said. "Come on out."

Richard quickly flushed again, but there wasn't enough water to make it go away. In desperation he said, "The toilet takes so long to fill!"

"Well, you don't have to fill it," Jimmy replied. A chorus of laughter echoed off the tile walls.

At his wits' end, Richard opened the stall door.

Jimmy pushed inside. "Whoa! Look at the size of that floater. You're not Richard the Second. You're Richard the Turd!"

All around the table the members of the coffee club sat silent. No one lifted a cup. The cruelest nicknames were the ones that could never be forgotten.

"Somehow I lived through the rest of that day," Richard said. "When I got home my father had started tearing up the house again. This time he wanted to build a Frank Lloyd Wright-style living room cantilevered over the backyard—something to show dinner guests how important an artistic director was."

"And that let the mice back in?" Jo asked quietly.

Richard nodded. "They built nests in the attic. For the longest time, little drips of smelly brown urine ran down the wall of my closet."

Marie pushed her coffee cup aside. "Please. This is not a conversation for breakfast."

"No, don't you see?" the bald man said, leaning forward. "The mice never existed. They're simply a manifestation of guilt, just as Eve's apple was a manifestation of original sin."

Gary narrowed his eyes, inspecting the bald man. "Who the hell are you, anyway?"

Richard picked up the roster and read, "Brendan Michael Monahan, born April 9, 1949 in Lynn, Massachusetts. Studied theology at Notre Dame. Served in a parish in Gervais, Oregon for sixteen years before renouncing the priesthood. Became director of the Marion County Food Bank. Married, adopted two boys." Richard looked up. "Anything I'm leaving out?"

Brendan tilted his cup a few degrees one way and the other, eddying the coffee. "I didn't leave the priesthood to get married, if that's what you're thinking. I just realized that rituals don't bring anyone closer to understanding life's mysteries. Instead of feeding wafers to the poor, I decided to give them boxes of real food. Instead of teaching altar boys Latin nonsense, I adopted a pair of Vietnamese orphans and taught them to be men."

"But you got married too," Gary said, smirking.

"Yes. Love is the greatest lesson of all."

Coffee Club considered this a moment in silence. Then Richard drained the rest of his coffee and set the cup down with a clank. "You're wrong about the mice. They had to be real. I can't forget them."

"That's an evolutionary survival instinct," Brendan said, holding out his hands as if to measure an imaginary box in the air. "Dangerous events burn into your memory as a warning. The fire that scorched your hand, the bee that stung your foot, the plant that made you sick — these are often our oldest and most persistent memories. It's nature's way of keeping us safe."

"Or God's way?" Marie asked.

"Yes. Or God's way," Brendan replied.

Richard frowned. "If that's God's way, he's brutal. He lets millions of happy memories drift away to make room for a few terrors."

Brendan brought his palms together. "And that's why he offers forgiveness for sins. Jesus is the mouse catcher of memory."

"No!" Richard banged the table with his fist. "That's not how the mice are at all. They're not sins. I didn't break the Ten Commandments by getting lost in the woods or embarrassing myself in a junior high school bathroom. Those were just painful moments, awkward experiences I can't get over. Jesus isn't a mouse catcher. He doesn't care about petty stuff like that. He's a rat catcher for real sins—things like adultery, sloth, gluttony."

Gary laughed.

"What's so funny?" Richard demanded.

"Those are exactly the things I don't want to forget." Gary patted his belly. "Messing around with the neighbor's wife, lying around drunk all weekend, stuffing myself with barbecued steak."

Brendan glared at him. "You're proud of your sins?"

"Maybe not proud," Gary replied. "Pride is your sin. But I sure as hell don't want to forget the good times."

"Enough!" Jo clapped her hands over her ears. She hummed loudly for a moment with her eyes closed. Then she lowered her hands and looked at the others. "We're not here to argue. I think religion and politics should be off the table,"

"Isn't health our only taboo?" Brendan asked.

"I don't care," Jo continued. "We're here to ask about Richard's mice. Personally, I want to know what happened to them."

"Yes, so do I," Marie said. Brendan and Gary nodded, albeit with less enthusiasm.

They all looked to Richard.

He shrugged. "I don't know. I'm told I married, moved back into my parents' house, and got a job with the parks department. They say I was living alone there at the age of eighty when a forest fire burned the whole house to the ground—mice and all, I suppose."

Marie caught her breath. "But you escaped?"

Richard shrugged again. "They found me wandering the streets in a different part of town. Apparently while running away I'd suffered some kind of stroke. Just like that, more than sixty years of memories were gone. I can't even tell you what my wife looked like. All that's left are the early years—the times I was tormented by mice."

In the pause that followed, a waitress approached the booth with a Styrofoam box and a pot of coffee. "Can I freshen up that cup for you, sir?"

"No, thanks," Richard said. "I just need a box for the rest of my muffin."

The waitress winked as she set the box on the table. "I came prepared. It's the same every Wednesday for you, isn't it?"

When the waitress walked away Gary called after her, "Hey! How about refills for the rest of us?"

But the waitress appeared not to hear him.

Richard silently put his muffin, several unopened condiment packets, and half a dozen napkins into the box.

Gary waved his cup angrily. "They're supposed to give us endless coffee."

Richard stood up. He turned the roster over, revealing that it was in fact a copy of the Medford *Mail-Tribune's* "Life" section.

"I don't understand," Jo said.

"I do." Brendan sighed. "Or at least I'm beginning to understand how little I understand."

"What on earth are you talking about?" Marie demanded.

"Yeah, what's going on?" Gary said.

Brendan pointed to the newspaper. "There is no roster. Every week our president-for-life comes here to read the obituaries to himself."

"Then we're—" Jo caught herself.

"Dead?" Gary asked, bewildered.

"I'm sorry," Richard said, tucking the paper under his arm. "Until next week, Coffee Club is adjourned."

With a heavy heart he walked out of the restaurant. As he made his way up the butte's spiral path, the retirement tower loomed before him, as dull as a library of blank books. The people he wanted to talk to were dead. Certainly none of the living wanted to ask about the few fragmentary diaries that survived, deep in the fireproof vault of his mind.

As always, before going back into the glass doors, he shuffled around to the back of the building, where a cluster of ancient pine trees remained near a recycling center. He opened the Styrofoam box and crumbled the remains of his muffin at the base of the largest tree.

As an offering to the mice.

THE BRIDAL VEIL
ROOSTER ROCK LABORATORY

The romance of the Old West had lured Regnar and Amalia Laibach to Oregon. It wasn't just childhood storybooks that inspired the two young doctors to abandon their jobs in Copenhagen's Rigshospitalet. They had researched rodeos. They discovered that the dustiest, sweatiest, most respected round-up of the Old West had been held in the Eastern Oregon cattle town of Pendleton each September since 1910.

The thought of those slim, tight-hipped cowboys in leather banging across the ring on bulls made Amalia order her husband to lie flat on his back in bed. She squatted above him, straddled his erection on her knees, and rode it up and down, her big breasts bobbing atop his cupped palms until he came like a six-shot pistol.

It was enough to make a girl throw back her head, wave her Stetson, and shout *Wahoo!*

Of course storybooks had played a role as well. When Amalia and Regnar had been fifth graders together in Denmark, they had read so many illustrated books about the West that they convinced their schoolmates to create a tribe. They invented "Indian" names by spelling their Danish names backwards.

After moving to Oregon, Amalia discovered how much she had misunderstood the West. But her romanticized vision survived in a series of dreams. Each dream began the same, with a mysterious book. Gilt letters on the faux leather cover spelled the words *Ailamas Skat*, Danish for "Ailama's Treasure." Inside, below a drawing of a winsome Danish-Indian princess with blond braids and a beaded buckskin skirt, was the caption, "The Quest for Enola."

Even in the dreams, Amalia realized this was a fantasy. Real Indian maidens do not have blond hair. But as a girl Amalia had wished to be just this way, as the romantic princess Ailama in the faraway land of Oregon.

Chapter One: Ailama

The beautiful blond princess of Oregon's proud Kramned tribe, Ailama grew up chasing butterflies, riding her Appaloosa pony across the prairie, and sleeping in a big, soft buffalo robe in her teepee. Most of all she loved playing with her two age-mates, Ranger and Snegom. Ranger was a quiet boy who told stories about the spirits behind the stars. Snegom was loud and boasted of the jackrabbits he hunted. None of the children had worries because Ailama's father, Strong Bow, was a great warrior who kept the tribe safe.

When they turned thirteen the children had to separate for their coming-of-age rituals. Ranger and Snegom sat alone on mountaintops, fasting and waiting for the spirit totems that would guide them as men. Ailama's ritual was different. She camped in a special wigwam by the rushing river, where her grandmother told her the secrets of womanhood.

Afterwards Snegom bragged that he had been visited by an eagle—a powerful totem that showed he would become a great warrior and hunter. He laughed that Ranger had seen only a crow, a silly bird that proved Ranger would grow up like his uncle, the crazy old shaman Sral.

That night Ailama cried herself to sleep in her buffalo robe. Ranger couldn't help that he had seen a crow! He wasn't crazy! Why couldn't everything stay the way it had always been?

When the Laibachs first opened their clinic in an old bank building on Pendleton's Emigrant Street, they were disappointed to discover that most of their clients were a lot like people in Denmark. The Laibachs did, however, have a number of genuine cowboys and Indians who came for consultation, and Ailama was dismayed that these clients had a perfunctory attitude about love. The men were typically no-nonsense ranch hands who used pumps to jerk off bulls and inseminate cows. The younger guys got drunk in bars, fought in parking lots, and showed up complaining to the Danish doctors about broken fingers and herpes. The older men drank themselves silly in front of television and showed up with diabetes and erectile dysfunction.

The cowgirls and Indian women who walked into the Laibachs' office, often dolled up with pearl buttons and leather fringes on their boobs, mostly complained about their men.

To be sure, America's frontier health system allowed the Laibachs to charge twice as much as they had in Denmark's state-run hospitals, but after three years in Pendleton they were no longer riding each other like broncos at night.

Searching once again for romance, they decided to leave their office in the hands of Kathy, their nurse practitioner, and sign up as shipboard doctors on California's Love Cruise.

A year later, shuttling between San Diego and Acapulco, they felt like medical commuters in sexual purgatory. And so they were willing to listen when a Pfisto pharmaceutical rep offered them a way out — even though they weren't sure whether his escape route might bring them a level farther from or closer to hell.

"You can pretty much write your own check," the young man said, distributing umbrellaed drinks on a slowly rocking table in the promenade deck's lounge. His teeth were as white as his sport coat, and his brown hair was the color of his tan.

"Why us?" Amalia cocked her head, tilting her shoulder-length blond hair to expose a pearl earring.

"This conversation must remain confidential." The young man smiled without mirth, a gesture that put no one at ease.

"Of course." Regnar did not lean forward to take his cocktail. He was a well-muscled man, with his hair trimmed as short as his stubbly beard. "Why us?"

"We've chosen a dozen teams from the world's top experts in human sexuality. Most of them work at university laboratories. But we want people with practical experience as well, front-line soldiers who have won their victories in the trenches." He held up his glass, offering to toast. When the Laibachs left their glasses untouched, he said, "We've been impressed with your success. Seemingly impotent couples with dysfunctional marriages sign up for your cruise as a last chance at love. And you help them. Two Danish doctors from the backwoods of Oregon, GPs with no academic credentials in sexual studies. Yet somehow the two of you have been working miracles. Wouldn't you like the freedom to explore the essence of human sexuality? It'll be like a paid vacation."

Regnar looked at his wife. They were both tired of the ship's lecherous old men, the worried wives, and the couples that should never have been together at all. Because the Laibachs made room calls, they had to be constantly on their guard. If a woman called, Amalia responded. If the client was male, only Regnar would go. Both doctors carried a black bag that contained much more than the Dramamine, condoms, and morning-after pills you'd expect on a cruise. Amalia had a library of videos to help uncertain women learn the delicate art of hand jobs. Regnar's bag of tricks included tips on teasing and delayed ejaculation. But most of their time was spent in counseling, training men to listen to their lovers' words, and women to forgive their lovers' flaws.

After the room calls died out between two and three each morning, Regnar and Amalia were often too tired to practice what they had prescribed.

They were ready to go back to Oregon.

"What do you want?" Regnar asked.

The young man smiled more broadly. "Pfisto wants to give you money. Enough money to buy a clinic wherever you like. You can hire your own staff. Be your own boss. Do whatever the hell you want." He took a drink without them.

Amalia shook her head. "We asked what *you* want."

The man leaned forward and lowered his voice. "We are seeking the holy grail of pharmacology."

Regnar rolled his eyes. "A female Viagra?" Half a dozen drug companies were already scouring the jungles for medicinal plants to help women love men. The market for such a drug, of course, would be even greater than for the pill that helped men love women.

"No." The Pfisto rep stared at the cocktail table, where a ring of water remained beside his glass. Slowly he used his fingertip to turn the circle into a square, speaking one word as he drew each line. "We. Seek. Love. Itself."

"Love itself?" Amalia raised an eyebrow.

"At Pfisto we've given the project the code name *Enola*—the opposite of *Alone*. Isn't that what you have been after all along?" The man put a dot of water in the center of his squared circle. "Not the mechanics of love. The world doesn't need hornier aphrodisiacs or more enticing perfumes. We need to find out what makes one heart care for another. People talk about lovesickness, but it's not a disease. The real epidemic is loneliness—the lack of love."

Regnar sat back in his chair. The young man might be an idiot in other ways—he might even be Mephistopheles on vacation—but what he said about love was true.

"We're willing to gamble that you can find Enola." The pharmaceutical rep reached into a bag behind his chair and took out a laptop computer. He set it on the table and lifted the lid, lighting an apple on the cover. Inside the laptop was a check for five million dollars, made out to Regnar and Amalia Laibach.

"This could be just the beginning," he said.

Amalia reached for the check. And at the same time, she noticed that the glowing apple on his laptop was already missing a bite.

Chapter Two: The White Spirit Bear

Ailama saw the first of the White Spirit Bears shortly after her sixteenth birthday. She had gone to the river to gather reeds. Her grandmother was teaching her to weave mats with beautiful patterns. Her father Strong Bow warned, "Do not stray far in your search, Ailama. The White Spirit Bears are spreading from the North Lands. They are dangerous invaders. One day they may come for our land too."

But Ailama's thoughts were already on the weaving she would make for Ranger in exchange for more of his stories. Her other childhood friend, Snegom, kept presenting her with the hides of the wild animals he killed—gifts that only made her sad. Ranger entertained her with tales of the trickster god Coyote, stories that made her laugh and think. She wanted to weave his stories into patterns of colored reeds.

When she reached the riverbank, however, she stopped in sudden fear. Her heart raced.

A giant, shimmering, silver bear was scooping a salmon from the whitewater with massive claws. It stood on its hind legs like a man, bit off the salmon's head, and turned a cold gaze past Ailama. An icy wind swept across the river.

This was no ordinary bear. She could see through its shimmering form to the river rocks beyond. She had the terrifying feeling that the White Spirit Bear was looking through her as well.

Ailama ran back to the village, rushed to her father at the campfire, and told him breathlessly what she had seen.

Strong Bow frowned, watching the flames. "This is a day of dark omens."

Ailama went on, "It killed our fish, but only its claws seemed real. The rest was—I don't know—like a cloud."

Strong Bow still stared at the fire. "I will assemble a war party with those of us who still have honor."

Ailama slowed, uncertain. "Has something else happened?"

Strong Bow said nothing.

"Father? What is it?"

He took her by the shoulders. "I have had to banish one of the tribe."

"Banish!" It was the worst punishment imaginable—being separated forever from the Kramned. "But who? Why?"

"He will live at Ice Lake, tending the horse camp in the mountains, where he can cause us no more harm."

Ailama clapped her hand to her mouth. "Ranger?"

"Never again speak that name."

"But what did he do?"

Strong Bow shook his head. "Some crimes cannot be spoken."

"Father!"

Ignoring her, he turned away and strode toward the corrals. "Snegom! Gather the warriors. We ride to battle at dawn."

For the rest of the day, as the men readied their weapons, Ailama asked people about Ranger's crime, but they either did not know or would not tell. She wanted to go to Ice Lake to ask Ranger himself, but she knew that she would then be banished too.

The next morning she sat alone on a rock above the village, watching the men ride out to confront the White Spirit Bear. Feathers flew from the warriors' raised spears. Bright streaks of paint turned their faces into fearsome masks. Snegom rode tall at her father's side.

What could Ranger's crime have been, she wondered? He was just a storyteller. He seemed the last person who might betray the tribe.

As she sat, a crow circled down from the mountains, cawing. It landed on a pine branch and wiped its beak on the bark.

Ailama watched the bird with a sad smile. "Maybe you are my spirit totem too."

The crow cocked a black eye at her and refolded its wings, as if it really were listening.

At that moment Ailama realized how much Ranger had meant to her, and how much she had lost. He had been more than a friend.

She looked up at the black bird. "If you see Ranger, tell him—"

She blinked, and a tear ran down her cheek. She could not speak.

The crow jumped from the branch and flew away, cawing.

When Regnar and Amalia returned to Oregon they checked in on Kathy, the nurse practitioner in their Pendleton office. All their lives the two Danish doctors had been looking for romance. Now that they had five million dollars to pursue the search in earnest, they weren't sure what to do.

"If you're supposed to research love—" Kathy began, but her voice drifted off as she looked out the window at the brown sagebrush hills above the rooftops of town. She was a former Umatilla County dairy queen who had earned her nursing degree at Eastern Oregon University. She did not normally drift into such reveries.

"Yes?" Amalia asked.

Kathy blushed, another thing the Laibachs had never seen her do before. "The most romantic place to go is a bed and breakfast."

Regnar nodded. This seemed a reasonable place to start. "Do you have a suggestion?"

Kathy lowered his eyes. "You might try Emily's Garden. It's just north of La Grande on Mount Emily."

"Perhaps we should make a reservation and check it out." Regnar took a phone book off the desk. "Is the owner's name Emily?"

"Not anymore." Kathy bit her lip. "But people say a young woman named Emily lived up there in pioneer days. The mountain got its name because so many cowboys from La Grande went there." She blushed again. "You know. To mount Emily."

Emily's Garden proved to be an 1894 Queen Anne ranch house surrounded by trellised roses, fruit trees, and cast iron benches. The owner, whose name was Rachel, apologized that she would be in town running errands when the Laibachs arrived, but she left a detailed note for them under the cushion of a wicker chair on the wraparound porch. The handwritten instructions told them how to find their way up a curving staircase to the Lilac Room. She encouraged them to pour themselves a glass of sherry from a decanter on the living room sideboard and informed them that breakfast would be served between eight and eight thirty.

A big brass bed with pillows dominated the room. White woodwork framed tall, lavender walls. Sunlight poured in through lace curtains.

Regnar and Amalia looked at each other. It was three in the afternoon. The romantic spark simply wasn't there. What was missing?

"I'll get some sherry," Regnar suggested.

"Here's a whole shelf of Zane Grey westerns." Amalia took down copies of *Riders of the Purple Sage* and *The Vanishing American*. "Let's read for a while."

And so they read in bed, turning pages, sipping sherry, and watching as the sunlight shifted across the Persian carpet. At six Regnar suggested they take a walk through the garden. The sun set behind the forested shoulder of Mount Emily. Meadowlarks sang. When it grew chilly Regnar and Amalia returned to their room to unpack the brie and crackers they had brought. They opened a bottle of cabarnet. But they still did not feel the urge to tear each other's clothes off.

Back on the bed, reading by the light of a tasseled lamp, Amalia finally closed her book and tapped its cover. "Maybe cowboys aren't the answer."

Regnar looked up. "I thought you were wild about them."

Amalia frowned. "Well, they may be sexy. It's hard to tell from Zane Grey's descriptions. But the men in his novels are mostly vengeful loners. They care about dead fathers and horses."

"So where's Enola?"

Amalia looked out the window. When she spoke again, it was in Danish. "Do you remember how we used to pretend we were Indians?"

Indianer. In the gliding, gulping dialect of their childhood, the word had not referred to Cayuse ranch hands, but rather to their own wild alter egos. The children in the fifth grade of the Ollerup charter school on the Danish island of Funen had become a tribe of blond *indianer*, prowling the beech woods and sharing secrets.

Once, after suffering through Lutheran confirmation classes together, their tribe had gone on the warpath against the village priest. On a moonlit Saturday night they had paddled a rowboat across Ollerup Lake to the church, climbed the spiral stair to the belfry, and howled like wolves. Running back down they had tripped on a rope and donged the big bell, which made them run even faster.

Even when the tribe graduated to the school in Svendborg they

THE OREGON VARIATIONS

kept their *indianer* nicknames. There were no outcasts. If someone threw a party, they went as a tribe or not at all.

"I remember telling myself that I'd marry a cowboy someday." Amalia shook her head. "But we were all *indianer*. We had a different kind of love — a love for the entire group. No pairing up. No dating."

"Not for you, maybe," Regnar said.

Amalia glanced to him. "You went on dates?"

"I wanted to."

"With who?"

Regnar looked down at his closed book. "Remember the cards you'd get on *Fastelavn?*"

Fastelavn was the Danish equivalent of Mardi Gras, marking the start of Lent and the end of the long, dark winter. Instead of parading, the Danes turned the festival into a Nordic Valentine's Day. Anonymous love poems appeared on girls' doorsteps. Only a row of pin pricks at the bottom of the card hinted at the number of letters in the secret admirer's name.

"It was you!" Amalia laughed, surprised that she had never before made the connection.

"I was the loneliest boy in town."

"I thought you didn't notice me until we were at the university."

Regnar shrugged. "By then I'd learned the trick was to rent cowboy movies."

Amalia tossed her Zane Grey novel aside. She put her tongue in the corner of her mouth. Then she began unbuckling Regnar's belt.

The next morning, when Regnar and Amalia went downstairs for breakfast, Rachel seated them at a long table with two other guests. She served them glass bowls of melon balls, strawberries, and blackberries. "Coffee is in the thermos. Is everyone OK with bacon in their omelets?"

They nodded.

"All right then. I'll leave you four to get to know each other." Rachel left for the kitchen.

After an awkward pause, the other couple introduced themselves as Bob and Sunny from Eugene. A balding man with a turtleneck, Bob explained that he was a hearings officer for the state labor bureau. He investigated complaints, mostly about employers who hired illegal immigrants and then refused to pay them. Sunny, with long hair and a peasant dress, said she practiced Nichiren Buddhist meditation techniques while Bob tracked down bad guys.

Bob asked, "So what brings you to Union County? Business or pleasure?"

"Both, actually." Regnar looked to Amalia, unsure how much to say about their project.

Amalia charged ahead. "We're doctors, researching sex."

"Oh!" Sunny dropped a melon ball.

"Love seems to burn with more intensity in some settings, don't you think?" Amalia continued. "Regnar and I are looking for the hottest place."

Bob leaned back, frowning. "Why Union County?"

"We've heard stories," Regnar admitted. "You know, about Mount Emily."

Bob laughed. "That old joke? If you believe that, you'd probably believe the other, about the taxidermist who walked into a bar."

"Hush, Bob," Sunny said.

For a minute spoons clinked against glass bowls as they finished their fruit.

Finally Regnar asked, "What about the taxidermist who walked into a bar?"

Bob set down his spoon. "He was from Eugene, with a hippie ponytail, a tie-dyed shirt, and sandals."

Sunny shook her long hair. "Bob, do you have to?"

But Bob was on a roll. "So the taxidermist walks into the toughest bar in La Grande, and all the cowboys turn to stare. The bartender squints at him and asks, 'Where you from, stranger?' The guy answer, 'Eugene.' The bartender scoffs, "Eugene! And what do you do in Eugene?' The guy stammers, 'I—I mount dead animals.'"

"Bob!"

Bob smiled. "Then the bartender looks around at the cowboys in the bar and says, 'It's OK, boys, he's one of us.'"

After breakfast Sunny stopped Amalia in the hall. "I want to apologize about Bob. He likes to tell off-color stories."

"That's all right," Amalia told her. "I think I needed to hear the worst about cowboy country. My husband and I really are researching places that focus love."

"You are?"

"Yes."

Sunny bit her lip. "Maybe I shouldn't tell you this."

"What?"

"Well, I've been to a lot of bed and breakfasts because of Bob's work."

Amalia waited. "Yes?"

Sunny leaned closer to whisper. "And there's one that *does* make a difference."

"Really? Where?"

"In the Columbia River Gorge. Between a penis-shaped rock and a cleft with a waterfall." Sunny looked both ways. "The Bridal Veil Rooster Rock Cabins."

Chapter Three: Heart Bane

That evening the warriors returned to the village somber and bitter. The White Spirit Bear had wounded two men and killed three Appaloosa ponies. The tribe's arrows had sailed through the Spirit Bear's shadowy body with no effect. Snegom had attacked with his knife. He had succeeded in cutting off one silver claw—the battle's only trophy. But the four remaining claws had raked Snegom's right arm, leaving strips of bloody flesh.

"You will tend to Snegom's wounds," Strong Bow had told Ailama.

"Yes, Father."

"When he recovers, you will be married."

"What?" Ailama looked at her father, open-mouthed.

"Snegom asked for your hand, and I have agreed. Today he

has proven his courage. He is the strong warrior the Kramned need as our next chief."

Ailama had never felt so torn. Of course she would nurse her childhood friend, but she did not want to marry him! She cleaned and dressed his wounds as well as she knew how. All the while Snegom shouted orders at her, demanding that she raise his pillow, wash his feet, and bring his pipe.

By the third day, although the wounds on his arm had scabbed over, Snegom began shivering with chills. Ailama brought a hot compress for his chest, but when she opened his shirt she stopped short. Just to the left of the center of his chest, where his heart should have been, was a shimmering hole.

"What's wrong?" Snegom demanded.

Ailama dropped the compress and ran to the teepee of Sral, Ranger's uncle. When she told her story, the old shaman shook his white-haired head.

"Snegom has Heart Bane," he said. "The real danger of the White Spirit Bears is not the salmon they take, but rather the disease they spread."

"A disease? Can anyone catch it?"

He nodded. "With time the victims become as lonely and greedy as the White Spirit Bears themselves."

"Is there no cure?"

The shaman looked down. "I am an old man, and have forgotten much."

For the next week Ailama watched with despair as the hole in Snegom's chest grew. Strong Bow called the tribe together for a war summit, but so many people had come down with chills that few attended. More and more they kept to themselves and began to shimmer.

One morning Ailama's grandmother took her aside. "Go to him, my child. Only he can save the tribe."

"Who?"

The old woman touched Ailama between the breasts. The wizened finger sank farther than it should. "You have begun to shimmer, Ailama. Look in your heart before it is too late."

Ailama tore open her buckskin blouse and saw with horror that a small patch of skin at the base of her neck had turned shiny.

"Heart Bane!" she cried.

"You have caught the disease while tending Snegom." Her grandmother lowered her voice. "Warriors will not save the tribe from the curse of the White Spirit Bear. We need a shaman, and Sral has grown too feeble for such a task."

"Ranger!" Ailama breathed the name.

"Go to him, child, and tell him of our need."

"But then I would be banished too. And he might catch Heart Bane from me."

Her grandmother sighed. "Listen to your heart while it still can speak."

Amalia and Regnar soon discovered that the Columbia Gorge had quite a reputation for sexual magnetism. Rooster Rock State Park not only had a three-hundred-foot phallic basalt splinter, but it also boasted a nude beach where women sunbathed topless and men paraded naked along the sandy Columbia riverbank. Just three miles away, the pioneer village of Bridal Veil had mostly vanished, but the Bridal Veil Rooster Rock Cabins still kept the old town's zip code alive. Each spring hundreds of young women brought their wedding invitations to be mailed from the inn so that the letters would bear the romantic postmark, *Bridal Veil, Oregon 97010.*

The cabins had been on the market for two years, first at $3.2 million, then at 2.9, and now at 2.7.

The Laibachs drove to the resort, fell in love with it, and bought it for $2.5 million. They spent another million replacing mossy roofs and installing gas fireplaces. They made no changes, however, to the eleventh cabin at the top of the waterfall's creek. In every experiment, Regnar insisted, it's important to leave a control.

They hired a staff of four: a groundskeeper, a maid, a receptionist, and a cook. Finally they posted advertisements in Portland for couples seeking more romance in their lives. The ads offered fifty dollars to committed but unsatisfied couples willing to spend a night participating in a discreet scientific study.

Within hours of the ad's publication the phone line to Bridal Veil was so jammed with applicants that the receptionist put everything on hold and yelled for help. "Dr. Laibach! And Dr. Laibach! Could you come out here a minute please?"

Regnar and Amalia had been working on a program in a computer room behind the lobby.

"Trouble with the applications?" Regnar asked. The receptionist, Clara Lee, was a dark-skinned beauty from North Portland. They had hired her because she had worked two years in a crowded Portland DMV office and could still smile.

Clara Lee cocked her head, wagging her shiny black hair. "I've entered the records for thirty couples in two hours, but I missed probably a hundred calls. The line's smoking. How many people do you need?"

"Just ten couples—well, eleven with the control," Amalia replied. "But we want a large enough applicant pool that we can sort it by the criteria."

Clara Lee put her hands on her hips. "The criteria are that they have to be committed and unsatisfied. Hello? That's practically everybody."

"Not everyone can take a day off for a scientific study," Regnar objected.

"Doctor, your study is about having sex. And you're paying them. Half the people on the planet would take a day off for that."

Amalia frowned. "Maybe we should reduce the remuneration?"

Regnar shook his head. "There's an ethical standard. And we have plenty of funding." He turned back to the receptionist. "Are you warning the applicants that they'll have to wear a device?"

"Yes." Clara Lee sighed and closed her eyes. "I tell them it fits behind your ear like a hearing aid. No one cares as long as it isn't a camera. They just don't want to be seen naked on YouTube."

Regnar tightened his lips. Although the device did not record video, it would be transmitting live to their computer room, charting the arousal levels of the participants based on electrical variations in skin conductivity. It wasn't the kind of graph everyone would want monitored during a romantic night out.

"Take as many applications as you can," Amalia told the receptionist. "We're holding sessions four nights a week for at least three months. We'll need a lot of people."

Clara Lee saluted. "Yes ma'am. And who do you want me to invite for opening night?"

Amalia leaned over to look at the receptionist's computer screen. "Email me the applications you've got so far. I bet we'll find our eleven couples there."

Chapter Four: Ice Lake

Ailama rushed across the village to her teepee. On the way she was surprised to see the shimmering form of Snegom floating toward the corrals. He had become a wraith, like the White Spirit Bears, translucent except for his teeth and his fingernails.

"Where are you going?" she asked.

He looked through her. "Bring me weapons. Bring me food."

"I'll fetch pemmican." She ran to her teepee to fill a pack with pemmican, but not for Snegom. A wraith was beyond her care. Would she become like that too, she wondered? Would the entire tribe dissolve in greed?

Ailama slung her pack over her shoulder and set out across the prairie. Only when she was out of sight of the village did she double back toward the mountain trail. She had never been to the horse camp at Ice Lake. The path turned out to be so faint that she soon lost it altogether. She struggled on, following Ice Creek up past waterfalls and fearsome crags. Brambles cut her hands and caught at her blond braids.

Late in the afternoon, exhausted, she crested the rocky rim of a high mountain valley. Here the creek suddenly grew placid, meandering through knee-deep grass to a milky-blue lake. Groves of pine trees clung to the slopes on either side, fringed with huckleberry bushes and wildflowers. A dozen horses looked up as she crossed the meadow toward the thin plume of a campfire. There, under the shelter of a shale ledge,

Ranger was hanging trout on a pole rack to dry in the sun.

He turned and exclaimed, "Ailama!" But then a shadow crossed his face. "You are not bringing good news."

She sank on a rock half a dozen paces away. When he stepped forward she held up her palm. "Come no closer."

He tightened his lips. "The tribe has Heart Bane."

She looked up, marveling. "How do you know?"

A crow hopped down from a pine branch and cawed.

Ailama asked, "Can shamans talk to crows?"

Ranger nodded. "Crows are the spirit forms of other beings. My mentor has taught me many things."

Ailama studied the bird, uncertain what other shape it might take. Then she turned to Ranger with the question that had been tormenting her. "Why were you banished?"

Ranger lowered his eyes. "The nephew of a shaman should not ask to marry the daughter of a great warrior chief." He looked up at her. "My crime is that I love you."

Ailama wanted more than ever to rush to his arms. Instead she touched the shimmering skin at the base of her neck. "I am not one to love. I too have been struck with Heart Bane, the curse of the White Spirit Bear."

Ranger tightened his lips. "And the others?"

"Snegom is already a wraith. Almost everyone else has chills. Within a week the tribe will be lost." She looked down. "Perhaps I am swayed by selfishness as well. I have come to ask if a novice shaman can help."

The crow cawed, a raucous cry.

Ranger asked, "Do you love me, Ailama?"

She nodded.

"Then trust me now." He stepped forward, lifted her chin, and kissed her full on the lips—a kiss as sudden as a summer thunderstorm.

For an instant she stiffened, startled. Then the warmth of his lips poured through her, filling her with joy.

When he finally released her he touched his fingertip to the infected skin at the base of her throat.

She looked down, bewildered. The shiny spot above her heart was all but gone. "You—you are the cure!"

Ranger shook his head. "Love will slow the disease, but a spirit curse can only be cured by a stronger spirit. The trickster Coyote keeps the cure in a cave behind a waterfall, deep in the Columbia River Gorge."

"A journey that far would take weeks! By then the tribe—"

"There is another way." Ranger closed his eyes.

Behind him the crow spread its blue-black wings. Then to Ailama's amazement, the wings spread wider and wider, changing to a rainbow of colors until they stood out to either side like great, feathered canoes. The giant bird began to caw, but its voice grew deeper and louder, rumbling like thunder in the mountains.

Ranger opened his eyes. "Unless you'd prefer one of Snegom's eagles, we could ride on my crow."

"A thunderbird!" Ailama exclaimed.

Everyone was nervous about the opening night of the Enola study. Regnar and Amalia stationed Clara Lee by the lobby door in a low-cut purple dress as a hostess. "Welcome to our social hour," Clara Lee said, flashing her melt-your-heart smile. "Doctors Regnar and Amalia are going to meet you all individually. In the meantime just make yourselves at home." She pointed to a table with fruit juices and vegetable dips by the lobby windows overlooking the waterfall.

Regnar and Amalia wore lab coats that gave them a professional look. They took the guests aside one couple at a time to ask a few questions. Pre-screening had guaranteed that the applicants were all between the ages of twenty- nine and forty, with no documented history of abuse, impotence, or infertility. In general these people were younger and healthier than the population the Laibachs had seen on the Love Cruise, but already many familiar, tiresome complaints had taken root: "He doesn't have time for me," and "She complains about everything I do."

By seven o'clock the doctors called all twenty-two of the subjects together at the table overlooking the falls. Maple branches waved in the breeze created by the cascade. The distant, rushing thunder played a constant background chord. The setting sun dappled the glen's rainforest jungle with glowing greens.

"Welcome to Bridal Veil," Regnar said, holding out his hand to the view. "Don't you wish all marriage counseling looked like this?"

Everyone laughed, and the nervousness eased a notch.

"We have some pleasant surprises in store for you tonight," Regnar continued. "You'll find drinks and appetizers in your cabins. We'll distribute suggestions for discussion topics and games. The packet for each cabin is different. Feel free to skip anything that makes you uncomfortable. Just be sure to wear these monitors." He held up a plastic transmitter the size of a curved pinky finger. "All you have to do is hook it over your ear and clamp the sticky tape onto your earlobe. Let's take a minute so everyone gets them on right."

Clara Lee and the two doctors helped people attach the devices. Then Amalia held up ten numbered folders, each a different color. "Before I can distribute the cabin assignments we need to ask one couple to volunteer to serve as our control, to make sure our study isn't skewed by some outside influence. Ten of the cabins have been upgraded for comfort and consistency. I'm afraid the eleventh is a bit primitive, without indoor plumbing. The couple there will still get a free night's stay, but not the stipend or the packet of tips that are part of the study."

The room fell silent. Skipping the fifty-dollar stipend was one thing. But no one wanted to miss out on the mysterious packet of tips for sexual stimulation.

Regnar said, "We can choose a control couple at random, but we'd really rather have a volunteer."

The couples looked at each other. Some whispered or shook their heads.

"Anyone?" Amalia asked.

Finally a red-haired woman sighed. "Zach and I will be the control."

"Melissa!" the man beside her objected.

Melissa shrugged. "Someone has to do it."

"Sheesh. All right."

Amalia handed out packets to the other ten couples. Then she stopped in front of Zach and Melissa. "Thanks for volunteering. Our groundskeeper will show you the way. It's close enough to the falls that the path can be slippery."

Zach pulled his mouth sideways. "Do we still have to wear the stupid hearing aids?"

"That would help us, yes."

That evening Regnar and Amalia sat shoulder to shoulder in the computer room, watching the early returns like politicians on election night. Twenty-two green lines jiggled across the screen. Occasionally one would spike or zigzag, as if a seismograph were recording minor tremors. But mostly the lines stayed flat.

"Look, there goes seven X," Regnar said, pointing to an uphill trend.

"But not seven Y," Amalia said. The Laibachs had code-named their subjects by cabin number and by chromosome. As they watched, seven X wavered and slowly sank back.

"It's still early in the evening," Regnar said. "They may not have taken their rations yet." Each subject had been allotted two hundred and fifty centiliters of merlot, thirty grams of dark chocolate, and half a dozen salmon canapes. Hidden in the canapes were a variety of test compounds, some of which had been difficult to obtain legally.

"Did cabin seven get the rhinoceros horn powder?" Amalia asked.

"No, tiger's teeth." He hunched before the screen.

Finally Amalia pulled his sleeve. "A watched pot never boils. Come on, I'm ready for my own ration of merlot."

"All right." They went out into the dim lobby, poured themselves glasses of red wine, and stood before the window. At night the waterfall seemed to give off a faint glow, as if it were a pale ghost shifting in the woods. Lights along the paths to the cabins twinkled as fern fronds waved before them, bent by the night breeze.

"I wonder if we've chosen the wrong place," Regnar said.

Amalia put her arm around his waist. "No, there's magic here."

"That doesn't sound very scientific."

"Maybe you can't put Enola in a bottle." She turned to face him, and their lab coats brushed together. He set down his glass. Then he kissed her, holding her head in his hands.

Before long they were taking off their clothes. He hoisted her onto the table and climbed up after her while the waterfall thundered.

Twenty minutes later, hastily redressed in underwear and lab coats, they returned to the computer room to check on the other couples. Six of the cabins were doing quite well, jiggling their little green lines up toward the red zone.

"Looks like some of the cabins are asleep," Regnar mused. "There's no response at all from number eleven. The couple there must have taken their monitors off."

Amalia knit her brow. "I remember them, Zach and Melissa. They said they'd wear the monitors, even though they are the control. Perhaps something's wrong. Can you show just the graph for cabin eleven?"

Regnar reduced the other ten graphs to icons at the bottom of the screen. In so doing he uncovered the rest of the eleventh cabin's graph. The two green lines were frantically spiking halfway to the top of the screen.

"My God." Regnar sat back. "They're off the chart."

"They didn't have tiger's teeth or anything," Amalia mused. "But they're sure passionate."

"You interviewed them. They were supposed to be unsatisfied with their romance."

"They said they were. They'd been to three different marriage counselors."

"Do they have children?" Regnar asked.

Amalia shook her head. "Not yet. But from the looks of things, maybe soon."

Regnar laughed. For a moment they watched the high, jiggling lines. Then he furrowed his brow. "I wonder what's so special about cabin eleven? It's a rundown shack. They had to chop wood to build a fire in the stove. Is that romantic?"

"It can be."

"Maybe there's something in the water."

"All the cabins have the same water."

"But cabin eleven is so close to the waterfall. And remember what the Forest Service told us? There's an endangered species of liverworts or something that doesn't grow anywhere else. Maybe the plant puts out spores that mix with the mist."

Amalia shook her head. "You're looking for Enola the wrong way. Honestly, I think our whole first round of experiments is missing the point. We're just trying out aphrodisiacs."

"That's the scientific method, eliminating the obvious first."

"But we're not scientists. Pfisto signed us up because of our intuition."

Regnar sat back. "And what does your intuition tell you?"

Amalia looked out the door to the dark lobby. "I think cabin eleven is different because the people there aren't being paid."

"Why would that matter?"

"No one wanted to give up the stipend. Zach and Melissa volunteered for the good of the group."

Regnar nodded slowly. "An act of selflessness."

"An act of love. Remember when we were *indianer*, back in Denmark? We cared more for the tribe than for ourselves. Maybe love is the opposite of greed."

"We could test that by switching cabins and stipends."

Amalia sighed. "That would only measure sex, not love."

"What else can we do? Love isn't quantifiable, but it presents as sex, which is."

Amalia stood up, sat on his lap, opened her lab coat, and pulled his head against her black lace bra. For a moment she just stroked his hair and let her heart bump her breasts against his cheek. "I'm glad you're a man anyway."

"Anyway?"

"Men think love is about sex. Women know it's really about romance. Try quantifying that, Dr. Laibach."

He twisted his head to look at her, and kissed her on the lips.

She smiled and pulled his head back to her chest. "There's more to romance than a good kiss."

"Teach me, guru."

"Romance," she said, swirling the graying hair at his temple, "is about waiting for something you want very much."

"Delayed gratification, then."

"More than that. Waiting for something impossibly beautiful."

"A fantasy?"

"A dream." She kissed the top of his head.

Chapter Five: Enola

Ailama and Ranger climbed onto the feathered back of the thunderbird.

"Hang on tight," Ranger said.

The giant bird hopped three times and sailed into the sky. Soon Ailama and Ranger were pointing out landmarks below: The great falls of the Columbia at Celilo, the snowy summit of Mount Hood, and the spire of Rooster Rock. The sun was setting when they finally landed at the misty pool beneath Bridal Veil Falls. Ailama put her arms around Ranger. "Thank you for this journey." Their hearts beat together for a moment.

Then he stepped back. "You must wait here."

"But—"

"Coyote is a treacherous bargainer. Here you will be safe."

"And what of you?"

"I know the risk. Please, Ailama." He kissed her again. Before she could say another word he turned and disappeared through the waterfall's mist.

Twilight had fallen. A pale, full moon was glowing through the woods when Ranger finally returned from the waterfall. His hair dripped and his steps were weary. He opened a small deerskin pouch. "There is enough for the entire tribe if you are careful. Use only a fingertip to put some on your tongue."

Ailama dipped a finger into the pouch, studied the red dust a moment, and touched it to her tongue. A great warmth poured through her, but she became drowsy as well. Dimly she recalled climbing onto the thunderbird's back. She flew through the night, held in Ranger's strong arms.

When she awoke, dawn was turning the sky red over Ice Lake. Beside the shelter Ranger was tending a crackling pine fire. "Eat this, Ailama," he said, setting cooked fish and pemmican on a slate rock. "You will need strength for your trek back to the tribe."

"Surely you are coming too?"

He shook his head.

"But you will not be banished anymore! Not after bringing the cure to Heart Bane."

"Spirit medicine comes with a price." He looked to the east, where a bright red glow revealed that the sun was about to rise above the dark shadows of Hells Canyon. He took Ailama in his arms, held her tightly, and whispered, "I will always love you."

At that moment a golden bead of sun broke the horizon, casting a ray upon them. Ranger drew in his breath. He grew lighter and softer in her arms. Then he burst into bluish-black feathers and flew into the sky. He circled twice, landed on a pine, and wiped his beak on a branch. Finally he cocked his black eye at her and gave a caw of such mournful longing that Ailama thought her heart would break.

Throughout the summer the Laibachs experimented, switching people and cabins. They even de-modernized one of the cabins, restoring it to its original primitive condition. They abandoned the aphrodisiacs early on—even the rare liverwort proved useless. Sex games helped some couples, but not others. Levels of passion were higher than normal in all of the cabins, no matter what they did. But cabin eleven was always the hottest, and if the couple volunteered to stay there without pay, the passion levels simply smoked.

"How can we package results like this?" Regnar asked, scrolling through screens of data on the office computer. The Pfisto rep was scheduled to come for an accounting the next morning.

"Let's stay in cabin eleven tonight," Amalia suggested. "I have an idea."

"Wow!"

"Not that kind of idea," Amalia chided. "Well, maybe. But I also remember something from a dream."

"Intuition?"

"Call it that if you like. Bring flashlights and raincoats."

By the time they had moved into the cabin, twilight had turned the woods to a grove of shadows. Regnar chopped wood and lit a fire in the wood stove. When the fire took hold Amalia put on a raincoat, opened the door, and whispered, "Follow me."

"Where?"

"Shh." With her flashlight shimmering through the ferns, she led him up the creek to the splash pool below Bridal Veil Falls. Sheets of water thundered into mist. Gusts of wet wind whipped their raincoats.

Amalia pulled the hood of her coat over her head. "Wait here."

"Where are you going?"

"To bargain for Enola. I know the risk."

"What are you talking about?"

"Please. Just wait for me." She kissed him. "Here you will be safe." Then she turned and walked through the waterfall. The gleam of her flashlight vanished behind the mist.

Regnar started to go after her, but then hesitated. She rarely gave him such strong orders. He waited, growing colder and more worried with every minute.

A pale full moon had begun to glow through the woods when Amalia finally reemerged from the waterfall.

"What did you do in there?" Regnar asked.

Amalia said nothing. She led the way back to cabin eleven. After they had hung up their raincoats she asked, "What happens if we find Enola?"

"Did you find it?" Regnar looked at her, astonished.

"I didn't say that. I want to know what happens if we give it to Pfisto tomorrow."

"We'd be rich. The rep promised ten percent of profits. For an elixir of love, that could mean billions."

"But what about Pfisto?" Amalia asked.

"They'd be rich too. Or at least their shareholders would. Did you really find something behind the waterfall?"

She frowned. "Controlling love means controlling people. The company that owns Enola would own the world."

Regnar opened his mouth, but then closed it without speaking.

The fire in the woodstove popped and crackled.

"Do you know what Enola really means?" Amalia asked.

"You mean, other than 'alone' spelled backwards?"

She nodded. "I looked it up. The *Enola Gay* was the plane that dropped the atomic bomb on Hiroshima. The pilot named the plane after his mother. She was named for a novel about a lonely girl tormented by the Prince of Darkness, the evil bird of death."

A sliver of moonlight played through the wavy glass of the window.

Amalia stood up and sat on Regnar's lap. "Love has always been strongest in this cabin. Especially when we ask people to give up something for the sake of the tribe."

"That's true," he said. "Usually it's enough if we ask them to give up fifty dollars."

"I'm asking you to give up more."

"How much more?"

"Billions."

Regnar looked up.

Then he kissed her so passionately that her head spun.

The next day the representative of the Pfisto pharmaceutical company drove a black Thunderbird to the Bridal Veil Rooster Rock Cabins. He strode into the lobby with a too-wide smile full of too-white teeth.

"Dr. Laibach and Dr. Laibach! So here we are, at your day of reckoning. My intuition tells me you have good news about the Enola project. What have you found that will make us all rich?"

Regnar exchanged a glance with Amalia. Then he shook his head. "I'm afraid we didn't discover anything you can use."

"Nothing at all?"

"Nothing you can use."

"Damn!" The Phisto rep stalked to the nearest wall and smacked his fist against it. "We spent five million dollars on this project."

Amalia eyed him coolly. "That's petty cash for Pfisto. Besides, you said you have eleven other teams looking for Enola. The others are scientists. For you, we were just a gamble."

The Pfisto rep shook his head. "They all came up empty handed too. But there was something special here, something about you. I could sense you were almost there. Two Danish doctors of love, in the romantic wilds of Oregon."

He looked out the window at the waterfall and sighed.

Epilogue: A Spirit Soars

The red medicine dust that Ailama brought to the Kramned tribe healed everyone except Snegom. He had already been so consumed by Heart Bane that he continued to wander as a wraith. The White Spirit Bears remained, claiming the best salmon and the best land, but the Kramned tribe survived in the high country under Strong Bow and his daughter Ailama.

In the evenings by the campfire Ailama retold the legends she had learned from Ranger. On special nights she also told the story of a young shaman, a man whose love was so great that he gave up his human form to save the tribe.

And sometimes in her dreams, or during the intoxicating beat of a pow-wow dance, Ailama thrilled to feel herself become a spirit crow. Only then was she free at last to soar with her one true love, a pair of spirits circling in the sky.

THE OREGON VARIATIONS

CRATER LAKE

PART TWO

HOT SHOTS

They were the best—the Hot Shots from the firefighting command center in Redmond. But now, as the seven of them huddled around the jump bay of the transport plane, surveying what had become of the little lightning strike in the Greenhorn Range of Eastern Oregon, no one spoke. What had been reported at 6:30 a.m. as a one-acre spot fire had exploded to twenty, a crescent of flames along half a mile of dry lodgepole ridgecrest. Downwind, through a ragged black veil of smoke, sunlight flashed on the tin roofs of Sumpter, a town of two hundred people just seven miles away, directly in the fire's path.

"We can do this," Taylor said, loud enough that his crew could catch his words over the rush of the wind and the roar of the props.

Crouching in their red jump suits and white parachute packs, the Hot Shots glanced at each other uncertainly. Even Austin, the affable Bend snowboarder who moonlighted as a stand-up comic, tightened his lips. Jeremy beamed, but then he always beamed. Built like a stand-up freezer, the football star from Lebanon had been hit often enough that he only had one expression left.

"Boss, we need backup!" It was Miranda, one of the famously responsible Gomez twins from Madras. The only two women to earn their way onto the Hot Shots, Miranda and Maria prided themselves in doing the work of one man—a superhuman firefighter who never slept. Working in twelve-hour shifts, the identical sisters could be trusted to hold a position on a fire line around the clock.

"Sorry, Binky," Kyle shouted back, "We're on our own." Kyle was the rich kid from Roseburg. Everyone knew the curly-haired young man was on the crew solely for the glory, and not the pay. He stood to inherit his father's construction company. Kyle called both twins Binky, a rude term of endearment shortened from the mixed-up phrase "binky stitches." In return they called him Buck, as in "Kyle, the bucking fast turd." In the crew's bass-ackwards language of Spoonerisms, the Shot Hots were a whole fam damily of hit sheds.

"Kyle's right," Taylor shouted. He was only a few years older than the others, but they had elected him captain by acclaim. Taylor was the college whiz kid from Salem. His judgment and strategy had saved their lives more than once.

"All the regular crews are fighting the Pasayten Complex and the Trinity Burn," Taylor continued. "We're alone out here, guys."

Loneliness was the curse of being the best. While an entire army of Pulaski-and-chainsaw crews had marched off to fight the long, slow fire wars in Northern Washington and California, the Hot Shots had been held back, just in case. Ostensibly they had been in Redmond to train fresh recruits at the firefighting center, but when the call came to pack their parachute gear, they had known it must be a mission only they could handle.

"But how, boss?" Jackson was shaking his head. He was the handsome kid from Corvallis, and his long sandy-blond hair shook past startlingly blue eyes. Even with the bulky red suit and the parachute packs, you could tell his shoulders were broad and his muscles hard. Wherever Jackson went, women turned to watch. Each time he bragged of another conquest, the Hot Shots responded in chorus, "It's a sham dame, Jackson."

Now Jackson pointed to the fiery ridge. "Seven guys can't contain a front that long."

"Not all at once, no." Taylor squinted, gauging the blaze. "But the west wind's light, so we've got maybe twenty hours before it burns into Sumpter. In the meantime, we can set back fires."

"Half a mile of back fires?"

Taylor nodded, thinking. The fire had just crested the top of a T-shaped ridge. For most of the front's length the flames would now be burning slowly downhill. "The ridge in the middle is the biggest threat. We'll drop there and start felling trees for a fire break halfway between the front and the town. While Jeremy finishes digging the fire break, two groups of three will fan out to the sides, lighting back fires. There's a big creek on the left that can anchor that half of the line. To the right, there's a dirt road. When we're done, we'll all meet back at the ridge to hold the middle with water packs."

"You want us to build a ring of fire," Austin said, his comic grin returning.

Taylor nodded. "A ring of fire that burns into the middle. The front line's already shaped like a big arc. We'll just finish the circle. Then we'll watch from the side while the fire goes out in a blaze of glory."

"To hell and back," Kyle said. He had a special fondness for the word *glory*. "I'm with you, boss."

At that point the pilot took off his earphones and shouted over his shoulder, "Are you guys jumping or not? I can't circle forever."

Taylor looked to his crew. All six of them held up their thumbs. "To hell and back, boss."

It had taken the Hot Shots four years to earn their name and their catch phrase, "To hell and back." They had been new hires, most of them just nineteen, the summer of the Tilly Jane burn on Mt. Hood. Seven kids who hardly knew each other, they had missed the order to pull out. Instead they had dug a line where the trees thinned at the 5700-foot level, and had stopped the fire a hundred yards below Cloud Cap Inn, the historic, shake-sided lodge from the 1880s. When the supervisor finally showed up and found them with their feet on the lodge's porch furniture, they were the rookie wonders. They called themselves the Hot Shots, but older crews scoffed.

The following summer they had parachuted into the Mule

Creek fire on the edge of the Wild Rogue Wilderness, just before the humidity dropped and the blaze blew up. They had already abandoned their fire line and were running for their lives when Kyle spotted a herd of elk trapped by the flames in Mule Creek's box canyon. Despite everything they turned back, called in a helicopter water dump, and held open the mouth of the canyon while a hundred elk and three black bears escaped. That night, when they hiked down to the Rogue River Ranch, sooty and exhausted, Jeremy carried in his arms a gangly bull elk calf, its fur singed.

But it was their third summer together that they went to hell and back. Lightning had shotgunned the Hells Canyon Wilderness with strikes. A maze of rimrock, the mile-deep Snake River gorge between Oregon and Idaho was no place to fight fires. It was designated wilderness, so the Forest Service decided to let it burn. Still, no one wanted to lose the Hat Point lookout tower. Built on the edge of the Oregon rim in 1948, the little seven-foot-square cabin atop an eighty-seven-foot tower had become a tourist attraction. Generations of Forest Service lookouts had staffed that panoramic box over the years, calling in smokes from summer thunderstorms. The Wallowa-Whitman supervisor put in a special request to the Hot Shots to see if it could be saved.

The seven of them had driven a rusty double-clutched International truck up into the smoke on the twenty-two-mile washboard gravel grade from Imnaha. A mile short of the tower, pine trees blocked the road, uprooted by hot winds from the firestorm ahead. This was a blaze they obviously could not defeat. After a moment of thought, Taylor decided they should hike on with ropes and fireproof Kevlar sheeting. They scaled the tower and rappelled down on four sides, wrapping the wooden structure as they went.

But sparks were already blowing through the hot air. As they ran back on the road, the truck ahead of them erupted in a ball of flame, its fuel tank rupturing with a boom. Behind them, a wall of fire was already sweeping past the Hat Point tower, leaving the wrapped cabin intact and unreachable.

The Gomez twins had argued to hunker down in the emergency

Kevlar bivvy tents. Statistically, two out of three people in fireproof tents survived, although smoke inhalation often left its mark.

Taylor would have none of it. He led them into Hells Canyon at a run—down six thousand feet of elevation in six miles, dodging rimrock cliffs and hot spots. At the Snake River they lashed together a raft of driftwood logs and steered downstream through gigantic whitewater rapids between riverbanks roaring with fire. Twenty miles later, when they drifted out of the smoke to the Forest Service outpost at Pittsburg Landing, they were no longer merely the Hot Shots. They were legends.

Officially, they had been reprimanded for taking unnecessary risks, but no one cared. They were the best.

"Now!" Taylor cried. With a grunt and a shove, the Hot Shots tipped a half-ton bundle of equipment out the jump door. At once a white nylon mushroom billowed free. For a moment, while the plane continued on its slow arc, they watched the load of tools, fuel, and water sway beneath the rapidly shrinking white dome of the parachute, drifting through the smoke toward a ridgecrest ahead of the fire.

"We'll jump as soon as we circle round again," Taylor shouted. "You know the order. Aim for the supply chute."

They buckled on shiny red helmets emblazoned with a proud circle of seven blue stars. Then they lined up, nervously rechecking the straps of their main and reserve chutes. No matter how many times they had jumped into the smoke, each of them always felt a flutter of doubt.

"Go!"

Jeremy jumped first, his chute red. Then Kyle with an orange chute, Jackson with yellow, Austin with green, and the twins with blue and violet. Taylor's indigo parachute completed the rainbow. They had chosen the colors out of sheer bravado. The pilot tipped his wing in salute before banking back toward Redmond.

Perhaps, Taylor thought, kids from Sumpter would spot the rainbow above the firestorm and rush to tell their parents that there was hope: The Hot Shots were on the way.

The drop itself rarely lasted more than three minutes, but these were always the worst. Dangling in silence, cut off from the team that made them great, each of them felt their sparks of doubt catch fire. There are no legends when you're alone. The forest coming up toward you is as dry and hard as the truth.

Jeremy had been a football star only until his senior year at Lebanon High School. At first his size and strength had been enough. But when a scout from Oregon State University came to watch the AAA quarterfinals, Jeremy had been so flustered that he scooped up a fumbled ball and ran the wrong way, doggedly shaking the tackles of his own teammates until he scored a two-point safety for the opposing team.

Kyle's father actually did own a construction company in Roseburg, but he wasn't rich. A bad back and a bout with depression had left him with more debts than assets. A firm young hand might have saved the company from bankruptcy, but Kyle had fled, spooked by the smell of failure.

Jackson, to be sure, had won his reputation as a ladykiller fairly, with the good looks of a romance novel hero. At seventeen he had knocked up a cheerleader and slipped into marriage. Two years and two kids later, he still hadn't learned to change a diaper. At first he had spent his days in the garage, tinkering with his motorcycle. Then he started taking longer and longer rides. One day he rode to Redmond and didn't come back.

Red, orange, yellow — the chutes drifted down into the smoke like wayward balloons after a party.

Austin, with the green parachute, had been happy enough snowboarding and cracking jokes. But then his parents kicked him out. Snowboarding and stand-up comedy, they insisted, were not life skills. Unless he enrolled at the local community college, they were cutting off his allowance. Austin held out for a year and a half, sleeping on sofas while he applied for snowboard scholarships and comedy gigs. When his money ran out, he escaped by joining a fire crew, too proud to admit his parents were right.

The Gomez girls from Madras should have been responsible. The eldest of eight, they had been born in a migrant camp outside of Woodburn, the first in their family with United States citizenship. When the feds raided the hop-picking crews and deported their father, their mother packed the family into a station wagon. They ended up in a vacant lot behind the St. Vincent de Paul store in Madras, living on food stamps. After Maria and Miranda graduated from Madras High, they left town. Shame kept them from going back to help their family. Instead they spent their firefighting pay on clothes, cars, and lottery tickets with guilt that wouldn't scratch off.

Green, blue, violet—the Hot Shots were descending one at a time.

Taylor, their indigo captain, was the only one who had been to college. As a kid, he had wanted to be a fireman. When he grew up his dream had grown up as well: He would earn an MBA and become a corporate titan. But after a single term at the U of O, skipping class to play video games and beer pong, Taylor's reckoning arrived in the mail as a report card during Christmas vacation. His father told him the Army would straighten him out, but his mother wavered. That spring he made them proud by joining the firefighting trainees. They were still proud. Every time Taylor visited them in Salem, they showed him the scrapbook of clippings his mother had collected from newspaper articles about the Hot Shots. They always told him, "You are the best." But inside, Taylor knew he had flunked out of the university, and had settled for the dream of a little boy.

The rainbow drifted through a layer of smoke that stung their eyes and crowded their lungs. When they broke through to the clear air beneath, they had only seconds to maneuver their chutes between trees. The half-ton supply drop had felled half a dozen pines. Jeremy crashed through the branches of a thicket nearby. Kyle and Jackson angled through slots in the stand of pines. Austin, the snowboard showoff, landed with both feet on the supply bundle and raised his fists in triumph.

By the time Taylor had landed, folded up his parachute, and made his way through the woods, six of the Hot Shots had gathered around the supply bundle. It only took a second to realize who was missing.

"Maria!" Taylor called.

Kyle cupped his hands and bellowed, "BINKY!"

A moment later a call returned from the treetops to the east, "Buck you, Kyle!"

The Hot Shots trooped through the woods to find Maria dangling from her chute in a bent pine. She was pumping her legs back and forth like a kid on a swingset. When she had swung high enough, she grabbed the tree trunk. Then she took out a Bowie knife and sawed off her parachute straps.

"Hey, Binky, those chutes cost money," Kyle objected.

"Might be," Maria replied, already clambering down branch by branch. It took the crew a moment to figure out she had really told Kyle to "Bite me." They all smiled except Jeremy, who had trouble unraveling word play.

Back at the supply bundle, Taylor distributed chainsaws and set the crew to work building a fire break across the crest of the ridge. For three hours they felled trees and dragged away the woody debris, clearing a hundred-foot-wide swath where the fire would be hardest to stop.

Most of the lodgepole pines were eight inches in diameter. Taylor counted rings: eighty-six years old. A beetle infestation had reddened many of the trees' needles, leaving dry poles that were lighter to fell, but more susceptible to fire.

A red sun was high overhead when Taylor called a halt for lunch. "Stoke up on Power Bars and Gatorade, guys," he told them. "This may be the last meal of the day."

"What's the plan, boss?" Jackson asked. He had stripped off his shirt. Sweat and smudges highlighted the muscles of his arms and chest. Miranda and Maria watched as he flexed his shoulders.

"The twins are with me," Taylor said sharply. "We'll walk out along the overgrown road to the north, clearing trees and debris for the fire line as we go. Jackson, I want you to go with Kyle and Austin down the creek to the south, doing the same. It'll probably take four hours before we're ready to start lighting back fires."

Jeremy, the big football linebacker, stood there frowning. "What am I supposed to do, boss?"

Taylor pulled a flat-bladed tool from the supply bundle. "You're the hoedad king. I want you to stay right here on the ridge, digging a ditch down to mineral soil between the creek and the road."

Jeremy nodded. This was a job he understood. Even after a swath of trees had been cut for a break, the fire could still creep across through the duff and roots.

"We'll be splitting up into three groups," Taylor said, "So leave your walkie-talkies on. Any questions?"

The crew looked at each other. Kyle said, "To hell and back, boss."

"All right, then. Let's build a line worthy of the Hot Shots." Taylor refilled his chainsaw tank, strapped a Pulaski onto his backpack, and led the Gomez twins down the ridge toward the dirt road. Halfway there he stopped for a look back. He saw Jeremy flinging dirt with his hoedad like a Ditch Witch machine.

No one could dig like Jeremy. During the long, rainy winters, when Taylor kept the Hot Shots employed as a reforestation crew in the Coast Range, Jeremy could plant an impossible two thousand Douglas fir seedlings in a day. Even the inspectors who came to check their work couldn't believe it. One miserable February, when the Hot Shots had landed a contract to replant a clearcut west of Philomath, they had decided to play a trick on a particularly nasty inspector. They set out at the crack of dawn, with Jeremy planting a back field where the work went fast. By one o'clock, when they broke for a late lunch, he'd put eighteen hundred trees in the ground. The inspector showed up about 1:30, as usual, and parked his pickup on the edge of log landing where he could oversee most of the clearcut. Instead of greeting them, he just sat there in his heated truck with the motor running, listening to the radio. When it began to drizzle, he turned the wipers on intermittent.

After a long lunch, Jeremy took a big bag of seedlings, lumbered like a bear down a hellacious slope to the bottom of a canyon, and slowly planted two hundred trees. At four o'clock, when Taylor finally honked the crummy's horn to announce quitting time, Jeremy dug a six-foot-wide hole in a very visible spot near the bottom of the canyon. He refilled the ridiculously large hole, leaving one little tree poking out. Then he climbed up the slope to the landing and told the inspector that he'd planted all two thousand of the trees he'd been allotted that morning.

The inspector smiled knowingly. He got out of his cozy truck, took a shovel, and struggled down the slope to the canyon, certain that he would find eighteen hundred trees buried in that big hole.

The Hot Shots laughed themselves silly, watching the inspector arduously dig, in the rain and the mud, only to find that it really did contain just one seedling, planted correctly.

Afterwards, driving the crummy back to Philomath, Taylor offered to celebrate by buying everyone dinner at the In'N'Out. As part of a Recession-buster promotion, the fast food hut was offering two hamburgers for a dollar. Instead of pulling into the drive-up, Taylor parked the van on a dark street where they could watch. Then he gave Jeremy twenty-six dollars and told him to walk up to the window by himself.

When Jeremy emerged into the hut's neon glow, with his clothes caked in mud, he could easily have been mistaken for a sasquatch.

"Can I help you, sir?" a voice squawked uncertainly from the drive-up loudspeaker.

"Uh, yeah. " The giant linebacker leaned over to the microphone. "Here's twenty-six bucks. Gimme fifty burgers and a small Coke."

Building their fire line in the Greenhorn Range was even harder than Taylor had expected. The sun had faded to a carmine glow on the horizon by the time the tired voices on the walkie talkie agreed that they were ready. They all met back atop the ridge to trade their chainsaws for fuel packs with flame torches. Jeremy had not only completed his trench, but he had also dug a line all the way around the supply bundle, as if to defend it with a dirt moat.

"All right Jeremy," Taylor said, "You stay here in the middle. The rest of us will trade sides so we can check each other's work and make sure the line's going to hold. Jackson, you go out the old road with Kyle and Austin. When you get to the end of the line we cleared, I want you to walk back a hundred paces before you start lighting the back fire. We don't want the flames to do an end run around our line."

"Right, boss." Jackson nodded, his long blond hair stringy with sweat.

Taylor squinted out through the trees. For the first time he could see the orange glow of fire. The front was burning closer. His nostrils flared at the smell of smoke and fear. The wind had changed. A cool evening breeze had sprung up behind them. That would work in their favor. But they still might lose this battle.

"Listen up, guys." Taylor said. "If anyone can hold this line, it's you. But this is no place for heroics. We're already on probation for taking risks. If the fire jumps our line, I want you to run for Sumpter. Understand?"

Heads nodded.

"All right. Walkie talkies on." Taylor held up his thumb. "To hell and back."

The crew responded as one, "To hell and back."

Taylor shouldered his fuel pack and led the Gomez twins south toward the creek. Jeremy's trench descended the side of the ridge to a clearing. The hooves of elk and cattle had churned a spring there into a muddy bog. Beyond the spring the creek ran four feet wide, its right-hand bank cleared of brush and trees. Jackson's group had obviously worked hard, slashing their way through the undergrowth of the canyon bottom. Their swath was hardly thirty feet wide, but with the wind and the dampness of the creek bank, it might be enough.

After hiking nearly a quarter mile down the creek, Taylor found the crackling edge of the fire, and his heart sped up. A knee-high ribbon of flames was creeping down the duff of the canyon slope, occasionally igniting bushes with a whoomf.

Taylor unhooked his walkie talkie from his belt. "Taylor here. The front of the fire is almost to the creek."

The handset responded with static. Then Kyle's voice cut in. "Roger that, boss. We've found fire too. It's already burned down to the road."

Miranda bit her lip. Maria held up her walkie talkie and asked,

"Is it stopping at the road?"

"So far, Binky," Kyle replied.

"OK," Taylor said. "Let's all start heading back to the ridgecrest, lighting back fires as we go." The plan was working. The outer tips of the crescent-shaped front had met their line. Now they had to complete the ring of fire and wait for it to burn out in the middle. Even if all went well, there would be no sleep tonight.

As they slowly walked back along the creek, Taylor held a metal wand at arm's length, dripping a line of flaming oil onto the duff above the cleared swath. Behind him, Maria and Miranda swung Pulaskis, touching up the fire break to make sure flames didn't spread the wrong way.

By the time they reached the muddy spring, the twilight had deepened enough that they turned on their head lights. Fuzzy white beams of light swiveled through the smoky air, turning tree trunks into shadowy bars. An orange curtain of flames shivered behind them. Overhead, the sky glowed an eerie red.

Watching the liquid flame drip from his wand, Taylor found himself wondering what the hell they were doing out in the Greenhorn Range. Everything was bass ackwards. And it wasn't just that he was lighting fires, when his dream as a child had been to put them out. For all their fame as the Hot Shots, there was no future in this work. It was a wrong turn, a dead end. Each of them on the crew had left a conflagration of unfinished business behind.

That winter, between tree planting contracts, Taylor had drifted into Salem's public library. He'd started reading firefighting narratives, but then had shifted to scientific journals about fire ecology. Fire, he had read, might be a good thing after all. According to the researchers, every Oregon forest has a natural fire cycle. The dry pine forests of Eastern Oregon typically burn every sixty to a hundred years. Layers of soot in the mud of mountain lakebeds had recorded the cycles as black stripes. If the forests aren't allowed to burn, many native plants can't reproduce. Overmature pine forests became targets for pine beetle infestations. Why was he fighting this fire, in an eighty-six-year-old stand of lodgepoles? If he'd stuck it out at the university, maybe he'd be calling the shots instead of lighting back fires. Maybe he'd be telling crews to wrap Sumpter in Kevlar, turn on a few sprinklers, and leave.

"Boss?" It was Austin, standing by the supply bundle with a flame torch in his hand. His white eyes stared out from a sooty face. "Is Jeremy with you?"

Taylor looked around, counting head lights: Maria, Miranda, Kyle, Jackson. The big linebacker was gone.

"Jeremy!" Taylor called, but the roar of the fire swept the word away. He unhooked his walkie talkie. "Jeremy? Jeremy, come in!"

The six of them gathered closer, listening to the crackle of static from the handset. Finally there was a click, and a small voice said, "Boss?"

"Jeremy? Where are you?"

"I did what you said."

"What?" Taylor demanded. "What did you do?"

"You said if the fire jumped the line, we were supposed to run toward town."

"But the fire didn't jump the line, Jeremy."

"Yeah, it did. It was coming up behind me on both sides. I barely got through before it cut me off." There was a pause. "But now I don't know. I was just following the top of the ridge, and somehow there's another fire in front of me."

The Hot Shots looked at each other, their faces long. They were tired, and sooty, and now scared as hell.

Taylor switched off his walkie talkie just long enough to say what they all were thinking. "Shit. He ran the wrong way."

Jackson looked at the curtain of flames beside them, his eyes wide. "We built a ring of fire, and Jeremy's inside it."

Maria lifted her walkie talkie. "Jeremy? You have your backpack, right? With your smoke mask and your Kevlar tent?"

"Yeah," the small voice replied.

"Then stay where you are." Maria lowered the handset and spoke to the others. "He can hunker down in the tent. Odds are he'll make it."

Taylor shook his head. "When that fire burns to the middle, it's going to plume out like a volcano. If we don't get him out of there, it's over."

"Jesus, boss!" Kyle was usually all for glory, but now there was real fear in his voice. "We built one hell of a fire. How are we supposed to fight our way back through it?"

"Like anybody else, with Pulaskis and water tanks." Taylor tightened his lips. He had already decided this would be their last summer together, whether or not they managed to struggle back through the mess they'd made.

Austin's voice wavered. "You're the boss."

"Not this time," Taylor said. "I can't make this decision for you. Everyone on this crew already has a reprimand on their record. We've been warned about taking risks. If we go after Jeremy, we'll never work on a fire crew again."

Miranda objected, "But we're the Hot Shots."

Taylor looked around at the sooty faces. "I'm telling you, if we try to rescue Jeremy, we won't be heroes. We'll be unemployed."

For a long moment the crew was silent, listening to the roar of the conflagration they had created.

Then Austin wiped his eyes with the back of his hand. "To hell and back," he said.

Jackson looked down at his boots and nodded.

"To hell and back," Kyle said wearily.

Maria and Miranda began distributing water packs from the supply bundle.

No one spoke as the six Hot Shots shouldered their Pulaskis.

They knew they were the only ones who could face down this fire.

They were the best.

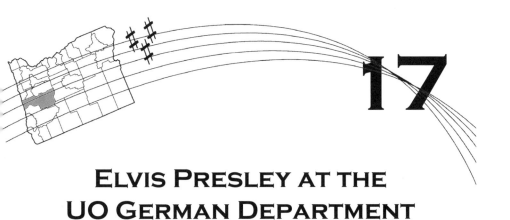

ELVIS PRESLEY AT THE
UO GERMAN DEPARTMENT

Messy den, messy den
Zoom steadily mouse,
Steadily mouse
Undo mine shots blight steer?

Slimy goo, slimy goo
Slime your voodoo Berkeley zoos,
Voodoo Berkeley zoos
Cross-eyed Aunt Eva's warden tart.

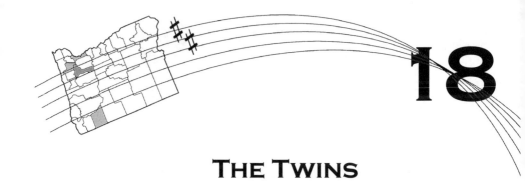

THE TWINS

Darryl had a gambling problem.

Ever since the twins were born twenty-three years ago, he left the house each Friday night to gamble away the weekend.

Darryl was otherwise a conscientious father, an accountant who made up for the family's losses to the penny. All week long he worked hard in his downtown Salem office, balancing the books.

Darryl and his wife Linda argued on Fridays, but they managed to hold their marriage together because of their twin sons. Over the years, Thomas and Lawrence had grown up, had girlfriends, graduated (or not), moved away, started professions (or not), and gone on to live their own lives. But the boys still loomed large in their parents' hearts.

For twins, the boys had turned out to be remarkably different. Thomas had become a lawyer in Medford, specializing in bankruptcy and divorce. He worked long hours and earned a decent salary, but never seemed to have a shot at real wealth or fame. He had married his high school prom date, Pam. He was a devoted husband.

Lawrence, on the other hand, had always been a happy-go-lucky adventurer, a goof-off who hit it lucky time after time. He dropped out of high school to build a sea kayak and paddle the length of the Oregon Coast. *National Geographic* picked up the story. Cameramen in helicopters filmed him confronting a pod of elephant

THE OREGON VARIATIONS

seals off Heceta Head and braving fifty-foot swells through the arches of Port Orford Reef. A ghostwriter wrote a bestseller about the trek, and the movie rights sold for six digits. Lawrence wasn't married but was popular among women.

The week before Darryl and Linda's latest fight, Lawrence had finished building a sixteen-foot Sitka spruce paddleboard by hand. On Monday he had taken his paddleboard on a ferry to a remote outpost on Queen Charlotte Island, off the coast of British Columbia. There he had announced that he hoped to become the first to paddle the 300 miles around the island. The Haida-Gai tribe rallied in support of his effort, chanting him off with drums and masks on the village beach. A float plane pilot volunteered to fly food and supplies to headlands along the route, but Lawrence said no. The only gear he planned to take on his long voyage was a wetsuit, a knife, and an iPhone with a satellite uplink. The world watched his postings, hour by hour, on the Internet.

On Thursday a TV reporter called Darryl at work to ask if he was worried about his son.

"A little," Darryl admitted. "I mean, I have the usual parental concern. But mostly I'm jealous. This is just the kind of adventure I wish I had the nerve to try."

When Darryl came home from work that Friday, he had big news. "Linda!" He hung up his coat in the hall closet.

"In the kitchen!" Linda called back.

As usual, Darryl took ten twenty-dollar bills from his wallet and put them in the purse Linda had left on a suitcase. He had learned to pay off the gambling losses in advance. Then he walked to the dining room. He took off his glasses and put them a pocket where they would be safe. He ran a hand over his balding head, straightening his wispy hair. Finally he called out, "This afternoon I got two telephone calls that are going to change our lives."

Linda appeared in the kitchen door. "What's happened this time?" She had put on a little weight over the years, but still had attractive arms. Today she showed them off with a sleeveless blouse and an apron.

Darryl took a decanter from the buffet. "You may need brandy first." He poured a shot glass half full.

"No, I don't. What's happened?" She took off her apron and tossed it aside.

"About an hour ago I got a call from Thomas in Medford. Pamela's pregnant. We're going to be grandparents in April."

Linda bit her lip. "You said there were two telephone calls."

Darryl took a sip of the brandy and set it aside. "It just gets better. I'd hardly put down the phone when Barbara called."

"Barbara?"They rarely heard from Barbara, although she was their favorite of Lawrence's many girlfriends.

"Yes," Darryl said. "And you'll never guess what she said."

Linda drew in a breath. "Go ahead. Tell."

"She's expecting too! Even Lawrence doesn't know yet. He's somewhere off the northern end of Queen Charlotte Island, out of cell phone range. But can you believe it? We're going to be grandparents *twice* this April!"

Linda stared at him. Her face had gone red. Then she leaned back, took a mighty swing, and slapped him so hard across the face that he staggered back.

"No!" she shouted. "I won't take it anymore. Ever since we learned that we can't have children, you keep coming home with stories about these two imaginary boys—the sons you've always wanted. For twenty-three years I've put up with your lies and your gambling because you bring home a paycheck. Well, this is the end! Imaginary children are bad enough, but I *refuse* to have imaginary grandchildren."

Linda strode to the hall. She grabbed her coat, slung her purse over her shoulder, and picked up the suitcase. Then she walked out the door and slammed it behind her.

Darryl cradled his head in his hands. He walked to the kitchen and got a pack of frozen peas to hold down the swelling on his cheek. Linda had hit him with more anger than usual. The eye might actually go black this time.

Finally he opened his cell phone and called Becky.

"Hi, lover," she answered. "So, how'd the wife take it this time?"

Darryl sighed. "Pretty hard. I dropped a big one on her. The twins are going to be fathers. Both of them, next April."

"Wow."

"Yeah, she's pretty shaken."

"She'll get over it," Becky said. "Your stories are all she's got."

"Sometimes she just seems so angry. She tells people *I'm* the one who spends the weekends gambling."

Becky laughed. "Well, in a way, I guess you are. Life is a gamble."

"You're my best bet." Darryl managed a smile. "So how are my real twins?"

"Looking forward to seeing you. Jonathan has a big science fair project about mathematics coming up. He's hoping you can help him with it. And you know Benny—he just wants you to go to the pool with him so he can try the scary water slide again."

"Those kids. I'll be there in half an hour. Love you."

As Linda drove off in her Toyota, her rage slowly began to settle. She might not have a credit card, but Darryl had put two hundred dollars in her purse.

By the time she reached the freeway she was already debating where she would go. Should she visit Thomas in Medford? He had a guest room, but she felt awkward barging in on the same day they announced their news. They might already be planning to convert the guest room to a nursery. Of course she could go stay in Lawrence's Portland apartment. But his apartment would be lonely while he was off in Canada.

Instead Linda decided to go visit her mother in Grande Ronde, by the Spirit Mountain Casino. Yes, she thought, the casino was always the most comforting place to retreat on the weekends when Darryl was gambling.

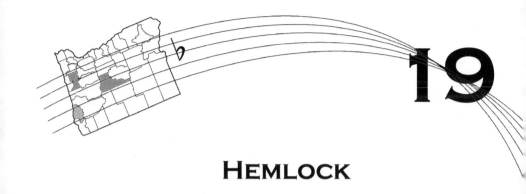

HEMLOCK

Day 1

My name is Myrna Penk. Remember that!

Today, a week before my sixty-eighth birthday, I am beginning a journal in defiance of fear.

The cause of my terror?

I couldn't start my car.

The problem was not one a mechanic could fix. When I sat behind the wheel I suddenly had no idea what to do next. Yes, I know—everyone has senior moments when you can't remember why you went to the basement. I've had memory lapses in recent years. But this was different. The knobs and dials in front of me had suddenly become an incomprehensible jungle of alien devices. Only in dreams have I felt so lost, showing up at the university to teach a class I had never studied, with lecture notes that turn out to be blank on every page.

My dear husband Norman laughed it off, but he consented to drive me to our family practitioner. She gave me a quiz that proved as frightening as any nightmare. "What is the capital of Italy?" It's Rome, of course, but I couldn't think of it. "Recite the alphabet backwards." Incredibly, I couldn't get past Z.

"There is no clinical test to confirm a diagnosis," she told me, "But you seem to be developing a form of dementia."

"Alzheimers?" I asked, aghast. "I'm a professor. The one thing I can't afford to lose is my mind."

"Then keep it as active as you can. Write a journal. Do puzzles. Plaque tends to build up on the neural connections in the brain. Each new thought strengthens the synapses and builds bypasses."

I sat there, working through my disbelief. As a child I had been appalled that my grandfather wore diapers. A degenerative brain disease was the worst fate I could imagine, and it had been lurking in my family history all this time.

Finally I asked, "How long do I have?"

I had chosen my doctor because she does not lie. She looked at her lap. "If the diagnosis is correct, anywhere from three to twenty years."

"We both know the diagnosis is correct." Now it was time for anger. "Tell me the progression and don't mince words."

"Well," she began. "Patients in the early stages of dementia have entire days of clarity. As the plaque spreads, they increasingly lose memory and cognition. They may panic or feel the urge to escape. Still, they often have lucid moments right up until the final months."

"The final months?"

She didn't look up. "Near the end, patients require full-time care."

Here I thought of my poor, sweet Norman, and I shivered. "Tell me about the end."

"Eventually patients forget how to swallow. Unless they are tube-fed they can't last more than a week. Then they forget how to breathe. At that point, medical options become severely intrusive."

"Not for me." I shook my head.

The doctor looked up and smiled. Clearly she thought I had taken to heart her suggestions about journals and puzzles. I would do all of that, of course.

But she misunderstood the nature of my resolve.

Day 2

I worry about losing things. Above all, I fear that I may lose the memories of my improbably lucky marriage with Norman, the romantic goofball who has brought me so much inspiration. At times I have been sorry we did not have children. I chose instead to earn my doctorate and pursue my career. To be sure, a child is another way to preserve memories. But now I am glad I did not pass on a flawed gene. A grandchild might only remember a distorted, decrepit version of me—something that might become their fate as well.

Last night on our way home I told Norman what the doctor had said. He pounded the steering wheel and called the doctor a quack. Then he announced that he would throw out every aluminum cookpan and every mobile electronic device in the house. He had heard that such things might cause Alzeheimers.

Back at home, I insisted that we do some research first. We sat before the computer screen, reading articles about dementia. The early symptoms were hauntingly familiar. Aluminum and cell phone usage had been scientifically discredited as factors, but genetics plays a large role. I told Norman about my grandfather, who wandered away from a Heppner nursing home in a blizzard.

When it was time for bed Norman kissed me, tears in his eyes, and said, "Tell me what you want for your birthday."

"My birthday?" I turn sixty-eight later this week, but we hadn't planned a party.

He nodded. "I'll do anything you want. I'll give you anything on earth. Anything."

I hugged him so tight he gasped.

Day 3

Western Oregon University dominates a claustrophobic hamlet called Monmouth. You can't escape students on the streets. Alcohol has been banned since the early 1900s. So Norman and I live three miles away in Independence, a blue-collar burg that serves as Monmouth's through-the-looking-glass twin. Here you can sit on your front porch and take deep, relaxing breaths with an India Pale Ale in your hand. But it does mean I have to commute.

This morning I pumped up the fat tires on my old red Schwinn. When the time came to set out, however, I tried the car first. The key turned. The parking brake released. The gear shifted to reverse. If I can't drive safely, of course I won't. If I can, I will. The main thing is to keep the mind active. To not lose what you have.

This term I'm teaching only one course, Food Science 101. After class I stopped by the WOU bookstore and bought a collection of *New York Times* crossword puzzles. The puzzles start out easy on Mondays and get harder each day of the week. The book I bought only has Sunday puzzles, the mind-mangling 21-by-21-square conundrums with sneaky hidden themes. I will solve them or die trying.

Day 4

Filled in four words on the first puzzle. They are wrong. Not good.

Day 5

Hello, Death?

Stand still so I can hammer you with this journal!

When I was growing up in Coos Bay, Death was little more than a mean fairy—the opposite of Santa Claus. Death was the bogeyman who takes things away instead of bringing presents. Death made my pet mouse Dana stop moving and sent my funny uncle Dwight on a long trip far away.

As a teenager, Death was simply uncool. I pretended he didn't exist. That made me able to jump off cliffs into mountain lakes and ride helmetless on the back of bad boys' motorcycles.

At seventeen Death turned religious, a black angel whose mighty wings could carry me through the portals of eternity. But the pastor who filled in the details about this mystic superhero at Bible camp made me suspicious by placing a consoling hand on my thigh.

My parents wanted me to study business at OSU so I could expand their Coos Bay deli into a chain. Instead I majored in science, probing the deeper mysteries of food. Why does popcorn pop? Which molecules make cooked eggs harden and pancakes bubble?

In my college labs, Death became another chemical quantum.

At first I exulted in this clarity. I had banished the bogeyman and debunked the religious fraud.

Then I met Norman, and questions of Life and Death melted into strange new emotions.

I didn't have a car when I was a student, so I signed up for Outdoor Program van trips to get out of Corvallis on weekends. One time we drove all the way to the Badlands east of Bend for orienteering training. Norman, a forestry major, raised his hand to partner with me in the field. OK, I thought, but he wasn't my type—a woodsy clown. Little did I realize how much I needed a woodsy clown!

We stumbled around in the Badlands—a labyrinth of snaking lava ridges and branching sandy draws—distractedly following an orienteering course of little stone cairns. We never did find the symbol ⊙ that marked the end point, the dotted circle that means "I have gone home." But we found each other. We—

No!

I can't do this. I would rather eat ground glass than keep a journal.

Day 5, later

We made love in the desert. This was unlike me. It is still unlike me. But it is very much like Norman. And I have to admit that our orienteering hike became the most joyous event of my young life, even if we never did find the damned dotted circle.

Day 6

My sixty-eighth birthday started out badly. Cleaning up after breakfast I put the milk carton and the cereal box in the dishwasher. I knew something was wrong, and it terrified me. I almost turned the dishwasher on, but couldn't figure out how.

Norman found me crying on the sofa. Even now I can't believe it, but I begged him to make love to me. Things were going wrong, and somehow it seemed this might make them right. He carried me to the bedroom, undressed me, and did a pretty good job.

Afterwards I must have fallen asleep.

The nap—or the sex?—cleared my mind. But now I am scared.

Day 6, later

For my birthday dinner—French toast! The only thing Norman knows how to cook!—he decorated the kitchen with sixty-eight red balloons, each marked in black felt pen with a small number and a word in block letters. They were strange words, things like OGEE, EROS, and ALAR. He had spread a sheet of butcher paper as a tablecloth on the kitchen island where we usually eat. In the middle of the paper he'd drawn a large thirteen-by-thirteen-square crossword grid, blank except for a pattern of black squares.

Luckily I was alert enough to figure out the game without being told. One by one I took down the balloons and fitted their words into the crossword, matching the little numbers. When I was done the thirteen-letter line across the center of the puzzle read ILOVEYOUMYRNA.

That earned him a big kiss.

Then he gave me a cube-shaped package wrapped in red velvet. Inside was something even more puzzling—a clear plastic block composed of a hundred and twenty-five smaller cubes. The block was held together by black magnetic letters embedded in the sides of all the little cubes. The five letters on each row of little cubes mostly didn't spell words. I took off the corner piece, about the size of a sugar cube. It had an "S" on all six sides. The three adjacent cubes all had the letter "A" on their sides. The entire block of cubes had been arranged symmetrically so that each face looked like this:

```
S A T O R
A R E P O
T E N E T
O P E R A
R O T A S
```

"What is it?" I asked.

"The magic cube of the Latins," Norman said. "A source of great power among Roman wizards. Your doctor said puzzles might help. If any puzzle can cure you, this is it."

Dear Norman. He believes in ghosts. He buys lottery tickets at the supermarket when he thinks I'm not watching. Still, I played along. "How does it work?"

"It's in Latin, an incantation about a sator named Arepo."

"What's a sator?"

"A sower of seeds. The whole thing says SATOR AREPO TENET OPERA ROTAS."

"What does that mean?"

"The translation is something like 'Arepo the farmer does his work with a plow.'"

I just looked at him.

"But that's not the point." He turned the block over. "See? It reads the same no matter how you look at it—upside down, backwards, in any direction. It's a three-dimensional palindrome, the only perfect five-letter crossword cube. It's been found inscribed on Roman ruins from England to Portugal and Syria. People claim it has all kinds of magical uses."

"Is there a perfect cube in English?"

He shook his head, obviously disappointed that I had not immediately caught his enthusiasm. "I wanted to give you something special for your birthday."

"I know." I hugged him. He wanted to give me a magic cure.

"Maybe there's something else you want?"

"Yes," I said. "Take me hiking again."

This caught him by surprise. I explained, "You and I met on a hike, but we've been so busy we haven't had time to get out for years."

"Where do you want to go?"

"Everywhere." I walked to the bookshelf and took down a copy of a local *100 Hikes* guide. "I want you to take me on every single hike, from cover to cover. Tomorrow I'll call up the dean and tell her I'm retiring for good."

"But what about your research?"

This is another reason I love Norman: He understood immediately how difficult it would be for me to drop my food science work.

For decades I had been developing marketing ideas for Oregon agricultural products. The cranberry farmers on the coast south of Coos Bay had been struggling, selling the same old jellied sauce for Thanksgiving, when my team invented a dried snack that was later marketed as *Craisins*. The filbert farmers in Linn County had been in a slump until we renamed their crop *hazelnuts*, processed it to a cream, and paired it with chocolate.

"I can continue my research here at home," I said. "One of the reasons we bought this house was its kitchen. It's big enough to be a food laboratory.

Norman nodded. "So be it."

And that was my birthday dinner. Now it's after one o'clock in the morning, but I can't sleep—partly because of the nap, and partly because my mind keeps clicking and churning. When I look into Norman's magic cube I see letters jumbled at all angles, a crazy honeycomb. That's how my brain feels. Neural charges are curlicuing around clogged synapses. I am changing. Already I am not who I was. When will I become unrecognizable, even to myself?

I couldn't tell Norman, but hiking and puzzling and this damned journaling are only part of my resolve. Next week I am going to a meeting of the Hemlock Society in Corvallis.

Someday, if I become a burden on the man I love, there is a danger that our love may be lost beneath the plaque, replaced by the cold horror of a sense of duty. No, please!

Suicide is not my Plan B. It is my Plan Z. We'll see how long I can remember to recite the alphabet forwards.

Day 10

We walked to Alsea Falls (Hike #3) on a glorious spring day. Big, three-petaled trilliums were popping out of the forest floor like Easter lilies. Back at home I plowed through a Sunday *New York Times* crossword, stymied only by a corner where the clue "French bread" turned out to have been EURO. It's still a victory.

Hurray!

Day 13

An unlucky morning. I started cleaning the windows with vinegar and newspaper. Soon I found myself rubbing the wallpaper. So scared. Norman set me to stacking pennies from our coin jar instead.

Day 17

Hemlock, humbug! Apparently the Hemlock Society has renamed itself Compassion & Choices. Anyway, I went to their meeting expecting that they would help. Oregon has an assisted suicide law, allowing physicians to prescribe lethal dosages. But at the meeting I was told I don't qualify. You have to get affidavits from two different doctors saying you have less than six months to live. My Alzheimers could drag on for years. Even if I were a week from death's door, I still wouldn't qualify. The law applies only to people with sound minds. The society members were appalled when I asked if the law could be expanded to cover dementia. That would be tantamount to euthanasia, they said, and would jeopardize their efforts to enact assisted suicide laws in other states.

I sat through the rest of the meeting, fuming. I only spoke again when they when they were discussing lethal drugs. "I'm a professor emeritus of food science," I said. "Do Oregon doctors prescribe hemlock?"

One man laughed out loud. Others looked puzzled or bemused. All of them, as it turned out, knew that the Greek philosopher Socrates had committed suicide by eating hemlock, but several assumed he had somehow eaten a hemlock tree, and most of the rest thought hemlock was an herb that grew only in Greece. A retired pharmacologist, who knew that poison hemlock does grow in Oregon, informed me that doctors could not possibly prescribe a wild weed. Medicines have to be refined, tested, and packaged by pharmaceutical companies.

"How can pharmaceutical companies test human poisons?" I asked.

"They can't." The man gave me a condescending smile. "No prescriptive drugs are intended specifically to serve as poison. Instead doctors prescribe a cocktail of barbiturates and other medicines in what amounts to a lethal dosage."

"A cocktail?" I repeated, aghast. "A mishmash of medicines for other purposes, with other effects? Why would they do that when the perfect drug is growing wild in roadside ditches?"

He shrugged. "Hemlock is not available as an actual drug."

"Perhaps that is about to change," I said, and stormed out of the meeting.

Day 21

Today Norman and I had our first argument in years. He came home from a consulting job on a private forest and found me in my kitchen laboratory, wearing latex gloves as I Osterized green speckled stalks into what looked like a celery smoothie.

"Yum," he said.

"Careful!" I warned him away with an elbow.

"What is it?" he asked, alarmed.

"*Conium maculatum.*"

"Sounds terrible."

"It can be. It's poison hemlock."

I explained about my visit to Compassion & Choices the night before. He had assumed I had been on a shopping trip to Corvallis. The more I told, the darker his expression grew. Finally he banged his fist on the counter.

"Damn it, Myrna, what are you thinking? I married you for better or for worse. I don't want you killing yourself. Most days you're fine. We've taken, what? Half a dozen hikes since your birthday. Don't you like living with me?"

"Of course! I love you more than anything, Norman." I would have hugged him, but my rubber gloves were spattered with hemlock juice.

"Then why mess around with poison?"

"Hemlock could be an important pharmaceutical product. Socrates used it two thousand years ago, but it's never been researched scientifically."

Norman still glowered. "This isn't like tinkering with hazelnuts or cranberries, you know."

I laughed. "True. The market for poison is smaller. No repeat customers."

Norman wasn't smiling. He glared at the bowl of green stalks. "Besides, I thought Socrates ate the tree."

I rolled my eyes. "The tree and the herb just happen to have the same common name. How could anyone eat a tree?"

"I don't know. The inner bark, I guess. Black bears chew on hemlock bark when they come out of hibernation, if they're hungry enough."

This stopped me, because I knew it was true. Foresters have complained so much about bear damage to hemlock trees that the OSU Forestry Department did a study to see what was so special about the bark. The cambium layer turned out to contain all kinds of nutrients.

"Hemlock bark wouldn't have killed Socrates," I countered. "It's healthy, full of Vitamin C."

"Well, if it's such a great food, why do sawmills throw it away?"

"Don't they make bark mulch out of it?"

Norman shook his head. "It's not acidic enough. Gardeners don't like it because it rots."

This also made sense. Especially in the spring, the cambium would be loaded with sugars. "It really might be a healthful food," I mused aloud.

Suddenly Norman put his two big hands flat on the counter. "Myrna, I've never meddled in your work before, but this is different. I don't want you dabbling with poison. Especially not now, when you're sometimes, you know, confused. Your specialty is food. I want you to study the other hemlock. Figure out how to make food from a tree."

I stood there, open mouthed. No one had really considered the commercial potential of either hemlock before. But I could sense that there was more behind Norman's sudden interest in tree bark.

"Why?" I asked.

"The two hemlocks are opposites. If one of them kills, I've got a feeling the other one might cure."

He looked aside, as if I had caught him hoarding Powerball tickets. He wanted to believe in a magic cure for my illness. If a Latin cube wasn't the answer, perhaps hemlock was.

Holding my gloved hands in the air I walked around the counter and leaned my head on his chest. "All right, my love. I promise to study the tree."

I didn't say I would give up on poison hemlock altogether. I know one of the two hemlocks can cure anything.

Day 23

Today I turned the SATOR AREPO block over and over, thinking of opposites. For the first time I took the block apart. Beneath the outer layer, the central 27 cubes turned out to be different. They spell

$$
\begin{array}{ccc}
L & O & C \\
O & N & O \\
C & O & L
\end{array}
$$

as a smaller magic cube. Inside them is a single L. Why?

Day 91

Diaries are always like this. You get a gorgeous blank book for your birthday. You write down everything for a few weeks: What you ate for breakfast. The cute boy you saw in the cafeteria. Then you start sharing your confidences with real people, and the diary gathers dust.

Almost every day I have a moment of terror when the alien gadgets return. A clock face suddenly becomes an unreadable pie, or my shoe laces stare up at me like puzzling noodles. Hiking helps. Then I feel as if Norman and I are running away from the gaps in my brain.

Day 123

Poison hemlock is embarrassingly easy to refine. This week, while Norman was at a conference in Portland, I boiled it down to lovely little crystals, like green salt. My tests show it really does have sugar and spice and everything nice—enough vitamins and minerals for a diet supplement. But it's one of the swiftest poisons on the planet. Who knows what it tastes like?

Day 307

A good day. Spring has come with a rush, and with it, the answer to our search for usable hemlock bark. Last fall, when we first started collecting, the sap had slowed. The bark stuck like glue. The cambium we scraped loose looked like red clay and tasted worse.

But after a cold winter, a sudden week of warm weather pumped the hemlock trees with sap. This morning Norman and I reeled off great strips of juicy bark from some freshly cut logs. Norman ran the strips through a planer and presented me with an entire barrel full of scarlet cambium mush. Even raw, it tastes wonderful—just to the left of pomegranate and a little to the right of sugar beet. Why hasn't this food source been tapped before?

Day 308

My driver's license is gone. Damn them.

Day 346

Refined, the sugars from hemlock bark are red crystals. They are exactly the same size and shape as the green crystals from poison hemlock. I have hidden the poison crystals in the back of a cupboard. Red and green. Stop and go. Go and stop.

Day 389

I have successfully cooked the red hemlock bark crystals into all kinds of things. Scarlet ice cream. Blood sausage. Sweet-and-sour salsa.

The Latin name for the hemlock tree, *tsuga,* looks like a mixed-up version of the word *sugar.* With every recipe I keep thinking: this dish would be the same in green, but fatal.

Day 402

Norman claims the tsuga foods are reversing my dementia. Instead I fear they are making him crazy. Who will buy the tsuga pops he wants to market? He rants about tsuga buns. And heaven forbid, tsuga pseudo chicken choo chew.

Day 581

Hike #85. Norman says we will finish all one hundred of the hikes in the book, but the trails are getting harder. I panic if he gets out of my sight.

Day 624

Why won't they let me vote? I walked three miles to Monmouth and pounded on the door of the library trailer. A man came out and said there is no election. Damn them!

Day 999

I can't do Sunday puzzles. Even Mondays make my eyes hurt. Today in frustration I smashed Norman's magic crossword block on the kitchen counter. Little plastic letters scattered. Later I picked them up. The magnetic letters stuck together in rows. First I spelled CARES, for Norman. Then ALONE, for me. The key turned on ROTOR. And there it was, a five-word magic square in English. ENOLA, the bomber of doom. SERAC, a pillar of ice. Impossible?

Day 1000

Norman helped me use a steak knife to scrape seven letters, turning E's into L's. Then we fit all of the 125 cubes back together, a perfect palindromic block in English:

```
C A R E S
A L O N E
R O T O R
E N O L A
S E R A C
```

He says it is the most powerful magic imaginable. I can now reassemble my brain.

Dear man.

Day 1101

My birthday. Seventy-one. Wrong by ten in base 4. Then it's gone, back to aliens. We did Hike #100, a horror of evils trying to take everything.

Day 1209

My mind is a stormy lake. Only underwater is it calm. No more puzzles. I don't always hear what Norman says. But now, finally, I see what he really feels:

He did love me.

He is afraid.

He is tired.

Day 1383

Norman hired a woman to watch me. He says he is going for a hike. But he is a man. I am losing him.

Day 1401

Back to the start. I remember we hiked in the Badlands, happy to be lost. Norman!

Day 1402

When the clouds part and my mind is clear, I know what to do.

I pour a circle of red crystals on the counter, with a green dot in the center. A trail sign to the man I love.

I will know the taste of Socrates.

I am Myrna Penk. Remember that!

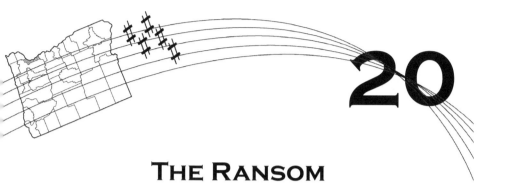

THE RANSOM

Brent Radley had fallen asleep over the tape machine when the doorbell rang.

Gah. How long had he been face first at his desk? He was supposed to be cramming for his history orals. Secretary Lincoln droned on from the recorder, reciting the San Francisco Address. Brent wiped filmy dreams from his eyes, glanced at his pocket watch, and shambled to the door in sticky clothes. Who the hell would disturb partnered student housing at eight o'clock in the morning?

No one, apparently. A cold eddy of soot swirled in the empty hall. But then he saw the note on the "Abandon Hope All Ye" doormat. The slip bore the familiar looping hand of his wife's fountain pen.

> Help! Brent! I'm being held hostage by a man who grabbed me on the street. He says you will never see me again unless you give him 5,000 Beaver Dollars. Leave unmarked bills in a brown paper bag under Sacajawea's skirt in the PNU commons by noon on Thursday. If you tell the police, I'm a goner. He means it, Brent!   – Your Esmeralda.

Brent frowned. His wife was always leaving him little notes — increasingly shrill notes, as if to bridge the gap as they drifted apart. But this missive gave him a shot of real fear. He walked back to the bedroom, just to check. No Esmeralda. She had stepped out last night for a veggie wrap at what — eleven?

Kidnappings were commonplace in the Confederacy, but until recently the Republic of Oregon had seemed immune.

He didn't dare call the police, of course — that never turned out well. How on earth was he supposed to scrape up five thousand in cash in two days?

Hell. He needed coffee before he could think.

Brent showered, shaved, put on fresh clothes, and went down the stairs, heading for Starbucks. He reached the sidewalk just as a streetcar chugged up to the PNU station. The tram hissed, blew a cloud of steam into the brick street, and clanged open its folding doors. No one got off. After a moment the doors banged shut. The engine belched a plume of black smoke and chugged on.

It was dead week at Portland National. A line of groggy students stood waiting in the Starbucks beside the station. Christmas lights blinked from a skinny Douglas fir decorated with coffee coupons. Brent joined the line at the same time as Sheila Andersen, the psychology grad from apartment 4G, upstairs. They had been through *Beowulf* together, a required English course that seemed useless to both their fields.

"Hi," Sheila said. She wore tall red boots and a bright yellow slicker that made her short brown hair look a little drab. After a moment she asked, "Something wrong?"

"No, no." The second no was a mistake. The line inched forward.

"You sure?"

Brent ran a hand over his jaw. He was tall, with a bony face that might have been handsome beneath a beard. "I don't know. Kidnappers may have taken my wife."

Sheila caught her breath. "Esmeralda?"

"Yeah."

Sheila studied him more carefully. "You don't seem very upset."

Brent sighed. "I don't know what to think. Since Esmy quit school in spring, we've been living in different worlds. She's always out, volunteering somewhere downtown."

"You're not even sure if she's been kidnapped?"

Brent unfolded the note from his coat pocket and handed it to Sheila. While she read it, he ordered a latte and a breakfast burrito.

Then the barista smiled to Sheila. "May I help you?"

"What?" Sheila looked up from the note, disoriented. "Oh, give me a pumpkin mocha."

She didn't speak again until she had steered Brent to a table behind a display of roasters. Then she laid the note on the table, leaned forward, and whispered, "Is someone in your family keeping indentureds?"

"No! Of course not."Brent turned aside indignantly. Indentured servitude had never been allowed in Oregon. The whole system was foreign, developed in the Confederacy a century ago to replace slavery with an underclass based on poverty, rather than race. But he could see why Sheila had asked. Since the civil rights riots of the 1990s, a radical underground movement had spread throughout the South, encouraging indentureds to ransom their way to freedom by kidnapping the wives and children of their masters.

Sheila raised an eyebrow. She wore no makeup, but her brown eyes shone. "And you haven't been involved with any foreign students?"

"Well, not romantically involved, if that's what you mean." Brent waved this objection away. The history department was full of foreign students, especially from California and Texas. Oregon had become a cheap place for undergrads to spend a year abroad. Because the Republic lacked oil reserves, it had never been able to adopt the automobile culture of its neighbors. To outsiders, Oregon seemed a strangely backward land of steam engines, sawmills, and bicycles.

"In that case," Sheila said, tapping the note meditatively, "I think you have received a most interesting demand."

"Interesting! What—"

"Latte!" A loud nasal voice interrupted. "Breakfast burrito! Pumpkin mocha!"

Brent and Sheila went to get their orders from the counter. When they returned, Brent asked, "How can you call a ransom demand *interesting?* They're threatening to kill my wife."

"Mm-hmm." Sheila sipped her mocha. "But the amount is so low. I mean, five thousand Beaver Dollars?"

"It's a hell of a lot to me," Brent retorted. "I'm buried in student loans, and I've got zero credit. If I asked my parents for that much cash by Thursday they'd laugh. No, worse. They'd go to the police."

"But you want her back." She looked at him over the rim of her cup.

"Esmeralda? Well, of course. I mean—" Brent faltered.

"You love her."

Brent lowered his head. For a moment he stared at the fern-leaf design in the foam of his latte, as if he might be able to read his own mind in the white swirls. Finally he looked up. "If Esmy is in danger, I've got to do something. That's what marriage means. I just don't know what."

Sheila nodded slowly. "Then perhaps I can help."

"You have five thousand Beaver dollars?"

"No, but my husband does."

Brent rolled his eyes. "I'm not going to borrow money from your husband."

"True. Frederick never offers loans. He's a sculptor, and he's so tight he squeaks. Last year he earned sixteen thousand Beaver dollars for his foundry work on that bronze Sacajawea statue. I haven't seen a cent of it. He says he needs it all for his studio downtown."

"How is this supposed to help?"

Sheila shrugged. "Kidnap me."

Brent blinked. "What?"

"You need five thousand by noon on Thursday, right?"

"Right."

"If you kidnap me, I'll write a ransom note to Frederick demanding ten thousand by noon on Wednesday."

"You can't be serious."

She stirred her pumpkin coffee with a spoon. "Actually, Frederick and I haven't been getting along all that well. He spends his days at the studio. More and more, he forgets to come home."

Brent glanced to either side before whispering, "But you're talking about committing a crime."

"Maybe not." She pointed to the tortilla chips on his burrito platter. "Are you going to eat those?"

Flustered, he rolled his hand in the air, a gesture even he couldn't decipher.

Sheila took a chip and dipped it in his cup of salsa. "The money belongs to me anyway. Partners are supposed to share their earnings, and Frederick hasn't. If we demand a ransom of ten thousand, you'll have five thousand to buy off Esmeralda, and I'll be five thousand to the good. Everyone goes home with their proper partners, and all is well."

Outside, a steam whistle blew as another streetcar pulled up. A bicyclist swerved to make way. When the tram doors opened, half a dozen students in wool overcoats stepped out onto the platform. Almost in unison they glanced at the gray sky and pulled their collars close. It had begun to hail.

The next day, Brent was sweating as he waited in the PNU commons for the ransom exchange. Half an hour before noon he had bought a plate of brightly colored noodles from the Thai Dye counter, but he was merely pushing the food around with his chopsticks, nervously eyeing the crowd. Sheila was in hiding, of course—in Brent's apartment, ready to go home to Frederick if the cash showed up on time. And where, Brent wondered, was Esmeralda? Perhaps chained in some basement by a radical Texan?

The whole situation had left Brent frightened, confused, and increasingly unsure that he was doing the right thing.

The plan had seemed plausible enough when Sheila explained the details in Starbucks. If Brent was going to kidnap Sheila, she obviously couldn't go back to her own apartment, even for a toothbrush. So she went home with Brent, furtively slipping into his apartment when the hall was empty. The ransom note they wrote turned out a lot like Esmeralda's, demanding that unmarked bills be left in a paper bag under the skirt of the Sacajawea statue. But this time the note said the abductor needed ten thousand Beaver dollars by noon on Wednesday.

Brent's heart had pounded as he crept up the stairs to leave the note at apartment 4G. Sheila had reassured him that her husband wouldn't be home then. Frederick, she said, always came back from his studio at two o'clock on Tuesdays, because that was the afternoon she prepared his favorite Danish dinner, a buffet she detested. She got angry just thinking about the smell of creamed cabbage, blue cheese, onions, and pickled herring.

Brent taped the ransom note to the door and hurried back downstairs. Only then did he realize how awkward his situation had become. For the next twenty-four hours he would be trapped in his own apartment with the hostage he had kidnapped — a woman he hardly knew.

When Brent closed the door he had trouble meeting Sheila's eyes. "You'll have to keep quiet," he whispered. "But other than that, you might as well make yourself at home."

"Then I'll go freshen up." She paused. "I assume the shower is in the same place in your apartment as in mine?"

"Oh yes, at least I think so." Brent fetched a fresh towel from the linen closet in the hall, almost tripping over his own feet. "Here. And you'll find — " he blushed as he waved a hand toward the bathroom " — women's things on a shelf by the shower."

"Thanks." When she took the towel their hands happened to touch.

Brent swallowed and pulled back his hand. A warm shiver had pulsed down his spine. "I'll be in the bedroom preparing for my orals," he said, and then caught himself. "I mean I'll be in the spare bedroom. I use it as an office. To study history."

"OK. I'll try to not bother you."

"No, that's fine. Really, make yourself at home."

"All right." Sheila smiled and walked down the hall.

Brent was left with a strange glow he hadn't felt for years. He turned on the tape machine in his office, but he had trouble concentrating on the elderly Abraham Lincoln's voice. Instead he heard the shower door open and water start to spray.

Brent looked out the window at brick dormitories and smoking chimneys. But that's not what he saw. He couldn't help imagining the steam-blurred shape of a pink body behind the shower's glass door.

For the next hour he listened guiltily as this intriguing new houseguest rummaged through his home. He knew this was no time for fantasies. His wife had been abducted. But the warm glow wouldn't go away. Finally the door to his office opened.

Sheila was wearing the white satin blouse and black pencil skirt he had bought for Esmeralda on their first Christmas — an outfit Esmeralda had immediately buried at the back of her closet. In her arms Sheila carried a tray with sandwiches and bottles of the home-brewed chocolate porter that Esmeralda despised. Somehow the shower had fluffed out Sheila's brown hair and pinkened her cheeks.

"I didn't want to interrupt," she whispered, "but I thought your studies might make you hungry."

"Oh! Is it time for lunch already?" Brent cleared his work desk, sweeping his notes aside to make room for the tray.

Sheila set down the tray. Then she sat in a revolving chair, crossing her legs with a swishing sound. "I feel so guilty," She gave a half-smile that dimpled her cheek. "I don't have any fresh clothes, so I borrowed some from your room."

"No, no." Brent held up his hands. "I said to make yourself at home." He uncapped the porter and clinked his bottle against hers. "Cheers."

"To my kidnapping." She took a drink and looked into the air, savoring the beer. "Chocolate. A hint of nutmeg? You could get a job as a brewmaster." She set out little plates for the sandwiches. "But I'm actually more interested in your history studies."

"Really?" Brent picked up a sandwich and took a bite. Prosciutto, pesto, and romaine lettuce on toasted olive bread. Either she was a magician, or she had really found all these things in his kitchen.

Sheila continued, "I spent my junior year of high school in France, so I missed the usual Oregon History course. I never did understand why Oregon isn't part of the United States."

"If I start telling you about the Missouri Compromise of 1820," Brent said, shaking his head, "you'll fall asleep."

"Maybe you could synopsize?" She gave a little shrug. "Psychologists say the best way to study something is to explain it to someone else."

He took another drink of porter. The potent brew gave him the courage to try. "All right. The problem was slavery." He paused, frowning.

After a moment Sheila encouraged him. "Yes? Go on."

"Well, the Southern states were afraid of being outvoted on the slavery issue, so Congress worked out a deal. Every time they admitted a free state, they had to admit a slave state for balance. If you let Maine join the Union, you had to admit Alabama."

"That makes sense, I guess."

Brent took another bite of sandwich. After he had washed it down with porter, he felt more confident. "The compromise worked until 1858, when Oregon wanted in as a free state. There wasn't any slave state for balance. Two Illinois politicians held big public debates about what to do. Abraham Lincoln wanted to admit Oregon and start a civil war. His rival, Stephen Douglas, was a man of peace. He came up with a cleverer plan — granting the Oregon Territory independence."

Sheila objected, "But why was the United States willing to give up so much land?"

"Britain had a claim on everything from California to Alaska at the time."

"I see." Sheila nodded. "So Douglas's plan avoided two wars at once, one with the South and one with Britain."

"Exactly. With Oregon out of the picture, Douglas easily beat Lincoln in the Presidential election of 1860. Then he appointed a 'team of rivals' to his cabinet, with Lincoln as Secretary of State. Together, they negotiated the—"

"Shh!" Sheila touched her finger to Brent's lips. She tilted her head toward the wall.

Footsteps were creaking on the hall stairs outside. The slow, heavy tread paused at the apartment's front door. Brent looked at

Sheila wide-eyed. Could it be the police?

Then the footsteps continued, creaking up another flight of stairs. Sheila closed her eyes.

An angry roar shook the stairwell outside. The door upstairs banged open. Furniture scraped on the floor overhead. Glass crashed. Footsteps thudded from room to room. At length the door slammed again. This time the footsteps pounded down the stairs all the way to the street.

Brent looked to Sheila. "What will Frederick do now?"

"Curse a lot." She shrugged. "My husband's not nice when he's angry. But he'll also find enough money for the ransom. Just like you're doing."

"Are men that predictable?"

Sheila gathered the dishes on the tray. "You're a better person than Frederick."

"That doesn't answer my question."

She carried the tray to the office door, smiling. Then she dipped to open the door handle with her elbow, twisting the black skirt tight across her thighs. The white satin blouse puckered open at the collar. Brent did not remember what, if anything, she said next.

In fact, the rest of that day became a blur. At some point they dialed to order take-out United States food, hamburgers delivered in a Buick by a kid from Chicago. Sheila found a bottle of Umpqua merlot in the broom closet. Brent vowed to sleep on the living room couch, but wound up in the double bed together with Sheila, twisted in sheets.

Brent woke up the next morning, guilty and scared.

"It's going to be a difficult day," Sheila told him matter-of-factly, reading the newspaper at breakfast.

"Difficult?" Brent whispered angrily. "While you sit here reading the funnies I'm probably going to be arrested for picking up a ransom."

She folded the paper aside. "Everything will turn out fine. You'll see."

Brent stalked angrily out of the apartment, not quite sure where he was going. He ended up at the riverbank, watching a stern-wheeler pull a barge of logs through the open Burnside Bridge. Dozens of streetcars waited on either side, snorting steam. Across the river, a row of gray windmills slowly twirled above the river-front bike path.

There were so many ways Sheila's plan could go wrong. Paying a ransom with a ransom was like fighting fire with fire. Wouldn't it have been cleverer, Brent wondered, if they had thought of a way to fight fire with water? Kidnappings were a symptom of a societal disease that didn't belong in Oregon. The whole history of the Republic had been about defusing conflict. He'd been led — no, seduced — into a criminal scheme. But now he was in so deep that there was no turning back. If he tried to apologize for the ransom note, he'd still go to prison.

At eleven o'clock, anxious and unhappy, Brent walked through the brick streets of Old Town to the PNU commons. There he ordered a paper plate of Thai noodles and waited. His stomach churned.

At five minutes to noon a man in a white fedora and a tan Burberry coat began pushing his way across the crowded commons. Brent quickly opened a copy of the PNU *Vanguard* as a screen. His heart was in his throat. He had only met Frederick Andersen a few times, but there was no mistaking the artist. With broad shoulders, a square jaw, and wire-rimmed spectacles, Frederick looked like the star of a gritty cinema show.

Peering around the newspaper, Brent watched Frederick make his way toward the Sacajawea sculpture in the middle of the hall. The life-size bronze Shoshone woman carried a baby in a cradle-board on her back. She stood atop a three-foot block of columnar basalt, striding out purposefully with her right foot.

Suddenly Brent was struck with an odd feeling that there was something familiar about this Indian girl, although he couldn't say what. Certainly the statue suffered from a design flaw, given its location in a food court. The striding right foot lifted the bronze skirt on one side, leaving a black gap about the size and shape of a recycling bin's mouth. Already Brent had seen a student toss a paper cup into the shadowy hole.

Frederick stopped beside the sculpture and glanced around the room. But then he did something Brent did not expect. Frederick slowly stroked the statue from hip to thigh, where the bronze skirt stretched tight over the striding right leg. In fact, Brent now noticed that the bronze was shinier in just this area. Brent frowned. Why wasn't Frederick delivering the money?

At length Frederick took off his spectacles and wiped a tear from his eye. He looked over his shoulder and nodded. Then he walked on, heading directly for the lobby doors.

Had the nod been a signal to the police, Brent wondered? Perhaps undercover agents were closing in even now to imprison him for kidnapping. Brent scanned the crowd, but all he could see was the usual mix of students. Many of them were obviously foreigners, lonely kids who wouldn't have the time or the money to book ship's passage home for the holidays. He felt particularly sorry for a Muslim girl in a blue burqa. There were so few Muslim women on campus that the full-body veil left them isolated — unintentionally shunned by people who simply didn't know how to react.

Nor was Brent sure how to react when the girl walked up to the Sacajawea statue, removed a white paper bag from a fold of her outfit, and stuffed the bag under the bronze skirt. Then she turned, striding out with her right leg.

For an instant the burqa stretched tight across her thigh.

Brent dropped his newspaper, open-mouthed. Suddenly he realized why the statue had looked familiar.

He vaulted from his chair, crashed through the crowd, and caught the woman by her shoulder. Then he grabbed the face flap of her veil and pulled the cloth up over her head.

She glared at him, her eyes filled with hatred.

Two nearby students jumped in, trying to wrestle Brent away.

But the woman in the Arab dress merely said, "Let him go."

The students paused, obviously puzzled.

"It's all right," Brent said. "She's my wife."

That night, lying beside Sheila in bed, Brent crossed his arms on

his chest. Tomorrow morning he would face five history profes-
sors for his oral exams, but a new feeling of confidence had swept
aside his fears.

"How did you know?" Brent asked. "Did you realize Esmeralda
must have been the model for the Sacajawea statue?"

Sheila ran her finger along his arm. "No, you're the only one
who would recognize something like that."

"Then how?"

"The ransom note you showed me at Starbucks seemed odd.
The amount was low and the tone was wrong. I knew your family
probably wasn't involved with indentured servants, but I had to
ask. Then you said your wife spent her time volunteering somewhere downtown. I just put two and two together."

Brent shook his head in wonder. "Still, it seems like a lucky
guess."

"Not really. I'd seen Frederick watching your wife in the hall
a time or two. He's faithless and greedy. I knew he was using his
studio for an affair. I should have realized sooner that it was with
Esmeralda."

"You're not upset that I split the ransom money with Esmeralda?"

Sheila shrugged. "She'll need it, living with Frederick. Besides,
five thousand seems fair. It was the price she chose for herself."

"And to think how angry I was at you this morning!" Brent said.
"It turned out you'd hit on the cleverest solution of all."

"Every plan has trade-offs."

"Trade-offs," Brent repeated. He liked the word.

THE STARTER

Gabby was a resident alien in Oregon—I think from Gabon, although her skin was more bronze than the cocoa brown you expect from Africa. I met her at a cancer clinic where I was having my remaining breast checked, yet again. I'm one of those high risk people who gets cancer at the drop of a hat. My mother died of ovarian cancer.

Why are reproductive organs so vulnerable? Men are always getting prostate cancer. I don't know what a prostate is, but I think it's part of their equipment.

Anyway, I figured Gabby's cancer issues must be even worse than mine. The only reason she had gotten a green card to live in the US was for treatments. Chemo had left her as bald as a brown egg. She didn't wear a wig to cover her scalp—a pride thing, I guess.

Did I mention that Gabby was hot? Usually I'm not attracted to other women, but Gabby had this lovely, sinuous walk. When she entered a room her erotic glow raised the temperature five degrees. For me, her baldness only made it worse. I found myself fantasizing about the other shiny, smooth curves slithering beneath the loose cotton prints she wore. I didn't have the nerve to tell her about my crush, but I kept finding excuses for us to be together.

One day, after I was pretty seriously hooked on Gabby, she told me she had to go to New Mexico for a special two-week radiation session. "Two weeks? Gabby! That sounds serious."

"Not so very bad, this one," she said in her lilting accent. Gabby's voice was as intoxicating to me as a rum drink on a beach with coconut palms. "I go for this treatment every year. I don't know why they insist on isolation."

"They do?"

"Yes. They won't let patients talk until it's over. But now I have a favor to ask. While I am gone, maybe you can take care of my starter?"

"Sure," I said, without missing a beat. Then I asked, "What's a starter?"

She shrugged, exposing a shiny shoulder under her loose wrap. "It's a bowl of dough."

"Oh, you mean starter for sourdough bread?"

"Yes, like that. It has been in my family for generations."

"Wow," I said, impressed and a little worried. If I goofed up and let her starter die, I'd be in big trouble. "Is it hard to take care of?"

"No, you just keep it in the fridge. But you have to feed it every day." She took a tin out of her purse and removed the lid, revealing a gray powder. "Mix a spoonful of this food with a little water and put it in the bowl. You would do this for me?"

I know it sounds silly, but when I drove Gabby to the airport I felt a little less lonely knowing the starter was home in my refrigerator. At the security checkpoint, where we really had to say goodbye, I was suddenly so choked up I couldn't say anything. I just looked at her—and here's the amazing thing. She read my eyes. Or maybe she had seen through me all along. Anyway, she took my head in her hands and gave me a kiss full on the lips—so passionate, so warm that my knees turned to jelly.

Men don't understand how to do this. For them a kiss is just a waste of time, a warmup to get you ready for sex. But Gabby? I almost melted when I felt her tongue exploring beyond my lips. Portland is a city where you can get away with a lot in public, but I wasn't sure two women should be necking this heavily at the airport.

Back at my apartment that night I slept like a baby, still drifting in a warm fog from Gabby's goodbye.

The next morning, after feeding my cat Mittens, I mixed a spoonful of the powder with water and poured it into the bowl in the refrigerator. Taking care of starter was almost too easy. I wished I could be doing more for Gabby. I would have been happy if she had plants to water and a dog to walk, too.

On the morning of the second day I was disturbed to notice an X-shaped crease on the surface of the dough, like a hot cross bun. The slits looked as if someone had quartered the dough with a long knife.

Could my brother Kevin have done something weird like this? He had a key to my apartment, and I'd asked to borrow his cordless drill, so he might have dropped by while I was at work. But why on earth would he attack the dough in my fridge? And as far as I could tell, he hadn't left his drill. The next most likely explanation, that I had started sleepwalking with a knife, was even more troubling.

On the third morning I went straight to the fridge, even before starting the coffee machine. To my dismay the dough had turned grainy, like tapioca. Clearly I was doing something wrong. For some reason the starter appeared to be curdling. Gabby's instructions had seemed so simple. Perhaps I should have been mixing the powder with colder water, or with less water. If Gabby came back from New Mexico to find that I had ruined her starter, I'd be mortified. This stuff had been in her family for generations. It might be one of the few mementoes she had been able to bring from her homeland.

Before leaving for work I carefully mixed a spoonful of powder with a small amount of very cold water and poured it into the bowl. Then I turned the refrigerator's temperature dial down a number, closed the door, and hoped for the best.

The fourth day I was relieved to see that the graininess was gone. The colder setting must have helped. The dough's surface was even smoother than before, and perhaps a little shiny, almost like Gabby herself. There was a slight depression in the middle. I put the food in there.

By the end of the week my fears returned. The dough was clearly changing shape. Two small bumps, one on either side, had gradually grown into sausage-shaped appendages. What on earth?

Before long I began to notice that food was missing from my fridge. One day an egg was gone. Then an old piece of cheese— I found just the wrapper. The dough's appendages were always folded across the top the same way, and the lid was in place, but there was obviously something very odd about this sourdough. I decided I had to contact Gabby, despite what she'd told me about the isolation policy.

I called the radiation clinic in Alamogordo, but they wouldn't let me talk to a patient. With my heart beating a little faster, I asked, "Can you at least tell me if she's OK?"

"Gabrielle's condition should be stabilized in a few more days," the voice on the phone replied.

"Stabilized? What does that mean?"

"It means stabilized."

Now I was getting angry. "What kind of cancer clinic is this, anyway?" All I knew about Alamogordo was that the government had tested nuclear bombs there in World War II.

I heard an exasperated sigh on the other end of the line. Then there was a click and the line went dead.

I decided to try sending Gabby a text message instead. "WHATS WITH UR STARTER? I THINK ITS GROWING. LUV U!"

A few minutes later Gabby replied, "ITS OK FOR STARTER 2 GRO. THX 4 KEEPING IT! C U NXT WK. XOX."

I fired back a series of questions, but Gabby merely responded, "CANT TXT ANYMOR. BYE."

The next day I couldn't open the fridge at all. I tried to pry the door open with a screwdriver, but gave up when I started damaging the paint. Gabby still wasn't answering text messages—I figured she was either in a therapy session or they'd confiscated her phone. I was getting desperate, already late for work, so I called my brother Kevin.

"Hi," Kevin said. "You still want that cordless drill?"

I'd forgotten about the drill. "Maybe. What I really need is for you to come over and take the hinges off my refrigerator door."

"Why would you want to do that?"

"I can't get the door open." No way was I going to tell him that my fridge had been possessed by bread dough.

"Have you tried pulling the handle?"

Kevin can be such a pain. "Yes. I've tried everything. It's really stuck. Can you come by this morning?"

"Sorry. I'm too busy today to dismantle refrigerators. You'll have to starve till tomorrow."

The doorbell woke me up at six thirty the next morning. By the time I could throw on a bathrobe and get to the kitchen, Kevin was already standing there with the refrigerator door open. On his way in he hadn't bothered to turn on the kitchen light, so the little bulb in the fridge cast his shadow larger than life on the wall—as if there were a giant demon in my kitchen, and not my brother.

"How did you get it open?" I asked.

"Watch closely." He pushed the door shut with his index finger. Then he hooked his little finger on the door handle and pulled it open.

I've learned to ignore Kevin's sarcasm, but my jaw dropped when I saw the inside of the fridge. The starter bowl was empty. The dough was gone!

I breathed the words, "Oh. My. God."

Kevin rolled his eyes. "Get a grip. You're so inept you're a menace."

He walked out, shaking his head. I just stood there in the kitchen, too terrified to think clearly. Which was more horrible—that I had lost Gabby's heirloom dough, or that it might be loose in my apartment?

Suddenly the alarm clock rang, and I nearly jumped out of my skin. But the familiar alarm also triggered my familiar morning routine. No matter how weird my life had become, I would need to go to work. I spent a few minutes searching my apartment for the missing dough. Then I showered, dressed, ate some yogurt, and fed the cat.

I considered leaving some of the starter's food on a saucer in the fridge. If I left the door open, it might lure the dough back. But how could a lump of starter move anyway? And leaving the refrigerator open would send my electric bill through the roof. The whole thing was ridiculous. I closed the door and hurried off to work, imagining that the nightmare might go away on its own.

After work that evening the bowl in the fridge was still empty. But the cat food bowl on the floor was empty too, and I don't think the cat had eaten it. I found Mittens hiding on the top of my bookshelf, looking freaked with her eyes black and her fur on end.

What kind of sourdough would eat cat food? I searched the house again, more carefully this time, but still found nothing. The cat retreated to my bed for the night, her ears up like satellite dishes. As a test, I put out two bowls of cat food, one in the bedroom for Mittens, and one in the kitchen. Then I locked the bedroom door, stuffed towels under the door, and tried to go to sleep.

Mittens didn't touch the cat food in my bedroom all night. She never left my bed. But when I unlocked the bedroom door in the morning, the cat food bowl in the kitchen was empty. So I had proof. Gabby's starter was out there somewhere. An alien growth, loose in my home.

I thought about calling an exterminator, but what would I say? That I had bread dough hiding in the house? Besides, did I really want to kill it, whatever it was? I had made Gabby a promise, sealed with a kiss.

For the final three days until Gabby's return I locked my bedroom door at night and left cat food in the kitchen. No matter how much food I put out, the bowl was always empty the next day. On the last night I left the entire bag of cat food open. In the morning the bag had been emptied as if by a vacuum cleaner.

When I finally picked Gabby up at the airport, she looked radiant. She held out her arms and gave me a big hug. Suddenly the recriminations I had been saving began melting away. When I finally found words, all that came out was an apology.

"I can't find your starter," I admitted. "I think it must be somewhere in my apartment."

"Let me take a look," she said.

"You're not angry?" I asked. What was I saying? I should have been demanding an explanation, accusing her of planting a monster in my refrigerator.

"I understand," she said. Her smile miraculously calmed my fears.

Back at my apartment Gabby went from room to room, whistling softly through her teeth. From behind a cabinet, where I wouldn't have thought anything could hide, a shadowy form slowly emerged. It oozed forward and swelled. Gradually it took the shape of a little bronze baby, with smooth skin like Gabby's and slits for eyes.

"Oh, look how you've grown!" Gabby exclaimed. "You've been eating too much, you greedy thing."

I should have been scared to death. In just two weeks the starter had turned my life upside down. I knew it was dangerous, a cancerous stowaway. But I had nurtured it from the first.

And I felt a flush of pride when Gabby wagged her finger at the baby, berating it with the concern of a mother, "If you're not careful, my little one, you'll end up having to go for radiation treatments too."

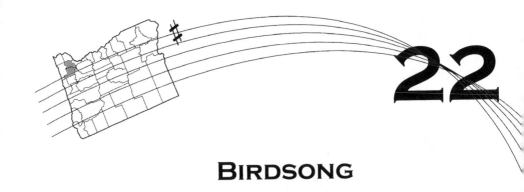

BIRDSONG

Gerald learned Vietnamese before he learned bird.

He was majoring in linguistics at Linfield Cellege, with a minor in environmental studies. As a junior he signed up to spend a year abroad teaching English in a rural Vietnamese school.

Gerald chose Vietnam to make up for his Grandpa Bob, a military attache from the Vietnam War who prided himself in not knowing a single word of Vietnamese. After the war Grandpa Bob had been assigned to resettle refugees in Oregon. He still laughed about the Hmong tribeswomen from the Laotian highlands who had chipped the enamel bathtubs in their Gresham apartment, washing clothes with rocks. Grandpa Bob had housed one Vietnamese family temporarily in a Rockaway Beach cabin, and had found them sweeping the lawn with brooms. When they moved out they followed his winterization instructions by leaving a quarter cup of antifreeze in each sink—balancing it carefully atop the drain in a paper cup. Grandpa Bob's cupboard was still full of lychee nuts, the flowery canned fruit given to patriarchs as a sign of respect.

As far as Gerald was concerned, the best way to show someone respect was to learn their language. But Vietnamese turned out to be harder than he had thought. Each vowel could have six different tones—a tense rising inflection, a breathy falling, a harsh falling, a mid-level note, a swoopy questioning, or a gulped warble. For example, Gerald learned that the word for lady is *ba*. If he said it with the wrong sort of tone, however, people might think he was talking about a poison, a governor, a residue, randomness, or the number three.

The Vietnamese host family who met Gerald at the Hanoi airport had similar problems with his name. No matter how he coached them, "Gerald" came out sounding either like "carrot" or "salad." Finally they made up an honorific title for him, which pleased Gerald so much he beamed. Everybody smiled a lot in Vietnam.

For the first three months the people of the village treated Gerald like a visiting prince. The school principal held a banquet in his honor. An extremely beautiful college girl was assigned to accompany him as a translator on day trips. Together they visited the notorious "Hanoi Hilton," the former prisoner-of-war camp renovated as a tourist attraction. They went swimming at a South China Sea beach, and she let him kiss her between waves. Gerald had never thought of himself as particularly tall, but here he towered above the locals wherever he walked. Often a gaggle of excited children danced behind him.

For the second three months the villagers treated him like a visiting student. The beautiful girl returned to her studies in Da Nang. A retired English teacher from the school agreed to accompany him on birdwatching forays—Gerald's other passion—but didn't know the birds' names, even in Vietnamese.

For the final three months the villagers treated Gerald like a visiting laborer. The principal informed him that his duties would now include tutoring students after school. Gerald needed new clothes, but the shops didn't carry anything nearly large enough. When he asked in his best Vietnamese about extra-large special orders the shopgirl simply shook her head. When he persisted she responded in English, "Bye-bye!" The only place with fast enough Internet access to Skype was the modern Hanoi Hilton, and although Gerald was running too low on cash to afford lunch there, he took the bus to Hanoi on weekends to sit in the alley behind the hotel, where he could talk with his old Linfield roommates on his laptop screen.

The day before Gerald's plane left for the US, he finally translated his honorific title. The name that his host family, the school staff, and the villagers had been using for Gerald for the past nine months meant "Idiot Foreigner."

On the flight home Gerald stared out the window hour after hour at the empty ocean below. He had tried to learn their language as a sign of respect. But he was too different to be accepted. In Linguistics 101 he had learned that every language is composed of dialects, and every dialect can be broken down into idiolects, the nicknames and slang that mark you as a member of a family or a neighborhood. Learning a language is not enough to fit in.

In the movies, Hollywood had made the Lone Ranger's sidekick speak a parody of pidgin English to show that a Native American could never be completely accepted as an equal by a white lawman. And they had named him Tonto, which doesn't mean "friend" or "comrade" or even "lovable fool" in Spanish. It just means "stupid."

Gerald had gone to Vietnam imagining that he was the Lone Ranger. But all he had been was *tonto*.

Back in McMinnville, Gerald switched his major from linguistics to environmental studies. After graduation there were no job openings for ecologists, so he agreed to a stint as an intern doing bird counts in the Tualatin River National Wildlife Refuge. He rented an apartment in Sherwood and rode to the refuge on the first Tri-Met bus each morning so he could set up his parabolic microphone and digital recorder in time for the dawn chorus. He had learned that bird counters rely mostly on calls, and not on actual sightings. Sunrise is when the birds are most verbal. They sing their hearts out claiming territory, showing off for females, and greeting the new day.

Soon Gerald could recognize quite a variety of bird calls. Yellowthroats cry, "Twitchety-twitchety-twitchety" from the brush. Song sparrows sing a five-note tune that seems to say, "I am a SPAR-row!" Western flycatchers ask, "What? What? What?" from the creekside alders. Swainson's thrushes pour out a delightful spiral of flute notes.

The most beautiful and varied song of all, however, was the melodious warble of the red-winged blackbird. And this was what got Gerald's research published in *Nature* magazine: He learned to identify the call of a single, unique bird.

BA-31, as Gerald identified the blackbird in his notes, was a young adult male. The bird had gray claws, black eyes, and a particularly board red stripe on the shoulder of each wing. BA-31 claimed three acres of cattail reeds in a marshy oxbow of the Tualatin River. When BA-31 wasn't actively foraging for insects, pestering vagrant hawks, or chasing away other male blackbirds, he liked to stand on the tallest stalk in the cattail swamp and sing.

What a song! From the blind where Gerald hid with his microphone and headset, Gerald could close his eyes and imagine he was in an orchestra pit, listening to a symphony tune up. Trills, scales, warbles! The harmonies and discords ran together so fast it sounded like dozens of musical voices instead of just one bird.

Gerald had been recording BA-31 for a full year, replaying the songs back in his spare time during the evenings, when he experienced his Helen Keller moment. Suddenly it hit him: Each part of this bird's song had meaning. The warbles and trills were not random. They represented ideas. BA-31 was singing a language—an idiolect that the other red-winged blackbirds of the Tualatin River National Wildlife Refuge could understand.

In his pathbreaking article for *Nature,* Gerald identified a basic twelve-world vocabulary and a rudimentary grammar for red-winged blackbirds. Much as in Vietnamese, Gerald discovered, the same note could have entirely different meanings if it was sung with a different tone—falling, trilling, or warbling. He was able to show that BA-31 could alert his neighbors to the presence of three different kinds of predators—cats, owls, and hawks—by using three different tones. The rest of blackbird grammar proved more difficult to decode, but the phrasing of a song seemed to indicate an object's position in relation to the sun. Repetition suggested that the object was closer, either in terms of time or place. Gerald speculated that BA-31 was such a good subject for study because red-winged blackbirds are nearly as intelligent as crows or jays, and yet can vary their song nearly as much as macaws or keas.

By the third year of Gerald's study, BA-31 had become so famous that ornithologists from all over the world were asking Gerald if they could come to conduct their own research. Gerald generally said no, in part because he himself had landed a National Science Foundation grant to continue his work. The *New York Times* ran a spread in the "Sunday Science" section, nicknaming the celebrity blackbird "Rosetta." The article hailed Gerald's work as the key to unlocking the hieroglyphics of avian communication.

In the fourth year of Gerald's research he allowed an Australian biologist named Jack Fitzroy to help him. Jack was a talented writer and offered to put Gerald's work together as a book. That winter Jack stayed on at the Tualatin preserve while Gerald went on tour, lecturing around the country. Gerald filled college auditoriums and library lecture halls with people eager to hear the "Doctor Dolittle of Oregon" tell about his breakthrough.

In the spring of his fifth year at the preserve Gerald held a press conference at the bird blind to let journalists hear Rosetta for themselves. The red-winged blackbird was older now, but still clung to the highest cattail in the swamp, singing like a diva.

A few days later Gerald was working with Jack Fitzroy when Jack said, "I wish you'd stop talking to the bird in English."

This stopped Gerald short. "Was I?" Without paying much attention to it, he had in fact begun muttering while he worked.

"If you're going to talk to the bloody thing," his Aussie assistant said, "You might as well talk in bird."

"How? I can't make the sounds Rosetta uses."

Jack shrugged. "We've got enough recordings. We could cut up Rosetta's songs and write a computer program that reassembles them differently, depending on what you want to say."

Gerald wished he had thought of this himself. A touch of jealousy made him look for flaws in the idea. "I'm not sure Rosetta would like a recorded song." Gerald had always objected to amateur birders who used cellphone apps to attract owls or warblers by playing recorded birdsongs. "Recordings just confuse birds."

"It's only confusing if the recording says something weird, like 'Here come the elephants" instead of 'Here come the birdwatchers.'"

Gerald smiled. "Maybe."

"I could put a program together, if you like."

"Wouldn't Rosetta think it's strange to hear his own voice talk back to him?"

"Listen mate," the Australian replied, thickening his accent on purpose, "Everything you blokes say sounds strange to me."

Gerald laughed. "All right. We can try."

That summer Jack cut and pasted audio clips, trying to assemble a dictionary of red-winged blackbird. It turned out to be more difficult than Jack had thought. When they tried out the recordings in the field, Rosetta really did seem confused.

By then Gerald was busy scheduling his next "Doctor Dolittle" tour. This time he planned to travel around the world, lecturing in thirty cities between November 15 and February 1. What he needed was a book about his work to sell on the tour. Jack was supposed to have been writing it for the past year. Gerald kept asking when a draft would be ready for him to review.

In reply Jack just shook his head. He began spending more time alone. In August, even before Rosetta migrated south, Jack returned to Australia.

Gerald was sorry to see Jack go, but he had other things on his mind. The Telezon cell phone company had offered him $6 million for the rights to use Rosetta's story in an advertising campaign about new worlds of communication. Gerald refused, but when the company's president called him in person, he reconsidered. Instead of paying him $6 million outright, Telezon was willing to donate $12 million to the charity of his choice. Would Gerald be interested, the president asked, if they created a Dolittle Foundation to carry on his studies?

By October the Dolittle Foundation had a board of directors, a staff of six, and an office in downtown Portland's Yeon Building. In addition to the $12 million start-up grant, pledges were rolling in from around the world. And then on November 13, two days before his Dolittle Tour was set to open in New York City, Gerald received a disturbing email from the foundation's new secretary. The owner of Samson's Book Bunker, an independent Portland bookstore, had called with a warning. Bookstores had been sworn to secrecy by the publisher, but a book by Jack Fitzroy was being released tomorrow night, at the exact same time that a "Thirty Minutes" documentary on Rosetta was scheduled to air on television. The secretary suggested that Gerald might want to watch the program.

That evening, alone in his Manhattan hotel room, Gerald clicked through his television's channels until he found "Thirty Minutes." He paled when he read the opening tagline: "Do Little and Lie a Lot."

While a robin chirped in the background—the same stupid call, over and over—the "Thirty Minutes" anchorman frowned at the camera. "Gerald Tilton claims he can talk to birds. For a twenty-seven-year-old intern with a bachelor's degree from Linfield College in McMinnville, Oregon, Mr. Tilton certainly has seemed an unlikely candidate to soar to international stardom. Tonight, with reports from his own assistant and from top ornithological scientists, we'll learn the truth: The famous blackbird Rosetta, the miracle who serves as the wings above Mr. Tilton's wind, is an ordinary bird that can't decipher its own call. In fact, the only language we can be certain Mt. Tilton understands is when money talks.

Gerald watched in shock as Jack Fitzroy—the writer whose career he had been trying to boost—shared recordings, notes, and interviews with the "Thirty Minutes" team. How had they gotten footage of Gerald's puzzled expression when Rosetta didn't seem to respond to its own call? Nowhere did they say that reassembling and replaying Rosetta's call had actually been Jack's idea, and that Gerald had doubted it from the start. Then they interviewed a research team at Cornell University's Ornithology Lab in upstate New York. The scientists there had been trying for months to duplicate Gerald's work using red-winged blackbirds bred in captivity, but they had been unable to isolate any intelligible vocabulary. Gerald leaned forward, straining to hear the birds. The tame blackbirds had spent their whole lives in laboratory cages.

As far as Gerald could tell, they really were gibbering. The scientists played their calls side by side with Rosetta's. The anchorman laughed and said they sounded the same to him. To Gerald, however, Rosetta was explaining that mosquitoes were arriving in the dusk. Couldn't anyone else hear that?

The lowest blow was yet to come. The "Thirty Minutes" anchorman announced that public records from the Dolittle Foundation revealed that the nonprofit had not yet funded a research project or bought a single refuge. Where was the foundation's $15 million in assets being spent? Skipping over the fact that the foundation had been in existence just six weeks and could hardly have been expected to buy refuge property so quickly, the program cut to a video clip taken that very morning. The television screen showed Gerald stepping out of a limousine at his Manhattan hotel. Videos followed of Gerald at sunny resort pools and expensive restaurants—all places he had been invited by hosts on last year's tour. The producers of "Thirty Minutes" hadn't actually lied, but by choosing facts and arranging the film clips they created the impression that Gerald was a self-aggrandizing con artist.

The show ended with a final question for Jack Fitzroy. The anchorman looked at him earnestly. "I understand you'll have more details about Mr. Tilton's deceptions in your upcoming book, *Do Little and Lie a Lot.* When will it be published?"

"It's available as we speak, both as an eBook and in bookstores everywhere." Then the Aussie traitor looked straight into the camera. "I'm sorry, Gerald, that it had to end this way."

The Dolittle Tour collapsed before it began. The Dolittle Foundation folded a week later when Telezon withdrew its support. Gerald fled from the whole nightmare, retreating to his Sherwood apartment. He disconnected his phone and switched email addresses. When reporters accosted him on the sidewalk, he walked on by.

That winter Gerald replayed the audio clips of Rosetta's songs. For the first time, he realized that Rosetta was using different names for different redwinged blackbirds. Individual birds had unique names! He started to write an article about this new discovery but soon gave up. He wasn't as convincing a writer as Jack Fitzroy, and no one would publish an article by Gerald Tilton anyway.

In February Gerald received a long, hand-written letter from the principal of the Vietnamese school where he had taught English. Word of his difficulties had spread even to their remote village. The principal assured Gerald that the villagers still supported him. If Gerald wanted to teach English or ecology, there would always be a job waiting for him.

Gerald wrote a nice letter back, declining. He wrote in Vietnamese, for the same reason that the principal had struggled to write a letter in English—as a sign of respect. But Gerald knew he would always be the Idiot Foreigner there.

That May Gerald concealed himself in the bird blind at the Tualatin River refuge, waiting for Rosetta to return from the winter migration. Listening with headphones in the blind, Gerald heard Rosetta before he actually saw the bird. Rosetta's song was as familiar and as welcome as the voice of an old friend. And now he could understand that Rosetta was greeting individuals: Hello, Big Tail! Hi, Fast Flier! It's good to be home, Blue Back.

Gerald could understand it all. Smiling broadly, he stepped out from the blind, shielded his eyes against the morning sun, and waved to the red-winged blackbird on the tall cattail stalk.

Rosetta replied with a song that included a new word. Could it be that Rosetta had a name for Gerald as well?

Gerald listened more closely. Yes! Rosetta had been addressing him by name all these years. Here at last was a breakthrough that might restore his reputation. Only Rosetta had the power to revive the Dolittle Foundation and put the Dolittle Tour back on track.

Gerald concentrated on the call. Rosetta's name for him had two parts, much like Blue Back, Fast Flier, and the names for other individuals.

"Look!" Rosetta sang. "There's **** **** again!"

Then Gerald recognized the words.

Rosetta's name for him was Hawk Shit.

That afternoon as Gerald waited at the Tri-Met bus stop on Highway 99W, he watched the cars roar by in the rain. His name was Hawk Shit. He was feared and despised by the red-winged blackbirds he had studied for six years. He had learned their language as a sign of respect, but he would never be accepted. He had wanted to gallop into their midst like the Lone Ranger. But instead he had just been *tonto*.

When the bus pulled up and the door folded open with a squeak, Gerald reached into his pocket and realized it was empty. He looked up at the bus driver helplessly. This was the final blow.

"I don't have any money," Gerald said.

The woman in the driver's seat waved him in. "That's OK. You ride here all the time. Another day you can pay double."

He climbed the steps with his awkward backpack of audio gear and stood in the aisle, his raincoat dripping. The bus was nearly full. A young woman with short black hair and a Trader Joe's bag scooted from an aisle seat to the window to make room. She didn't have to smile at him, but she did.

When he sat down and the bus started, Gerald marveled that he could understand every conversation on the bus without even trying. A large man in the seniors seats didn't think the Ducks would make the basketball finals. Two boys behind him bragged that they would soon be getting learner's permits from the DMV. An elderly woman across the aisle said the best hair stylist worked in a little place in King City. The entire bus was full of people who spoke his idiolect.

"Kind of a rainy day for a hike."

The black-haired girl beside him had put this statement out in front of her, but Gerald understood at once that it was really a question, and that it was aimed at him.

"Actually, I work at the wildlife refuge." Gerald shifted the backpack of equipment onto his lap. "I record birdsongs."

The girl looked at him more closely. "So you can tell one kind of bird from another?"

"More than that. I want to understand what they're saying."

"Really?"

Gerald closed his eyes, appalled by how much he thought he could read in the tone of a single word. The girl had shifted seats because she did not find him unattractive. She had never heard of the Dolittle Foundation. She did not like to look for dates in bars, but was also suspicious of men she met on buses.

"Can you do that?" she asked. "Can you understand birds?"

Gerald sighed. He didn't know what to say.

NINETY ON A TANGENT FARM

Bev dropped her spoon.

"Well now!" Laura laughed, her chin shaking. "That means a man'll come visiting."

"You think?" Bev straightened her apron. "Then maybe he'll bring money. My left palm's been itchy as poison oak."

A cloudy-eyed collie pawed Laura's sleeve. "Down, girl! Well, my ear's been ringing since dawn."

Bev's cup stopped in mid-air. "Which one?"

"Guess."

"Left?"

Laura grinned. "Nope. Reckon that means somebody's talking bad about me right now."

She looked out the rain-streaked window, across fields of stubble, and her smile faded. "I wonder who?"

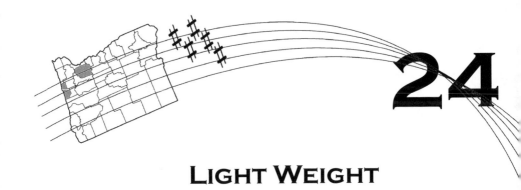

LIGHT WEIGHT

Daniel's genius burned brightest in the stormy half light of midwinter. When the ebb of tourists turned Oregon's coastal towns to yawning tidal flats of rainy asphalt, no one stopped at the Beauchamp Atelier to "Blow Your Own Glass Float For Just $30."

Alone in the hellish orange glow of his furnace, Daniel dreamed sheer silica into incandescent millefiori fireworks.

And so he did not see the pale stranger who slipped in the door with a black bag to watch him work one drizzly Monday morning in January.

Sweat ran down Daniel's pock-marked face as he dipped a fiery pigtail of molten glass from the roaring oven. Then he spun the blowpipe with one hand, dipped a second pipe with the other, and twisted the pigtails into a glowing helix. Since his accident in Chihuly's Tacoma studio, Daniel had learned to work alone. He had started as an assistant, snipping hot glass, dipping blow tubes, and wetting wooden shapers for master artisans. One day he fumbled a hot pipe into the furnace, spattering droplets of glass. He had screamed as if his face were melting, and it nearly had. Miraculously his eyes had been spared. But the pitted flesh had changed him. He became his own master. He opened an atelier in an abandoned appliance showroom in the lonely coastal village of Taft, at the far end of Lincoln City. He hired no help and asked nothing of women. He grew skeptical of reality. Instead he focused on inner beauty, seemingly spinning his creations not from glass but from pure light.

Daniel used an awl to score the base of his double spiral. Already the sculpture was starting to resemble twining strands of kelp. He gripped the glass with wooden tongs and rapped it lightly to free it of the pipe. Finally he turned and saw the stranger's dark eyes.

The man did not meet his gaze. "You work alone, Mr. Beauchamp. That is good. It is also very rare."

The man spoke with an accent Daniel did not recognize. He wore black jeans and a gray sweatshirt that read, "Property of Alcatraz." The skin of his face seemed so translucent that Daniel imagined he could see the ghostly shadows of gray cheekbones and blue veins within. Daniel almost expected the stranger to announce that this was a robbery — but the only thing to steal in the atelier was art.

The man surveyed the display shelves, as if he were thinking the same thing. "I am told you are Oregon's most accomplished creator of glass spheres."

Daniel responded with a slow nod. "Lincoln City hires me to make glass floats." It was his most reliable source of income. Years ago, visitors to Oregon's beaches had delighted in collecting Japanese fishing floats. Made of cheap green glass, the balls had ranged from the size of grapefruits to basketballs, depending on the kind of nets they were designed to support. When storms broke the floats loose, they could circle the Pacific for decades. Barnacles and bits of net often clung to them when they finally washed ashore. Determined beachcombers rose before dawn, searching the driftwood flotsam with flashlights to discover what the night tide had brought. After fishermen in Japan switched to plastic and Styrofoam floats, the supply of glass spheres dwindled. Old timers claimed the best ones were still out there, carried by high midwinter tides to circle forever in a secret North Pacific gyre far from the shipping lanes, somewhere in the never-never sea between Oregon and Hawaii. Meanwhile, the Lincoln City Chamber of Commerce had sought to boost tourism by salting the beaches in the off season with colorful glass spheres blown at the Beauchamp Atelier.

"For just thirty dollars," Daniel said, watching the stranger, "I can help you make a float of your own."

"No." The man put a finger to his chin, a gesture that suggested he was either thinking or asking for silence. "I will give you ten times this amount if you attempt to create a sphere to my specifications. And I will give you one hundred times this amount if you succeed."

Daniel frowned, doing the math. Three thousand dollars for a single float? "What do you mean, succeed?"

The man smiled, exposing uneven teeth. "Is there perhaps a place where we can discuss this more comfortably?"

At the Cape Foulweather Coffee Company, a block up Highway 101, wooden seagulls stood bolted to the weathered gray railing of a drizzly deck. Inside, burlap coffee sacks from Columbia and Costa Rica hung from the ceiling. Daniel ordered his standard lunch, a Reuben and a mocha. The pale man merely said, "Tea. Earl Grey. Hot," as if he imagined himself a Star Trek captain. They sat at a table beside a mirrored wall that made it seem as if there were four of them in the middle of a large, empty room.

"My name," the pale man said, "is Vasily Luchabnek. I am a physicist."

Daniel nodded warily. "Well I'm an artist. I know nothing about physics, and I don't trust scientists."

"Better and better." Vasily lifted his tea cup as if for a toast. Then he paused. "But I wonder, do you mistrust science for the right reasons?"

Daniel sipped his coffee without toasting. "Art provides me with beauty and truth. What has science given us except fear and deception?"

"Perhaps in Lincoln City you are safe from science?"

Daniel heard the sarcasm and narrowed his eyes. "Nope. Tonight the marine science center is holding a community meeting. I've heard it all before. One speaker will warn that the continents are moving. Any day Oregon will jerk thirty feet to the west and a tsunami will wash Taft away. Someone else will claim that my glass furnace has warmed the planet, and river floods will wash Taft away."

"We are all doomed," Vasily said.

Daniel glanced at him from the side. "Where are you from and what do you want?"

"I grew up in Vilnius, Lithuania. After university I won a research grant for LIGO. You know it?"

"The little plastic bricks?"

Vasily shook his head. "Not Lego. LIGO stands for the Laser Interferometer Gravitational-Wave Observatory. The project uses two identical cyclotrons, one in Louisiana and one in Eastern Washington, in an attempt to detect gravity waves. In each cyclotron, two four-kilometer tunnels connect at an angle. In the middle a one-way mirror switches light on or off through a forty-kilogram artificial sapphire. Currently the mirror only works on a single wavelength of light. My assignment was to find a more versatile one-way mirror. One that works for all wavelengths."

Daniel took a bite of his pastrami sandwich, only half listening to this jargon.

"I was fired before I could find this mirror. The LIGO program was cut sixty percent. I got a job with Mentor Graphics in Wilsonville, developing plasma screens. But on my own I kept working on mirrors. And now I have found it."

Vasily unclasped his black bag. He withdrew a jelly jar half full of what appeared to be black mercury.

Daniel set down his sandwich, suddenly focused on the strange, viscous liquid. In his career he had seen countless colors of molten glass, but nothing so utterly black — so devoid of light.

"What on earth is it?" Daniel asked.

Vasily swirled the jar, momentarily turning the liquid from black to silver. "A metal polymer. A thin coating on very clear glass creates an absolute one-way mirror for visible light. Photons pass one way, but not the other."

Daniel considered the possibilities. "So you could use it for — what? Mirrored sunglasses?"

"No. The glasses you suggest would be silver on one side but black on the other. You would see nothing. Still, there may be other applications."

Daniel reached for the jar, but Vasily pulled it back. "I need to conduct a test," Vasily said. "This is why I want to create a glass sphere. The difficulty is that the coating must be on the inside."

"The inside?" Daniel frowned.

"The polymer has high surface tension, like glass. Perhaps you could blow it like glass, inside?"

Creating a sphere within a sphere was one of the greatest challenges of glass art. A float like that would be worth three hundred dollars. Daniel held out his hand for the jar. This time Vasily relinquished it. Daniel tilted the jar slowly, studying the eerie void within.

"All right," he said at length. "I'll try."

After lunch Daniel added lead shavings to his furnace. He rarely worked with lead crystal because of the danger and expense. While the furnace melted the mixture he practiced blowing the polymer with several sizes of pipes. Before long he was able to puff a bubble that resembled shiny black chewing gum. Vasily guarded the jar of polymer jealously, but still did not notice when Daniel switched blowpipes, leaving one loaded with polymer at the back of his rack.

When Daniel felt ready he blew a five-inch ball of hot lead crystal. At this point most glassblowers would need an assistant to keep the sphere spinning so the hot glass wouldn't sag. Daniel, however, had invented a wheeled rack with a variable electric motor for just such a purpose. While the hot reddish sphere slowly rotated, he inserted a second blowpipe on the opposite end. Slowly he blew a bubble of polymer inside. Vasily stood so close that his pale skin glowed pink.

With Daniel's final puff, the inside sphere adhered to the crystal. As suddenly as a thrown light switch, the red ball turned black.

"Ah!" Vasily gasped.

Daniel twisted loose the polymer blowpipe. He heated the scar with a small blowtorch until it melted smooth. Then, holding the sphere in a wooden cup, he broke off the first blowpipe. By this time the glass had cooled so much, however, that the second scar proved harder to heal. After a minute Daniel turned off the blow-torch. As the glowing red navel dimmed, the ball before them seemed to sink into another world — a surfaceless hole in the fabric of light.

"Oh, my beauty," Vasily breathed.

For an instant Daniel feared he had been tricked into creating something that should not be. That a scientist would dare to use the word 'beauty' gave him chills. But the sphere spoke to him with its own silent language, mysteriously melding science with art. In all of his work Daniel had sought to capture light, to use glass to trap inner beauty. The pale stranger had made this dream a possibility.

Daniel handed Vasily a pair of mitts. "Be careful. It's still quite warm."

Vasily cradled the ball, marveling. "I feel as if I am looking at myself."

What a peculiar thing to say! And yet Daniel realized he had the same thought. Since his accident his talent had been hidden behind a disfigured face: beauty within ugliness, light within the dark. But was that really what the scientist meant?

"I have known autism all my life," Vasily said, as if to the sphere and not to Daniel. "The world bombards me with data. I take it all in, but cannot release it. Someday I feel I may explode. It is my ter-ror, and my dream."

Vasily replaced the sphere in the wooden cup. Then he with-drew a flashlight from his bag and aimed a bright beam at the glass ball. At first it seemed that the light was vanishing as if into a bot-tomless cave. But when Vasily turned the globe, a white ray from the back shivered across the studio.

Vasily sighed. "There is a flaw. There will always be a flaw. No one can create a perfect sphere within a sphere."

Daniel's face flushed red with anger. He tried to avoid showing this kind of emotion because he knew it lit up the white scars of his face in an unflattering display. Without a word he dipped the blowpipe back into the furnace. He had been too cautious the first time, allowing the glass to cool. Now he hefted a blob of molten glass, turned it round, blew it into a bubble, and quickly set it onto the motorized rack to spin.

"The polymer," Daniel ordered.

Vasily reluctantly reopened the jar. Daniel took a second blow-pipe and drew up nearly all of the remaining black liquid. At once he attached the second pipe to the spinning sphere and blew. This time when the globe went black he immediately broke it loose and heated the scar with the torch. The entire operation had lasted less than a minute. The glass ball was still so hot Daniel had to shift it from one wooden cup to another.

But this time, when Vasily shone his flashlight on the sphere, the light simply disappeared. In fact, the ball itself seemed to vanish, a thing with no surface—the absence of a thing.

"What happens to the light?" Daniel asked.

Vasily took what looked like a cell phone from his bag, waved it around the sphere, and checked the device's screen. "Nonvisible wavelengths eventually leak out."

"And that means?"

"Infrared, ultraviolet. My research continues." Now that the glass had cooled enough to touch, Vasily seemed in more of a hurry. He took a small electronic scale from his bag, weighed the sphere, and noted the number. Then he took a roll of aluminum foil from his bag. He tore off a piece, wrapped the sphere, and packed it in the bag.

When Vasilyl reached for the other sphere, however, Daniel held it away, clicking his tongue. "Have you forgotten our deal?"

Vasily said nothing. He pulled a checkbook out of his back pocket and wrote a draft for three thousand dollars.

Daniel took the check but kept the sphere. "Three thousand was for success. Three hundred is for the attempt."

Vasily wrote a second check, this time for three hundred dollars. Then he snatched away the sphere, lifted his bag, and slipped out the door as silently as he had come.

Of course Daniel created another black sphere that afternoon—as much for Pablo as for himself. Daniel had orchestrated the shell game of polymer-filled blowpipes because he had never seen a perfectly colorless medium before. He prided himself in keeping a collection of his most interesting floats on his trailer balcony for Pablo, his pet seagull, to judge.

The trailer park where Daniel lived was little more than a puddled gravel lot between Kari's Kandi Kitchen and the Dumpsters of Jerry's Thriftway. Daniel had bought the rusty single-wide of a recently deceased Army vet as a statement, and not just because the trailer was cheap. Even the real estate broker had cautioned him about the flats of Taft's old quarter, where tsunami warning signs depict a little blue man frantically scrambling up cliffs to escape the scimitar curls of blue waves. Daniel scoffed at that doom, but he also wanted to demonstrate the principle of inner beauty.

Now, when Daniel climbed the rotten steps, opened the shabby aluminum door, and threw on the lights, he stepped into a bright undersea grotto of glass. Red snappers and bluefin tunas made of glass swam through a crystal chandelier. Starfish sconces glowed orange from a seaweed wall of shimmering silica.

At the back door a live seagull squawked impatiently.

"Hold your horses." Daniel set a brown paper bag gently on the glass kitchen counter. Then he got a tin of sardines, a box of RyKrisp, and a bottle of beer—his usual back-porch dinner. The gray-and-white bird was already hopping along the row of glass balls, tilting his orange eye to watch Daniel from various angles. Daniel popped open the sardine can by its metal ring and lifted a greasy fish by its tail. At once Pablo beat the air with his wings, hovering just long enough to snatch the sardine in his yellow beak. The gull fluttered back to the edge of the porch and settled on a swirly green-and-blue ball.

"Oh, so today you think the Earth ball is the prettiest?" Daniel asked. "Just wait till you see what I blew today." He went back to the kitchen, opened the brown paper bag, and took out the black sphere. He couldn't help but stare at the void before him. Why had the pale scientist weighed the other sphere? To prove that it was really there? Daniel turned on the metric kitchen scale he used for French recipes, set his glass sphere on the tray, and waited for the green numbers to stop flashing.

One hundred sixty-nine grams. So it did exist. Although it seemed to have no surface, it cast a hard black shadow on the counter.

Daniel took the sphere out to the porch, rearranged the row of glass floats to make room, and set it in a slot near the seagull.

Pablo cocked his head. He pecked at the sphere tentatively. Then he hopped past it to a crimson ball, spread his wings for balance, and screeched, *Kyee-ki-ki-ki-ki!*

What kind of noise is that?" Daniel asked, opening his beer on the arm of his folding chair. "A laugh or a cry?"

In the distance the muffled roar of surf suddenly rumbled louder, as it often did when a large wave broke with the night's incoming tide.

In the morning, after scrolling through the online *New York Times* while eating corn flakes, Daniel took the Lithuanian physicist's checks to the Lincoln Bank. A teller ran them through a scanner, stamped them, and handed them back along with a receipt.

"Did they clear?" Daniel asked.

The teller smiled at him. She was hired to smile, even at a face like his. "It usually takes one business day for funds to be available. You can check your account tomorrow."

He nodded, folded the checks into his pocket, and walked back along Highway 101 toward his studio. Even though the rain clouds had cleared, and a weak January sun was struggling to dispel the bay's morning mist, he knew no one would stop today to blow glass floats. The checks would either clear or they wouldn't. He would continue work on his kelp forest project—a grand piece of installation art that would be perfect for the Lincoln Bank lobby, but which would probably end up decorating his laundry room. He would eat sardines with Pablo in the evening, and nothing would have changed.

Daniel's prediction was almost right. Not a single tourist visited the atelier for the rest of the week. The checks cleared, lifting his account balance out of the danger zone. He blew some glass floats, knowing that Jennifer from the Chamber of Commerce would want a selection for the tourism project when she dropped by on Friday.

But he was wrong about Pablo. The seagull refused to eat sardines, even when Daniel laid them enticingly on the blue-green Earth ball. The bird hopped back and forth, cocking his head toward the black sphere and squawking, *Kyee-ki-ki-ki-ki!*

By Friday evening, after four improbably sunny days in a row, Pablo refused to land on the porch at all. Instead the bird circled above the trailer park or landed on the pink roof of the Kandi Kitchen. Daniel felt desolate. The seagull had been his closest friend. When Daniel turned off his porch light for a better view of the seagull, he noticed with some puzzlement that the white stripes of the American flag on his porch were glowing bright blue in the night. The yellow palm trees on his Hawaiian shirt were glowing green.

Suddenly the doorbell rang, and he jumped. Then he remembered it must be Jennifer, the Chamber of Commerce woman. Usually he gave her a bag full of reject floats—the ones Pablo judged unworthy. This time there was no doubt: The black sphere had to go. But when he picked it up, he noticed with alarm that it was warm. His teeth and shirt buttons glowed crazily. If he gave the Chamber a haunted float like this, they'd cancel his contract.

The doorbell rang again. In that moment Daniel felt so angry at the glass sphere—it had alienated his seagull friend and might jeopardize his best customer—that he threw it as hard as he could into the night, hoping the glass would shatter. Instead it thumped, apparently unbroken, into a patch of weeds near the supermarket Dumpsters. Daniel turned away, switched on the porch light, and hurried through the house to answer the door.

"Is everything OK, Mr. Beauchamp?" Jennifer wore trim white slacks and pink sneakers. Long blonde hair draped in curves over her fuzzy pink polar fleece jacket. "When I didn't see a light I was beginning to get worried."

Daniel looked down. He was easily flustered by beautiful

women. "No, I just—" he searched for words. "I just turned out the lights to watch for my pet seagull."

Jennifer wagged her finger. "You shouldn't feed them, you know. They're wild animals." Then she peered past him into the trailer. "Don't you have the floats ready?"

"No. I mean yes." He held open the door. "They're on the back porch. Tonight I thought I'd let you choose."

She followed him through the living room and kitchen, marveling at the brightly colored glass that hung from nearly every surface. "Aren't you afraid of breaking something?"

Without reply he opened the porch door and held out his hand to the row of colored spheres. "Take your pick."

Daniel knew it was pointless, trying to impress a beautiful girl. Or was he really trying to punish a fickle seagull? Either way, it was too late to turn back now. Jennifer picked the Earth ball, the crimson ball, and two others he had not meant to lose. Then she gave him the usual check for a hundred dollars, said good night, and left.

Daniel turned out the lights and returned to the porch.

"Pablo?" he called, his eyes damp. His hands still felt hot where he had touched the black sphere. His face was warm.

Later, when he got ready for bed and looked in the bathroom mirror, he realized that his face and hands were red, as if from sunburn. What had the Lithuanian physicist said might leak from the ball? Not X-rays, but something else. Perhaps ultraviolet rays—the ones that cause sunburn?

Whatever it was, it didn't matter now. He had thrown the ball away. Tomorrow was Saturday. He would blow a new Earth ball and Pablo would return. On Monday, his day off, he would close the shop and walk the beach all the way to the cafe at Roads End. Pablo would fly above him along the beach, screeching impatiently for the fish and chips waiting for them at the cafe. Nothing would have changed.

Daniel's prediction was almost right. On Saturday he blew a blue-green Earth ball, better than the first, with a tricky silver moon inside. Pablo came screeching back. On Monday Daniel hiked seven miles along the beach to Roads End. The seagull followed overhead like a kite on a string. On Wednesday the *Lincoln Tidings* ran a color feature about the lucky tourists from Seattle who had found unusually spectacular glass floats among the driftwood that weekend. The publicity brought a crowd into the Beauchamp Atelier the next weekend to blow clumsy green ovoids.

More than two weeks had passed since the odd physicist had brought his jar of polymer to the shop, and Daniel had nearly forgotten the whole thing. But then news came of a terrorist attack near Portland.

At the coffee shop where Daniel ordered his mocha and Reuben, the customers were all watching the television on the wall. A huge explosion had destroyed more than a square mile of the Boones Ferry Road area outside Wilsonville. Witnesses told of a blinding flash, a deafening boom, and a mushroom cloud. Everyone wanted to know how a terrorist cell could have developed an atomic bomb, and why they would target a suburban farm in Oregon. Shaky video footage from an Interstate 5 traffic helicopter showed a smoking crater perhaps five hundred feet in diameter, surrounded by scorched terrain. The death toll remained unknown, although dozens of people were being evacuated with burns and eye damage. Finally a government official reported that the blast couldn't have been caused by a nuclear device after all. Radiation levels were normal. There was no need for people to rush about in search of fallout shelters. The entire disaster might well have been caused by something as simple as a lightning strike on a fertilizer silo. Above all, the official said, everyone should remain calm. There was no imminent danger of a second such explosion.

Daniel frowned, struck by a sudden fear. He abandoned his lunch and walked back to his trailer. Where had he left those canceled checks? He had emptied his shirt pockets before doing the laundry. He opened the laundry room door, dumped the garbage basket on the floor, and rummaged through the debris.

Finally, beneath wads of lint, he found the three-hundred-dollar check. He spread it smooth on the floor and read the name in the upper left-hand corner:

Vasily Luchabnek
26515 SW Boones Ferry Rd.
Wilsonville, OR 97070

Was it possible, Daniel wondered, that the explosion wasn't caused by fertilizer, but rather by Vasily's experiment—by the glass sphere Daniel had helped create?

Daniel ventured out of his trailer, cautiously approaching the weedy area where he had thrown his own black sphere in anger more than a week ago. Since then garbage trucks had emptied the Dumpsters behind the supermarket. Hundreds of people had walked by on their way to the beach. Kids had ridden dirt bikes nearby. Anyone might have taken the strange black globe.

But it was still there, lurking ominously in a circle of dead plants withered by heat. Daniel backed away from the globe. Perhaps he was overreacting. It was just a glass float, after all. On a hunch, he decided to weigh it again. He went back to the trailer, smeared sunscreen on his face, pulled on a thick coat, and put oven mitts on his hands. Then he returned to the weeds. When he picked up the sphere it didn't seem very different. Although it had been in the sun for many days, the glass felt only slightly warmer than when he had thrown it away.

He carried it to his kitchen, set in on the scale, and waited for the green numbers to stop.

One hundred seventy-two grams.

He gave a sigh of relief. The sphere's weight was essentially unchanged. What had the scale read on the first day? A hundred sixty-nine? He reset the scale and tried again, just to be sure. Again the blinking lights stopped at one seven two.

Daniel frowned. The scale's plastic tray was getting so warm he was afraid it might melt. He moved the sphere to the stainless steel sink.

Then he walked to the living room, opened his laptop computer to a search engine, and typed in the question, "How much is 3 grams of light?"

A moment later the screen filled with blue links, most of them useless: "Low low prices on 3 grams of light!" "Books on 3 grams of light, starting at just 99 cents!"

But there was also a link to an online chat service called "Ask an Astrophysicist," sponsored by a library at Cal Tech.

Daniel did not like scientists, especially from big universities, but he retyped his question on the chat page.

A minute passed before a reply appeared: "Photons do have mass, but weight is meaningless in space. Where are your 3 grams of light?"

Daniel bit his lip. Telling the truth, that the light might be trapped in a glass ball in Oregon, probably was not a good idea. Instead he typed, "Suppose they are on Earth. Is this dangerous?"

The reply came back: "What wavelengths of light? Some have more energy than others."

Daniel tried to recall what Vasily had said. He typed, "Only visible light, I think."

A minute passed with no response. Then two minutes. Then five. After ten minutes Daniel was about to give up when the screen flickered. "Three grams of visible light focused on the Earth's surface would have the energy of a thirteen megaton thermonuclear device."

There was a pause, and then the screen added, "What is your location?"

Daniel quickly flipped the laptop shut. He walked back to the kitchen and studied the ball in his sink. Then he covered it with an aluminum tray, took a can of beer from the fridge, and settled into the lawn chair on the back porch. He needed to discuss the matter with Pablo.

The seagull hopped from one sphere to another, examining Daniel quizzically.

"I know, I know," Daniel said, popping the lid of the beer can. He took a long swig and closed his eyes. "But it was my dream. Pure light, pure beauty, captured in glass. You're supposed to follow your dreams, aren't you? That's what Paul Coelho always said." Daniel had once tried to learn Portuguese in order to read the untranslated books of Coelho, the literary alchemist from Brazil who spun stories into gold.

Pablo stopped beside the new Earth ball, as still as the wooden birds on the coffee shop railing.

"Don't give me that," Daniel scowled. "I wasn't after the money. I'm an artist."

The seagull cocked his head.

Daniel took another drink of beer. "My problem was getting mixed up with scientists. They say they can cure all your problems. Hell, they even invent problems to solve. They talk about the end of the world as if it's actually their goal."

The seagull lifted his wings, as if preparing to fly, but then tucked them back in place.

Daniel stared at the bird, dumbfounded. "That's true. Vasily said he felt like he was about to explode. He said it was his 'terror and his dream.'"

The seagull screeched, *Kyee-ki-ki-ki-ki!*

"All right, so he knew all along. But art isn't science. I'm not blowing anyone up for enlightenment. Art doesn't destroy, it creates."

Kyee-ki-ki-ki-ki!

Daniel tossed his beer can into a wastebasket, slam dunk. He thought for a long moment. Then he went to get a tin of sardines for his seagull friend.

That evening a full moon rose like a glowing glass float, pocked with flaws. For six hours it pulled the ocean into Siletz Bay. Even the river couldn't escape. The estuary filled and filled. Water buried the clam flats and climbed the tarry pilings of Taft's dock. By midnight the bay could hold no more. Waves crashed on the bar with a syncopated thunder, fighting the bottled-up river. Harbor seals on the sandy tip of the Salishan Spit looked up, sniffing the change of tide. A beach log floated loose into the surf, as if it too sensed a rare chance to make a break for the open sea.

A single silver figure knelt at the mouth of the bay, where the current of the outgoing tide is swiftest. Midwinter moonlight washed him free of imperfection.

His warm hands held a black void above the water. "Follow your dreams, my beauty."

At first he had regretted leaving so much behind—his studio, his work, his home. He would miss Pablo most of all. But true art demands sacrifice.

He closed his eyes, ready now.

Slowly the black sphere took him in, dissolving him heart-first into the light. Then the glass relaxed, settling onto the water with its master. And Daniel floated away on the midwinter tide, toward the current that swirls forever into the North Pacific's gyre.

HEAVENS GATE

When Kitti Moulton finally decided her cancer treatments had become too awful she quit the Portland Opera, sold her Hillsdale duplex, and chartered a light plane to the Wallowa Mountains, the dramatic northeast Oregon range where she had spent her happiest vacations.

The Realtor who met her at the Enterprise airport introduced herself as "Sharon Acheron, Agent of the Sticks. Welcome to God's country."

Sharon wore jeans and drove a big dusty pickup. She didn't seem fazed that Kitti wore a scarf over her bald head, or that she could only speak in a whisper, or that her luggage included a virginal, a suitcase-sized keyboard instrument from the Renaissance.

"Let's start at Heavens Gate," Sharon suggested, steering her pickup down a gravel road between red barns and green alfalfa fields. Out Kitti's window the Wallowas rose like a purple castle, with patches of snow clinging to parapets.

"What's Heavens Gate?" Kitti whispered.

"The House of Tomorrow," Sharon replied, eyes on the road. "A five-acre ranchette carved out of the Zumwalt Prairie Preserve by a former Nature Conservancy donor. Just one bedroom, but high-tech everything. And a bonus view of Hells Canyon."

"Halfway between heaven and hell?" Kitti laughed breathily.

Sharon nodded. They talked about finances for half an hour as

THE OREGON VARIATIONS

the road narrowed and the farms gave way to rolling grassland. Then Sharon turned up a drive that spiraled to a glass chalet atop a knoll. The front door opened when Sharon placed her hand on a scanner. Lights dimmed on and off automatically as they walked the halls. The kitchen gleamed with silver, the galley of a starship. A red Chevrolet Volt charged on a cable in the garage. But what won Kitti's heart was the endless lap pool. Hidden pumps in a glass solarium sent a current of water along a six-foot-wide swimming lane. A single clap of the hands made the current speed up. A double clap slowed the flow. Three claps reversed direction, so you could swim towards the view of Hells Canyon instead of the Wallowas.

"This is perfect for my therapy," Kitti whispered. "Everything's perfect."

"Don't you want to see other homes?"

"No, I'll take this one."

"OK," Sharon replied. Then she added, "I should tell you that this property is covered by an agreement with the Nature Conservancy."

"That sounds even better."

Sharon hesitated. "The contract has a clause allowing the Conservancy to buy the property back at the same price if you decide to sell, or if—" her voice trailed off.

"I know," Kitti whispered. "If I die. Sure, I'll sign that."

Sharon breathed easier. "Good. A Nature Conservancy caretaker tours the preserve on a schedule, checking on things. Don't be surprised if Pete drops by every three days or so."

"Pete?"

Sharon smiled. "It's all part of the package."

The alpha male stopped at the edge of the pines, lifted his nose, and sniffed the evening air. The Buckhorn elk were still six hours ahead. They would probably reach timber before dawn. Pete was moving toward the Imnaha for the night. A juvenile badger was still digging up ground squirrel tunnels by the abandoned stock pond; the scattering rodents would be easy prey. But there was something else in the wind—something new and troubling. A woman. A dying woman. Yes, that was it: The glass house with the bogus alarm fence was occupied once again.

His yellow eyes scanned the horizon. Each new human home intruded on his territory. He sniffed again, wondering. Why had she come to his domain?

That afternoon Kitti drove the Volt back to Enterprise, following Sharon's pickup so she could learn the route. They stopped at the bank for Kitti to open an account. In Sharon's office they signed papers. Then Kitti bought a month's worth of groceries at the Safeway and drove back to Heavens Gate.

She had unpacked the car and put most things away when she suddenly woke up to find herself lying on the hall carpet. Fuzzy colored lights swam through the darkness. Her head felt like a cracked coconut.

A seizure: She had suffered another seizure. The doctor at OHSU had told her this would happen more frequently unless she let him cut open her brain to remove the tumor.

Kitti sat up, and the lights in the hall automatically turned on She crawled down the hall, opening doors in search of the bathroom. When she finally found it, she discovered that she had not yet unpacked her toiletries, including her headache medicine. She drank three double handfuls of water and let the tap run over her bald head.

She knew the seizures would kill her eventually. She would fall where there was no carpet, or she'd drown in that lovely new pool. Perhaps she would simply go to sleep in her bed and never wake up. She had accepted these risks. But it wasn't fair to endanger others. Unless there was some way to predict the seizures, she would have to give up driving. Then she would really be alone.

Had there been a warning? She remembered putting away the food, finding the refrigerator hidden in the knotty pine paneling. She had been walking back to the garage for a box of clothes when she heard a strange sound. She had stopped in the hall, listening: A breathy, muffled sound. An animal sniffing—unafraid and

THE OREGON VARIATIONS

curious. It had seemed so close.

And then she had awakened on the carpet.

The next day Kitti set up her virginal in the living room and began working her way slowly through the *Goldberg Variations*. If she couldn't sing, at least she could try to play the fourth and final set of Bach's musical exercises. The problem was that the pieces became more difficult the farther you went. And whenever she stopped, the silence was deafening.

She walked out onto the patio to survey the view — from the dark rim of Hells Canyon in the east to the bright granite peaks of the Wallowas in the west. In all that vastness she could not see a single person. This was what she had wanted, wasn't it? The solitude to explore deeper questions? But now she wondered if loneliness itself was the question.

She thought of Pete, the Nature Conservancy employee. What kind of caretaker was he? Perhaps he was a wild, sniffing animal, curious and unafraid.

By the third day Kitti found herself watching the gravel road from Enterprise, wondering which of the distant dust clouds might be the mysterious Pete, coming to check up on her. When she went for a swim that evening she directed the lap pool's current so she could breast stroke toward the mountains, keeping an eye on the road. But the few headlights turned aside long before Heavens Gate. The real estate agent had said Pete would come by every third day or so. Maybe today was the "or so."

Finally Kitti clapped her hands three times to change the current, and swam toward Hells Canyon instead.

That's when she saw the man on horseback riding up the butte. He wore a black hat — weren't good guys supposed to wear white? A rifle stuck out behind his saddle. He swung down and tied his horse to the patio railing. His spurs jangled as he walked around to the front door.

Kitti realized with some horror that she had left her clothes in the bedroom. Although she lived in a glass house, she hadn't seen anyone for three days, so she had worn a short white bathrobe to the pool.

The doorbell rang.

She scrambled out of the pool, cinched the terrycloth robe around herself as tightly as she could, and hurried through the house, leaving splattered footprints.

Before she could reach the bedroom, the doorbell rang again.

She had performed enough on stage that she stopped. Nobody rings twice for Kitti Moulton to make her entrance. She thumped back to the front door, barefoot, and opened it wide.

The man standing before her hadn't shaved in several days. Was he thirty, or forty? He wore a dusty jeans jacket. He touched the black brim of his cowboy hat with a gloved hand.

"Ms. Moulton?" He lowered his gaze slowly from her bald head, assessing the bare V of pink skin below her throat, the belt cinched about her waist, and the dripping legs beneath the terrycloth.

"I suppose you're Pete," she whispered, raising her head. "I didn't know the Nature Conservancy hired desperadoes."

"They hire wildlife biologists." Pete looked back to her eyes. "My job is to keep the Wallowa wolf pack out of trouble."

"Well. I'm not part of that pack."

"But you're in their territory. The Nature Conservancy has an interest in this house. They've asked me to drop by whenever I'm in the area to see if there's anything you're lacking."

"You mean, like clothes?" Kitti wanted to see how easily he would ruffle.

Pete smiled. He had a nice smile. "Anything you need, I'm here to help."

This time Kitti was the one who looked down. He had spoken the word "anything" with the casual command of a baritone star. She held the bathrobe together at her neck and said, "I'm fine."

"Then I'll be riding on." He touched his hat again and walked back around the house, each step accompanied by the timpani of his boot heels and the fading cymbals of his spurs.

Suddenly she wanted to call him back, to talk with him a little longer about something—anything. Pete was the only person she was likely to see for days, and she had sent him away like a pan-handler. She hurried through the house to the living room. When she opened the patio's sliding glass door, Pete was untying his horse.

She didn't know what to say.

He looked up.

"Where will you go?" she whispered.

He cocked his head to show he hadn't understood. "I suppose you have to whisper because of the cancer?"

She nodded. A cold wind from the mountains made her shiver.

Pete retied the horse, walked halfway to the glass door, and stood there, waiting.

Kitti bit her lip. She didn't have time for second chances. "I just wondered where you were going tonight."

"There's a shack toward the Imnaha."

"It's getting dark."

"Palooka knows the way."

She braced herself and whispered, "You could stay here. There's a hide-a-bed, and I made too much eggplant parmesan."

He studied her a while. Then he nodded and went to unsaddle his horse.

Pete knew his way around the house surprisingly well. He took a shower while Kitti changed into dark blue slacks and a ruffled cream blouse. She tried on a few of the wigs she had brought, but decided to leave her head bare. When she came out of the bed-room, Pete was in the solarium swimming the crawl toward the mountains. She should have been miffed that he hadn't asked per-mission, but he was naked and was swimming away from her in the brightly lit glass room. She watched the shiny muscles of his tanned shoulders flex with each stroke. Through the spray of his rhythmically pumping feet, his small white buttocks twisted left and right.

Kitti took a deep breath and went to the kitchen to heat up the eggplant. Ten minutes later Pete tapped on the half-open kitchen door. "Were you serious about dinner, Ms. Moulton?" He had shaved, exposing a bony jaw. His wet brown hair had been slicked back. Somehow he had found a clean blue shirt, but the jeans were still dusty. He was at least ten years younger than her. She should have been ashamed by her thoughts, but there just wasn't time.

"Call me Kitti," she whispered.

"Kitti. I like that."

While she filled his plate a faint howl drifted in from the night outside. She tilted her bare head toward the window. "Should I be afraid of your wolves?"

"That's a coyote. Wolves have a longer, lower song. You'll know it when you hear it. But no, you don't need to be afraid."

"Why not?"

Pete took a bite and raised his eyebrows, savoring the mix of sharp cheese, sweet tomato sauce, and musky oregano. Only when he had wiped his lips with a napkin did he speak. "Because, Kitti, no one has ever been killed by a wolf in the history of Oregon. Or by a bear or a cougar, for that matter."

"Never?"

"Never. Predators do everything they can to avoid people."

"But you hear about attacks."

"Provoked, misinterpreted, exaggerated. Often fabricated outright. When wildlife biologists are actually called in, we always find it's the wildlife that died." He loaded his fork. "My job is to keep Cerberus alive."

"Cerberus?" Kitti sat back. "I thought that was the three-headed dog who guards the gates of hell."

Pete nodded, chewing. He took a drink of water and said, "He's the new alpha male. He may not have three heads, but he's got three names. The tag on his collar says OR-7. That's how he's known to science. When he was two years old the Imnaha pack kicked him out. He wandered all the way to California and back, through half the counties in Oregon, looking for a mate. Nothing. When he returned to Wallowa County he killed the old top dog and took his place. By then environmentalists had named him Journey, the guardian of the gates of heaven. Ranchers call him Cerberus, guardian of the gates of hell. Three names. Same wolf."

"Maybe the same gate," Kitti whispered.

Pete put down his fork and looked at her. "You're not treating your cancer, are you?"

She shook her head.

"Are you in pain?"

"That's why I stopped the treatments," she whispered. "It was bad enough when they cut out my larynx. I lost my job and had to reinvent myself. But then it spread to my spine and started a tumor in my head. The radiation and chemo have to be strong enough to kill the cancer without quite hard-boiling your brain. That's when I lost my husband."

Pete lowered his eyes. "I'm sorry."

"Don't ever marry a musician. Their world is barely big enough for one ego, let alone two. Great lovers. Lousy partners."

When Pete didn't say anything, Kitti asked, "You have a sweetheart?"

"Sometimes."

"You want one tonight?"

That made Pete lift his head. "You sure?"

She put her hand on his. "I haven't had sex in three months. I never thought I'd miss it this much."

He turned her hand over, lifted it, and kissed each of her fingertips one at a time. A sudden tingling made Kitti catch her breath. How could such a simple gesture be so electric?

Slowly Pete ran a finger up her arm. At the same time he stood to move behind her. When his finger reached her shoulder he pressed himself against her back. His strong hands kneaded her shoulders a moment. Then his fingers slid to the top button of her ruffled cream blouse.

For the rest of that week Kitti devoted herself to practicing on her virginal. She had come to Heavens Gate to search for answers about music, not loneliness. One of the greatest puzzles she had encountered as a musician was the theme buried in Bach's *Goldberg Variations*. The composer had written the variations at the request of an insomniac prince. The nobleman wanted something his harpsichordist Goldberg could play to lull him to sleep. Thirty-one repetitions of a seven-note melody should have been simple and soporific. But Bach turned the work into a treasure map, flipping and shifting the theme with each piece, echoing it in musical rounds. Often he hid just one note of the true melody in each measure. The prince had lain awake listening, so enchanted that he rewarded Bach with a cup full of gold coins.

On the afternoon of the fifth day, Kitti awoke with her head on the keyboard, swimming in colored lights. The lights were brighter. The headache was worse. She was scared.

The score on her virginal stood open to the twenty-fifth variation, the darkest of Bach's works. Known among musicians as the "Black Pearl," the piece had allegedly been composed as a metaphor for Christ's suffering on the cross. The piece began with three sharps, but kept piling on accidentals until it became a cacophony of black notes. Near the end it cried out with the most excruciating chord in all of music — a painful, jangling seventh — at the moment God died.

Now she remembered: Throughout the Black Pearl she had heard the whimpered animal warnings of the gate's guardian. But she had kept playing. The same animal voice had presaged all of her seizures. Why did she always hear a wolf before blacking out?

The glass house felt cold. She wanted Pete to come hold her.

Orpheus once stole into Hades by soothing Cerberus with his harp.

Journey was not so easily fooled. He knew people were trouble. He made the pack circle wide when they smelled a dead cow by a dirt road. Had the cow been hit by a speeding metal machine? Had it tried to birth a breach calf? The smell was different, and when he ventured close enough to see the puffed-out carcass, he knew. It had died of bloat, eating the poisonous weeds that grew near an old hay storage shed. A cow has four stomachs, so gas can be fatal. You don't want to be the first to bite into a carcass like that. Vile green soup spews out.

But dead meat is dead meat, so Journey led the pack closer. He bit into the neck cautiously. The blood was still warm. Two of his pups lunged for the belly, the idiots.

Suddenly there was a flash and an explosion. This wasn't right at all! Journey barked for retreat. The pack ran into the night.

They regrouped at a temporary lair in a thicket. One younger she-pup straggled in late, dragging her rear leg. The blood speckling her side smelled of shotgun. The pack licked and licked, whimpering. But Journey knew she was lost.

"You're late," Kitti whispered when Pete tied his horse to her patio railing on the evening of her eighth day at Heavens Gate.

"Lost a wolf," Pete said. He stood his shotgun against the glass wall. Then he unbuckled the saddle and carried it toward the patio door."

"You think I'm going to invite you in?" Kitti asked.

He stopped. "Aren't you?"

She sighed. "Yeah. I've been watching for you for days. What took you so long?"

"Shit happens."

"Don't tell me it was Journey?"

"Nope." Pete tossed his black hat on the sofa and lumbered off toward the shower. "It was his daughter."

Kitti had to wait ten minutes before Pete came out of the shower. "Are you telling me that Journey's daughter is dead?"

He tied a blue towel around his waist. Beads of water still clung to the short brown hair curling on his chest. "No, we're sending her to a wolf rehab farm on the coast near Reedsport. Buckshot crippled her left haunch, though. She'll probably run again in six months, but we'll never be able to release her in the wild."

"Was it your shotgun?" Kitti glanced to the weapon beside the door.

Pete walked over, cracked open the breach, and showed her the oddly lumpy shells. "Bean bags. No, she was shot by Aaron Ferguson, a rancher's son. The boy said he'd seen the wolves tear the throat out of one of the Ferguson cows. He said he was afraid they would come for him next."

"Do you think that's true?"

"Yes."

She sighed. "I thought you said wolves don't attack people."

"They don't, but it's true a boy might be afraid." He sat on the sofa and looked out the window at the mountains. "That cow had a jagged wolf hole in her neck the size of your hand. But her belly was also about to burst from bloat. I can't prove which killed her."

"What do you think?"

"Here's what I know. This morning at breakfast old Hank Ferguson told his sixteen-year-old son to go cut some weeds that had sprung up near a hay shed. Hank was afraid the cattle would eat the weeds and get sick. But it's summer vacation, and the sixteen-year-old boy decided instead to get in his truck, pick up a girl, and spend the day at a chocolate shop in Joseph."

"You know all of that?"

Pete nodded. "Now here's what I think. By the time young Aaron got around to checking on those weeds, a cow really had died of bloat. At that point the boy had two choices. He could go home and confess that his laziness had cost the ranch a fifteen-hundred-dollar Hereford. Or he could hide in that hay shed with his shotgun until the wolves smell a dead animal and come to clean it up."

Kitti covered her mouth with her hand.

"If the boy tells the truth he'll get a tanning and probably lose his truck. If he waits in the shed the ranch gets a fifteen-hundred-dollar government check for the cow and there's one less wolf."

"But that's murder," Kitti whispered. "It's also cheating the government."

Pete looked up with a sad smile. "You heard about the restitution claim by a rancher in Montana? Last winter they had a sub-zero cold snap and five hundred of his sheep were killed in one night. By a wolf."

"Are you going to let the Ferguson boy get away with this?"

Pete shrugged. "What would happen if I told Hank that the heir to his ranch is a liar? As it is, the boy seems pretty sorry, and I think his dad suspects. Until recently they wouldn't let me on their ranch at all. The only time I've been there was last week, when they lost a pet goat out of their yard. They blamed that on wolves too. I told them the tracks were made by coyotes."

"We heard coyotes howling last week."

Pete nodded. "Today the Fergusons let me put fladry around their yard as a test."

"Fladry?"

Pete reached over to his jeans jacket and pulled out a strip of bright red plastic. "If you hang red flags every eighteen inches on a fence, wolves won't cross it. Coyotes don't care. No one know why."

Kitti pondered this. Wolves were mysterious animals. And a range rider's job involved more diplomacy than she had imagined.

"Listen," Pete said, standing up and straightening his towel. "You mind if I use that lap pool again?"

"No, but this time—" Kitti hesitated.

"What?"

"Can I join you?"

Pete broke into a slow smile.

"It's not that," Kitti said, blushing. "Well, it is. But I'm becoming afraid to go in by myself."

He studied her. "Is your cancer causing trouble?""

"Just blackouts, but I think they're getting worse."

He pulled her by the hand. "Come on, then, let's swim together."

"Let me change first." She slipped loose of his hand and hurried to the bedroom. For some reason she felt shy about undressing in front of him. But she had gotten used to living in a glass house. Once she was naked, she had no problem walking back through the house with just a towel. At the pool she dropped the towel on a yoga mat and slipped into the water with him.

For the first few minutes she swam slowly after him toward the mountains. Sunset melted cottony purple clouds from the summits. Then he clapped his hands to speed up the current, calling out, "Catch me if you can!"

Of course his kicking feet were hard to grab, and there wasn't room to pass, so she finally clapped her hands three times. That turned the current around and sent him chasing her toward Hells Canyon. When he actually caught her ankle and started reeling in her leg, the current swept them both into a jumble of arms and hips against the screen at the far end. He squirmed around until the current was pressing her against him, her wet breasts flattened to white ovals on his chest.

He kissed her ear and whispered, "Let's get out. I have an idea."

Kitti had the same idea. They climbed out to the yoga mat and made love, his wet, muscled body slowly sliding back and forth across her smooth skin. They came at the same time, one wave of joy after another. Then they lay side by side, listening to each other's breathing until the room lights assumed they were gone and dimmed to nothing.

A first star flickered in the mauve sky above the Wallowas. The sight made Kitti sad. You were supposed to wish on the first star of the evening, but she knew her wish would never be granted. Instead she raised herself to one elbow, touched a finger to Pete's lips, and whispered, "I'll heat up some pizza."

Half an hour later, the magic of their twilight swim had given way to a Red Baron pepperoni and two cans of beer on the kitchen counter.

Pete frowned. "I don't actually know much about you, Kitti. I mean, you have a strange little piano in the living room."

"It's a virginal."

"A what?"

"A small harpsichord that plucks the strings. It was built in Italy four hundred years ago. In the 1820s a shop in London restored and repainted it."

"You see?" Pete said. "I'm missing out on most of the story here."

"What do you want to know?"

"For starters, where are you from?"

"Lakeview." She took a drink of beer.

"Really? That's cowboy country. You don't seem like a ranch girl. I mean, other than the beer."

She sighed. "My parents started out on ranches, but they were deaf. My mother was born that way, and my dad was shaken so badly as a baby that he lost his hearing."

Pete set down his pizza. "Ouch."

"Back then disabled kids were sent to institutions, so they both wound up at the School for the Deaf in Salem. They grew up together, learning to sign, sharing rides home for vacations. When they graduated they got married and tried out various jobs in Lakeview—busing tables, bucking hay bales. Nothing really worked out until they found out they could make a decent living by taking in deaf foster children. By then the state was trying to mainstream deaf kids in regular schools. I grew up as their own biological miracle child, the voice of an angel in a mute house."

"They must have loved you very much."

Kitti peeled the pepperoni off her pizza and laid it aside. "Too much, perhaps. Because I was able to sing, they sent me to a boarding school in Portland for voice lessons."

Pete frowned. "The opposite of the School for the Deaf. But another institution."

"Exactly. Still, I was a star student. I made them proud by touring the world as an operatic alto. I married a violist. We did the Oregon Bach Festival in Eugene each summer with Helmut Rilling. We bought a house in Portland, where I got steady work with the opera."

"Until you developed laryngeal cancer."

"Yes." Kitti took another long drink of beer.

Pete began eating her pepperoni. "A while ago you said you had to reinvent yourself. How was that?"

She shrugged. "I knew American Sign Language. I did sign interpretation for operas, lectures, and plays."

"Spunky girl."

She smiled. "I was good at it, too. Especially for the operas in English, where they don't project superscript text above the stage. I signed so creatively that deaf people would come to concerts just to see me."

Her smile slowly dimmed. "And you know the rest."

Pete stood behind her chair and kneaded the muscles in her shoulders.

Journey perked his ears toward a sound in the night. The wind off the mountain slopes carried a faint echo of gunshots. He thought he recognized that pattern. When he heard a snatch of shouting a moment later, he was sure. Elk had triggered the motion sensor alarm at the McCully alfalfa fields. Loudspeakers broadcast a variety of threatening sounds that the elk had learned to ignore: gunshots, cowboys yelling, sirens, and even the thumping beat of the metal machines that fly. Real people might hear the alarm and come to chase the elk out of the alfalfa, but Journey doubted it. The alfalfa people didn't live nearby, and they didn't like to drive out to the irrigated fields in the middle of the night. Besides, elk didn't pay much attention to people anyway, especially not if the herd was chowing down on top-grade browse.

Elk needed wolves to teach them a lesson.

Journey roused the pack with a few sharp yips and led the way, sprinting across the prairie. The V of deadly shadows raced mile after mile toward the mountains. As they neared the loudspeakers, Journey slowed the pack to a trot. They panted, their long tongues hanging out. When the recorded cowboys began shouting again, a he-pup wrenched his head around, his yellow eyes wide with fear. Journey ignored him, trotting on to the eight-foot wire fence that was supposed to keep elk out. Strobe lights beside the loudspeakers blitzed the field with flashes. This too was supposed to scare elk. Instead the strobes outlined what appeared to be the entire Wallowa herd. Five hundred animals, plowing their way across the field, their heads carelessly hidden in deep alfalfa.

Journey didn't have to look far to find a hole in the fence large enough for a wolf. He waited until the entire pack was through. The smell of the elk made their nostrils flare and their blood race. Journey scanned the pack's circle of yellow eyes, sensing their lust for the chase. Then he turned toward the herd, crouched, and launched himself forward.

Almost at once a bull elk lifted his head, alfalfa hanging from his muzzle. He tilted back his rack of antlers and barked. Five hundred shaggy dark heads rose in unison, sniffing the air, perking their ears.

Wolves!

A cow elk bolted for the low spot they had beaten into the fence. A dozen others followed, and then a hundred.

A phalanx of eight big bulls stood their ground, their antlers lowered to meet the attack. But Journey swung wide, and the pack circled after him, already smelling the fear of the calves in the rear. Three of the bulls managed to turn and charge.

Journey yipped to hold back the pack. He couldn't afford to lose another wolf, not so soon after the she-pup had been taken. There were safer ways to take down an elk than by facing the antlers of a thousand-pound bull. Journey snarled, curling his lips to expose yellow fangs. At this signal the pack split up. Hidden by the alfalfa, wolves seemed to be everywhere, darting out of the dark to harass the bulls and slip past. The terrified bulls broke for the fence. A panicked yearling with his spike antlers in velvet misjudged the jump, caught a hoof in the wire, and went down. The rest of the herd escaped, but the wolves pounced on the young bull, ripping , tearing, and slashing until the fur on their heads was covered with the hot blood of the kill.

By the third week at Heavens Gate, Kitti was suffering blackouts almost daily. Her headaches were worse. On the evenings when Pete failed to show up, the glass house felt as lonely as a spaceship between stars. She fought her way through the most difficult of the *Goldberg Variations,* and was rewarded late one night when she turned the page to the thirtieth-first and final piece, titled "Quodlibet." It was a joy to play! An easy, harmonious crowd pleaser with the seven-note theme walking plainly through the measures, one note at a time, in the base, while the right hand fiddled with a variety of pleasant asides.

Then she noticed a footnote in tiny print at the bottom of the page. She didn't recall seeing this text before. Puzzled, she took a magnifying glass from the living room table and held the page up to the light.

"Do not be deceived by the obvious return of the theme, hidden since the opening Aria!" the footnote warned. Kitti frowned and read further.

"The Quodlibet is a four-part fugue in disguise, weaving in no fewer than three popular folk songs of Bach's day. The first of these, 'You Haven't Been to See Me For Ages,' is a tongue-in-cheek complaint about the long-lost theme. The second folk song takes a pot shot at the many frivolous variations you have just endured, using the lyrics, 'Cabbage and turnips have driven me away. If my mother had cooked me meat I would have stayed home longer.' The final folk song is a student hiking tune, suggesting that you have more to learn before your journey ends."

Kitti set the magnifying glass aside. Her headache had returned. She was confused, tired, and hungry. She left the keyboard and walked to the kitchen to boil an egg.

First there was a yip. Then the thrum of paws, running through the prairie. When she opened the refrigerator and heard the panting of a wolf, she was scared. If this was the opening aria of another seizure, she didn't want to be in the kitchen, a room full of sharp corners and granite floors. She hurried to the bedroom. She barely managed to throw herself onto the quilt before the world went black.

When Kitti regained consciousness the sun was in the west, surrounded by great swirls of colored lights. Her head pounded. Her stomach also ached, but it took her a while to realize this was because she was desperately hungry. She was still lying atop the bed. Her clothes were limp with sweat.

Eventually she gathered enough strength to get up, peel off her clothes, and take a shower. Then she dressed in yoga clothes — this wasn't a day when Pete was supposed to visit — and went to the kitchen. She boiled half a dozen eggs, ate them all, and was still hungry.

The digital wall clock didn't surprise her (why shouldn't it be four in the afternoon?) but the date was a puzzler. Thursday the twenty-second? She had blacked out on Tuesday night. Could she really have slept for a day and a half? More frightening was the realization that the blackouts were getting longer. She might not wake up from the next seizure at all.

Kitti drank a quart of orange juice, practiced her yoga exercises, and listened to Pachelbel. She had sagged onto the sofa with her eyes closed when she was startled by a tapping at the glass door.

Pete slid open the door, balancing his saddle on his shoulder. "Weren't you expecting company?"

"No, I mean—" She blinked at him, bewildered. "I sort of lost a day."

He set down his saddle and knelt beside her, his elbow on his dusty knee. "Are the seizures worse?"

She nodded.

"Listen, Kitti. This would be the time when you tell me to drive you into town. Heavens Gate is awfully remote for someone in your condition."

"I know the risks." She pursed her lips. "You don't know what hell is until you've seen what the doctors in Portland would do."

"All right. Then what do you want me to do?"

"Seriously?"

"Seriously."

She smiled. "What I want is for you to make me dinner, tell me about your day, and put me to bed."

"Done." Pete stood up. "You got eggs?"

"Anything but eggs," Kitti pleaded. "I just ate six."

"OK." He ran his hand over the stubble on his jaw. "How about pancakes?"

"Sounds wonderful."

As it turned out, Pete was such an inexperienced cook that Kitti had to coach him all the way through the pancake process. But this was fun. She hid a grin when he didn't know what baking powder was. Then he poured the flour into the milk and couldn't get rid of the resulting lumps, even with an eggbeater.

"How's the wounded wolf?" Kitti asked.

Pete poured four circles of batter into an iron skillet. "She's in good hands. She'll probably wind up at the Winston Wildlife Safari."

"What about the boy who shot her?"

"Haven't heard from the Fergusons since they let me put fladry on their fence. I guess they haven't lost more goats." Pete frowned. "It kind of surprises me, though, that the coyotes haven't struck again. And that the wolves are letting them get away with it."

"What do you mean?"

"Well, wolves usually don't pay much attention to coyotes. Wolves aren't particularly fond of coyotes in their territory, but it's like a cop with bicycles thieves. A cop isn't going to bother tracking down a missing bike here and there. But if the thieves start stealing cars, the cop cracks down hard."

Kitti pointed to the smoking pancakes. "I think they're done."

"Oh, sorry." He scooped the blackened disks onto a plate. "Can you eat these?"

"With enough butter and syrup, I could eat a Presto-Log."

Pete poured the batter for another four pancakes. "The week's big wolf news is from the foot of the mountains."

"Oh?" Kitti tried a bite of pancake. It was charred, but she was hungry.

"Journey took the pack over to the McCully hayfield, just three miles from Joseph. The McCullys have tried everything to keep elk out of that alfalfa farm. Nothing worked until Journey showed up. He spooked them right back up into the mountains."

"So Journey's a hero in Joseph?"

Pete laughed. "A wolf three miles from town? People are locking up their pets at night."

Kitti set down her fork. "You can't win, can you?"

"Ten years ago there weren't any wolves in Oregon. Now that they're back, it's taking some time to put our house in order. But we'll figure it out."

After the pancakes, Pete stood behind her chair, rubbing the muscles at the back of her neck. "Anything else you need?"

"Thanks, Pete, but not tonight."

"You have a headache?" He smiled.

"I'm just tired. All I want is to lie in bed with you beside me."

"My pleasure."

While Kitti went to prepare for bed Pete fetched a small sack from his saddlebag. She was lying in her nightgown, propped up with a pillow, when he ceremoniously opened the bag above the bed.

"What on earth?" she asked.

He poured out a clattering stream of gold coins onto the quilt. It took her a moment to realize they were actually chocolate coins wrapped in gold foil.

Pete grinned. "I used to get chocolate money as a kid in my Easter basket. It's silly, but when I was at the chocolate store in Joseph checking up on the Ferguson boy, I saw a bag of coins and thought of you."

Kitti peeled back a doubloon to expose dark chocolate. "You are the sweetest man ever."

His hand tipped the brim of an imaginary hat. "It's not always easy working in God's country. But it's all part of the package."

Journey smelled blood in the night air, and he wasn't happy about it. There was too much blood, and it was too close to the house with the shotgun boy. This wasn't a job for the pack. The house was dangerous. Journey trotted off from the lair casually, in the wrong direction. Then he circled around and headed toward the blood by himself.

As he neared the ranch he decided the smell belonged to a goat. Something had slaughtered it silently near the ranch house. A rival wolf? If so, it was a daring foe and an expert killer.

Journey crept closer. But he stopped in confusion at the edge of the yard. Fladry! The entire yard was surrounded by a wire with the red flames of Hades. No wolf in its right mind would cross that boundary! Then who?

He crouched behind a sagebrush, waiting. The full moon rose free of the clouds over Hells Canyon, casting the house and the metal machines in white. Still he waited.

The moon was high when two shapes loped out from the shadow of a metal machine. They turned their heads warily left and right. Then they ducked through the red flagging as if it weren't even there.

Coyotes!

Journey bared his teeth with rage. He shot forward, sprinting with his ears back. He lunged for the neck of the first coyote, but it twisted aside and Journey hit it full in the flank. The blow sent the coyote rolling. Incredibly, the second coyote dared to nip at Journey's leg, narrowly missing the hamstring. Journey spun and charged, snarling. The two coyotes took off in opposite directions. Journey let the first one escape; the one he had bowled over would learn respect another night. For now Journey was determined to chase down the one that had nipped his heel.

Journey and the coyote tore across the prairie, their tails streaming behind like the feathered shafts of arrows. Journey was twice as large and much faster, but the coyote in front zigzagged, throwing Journey off his stride. Time after time, Journey lunged and missed as the coyote dodged. Two miles they ran — then three — then four. Journey didn't care if he had to run all night. Finally, at the hill with the glass house, the coyote faltered enough that Journey bit off half his tail. The exhausted coyote sprinted another hundred yards up the butte. Then he turned, ears back, in the desperate hope that this submissive pose might spare his life.

Journey broke the coyote's neck with a single bite. He shook the limp gray body like a rag. Then he tossed it aside, threw back his head, and howled.

He pawed the coyote's carcass for a while, catching his breath. Only then did he look up and realize where he was. Above him the moon glinted off the glass walls of the woman's house. The dying woman was an intruder on his territory too. Journey reigned over this prairie between worlds. Insolent coyotes were to be punished with death. Elk lived by his rules, or not at all. But people were spirits of a different order. Even a dying woman filled his heart with uncertainty.

Damn her!

Journey looked to the moon and loosed a long, terrifying howl of anguish. He was a god!

When Kitti awoke, Pete was no longer in her bed. She sat up to look out the window. His horse was gone. She yawned and stretched, marveling that every part of her felt good. She showered. Then she dressed in her black concert gown, just for the hell of it. She even put on a cute little blond wig. Why not?

In the kitchen she tossed out the leftover black pancakes with a laugh. Instead she poured a bowl of granola. The yogurt containers in the fridge had started to puff out, so she opened a can of evaporated milk. As she sat at the granite breakfast bar, eating her cereal, she decided this would be a day to straighten up. She had unpacked in a hurry and had never really taken the time to clean house thoroughly.

So she put *The Magic Flute* on the music system and spent the day whispering along with the Queen of the Night as she breezed about the House of the Future, putting her affairs in order.

Kitti lit a candle to accompany her dinner, an excellent frozen beef stroganoff with two cans of beer. For dessert she opened a bottle of Terminal Gravity, a wildly hoppy India Pale Ale from the brewpub in Enterprise. She wished she had bought more of this peculiar dessert when she stumbled across it on her Safeway shopping trip almost three weeks ago.

Feeling a little light headed, she walked out to the living room, stood before the virginal, and bowed to an imaginary audience. "I shall now attempt," she whispered grandly, "to perform the entire keyboard works of Johann Sebastian Bach."

Of course she didn't have Bach's entire oeuvre on hand, but she had four full music books. So what if it would take half the night to play them all?

She sat down and opened the virginal, revealing the painting on the inside of the lid. It might have been a scene from a Jane Austen novel: a young woman in a long blue gown by a riverbank in the English countryside with a shaggy hunting dog leaping attentively at her side. Kitti opened the two-part inventions on her music rack, covering up most of the woman and the dog. Then she poised her curved fingers above the pear and cherrywood keys, and began to play.

Never had she played so beautifully! Every hour or so she bowed and announced a five-minute break.

By three in the morning she had worked her way through the *Goldberg Variations* to the final Quodlibet. The footnote she remembered at the bottom of the page was no longer there. Had she imagined it? Instead she now noticed the instructions, "Aria di Capo e Fine." She wasn't ready to go to bed, and the audience was applauding for more, so she turned back to the opening aria and played it again.

This time every note in the aria made sense. The theme was clear, one note per measure, walking through the piece as steadily as birthdays had walked through the years of her life. Ornaments and trills filled the story with all manner of frivolous fun, but they didn't change the clarity of the melody.

When she finished the audience sat silent, too spellbound even to applaud. Kitti began to close the music book.

Suddenly a howl rose up from the audience outside. It wasn't the jeer of a concert hall or the yip of a coyote, but rather the long, low voice of Journey.

Pete had said she would know the call when it came.

Solemnly, Kitti set the book of variations aside. She closed the lid of the virginal. Then she walked to the bedroom, set her wig on the nightstand and lay down on the quilt. The full moon shone through a skylight, illuminating her in a rectangle of silver. The mountains she loved rose in silhouette at her feet. Hells Canyon, the dark chasm she feared, lay at her head.

When Journey howled again — longer and more hauntingly this time — she closed her eyes and followed the call across.

Winter snows had frosted the Wallowas when Sharon Acheron met Nancy Fishbaum at the Enterprise airport. While Sharon drove her client out the long gravel road to Heavens Gate, they talked mostly about finances. At the house, Nancy admired the sweeping view, the space-age kitchen, and the electric car. But what really won her heart was the endless lap pool.

"This is perfect for my therapy," Nancy exclaimed. "Everything's perfect."

"Don't you want to see other properties?"

"No, this is it. I'll take it."

Sharon hesitated. "I should warn you that this particular property has a contract clause allowing the Nature Conservancy to buy it back at the same price. If you decide to sell, or if—" her voice trailed off.

"I know. If I die," Nancy said. "Sure, I'll sign that."

Sharon breathed easier. "Good. Pete will drop by every three days or so to see if there's anything you need."

"Pete?"

Sharon nodded. "It's all part of the package."

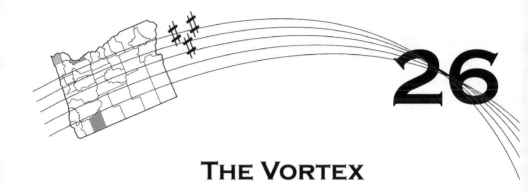

THE VORTEX

"Visit the *Oregon Vortex!*" the billboard shouted. "Home of the *House of Mystery!*"

Brian knew it was a tourist trap, but he pulled off Interstate 5 at the Gold Hill exit anyway, figuring he needed a chance to stretch his legs—and perhaps lighten his spirits after a stressful week in San Francisco. Did it matter that the corny Vortex billboard had a "For Sale" sign in the corner?

Following arrows, he drove through a yuppified gold mining town where ancient brick buildings housed beauty salons and wine tasting rooms. Then the signs sent him up a canyon past trailers and horse barns and slopes full of madrone trees. He pulled into a gravel parking lot and walked a narrow bridge across a creek to a gift shop.

"Welcome to the Vortex. Just one?" the girl behind the counter asked.

Brian checked the prices posted on the wall. "Sure." He could afford ten bucks, even on a whim.

"You'd better hurry. The tour's about to leave." She slid him a ticket. On the front was a drawing of what looked like a glowing green basketball. Wavy text below the illustration explained, "The Oregon Vortex is a spherical field of force, a glimpse into a strange world where the improbable is commonplace and everyday physical facts are reversed."

For the next forty minutes Brian and half a dozen other bemused tourists were herded by a vivacious teenage guide through the woods to a sagging wooden shed, where the sloping floor made people stagger to the left. A ball that rolled out the window on a plank miraculously rolled back, apparently uphill. An old broom stood up on its bristles, balancing at a weird angle. But people didn't really look shorter or taller depending on where they stood, despite what the tour guide said.

Back at the gift shop Brian asked, "So this place is for sale?"

The girl at the register cocked her head. "Not the whole place. Just the Vortex."

"And what exactly is the Vortex?" Brian asked.

"You know." The girl shrugged, chewing gum. "A spherical field of force."

Gert Samson, owner of Samson's Book Bunker, had learned her business the hard way, through years of battle. When wounded, she retreated to strategize in the solitude of the rare book room, a windowless sanctum on the fourth floor. Amid leather spines, marbled endpapers, and gilt lettering she shoved aside her desk's laptop computer and uncapped a Monteverde fountain pen. Some lists should be executed only in ink. Such was the secret archive of her war with Amazon, the giant that had laid waste to so many other Portland bookstores. So far the battle list had been a litany of strategic retreats:

> *Train Brian.*
> *Don't cut staff.*
> *Sell pens, not iPads.*
> *Host events with real, live authors.*
> *Create a web page.*
> *Cut hours, not staff.*
> *Sell toys along with children's books.*
> *Post a blog of staff picks.*
> *Don't cut staff, but don't replace those who leave.*
> *Sell puzzles among the fiction.*

Start selling the rare books on eBay.
Start cutting staff.

Gert tightened her lips. Employees were like family. The giant must think he was winning, sucking her into the black hole that had swallowed Murder By the Book, The Catbird Seat, and so many other stores. But Samson's had bunkered in this old brick building for a century, and like every successful giantkiller, Gert had one last weapon in reserve. She touched the gold nib of her pen to the list, writing in careful longhand,

Give Brian the Box.

Gert remembered the day thirty-seven years ago when her father had suddenly retired, announcing that he wanted to write a novel about runaway missionaries in a vineyard. "You already know how to run the bookstore," he had reassured her. "The rest is just good judgment." Gert had asked, "But how do you get good judgment?" He had replied, "Experience." "And how do you get experience?" Her father had laughed and said, "Bad judgment."

Perhaps because of that memory, Gert hesitated a day and a half before calling in her son.

With his pants hanging low, Brian shambled into Gert's rare book bunker sleepily, as if he still stayed up all night playing online Scrabble. Now that he no longer lived at home, Gert didn't know how he spent his nights. The quiet young man became more of a mystery to her each year. But perhaps that is what you need in a secret weapon, she thought. Perhaps that was why her father had trusted her.

"So what's up, Mom?" Brian shook stringy hair out of his eyes. "Trying to hack into Amazon's high command again?"

For a moment Gert considered changing her mind. "No, we can't attack the giant head-on. Instead I want you to drive to San Francisco."

Brian blinked. "Why?"

"To open a branch. I'm tired of retrenching, and to be honest, we're up against a wall."

"You're mixing metaphors, Mom."

"Don't talk back. We need to turn our nest egg into a cash cow."

Brian bit his lip. He had investigated the bookstore's cash flow. There was no reserve. All he had found was a slow cash leak. When he found out which employee was pilfering from the till, they'd be able to cut one salary. That might be enough to buy the store another few months before the lights went out.

Gert unlocked a desk drawer. She lifted out a stack of ancient check registers. Then, to Brian's surprise, she removed a wooden panel that served as a false bottom. From the space underneath she withdrew an old-fashioned Roi-Tan cigar box. Gert set the box on the desk and flipped back the lid.

Bundles of hundred-dollar bills lay packed inside like Monopoly money.

Brian opened his mouth. But then he closed it again. Suddenly he was struck by the suspicion that he had found the embezzler. Could his own mother have been dipping into the till?

"I know how surprised you must be," Gert said. "Every week for twenty years I've managed to set aside two hundred-dollar bills. When times were tough it was hard to keep my resolve. But I knew times could get tougher, and that's when we would need an emergency fund most."

"So you've—" Brian wanted to say *stolen,* but that wasn't true. She owned the store. "You've collected a million dollars in a cigar box?"

"Use your head." Gert marveled that a knack for numbers could skip generations. Her grandfather Friedrich, the founder of the Book Bunker, had been as cagey a businessperson as herself, but her father and her son seemed to only understand words. "It isn't a million dollars. Twenty years times fifty-two weeks times two hundred dollars is a little over $200,000."

"Whatever. And now you want me to use it for some kind of investment?"

"Someday soon I'll have to retire, and then the whole business will be out of my hands." Gert pushed the cigar box toward him.

Her eyes dampened as she added, "You already know how to run the bookstore. The rest is just good judgment."

She had been hoping that Brian would ask how to get good judgment.

Instead her son cast a strangely distant look at the cigar box. "Wallace Stevens once said that money is a kind of poetry."

"Wallace Stevens?" Gert asked. "The poet?"

"Yeah, he sold poetry, so he knew what he was talking about. But Stevens was smart enough to keep his day job. He worked at an insurance agency in Connecticut."

"Brian, I need you to focus. The fate of the Bunker is in your hands."

"I know, Mom." Brian tucked the cigar box under his arm.

Brian's trip to San Francisco had not gone well. He found a dozen bookstores that had closed or were about to close. He could make a down payment on one that was small, or buy a large warehouse in an out-of-the-way district, or rent a large space at a good location for eighteen months. None of these seemed like a good option. He went to Berkeley and talked to the former owners of Cody's Books. They said the only things they had sold before going under had been video games and toys. Bookstores were dying. People bought from Amazon, the evil giant. "You'll need a miracle to keep Samson's alive."

Brian was driving back to Portland when he saw the sign for the Oregon Vortex. This was exactly the kind of frivolous detour his mother had never allowed on road trips. Perhaps that's why it was irresistible.

"How can you sell a force field?" Brian asked.

The girl at the gift shop shrugged. "Let me get the owner. I think she's in back."

Five minutes later a wrinkled old woman in a green paisley bathrobe hobbled up to the ticket desk. "You? A long-haired kid wants to buy the Vortex?"

Brian laughed uneasily. "No, I was just curious. If the Vortex is so important, how could you sell it?"

The old woman eyed him darkly. "The Vortex is an ancient spirit. But like you, it is curious. It discovered gold here in 1853. Since then it has grown tired of the House of Mystery. The Vortex is looking for a new home."

Brian shook his head. "I've done the tour. It's claptrap hokum. Nobody's going to buy a cutover forest with a crooked shed."

"The forest and the shed are not for sale," the old woman replied.

"Then what are you actually selling?"

The old woman crooked her finger toward a window overlooking the creek canyon. "Hope. Magic. The Vortex is a power that can bring down giants."

For once Brian found himself at a loss. "Giants? And where is this Vortex of yours?"

The old woman unlocked a drawer beneath the counter. She withdrew a Roi-Tan cigar box. "The treasure temporarily lives in here. With it I will sell the rights to the name of the Oregon Vortex. We will rededicate our tourist destination as the Ranch of Mystery. The only true and original Oregon Vortex will be yours."

Brain swallowed. "At what price?"

The old woman smiled. "Two hundred thousand dollars. In cash."

How could she have known that Brian had exactly that much in a similar cigar box in his Subaru? The coincidence was uncanny. Brian reached for the lid of her box.

"No." She pulled the box back. "You must not open the box until you are safely in the Vortex's new home."

"You won't even let me look? How do I know the box isn't empty?"

She tilted the box slightly. Something rattled, as if it were rolling to one side. "The power of the Vortex is spherical. You can choose its new center. But I warn you: Once you lift the lid, a century may pass before the spirit will be willing to go back into a box."

Even Brian couldn't explain why he suddenly wanted so badly to possess this box. Perhaps because he would be embarrassed to return from San Francisco without an investment. Perhaps because it seemed like an even trade, one cigar box for another. But there was something more, something he couldn't explain.

The old woman had caught him with the word *Hope*.

Back in Portland, Brian's doubts multiplied. Rain pelted the dark streets. The bookstore had closed for the evening but the windows were lit, so he knew his mother must be working late. As he walked up the stairs to the rare book room the cigar box seemed less valuable with each step. Instead of $200,000, he now had a box that rattled mysteriously. He was beginning to suspect that his mother might not be pleased.

When Brian opened the door of the rare book room, his mother looked up from her computer screen with a smile of relief. "Thank God you've brought it back."

She had always reminded Brian of a bulldog, with her gruff manner and stocky frame. But now Brian realized how much she looked like a bird. Age and worry had made her fragile. The bones stood out on her face. Her neck seemed to have shrunk to wrinkles of skin. His mother had grown old.

This realization was so overwhelming that it took Brian a moment to register what she had said.

"Brought it back? You mean the box?"

"Of course. You didn't open a branch in San Francisco."

"Yeah, I decided not to." Brian frowned. "All the bookstores are closing down there too. So I was driving back, and — "

"Stop!" Gert's bulldog voice had not aged. "You did the right thing. And to think I've been lying awake worrying. The Samson blood runs strong."

"Actually," Brian began, his long hair hanging over his face.

But Gert was unstoppable now, her old strength returned. "You are the great-grandson of Friedrich Samson, the silent partner of Arnold Blitz and Henry Weinhard."

Brian had heard the story before. His mother repeated it whenever she was battling back from another Amazon setback. He knew not to interrupt.

"Friedrich was a business genius, a teetotaler who owned a brewery." Gert reached for a black-and-white photograph at the back of her desk. A broad face with a handlebar mustache stared sternly into the camera's eye.

"When Oregon introduced Prohibition in 1916 he was smart enough to sell his share of Blitz-Weinhard. While the brewery struggled, bottling root beer and sodas, Friedrich opened a bookstore in a warehouse across the street. It was an instant success. The man understood Portland."

Gert sighed. Brian disliked the next part of her monologue, but he waited for it anyway.

"Grandpa Friedrich died before I was born, and my father took over the bookstore." Gert set the photograph back, her voice cold. "Before I was old enough to know better, he had squandered our fortune remodeling the building. Ever since, it's been an uphill struggle to balance the books and keep the store afloat."

The mixed metaphors made Brian wince. "I'm not like those people, Mom."

"Yes you are." Gert took the cigar box from him and set it on her desk. "You brought back our fortune. Now we can do what we should have done all along. Instead of shooting from the hip, we'll double down on what worked for Grandpa Friedrich: selling books."

Gert opened the cigar box.

Inside was a single, round pine cone. In the darkness of the otherwise empty box, its bristles glowed a faint green.

"What the hell?" Gert muttered.

"I traded the money for an investment, like you said," Brian said.

"You traded $200,000 for a pine cone?"

Brian shrugged. "The old woman who sold it said it was magic."

Gert's voice rose threateningly. "A *magic* pine cone?"

"It's the Oregon Vortex, Mom. A spherical field of force." Without much conviction he added, "See? It's glowing."

"It's glowing because somebody has sprayed it with glow-in-the-dark paint." Gert's face had turned red. She lifted the pine cone in her shaking hand. "Did you really trade our fortune for *this?*"

Brian nodded fearfully.

"Idiot!"Gert hurled the pine cone against the bookshelves on the wall. Then she pounded her computer keyboard with her fist. "That's it. I'm out of here."

"What do you mean?"

"Quitting, leaving, giving up. I'm retiring."

"But Mom!"

"You threw our money down a rat hole. Now you can try digging out on your own." Gert looked about the room, as if checking to see if she had left behind anything she really needed.

"But what will you do, Mom?" Brian asked.

She took a long breath. "I'll move to our cabin in Cannon Beach. Maybe I'll start writing that history book I've always talked about."

This was the moment when Brian might have changed her mind. He could have apologized for a stupid mistake and begged her to stay on. Instead he stood there silently, his eyes lowered.

Gert put the photograph of Friedrich Samson in her purse. Then she walked to the door and paused, looking back at her son. "You're not an idiot, Brian."

"You don't think so?"

She tightened her lips. "You're a mystery. A dreamer. I'll never understand what makes you tick. But as of this moment, you are the sole owner of Samson's Book Bunker."

Her voice was thick as she added, "Good luck, son." Then she closed the door and strode past the bookshelves of the art & architecture section. She clomped down the stairs, turning off the lights on each floor as she went.

Perhaps the lights in the rare book room had been left on a timer, or perhaps they were somehow wired to the electrical system in the foyer, because all of the lights went out when Gert left the building.

Brian found himself alone in dark. Even the ghostly shimmer of the laptop screen did little to dispel the gloom. His mother had left the computer running on a page from Amazon.

Amazon was the giant lurking in the room, the bane of independent bookstores. The Samsons had held out for years. But now it looked as if the giant had finally won.

Brian sank into a chair, buried his face in his hands, and cried. How, he wondered, had he managed to ruin everything so thoroughly? If he wasn't an idiot, then he was surely a heartless wretch for disappointing his mother. He was a fool for wasting a last chance to save the family business. And he was a sucker for letting a crazy old lady in a tourist trap con him into buying a pine cone for $200,000.

For a long time he sat there, alone in the dark, doubting everything he had done.

But Brian was young enough, and resilient enough, that he eventually sat up, wiped his eyes, and looked around. He owned the store. The rare book room was now his office. Even if he had squandered a fortune and lost the aid of a seasoned businesswoman, he was not entirely without resources. The bookstore had no debts. The cash leak had been stopped. He had a loyal staff, although their numbers would necessarily decline as the store withered.

And of course he had a pine cone.

Where was the damned thing, anyway?

His mother had thrown the pine cone so hard that it had knocked a book or two off the shelf. Apparently the cone had fallen back between the bookcase and the wall. Now that Brian's eyes had adapted to the dark, he could vaguely see a greenish glow behind the books.

Brian turned on the room's overhead lights — which now seemed to be functioning fine — and inspected the gap in the bookshelf. Standing akilter on the left of the hole was an autographed first edition of Ken Kesey's *One Flew Over the Cuckoo's Nest*. To the right was Bernard Malamud's *The Magic Barrel*. He took these volumes carefully off the shelf so he could reach his arm down behind the bookcase for the pine cone.

Brian was expecting to find *A Wizard of Earthsea*. Ursula LeGuin's fantasy trilogy seemed the most likely thing to have been shelved between Kesey's K and Malamud's M. And so he was puzzled when his hand bumped into something hard and round, apparently attached to the wall.

A doorknob?

Brian sat back, thinking. The room on the other side of the wall held the military history collection. It was not supposed to have a door on this side.

Curious now, he began emptying the bookcase, stacking the volumes beside the desk. Even then the wooden shelves proved tough to budge. The bookcase had been nailed to the wall in three places. At this point he would normally have hesitated. But now that he owned the store, he simply braced his foot against the wall, gripped the bookcase with both hands, and yanked it loose. Plaster flew as the nails ripped out.

Behind the shelf an antique ceramic doorknob protruded absurdly from a smooth wall. On the floor below it lay the pine cone, along with the *Wizard of Earthsea*, a rubber ball, and a Twinkies wrapper.

Brian tossed the pine cone into its cigar box and stacked the LeGuin books with the others by the desk. Then he put his hand on the doorknob. It turned with a click, but opened nothing. He thought about this a moment. He tried rattling and jerking the doorknob. When this had no effect he kicked the wall. A hairline crack appeared in the plaster—a large, rectangular crack that suggested a door.

At once Brian thought of his grandfather, the man who had wasted the family's fortune remodeling the building before his mother was born. What had his grandfather changed that proved so expensive? Was there something he had wanted to hide? Obviously Brian's mother had never discovered this door.

Brian fetched a hammer and a screwdriver from a broom closet. Then he set to work chiseling plaster. Slowly he revealed an old-fashioned, five-panel wooden door. He used the hammer's claw to pry loose a long strip of baseboard molding that had been nailed across the bottom of the door.

Finally he tried turning the doorknob once more. This time the door swung toward him, squeaking painfully. Behind was a brick-lined shaft with a small metal landing. A chimney? No, when Brian looked down the narrow shaft he could see a wrought-iron staircase spiraling into the void. Above him a pyramidal glass skylight glowed with the lights of the city. He knew that similar antique skylights graced ceilings throughout the fourth floor. Brian remembered counting a dozen of them as a boy, on the day he had sneaked up the back fire escape to the roof. He had never thought to count the skylights from below. Were there otherwise only eleven?

The brick shaft had no obvious light switch, and he didn't have a flashlight, so he unplugged the laptop computer and used its glowing screen as a light. Spiderwebs spanned the iron railings of the spiral staircase. The musk of old books and earth rose from the depths. To his surprise there was no door on the third floor, nor on the second. The iron stair kept spiraling down.

At the bottom of the shaft the steps ended beside an arched brick portal. Cobwebs and dust obscured a sign across the top. Brian brushed it clean with his sleeve. Then he held up the laptop for light. Art Deco lettering spelled out the words, *Fred Samson's Book Bunker.*

Why would his great-grandfather Friedrich have built an entrance to the bookstore at the bottom of a shaft?

Brian opened the metal door beneath the arch. Beyond was a broad hallway, its tiled floor strewn with rubble. As far as Brian knew, the building did not have a basement. But the musty air and the vaulted brick ceiling told him he was underground.

Glass-doored bookcases lined the hall. Brian opened one at random and took out a dusty hardback. The blue eyes of a beautiful woman gazed from the sky above a Coney Island carnival. It was F. Scott Fitzgerald's *The Great Gatsby.* But this was a first edition from 1925, apparently new. The next book Brian pulled out was a paperback, its cheap brown cover seemingly fashioned from a grocery bag. The old German lettering inside a red frame read, "Franz Kafka—*Das Schloss.*" But this wasn't a reprint. It was the original Prague press run from 1926.

Such books might have been commonplace in the roaring twenties, but they were treasures now. Brian ventured onward, holding the laptop ahead of him as a dim torch. To his disappointment, the bookcases soon ended. Instead the hall opened up into a large room where clusters of tables and chairs retreated into the darkness amid pillars. Cobwebbed chandeliers hung in each arch of the vaulted ceiling. Had it been a meeting room, Brian wondered?

He explored to the right, scouting the perimeter. Framed on the brick wall were old photographs of German marching bands, horse-drawn fire brigades, and leather-helmeted football teams.

After fifty feet he discovered another hallway, a sort of tunnel, faintly lit by rows of small purple squares in the ceiling. He puzzled a moment about the purple lights. When a shadow passed across them, he realized they must be embedded in the sidewalk beside the bookstore. He had walked over these purple squares countless times on his way to work. Now that it was night, they were lit from above by streetlamps. Pedestrians overhead darkened them in passing.

He was in a forgotten basement of the bookstore building. And judging from the position of the sidewalk squares, the tunnel extended underneath the street toward the Blitz-Weinhard block. He ventured farther into the tunnel, but it ended after a few yards, blocked by barrels, bottles, and debris.

Suddenly Brian realized what the tunnel meant. He turned around and strode to the center of the large room. A huge crystal chandelier hung above a wooden dance floor. Behind it rose the carved woodwork, beveled mirrors, and dusty bottles of a gigantic, ornate bar. And framed on the wall above the middle of the bar was an oil portrait of a stern, broad-faced man with a handlebar mustache.

Friedrich Samson had obviously been a cleverer businessman than the family stories suggested. When Prohibition arrived, he had opened a speakeasy in a basement across the street from the brewery, delivering illegal barrels through a tunnel. The bookstore above ground had primarily been a decoy. Thirsty clients would have climbed to the rare book room on the fourth floor, opened a hidden door, and descended a spiral staircase to Samson's real Book Bunker. Friedrich had obviously understood Portland.

Friedrich's son, however, had abandoned the old tavern. He

had plastered over the entry door. He had lost the goose that laid golden eggs.

Brian set the laptop on the bar and looked out into the dark arches of the old speakeasy, already considering options. He would change as little as possible. "Fred's Book Bunker" was the perfect name for a pub beneath the bookstore. He might even be able to reopen the tunnel, adding a wheelchair-accessible entrance to the condos and shops of the old brewery block.

But would it be enough? Brian glanced at the laptop. The screen was still lit with a page showing Amazon's logo, a curving arrow that resembled a crooked half-smile. The giant may not yet have won, but he was smirking. And he was coming.

Brian noticed that his mother had been trying to hack into Amazon's high command yet again, a hopeless attempt by a desperate woman. A row of black dots showed that she had even tried typing something into a password box.

Or no—now that Brian thought about it, the last thing his mother had done was to pound the keyboard. She had been in a such a rage after opening the Vortex box that she had thrown a pine cone at a bookshelf, inadvertently revealing a doorknob that led to the family's lost treasure. Only then had she hit the computer with her fist.

Who knew what gibberish she might have typed with her balled hand in that moment of anger? The password screen hid the actual characters, displaying only black dots.

An eerie presentiment made Brian's skin prickle.

He lifted a finger over the keyboard.

Carefully, he pressed "Enter."

Instantly Amazon's smirk vanished, replaced by the greeting, "Welcome, Jeff Bezos." A moment later the entire hierarchy of Amazon's internal system began scrolling onto the screen.

Brian's mind raced. It was 11:43 p.m. In a few hours the real Jeff Bezos would walk into his palatial Seattle headquarters and regain control of his empire.

Until then, however, an ancient, curious spirit had taken over as CEO of the world's largest virtual bookstore. They were entering a strange world where the improbable is commonplace and every-day physical facts are reversed.

The Oregon Vortex had hacked into Amazon's mainframe.

And Brian had a feeling the giant was going down.

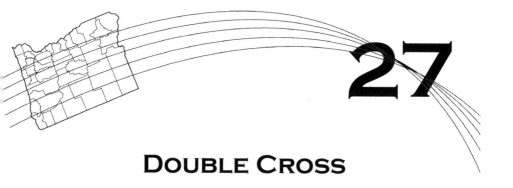

DOUBLE CROSS

ACROSS

1 One sixteenth of a peck
5 Champagne type
8 Raised trains in Chicago
11 Vandenberg, e.g.
14 Spark _____
18 Peter Pan pirate
19 Jazz singer Fitzgerald*
20 Sass
21 G.I. battle chow
22 Verdi opera set in Egypt
23 Hexagonal bar wrench*
24 Rule with an iron fist
26 Common flour bag weight*
27 Airplane crash cause*
28 Basin or pool
30 Tongue twister by the sea-
   shore*
33 Among, to poets
35 Main dinner selections
36 Response to dis?
37 Mist bit
41 Debutante's crown
42 A _____ whipped cream*
46 Frequent Presidential candidate Paul

47 The die that Caesar cast
49 Metric vols.
50 Of inferior size or strength
51 Lager alternative
52 Dread and wonder
53 Certain US cars, for short
55 Ways
56 USFS backroad identification*
57 Nil, in Nogales
59 Grammarian's response to
   "One of you is chosen"
61 Comedian Poundstone of
   NPR's "Wait Wait"
62 Riverbank, in Ravenna; summer, in Warsaw
63 Dwarf garden guardian
65 Frank Lloyd Wright's 1936
   house style
67 With 76 Across, Donovan's #2
   hit in 1966*
68 Common can size*
69 Symbol that is the key to
   starred clues in this puzzle
72 Mary's hail
73 _____-Unis
75 The heart of Poe's short story*
76 See 67 Across*

79 Not any (archaic)
80 More secure
83 Oak fruit
85 South American capital
86 Globe
87 Light between red and green
88 Puts in the bank
90 Jodie Foster drama of 1994*
91 TV police intelligence squad
92 Valuable Pinochle cards
93 AARP targets
96 Kind of product support
97 Self esteem
98 Old TV's Jed Clampett, for one*
100 Facials
102 Power tool brand

104 _____ and outs
105 Em and others, to Dorothy
107 Blessed sign for a Broadway angel
108 On-site rug cleaners' specialty*
113 Rubbish
117 _____ ease*
118 Sprite
119 What makes dandelions hard to pull
121 Roosevelt or Mercury
122 Big book
123 Big bird
124 Big verse
125 Miss or infant follower
126 Large Cascade lake near

Willamette Pass*
127 Rats in reverse
128 Kind of ship or tale*
129 Kind of light or scare
130 Kind of mate or phone*
131 Cuts, as a tree*

DOWN

1 Univ. qualifying prep test
2 World champion's boast*
3 Want
4 Kind of car fuse
5 Nero's but
6 New York harbor island*
7 Backwoods storage spot
8 Springy
9 Verbatim
10 Contestants at a kind of bee*
11 Out of proper order
12 Shake riving tool
13 Eye-widening, poisonous herb*
14 Persian tongue
15 Bud or Miller option
16 Political family that won elections in Oregon, Arizona, Colorado, and New Mexico*
17 Irks*
25 Home on the range?
29 Fragrant homestead bloom
31 Ocean
32 Ride and Forth*
34 Ancient Indian capital
37 Sturm partner
38 Mountain ash
39 Where to find George Washington's portrait*
40 Prepares to golf
42 Twin
43 What never meet, in geometry*
44 Too ____ cut the mustard
45 Guy*
48 Warning, in Italy
50 Few, in France

54 Fatter
55 Crazies
58 Friendship
60 Kind of peace
61 Farfalle, for example
62 Flatten
64 Dawn goddess
66 Personal code, for short*
67 The shortest month
70 Rub it in, after a victory
71 What speakers don't want a case of
73 Cain's son
74 Foot bones
77 Greek alphabet ender
78 Porcine relaxation hangout*
80 What a rose may do, regardless of name*
81 Competently
82 Gave a meal to
84 Kisses a while
87 Kind of acid
89 Word with night, polo, or dress
93 One of two per state
94 Resell, as a stock
95 Lost one's knack
99 Acrimonious
100 Utility regulatory agcy.
101 Fortune teller
103 Lead-in to the Dance or the Flies
105 Completely occupied*
106 Indifferent to joy or grief
108 At ____ end
109 Distribute*
110 New World camel relative*
111 Michigan town and college
112 Flounder
114 Assistant
115 Odor*
116 ____ bells! (exclamation)*
120 Archer Wilhelm*

(Solution on page 337)

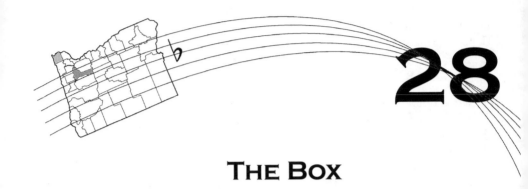

THE BOX

I loved my father, but he was a hoarder. As his middle child, an awkward daughter, I felt like another one of the bobble-head go-go dolls atop his refrigerator. One of the extra toasters lining his basement steps.

After Mom died he blamed the three of us grown children for the clutter, saying he'd have plenty of room if we only cleaned our stuff out of the attic.

What stuff?

Then the implanted device that jolted his heart gave out.

Tears.

Funeral.

My little sister Celeste inherited the old house in Keizer, so she had to deal with the stuff. Her husband Rick hauled eleven trailer loads to the dump just to make room for the garage sale. But Celeste also found a cardboard box with my name in the attic. One day she dropped it off on my porch.

I loved my father, but I left that box sitting out there for a month. I recognized his handwriting. In a slightly dyslexic mix of upper- and lower-case letters he had penned "GooDwiLL." Then he had crossed it out and written "CoRDeLia."

After my sophomore year at Clatsop Community College I had quietly moved in with my boyfriend Jon. When I confessed this at Christmas over highballs, Dad told me I'd always been trouble. He said I was now dirtying the family's good name.

The next day I drove back to Astoria and went straight to the county courthouse with Jon so I could get rid of the family name.

Too late.

By then Dad had cleaned all trace of me from my old bedroom. The box on the porch suggested that he had originally planned to send me to Goodwill, but had commuted the whore's sentence to exile in the attic. My stuff really had crowded his house. And now it crowded my porch.

In the dream my father was a surprisingly young man — perhaps thirty, with a full head of sandy blond hair and a boyish grin. I was so happy I could hardly sit still beside him on the front seat of the big blue Plymouth. Dad's college graduation tassels swayed from the rearview mirror. Earlier that week Mother had come home from the hospital with a baby sister that fussed and took up all her time. My older brother Doug had been given a bicycle to keep him out of the way. Dad had built me a play cupboard, complete with a toy sink. Now he was driving me to Fred Meyer to pick out paint.

"You'll paint it any color I want?" I asked.

"Any color at all. You can even pick out a few toys to outfit your new kitchen."

The dream skipped forward to a rainbow wall of paint sample strips. When I pointed out a light purple, the hardware man and my father exchanged smiles. But when I told Dad I didn't want toy pots and pans his smile dimmed.

"Honey, what are you going to do in your kitchen without pans?"

"I don't want to cook. I want to learn to draw so I can be an artist."

The colored pencils I pointed out in the store's art department cost an impossible fifty cents apiece. Dad stood in the aisle, frowning. We drove home in silence.

For years, as Celeste squalled and crawled and toddled, my purple cupboard became everything from a spaceship to a rabbit hutch, but never a kitchen. And my greatest adventures were in the worlds I colored cerulean blue and coral pink with the two prized pencils from my Dad.

The echo of that dream eventually persuaded me to bring the box indoors. My father had grown up an only child, so daughters had been as alien to him as Venusians. What might he have rescued from my childhood in that box?

Jon set the time capsule on the living room carpet as if it were a Christmas present delivered fifty years late. He took out his pocket knife to cut the strapping tape, but I shook my head. "Not yet."

"Why not?"

I just shook my head.

That night I dreamed again of Dad. This time he was in his late thirties, with a receding hairline and a few wrinkles beside his blue eyes. He wore a rumpled canvas hat with a shiny fishing lure. We were on the Little North Fork, staying at my uncle's cabin for Father's Day, like we did every June. Dad didn't know what to do with daughters, so he treated me like one of the boys. He baited my hook and gutted the silver steelhead I landed. In the evenings we'd sit around the kitchen table by kerosene lamplight, playing Seven-Toed Pete for matchsticks. I learned to bluff delight or dismay when the dealer turned up the two hole cards to complete our poker hands.

The year I turned twelve it became harder to bluff about who I was. I caught a beautiful twelve-inch fish from my favorite rock and called for Dad. He admired my catch, but then said, "You're old enough now, Cordelia. Kill it and clean it yourself. You know how. Just bend back the neck until you hear the spine snap."

That was the moment I had to choose: Was I a girl?

Dad watched with tight lips as I unhooked the fish and let it swim free. But the reprimand I was expecting never came.

"All right," I told Jon.

We brought the box into the living room and set our chairs on either side, as if for a child's tea party. I cut the strapping tape and

THE OREGON VARIATIONS

folded back the cardboard flaps.

On top lay Snookums, my childhood stuffed dog, worn to a brown lump.

Beneath were a set of four plastic plates with ballerina pictures.

Next came a "Learn And Do" school workbook from the Ginn Company. My few mistakes had been corrected in red by my second-grade teacher, Mrs. Stingley. "Is the duck happy to see Tom?" (I said no, but Mrs. Stingley said yes.) "Put a green X on the farm house." (I put an X on the barn instead of Tom's home.) Everything else I got right, including "Do trains plant wheat?"

I looked to Jon. "Even Goodwill doesn't want this junk."

He looked deeper into the box. "Hey, there's a talking book."

I shivered.

He took out *Chucko's Birthday Party*, a clown book about a man who magically appears in a sick girl's bedroom in an attempt to cheer her up. When Jon turned a plastic crank on the clown's red nose, Chucko's terrifying laugh rang through the decades.

"This thing's valuable," Jon said. "It's in mint condition."

"It's in mint condition because I feared it violently. What girl wants a creepy man appearing in her bedroom, laughing like a maniac? What was Dad thinking, giving me that?"

"It's just a clown," Jon said.

I closed my eyes and shook my head. "It's a nightmare."

"I could sell it on eBay in a minute. Hey, and look what else is in here."

I opened my eyes. Near the bottom of the box Jon had found an eighteen-inch-tall white plastic snowman. The toy had a stovepipe hat and a barrel-shaped metal grater in his belly.

At last I could smile. "It's my snow cone machine."

"How does it work?" Jon lifted the snowman's hat, exposing a hollow square chute in its head.

"You're supposed to put ice cubes under the hat and turn the crank on its back. Then I guess shaved ice comes out the stomach."

"You guess?"

My smile faded. "I never got to try it with real ice. It was a Christmas present. When I asked for ice, Dad said snow cones were for summer. He said no one makes snow cones in winter."

Jon frowned at the snowman "But you liked it anyway?"

"I shredded plastic bags with it."

We removed the rest of the box's contents in silence: A broken plastic Instamatic camera. A shiny pink belt. Half of a wooden backscratcher inscribed, "Chinatown."

Jon said, "It would have been better if there had really been a tape recorder in it."

I blinked. "A tape recorder?"

"Sure." He turned the empty carton around to show the picture of a 1970s reel-to-reel recorder on the side. "It's an old Sony box."

I leaned back, taking a deep breath. Now I recognized the carton. In the fall of my twelfth year — a few months after I quit fishing — Dad had announced that we were going to buy a tape recorder as a family project. He and my brother Doug were excited about this new technology, but I could have cared less. I was focused on drawing and skiing. I had filled my bedroom with pencil sketches of snowy mountains. I even joined a Boy Scout troop so I could try skiing for real. That was the year the Boy Scouts were experimenting with the idea of admitting girls. My neighbor Julie and I worked up the nerve to apply as Tenderfeet to Troop 34, the only local Scouts that hired a ski bus and gave lessons on winter weekends. All summer I picked strawberries and beans in the fields outside town to save money.

But then in September Dad announced he was contributing one hundred dollars to the family tape recorder project. Doug and I were supposed to chip in fifty dollars each. Mom apparently didn't count, and my little sister Celeste was just six, so she wouldn't have to contribute anything either.

For me, fifty dollars represented a month's hard labor in hot fields with no hat and no sunscreen. When I protested that I needed my savings for ski tickets, Dad laughed. Skiing was foolish, he said. A pastime for sissies.

The next day I confided my frustration to Julie. She told her Mom, who told my Mom. And my Mom told Dad.

I've never seen Dad so angry. What right did I have to go whining to the neighbors about our family projects? In this house everybody had to pull their weight. A family project was a privilege.

For the next two months I was grounded on Tuesday nights — precisely the evenings that Troop 34 met in the Episcopal church basement on High Street. And I still had to surrender fifty one-dollar bills from the locked lunch box in my purple cupboard.

The Sony tape recorder arrived the week before Halloween, special ordered through Pay Less. I wasn't allowed to use it because I might break the tape or jam the buttons. Instead Doug and my father mostly used it to record my little sister Celeste singing cute songs or saying the funniest things.

"Burn it," I told Jon.

"What?"

"Throw all this junk away and burn the box."

My husband looked at me with concern. "Slow down. At least we could recycle the cardboard."

In my dream that night Dad and I were both in our fifties. He now had a tonsure-like halo of gray hair. He handed me a present wrapped in light purple paper with pink holographic sparkles. I opened it to find a hardback copy of Madeleine L'Engle's *A Wrinkle in Time*, the young adult science fiction classic I had begged and begged for in the months leading up to my ninth Christmas.

"I'm learning, honey," Dad said with an apologetic smile.

"Too late." I shook my head. "You're dead."

In the morning, lying half awake, I remembered what had happened at the end of my twelfth year. The taboo on leaving the house on Tuesday nights ran out after Thanksgiving. That was when Troop 34 began their ski bus trips anyway. Somehow Julie and I found enough money to ski. We even managed to buy a few Christmas presents. To patch things up with Dad I bought him the neatest gift I could imagine.

It was only on Christmas morning that I began to have second thoughts. Dad held the large, flat, square present in his hands. "It doesn't rattle," he mused, "so I guess it can't be the tire chains I want. Maybe a calendar?"

He tore off the paper to reveal the latest record album by The Monkees, a television rock bank popular with preteen girls. Suddenly I realized he would never, ever play a record like this.

"Well," he said. "This seems like a gift we could all share. As family music."

After breakfast I put Chucko the talking clown on the desk in my husband's office. Jon really does enjoy selling oddities on the Internet.

Then I packed up the ballerina plates and all the other detritus of my girlhood bedroom. I carried the Sony box up the stairs to our attic. It wasn't easy finding a place for it. Over the years the attic has grown cluttered with boxes, mostly with stuff from the kids.

In my Dad's final years he began learning to let go of things. When we came to visit those last few times he surprised us by bringing out the family treasures he had packed away greedily years ago: the antique gate-leg table, the wind-up chiming clock, the wall barometer. "Take it," he would tell us, to our amazement.

I balanced the Sony box on a rocking horse. Then I began backing down the creaky folding staircase. Before I pulled the string to switch off the light, I took one last look at all the stuff I had hoarded in my attic.

The name "CoRDeLia" leered out at me from the teetering horse, the cry of a lost kingdom.

A great loneliness made me shiver.

I fear the coming dark.

I miss Dad.

TO SAY NOTHING OF THE DOG

"Which one are we supposed to harvest?" Tyrone asked. It was March 21, the equinox when all the world hangs in the balance between light and dark.

Roy put down the binoculars and looked again at the photograph. The face had a high forehead, a flat nose, and worried-looking wrinkles at the corners of his eyes. He might be any of the three men who were now standing in a snowy parking lot, bundled up in ski clothes for the four-day trek around Crater Lake.

"The guy in the red coat, I think," Roy said.

Even with the defroster on high, the windshield of the Dodge Ram pickup kept fogging. Roy wiped it with a paper napkin from the burger bag. Most of the two dozen cars in the plowed parking lot behind the National Park gift shop had brought kids so they could throw snowballs and build snowmen. Foreign tourists took pictures of each other. A few people ventured along a fifty-foot path through the drifts to shiver at the rim viewpoint on the edge of an unearthly blue void. In winter the lake looked like the hole of a frosted doughnut from outer space.

Only about a hundred people a year are daring or foolish enough to try skiing around the lake in winter. Most of those who set out turn back. Occasionally someone dies. Roy and Tyrone's client had said it would be the perfect spot for a hit job, but now Roy had his doubts. "I wish they'd take off their damned hats. Then at least we could tell them apart."

"Why not harvest all three?" Tyrone asked.

Roy shook his head. "Bad luck to waste meat."

The three men organizing packs, poles, and skis beside the Toyota SUV wore matching black knit caps embroidered with the letters CKS, which stood for "Crazy Kowalski Survivors." They had been friends since high school, when they had wrestled together for Bend under Coach Kowalski, a nearly neckless ex-Marine who taught US History while reading *Soldier of Fortune* with his feet on the desk. Since then they had gotten together each year on the fourth weekend of March, close enough to when they all had birthdays that their wives couldn't veto an all-guy trip. Usually they skied to a cabin where they could stay up late talking and drinking. Once they backpacked across Kauai. Another time they borrowed a sailboat to explore the San Juan Islands.

Now that they were turning forty, they had chosen a more serious athletic challenge—skiing thirty-three miles around an exploded volcano. Fifty-foot drifts covered the park road they would follow. Their backpacks bulged with thick down sleeping bags, thermal pads, and survival gear. Snow shovels and blinking avalanche beacons were strapped on the outside of the packs. For three nights and four days they would be out of cell phone range. If they needed help, there was no shortcut back.

The park rangers who had issued them permits that morning said everyone went clockwise around the lake.

"Let's go counter-clockwise," Josh suggested. He liked breaking rules. Still built like a wrestler, he butchered bison on his desert ranch near the lonely outpost of Burns Junction.

"But I thought—" Matt began, and then stopped. Matt had wrestled at a hundred and four pounds in school. Never a risk taker, he had become a computer wonk for a law firm in Scappoose, north of Portland. Weekends he escaped his wife by lathing candlesticks from exotic hardwoods in his basement.

"Wait," Gerald said slowly. He didn't mind risk, although his gambles rarely paid off. He ran a bakery and a bed and breakfast that comprised much of downtown Halfway, on the hippie fringe of the Wallowa Mountains. He sized up Josh. "Why do you want to ski around the lake backwards? Are you trying to throw followers off the track?"

The big butcher shook his head. "We're turning forty, old man. I'm in favor of anything that goes against the clock."

Tyrone scratched his stubble beard, puzzled. "I thought you said they'd ski the other way."

"It doesn't matter." Roy turned off the engine and opened the pickup door. A cold wind dusted snow across the floor mat. "The lake's round. We'll meet them on the far side."

"If we can figure out which one he is I'd rather do it here, as soon as he's out of sight of the lodge."

Roy pulled two pairs of snowshoes from the truck bed. "Pretend we're hunting elk. You've got to circle round and catch them by surprise. We're being paid extra to do this right."

Tyrone disliked dealing with clients, so he mostly left that end of the business to his brother. Clients were a pain. The East Coast game hunters they guided in fall fussed about heated tents and single-malt Scotch. The Hollywood fly fishermen who hired them in summer demanded barbecues and froo-froo wine. But it was worse in the off season, when the only clients were women. They weren't interested in hunting or fishing at all. They just wanted you to kill their husbands in very specific ways. Ten thousand dollars apiece almost made it worthwhile.

"They don't let you hunt elk in national parks," Tyrone muttered, strapping snowshoes onto his Danner boots.

Roy zipped the client's antique Colt revolver into a pocket of his brother's backpack. "We're not hunting elk."

The three Kowalski Survivors did not talk much until nightfall. Their packs were heavy, loaded with four days of supplies. Five miles in, where the snowed-under road skirts the cliffs of Vidae Ridge, the tracks ahead of them showed that day-trippers had dared to continue skiing the road to Sun Notch, rather than take the recommended avalanche detour, which added a mile.

Matt was dripping sweat, but still argued for the safety of the longer route. Josh wavered. Meanwhile Gerald simply plowed ahead, scoffing. So they all wound up crossing what turned out to be an icy avalanche chute. Crumbling snow cornices on the cliffs above had ripped out the orange snow poles marking the road. More rock and snow could come down any minute. They kicked their skis' metal edges into the icy slope, struggling for purchase.

At the Sun Notch viewpoint they were shivering so hard from exhaustion and relief that they didn't even take out their cameras. Sunlight had broken through the clouds, turning the lake into a glowing blue bowl. Phantom Ship, a small volcanic crag, jutted from the edge of the blue as if it really were a ghost ship, without sails or crew.

Someone had built snow shelters in the pass, perhaps the previous weekend, but the crude igloos had sagged or collapsed.

"We can't camp here anyway," Matt said.

The two others looked at him questioningly. They had outvoted Matt about the avalanche detour, and he had been right.

"If we're going to make it around the lake in four days," Matt said, "we need to put in at least two more miles."

The final two miles were an uphill slog. When the road crested a broad, windswept ridge they dropped their packs in the lee of a cluster of bonsaied whitebark pines. Without a word Gerald began assembling the white gas stove. He was the baker. Everyone knew it was his job to start dinner and soup and tea. Meanwhile Matt and Josh set up the two tents, as far apart as they reasonably could.

They ate freeze-dried beef stroganoff in steaming bowls, hunkering in a tree well as the sky turned red and died. Then, by the shivering beams of their head lamps, they all crawled into what they called the "party tent"—a four-season nylon dome full of Thermarest pads and thick down sleeping bags.

Matt uncapped the first night's bottle, a plastic fifth of Black Velvet. "To the Survivors," Matt said, distributing metal shot glasses.

"May they live long and prosper," Gerald added.

"To say nothing of the dog," Josh said. He tossed back his

THE OREGON VARIATIONS

whiskey and held out the little metal cup for a refill. "It's your bottle, Matt, so you go first. Spill."

Matt knew he wasn't being asked to spill whiskey, but rather a story. He filled all three of the cups and sighed.

"Come on," Gerald prodded. "Last year you were running around with a hot little receptionist from the law firm. Something to keep your candlestick waxed."

Matt had been dreading this moment. The three friends used their outings to catch each other up on their lives—particularly their sex lives.

"Well?" Josh asked.

"It's all over with Helen. She's crazy. I finally cut it off."

Gerald raised his eyebrows. "You cut off your candlestick?"

"No. Helen started missing work, wearing black mesh, and yelling about snakes. The lawyers fired her, and so did I." Matt frowned into his cup. "When I told my wife about the whole thing, she blew up. Home's been hell ever since."

Josh whistled.

"Why are the sexy ones always nuts?" Gerald mused.

"But that's just it," Matt said. "Helen really might be psycho. She's been sending me threatening notes, saying if she can't have me, no one can."

Josh nodded. "Then she's definitely nuts."

"I'm not kidding," Matt retorted, too loud for a small tent in the snowy wilderness. He lowered his voice. "I'm afraid of what she might do."

Later that night, when the full moon lit the tents like Chinese lanterns and the wind howled in the pine branches, Josh thought: It is not Helen that Matt should fear, but rather his powder keg of a wife. She might slip him a toxic cocktail one dark night in his woodshop. Then she could blame the crazy girlfriend and be done with both of them. At least here, in the lonely heart of God's country, Matt would be safe.

Roy and Tyrone had a difficult day as well, snowshoeing in the opposite direction around the lake. After trudging three miles they reached a different avalanche detour, on the side of a triangular butte called The Watchman. They dropped their packs beside a blue trail sign that pointed out the options. The detour route dived into a wooded valley, losing elevation they would later have to regain. The alternative was to continue straight, but drifts and avalanches had buried all trace of the road, leaving a steep sidehill. Skis might traverse a slope like that, but they had snowshoes . The slope would tilt their ankles at a painful angle.

"Let's camp here," Tyrone suggested. "We can take the detour tomorrow."

"You got the tent?"

Tyrone rolled his eyes. He opened his pack and pulled out a tan plastic bag, so new it still dangled tags: "Cabela's," "39.99," and "Made in Korea."

Roy loosened the string clasp and dumped the tent onto the snow. Flimsy aluminum pole sections and a plastic bag of pencil-sized pegs clattered onto a roll of desert-camo-colored plastic.

"This is shit," Roy said. He should never have trusted his younger brother to buy supplies. Usually they slept in a two-room wall tent on outings. This pup tent would blow away in the first gust.

"It looks better when it's set up," Tyrone offered.

Roy shook his head, then looked uphill. "There's a lookout on top of this butte. Let's try there."

Tyrone stared. "Are you kidding?" He was tired, and not in as good shape as his brother. He wanted to lose forty pounds, but not by climbing mountains in the snow.

"It'll have a roof and a stove." Roy was already putting on his pack.

The climb was only half a mile, but steep enough that they had to rest several times. Near the top, winds had sculpted the snow into frozen, cresting waves. Three inches of rime frost encrusted every needle and twig of the tortured trees, as if a Christmas decorator had gone mad with a flocking machine.

The fire lookout consisted of a wooden cabin atop a ground floor built of stone. Roy snowshoed around the upper story's railed porch, peering in through slits in the locked shutters.

"Nothing in here but a fire-spotting table," Roy called down to his brother. "The beds must be in the basement. Check the door."

"It's padlocked," Tyrone called back.

"Well, shoot it off. You need to practice with that cowboy pistol anyway."

Tyrone stood back and blasted six shots at the oversize lock, jerking it around but otherwise having no effect.

"Huh. Works in the movies."

By now Roy had tromped up for a look. "Try aiming at the hasp."

Tyrone reloaded, his fingers clumsy from the cold, and emptied another six rounds into the door frame.

This time the wood splintered enough that Roy's boot sent the door swinging. The cavern inside was so dark it took the brothers a minute to realize it was a museum. Signs described the lonely life of a fire lookout. The bunks had woolen blankets. A stack of firewood stood by the stove. It was better than a tent.

Roy took an oversized pair of binoculars down from a shelf. "From up here we can watch them coming. We'll stay two nights. Then they should camp within walking distance on the third."

Tyrone was already arranging kindling in the cast-iron stove, his cold fingers fumbling. "But we still don't know which of the three to take out."

Roy took a lighter from a Velcroed pocket on his thigh. "We don't need to know what he looks like."

"We don't? Why?"

Roy handed the lighter to his brother. "Because he snores."

Tyrone clicked a flame. "So?"

"Our client says you can hear him for miles. At home he uses a machine with a face mask to help him breathe at night. But out here the man's a buzz saw. The other two guys set him up in a little tent all by himself, far enough away they can't hear a thing."

"Oh, my." The flickering kindling lit Tyrone's crooked smile from the shadows. "This hunt might be easier than I thought."

The next morning the Survivors awoke to a still, cold dawn. High ice clouds streaked a steel-gray sky. Despite the cold and the previous evening's whiskey, Matt hummed as he melted a pot of snow on the hissing burner. Telling his story to his friends and sleeping twelve hours had pushed Helen into a different world. Soon there would be steaming hot cocoa and a double packet of oatmeal with maple sugar. Even the muscles in his legs seemed to remember the strain of the previous day with a certain satisfied pride.

By nine thirty they had packed up the tents and hit the trail, following the orange poles that would eventually tell snowplow drivers where to find the Rim Road. With no avalanche slopes ahead the three skiers made good time, kicking and gliding, taking turns at the front to break trail.

The route wove in and out to the crater rim in big loops, like the petals of a gigantic flower, traversing the glacial valleys that had been amputated when the mountain blew up thousands of years ago.

They stopped for granola bars and brownies at a dip in the rim called Kerr Notch. Already Phantom Ship had shrunk to a toy. Wizard Island, the cinder cone island beneath The Watchman, had dialed around the lake's big circular face to twelve o'clock.

By four, when they skied to a viewpoint beside Cloudcap, they had covered more than nine miles and were ready to camp. It was still early enough, however, that they had time to sculpt more luxurious digs than the night before. Matt shoveled a sunken ice bar with stools. Gerald dug a kitchen with a cookstove island. Josh tramped out a circular platform for the party tent on one side of the central restaurant, and built a smaller deck for the snoring tent over a low ridge on the other side.

Gerald, the baker, astonished them by heating mysterious sealed pouches and serving a four-star dinner of smoked salmon, rice pilaf, and chocolate mousse. He screwed together the bases and cups of three collapsible plastic wineglasses and poured pinot gris from what looked like a milk carton.

"Skoal," Gerald said, raising his glass.

"To the CK Survivors," Matt said solemnly.

"To say nothing of the dog," Josh added. The three friends

clicked their plastic glasses together and tucked into the meal without another word.

Gerald had brought the bottle that night, so they all knew it would be his turn to spill.

He said nothing as they cleaned up after dinner. A gray sunset turned the lake from mercury to lead. Only when they were in the party tent, passing a small silver flask of Grand Marnier did Gerald sigh. "I think Linda's trying to kill me."

"Linda?" Josh asked, amazed. "Your wife Linda? But you were getting along great. You built her a love nest halfway to paradise. You bake her pastries. What's not to like?"

Gerald frowned. "The bed and breakfast in Halfway is struggling. It's more work than she thought. But that's not the problem."

"Well?" Matt asked. "What is?"

"Me, I guess." Gerald hung his head. The flashlight on his forehead surrounded his face with a pale aura. "Linda wanted kids. When she turned thirty-nine she said she was running out of time. She blamed me. And I guess she was right."

Matt and Josh exchanged a silent glance. This was no time for a funny comment.

"She left me three months ago, but she must have been experimenting for a while, because she's six months pregnant, and it isn't mine."

Josh nearly whistled, but changed it to a breathy exhale. "So she's living with this guy?"

"Some idiot truck driver in Baker City. She's been pestering me for a divorce. She says she needs to marry the real father." Gerald looked up angrily. "But why can't I serve as this child's father? I've always wanted a kid too. And I love Linda. I need her. I can't run a bakery and a hotel by myself."

"You won't give her a divorce?" Matt asked.

"Why should I?"

"Motherhood does weird things to women," Matt said.

"Has she threatened you?" Josh asked.

Gerald rubbed his temples. "She says she won't be my wife anymore, but I can decide whether she'll be my divorcee or my widow."

Josh puzzled about this a moment. "If she's your widow, then — "
Gerald nodded. "Then I'd be dead."

Roy and Tyrone spent a leisurely day making themselves at
home in the Museum of Lookout Life. Tyrone fired up the woodstove until it glowed. Then he cooked a mess of pancakes and
methodically ate the entire pile. Every hour or so Roy took the
binoculars upstairs to the porch to look around. The binoculars
were a US Navy model with lenses the size of teacups. He rested
it on the railing while he scanned the lake's rim. A little after four
in the afternoon he spotted an orange dot that could only be the
three skiers' dome tent. They had made it halfway around the lake,
right on schedule. Their client had wanted her husband to commit
suicide there, at the farthest point from civilization. But it would
work just as well to let them ski another day until they camped
nearer to The Watchman. Roy was willing to let Mohammed come
to the mountain.

Roy went inside to tell his brother, and found him opening a
bottle of Jack Daniels. "Uh uh," Roy said, taking it away. "No
booze before a hunt. Think of your aim."

"I have been thinking," Tyrone said slowly.

"About what?"

"About this guy we're supposed to harvest. Is he bad?"

"He's stupid."

"Yeah, but is he bad?" Tyrone scratched his stubble beard. "All
the others have been bad people. You know, like Papa."

Roy set the bottle carefully on a shelf. Their father had in fact
been a bad person, with a violent temper. They had lived in a
cabin on the edge of Prineville, up against the dry pine woods of
the Ochoco National Forest. Their father had found work in the
Les Schwab Tire Center, back when Les Schwab still ran his tire
empire in person, wearing a white cowboy hat and demanding
"sudden service" from his employees. Workers had to run — not
walk — while on the job, and smile at every customer. Their father had bottled up his anger at work, but he uncorked it at home,
drinking heavily, shouting at the boys, and slapping their mother.

She wore nice things in defense, thinking that a low-cut blouse or a satin choker might stay his hand. One night, after he emptied an entire bottle, she put on her best armor, a fake chinchilla top that poofed out her chest with a haze of soft fur. Somehow this made their father even angrier. He attacked her with a piece of firewood, bludgeoning her until she fell unconscious on the stone hearth.

The two boys had watched, terrified, from a crack in the den door. Roy was thirteen, tall and skinny for his age. Tyrone was only eleven, but already weighed more. Never had they seen their father so crazed. Blood trickled from a gash by their mother's ear. She moaned faintly with each breath.

Their father put down the firewood. For a moment the boys thought he was going to kneel beside her — to say he was sorry, to tend to her wounds, to call for help. But instead he picked up the fireplace poker, an ugly length of bent rebar, and weighed it ominously in his hands.

"He's going to kill her!" Roy whispered.

"What can we do?" Tyrone asked.

Roy walked across the den to the elk antlers that served as a gun rack. He was tall enough now to reach the thirty-thirty their father kept loaded in case of intruders. Both he and Tyrone had taken hunter safety classes after school, and they had both gone on hunts with their uncles, but only the younger brother had actually shot a deer.

Roy held the rifle out in both hands. "You're the better shot. Scare him away until he sobers up. Then we can call a doctor for Mom."

Tyrone nodded. His older brother always seemed to know what to do, even when Tyrone himself felt confused.

Tyrone took the gun and pushed open the door.

Their father was supposed to have been scared. He was supposed to have run away. Instead he gave the boy a murderous look and rushed at him with the poker.

Tyrone really was a good shot. He aimed for the heart. A jury later ruled that he had fired the rifle in self defense.

For the next five years the two boys kept their mother from the indignity of food stamps by poaching meat off the National Forest. Tyrone racked up enough of a reputation for trophies that Roy suggested they start a guide service together. And then it had been Roy's idea to expand the guide service to help women like their mother—battered, cheated women who needed help to free themselves from bad men.

"Is he bad?" Tyrone asked again. "The guy who snores. Is he a bad person?"

Roy didn't turn to face him. "He's twenty thousand dollars bad."

The third day proved difficult for the three skiers. The snow had frozen overnight into a hard crust, so the lead skier kept breaking through. Matt was light enough that he could skate on the surface for several steps, but Gerald and Josh had little choice but to plow ahead like icebreakers, leaving a wake of buckled plates.

They stopped for a lunch of salted cashews and dried pears at Cleetwood Cove. In a few months, crowds of tourists would be hiking a dusty path from a parking lot down to a tour boat dock. But now only a Clark's nutcracker cawed as the skiers crunched slowly by.

By four thirty they had skied as far as the Devils Backbone, a fin of lava rock a mile short of The Watchman. They were too exhausted to go farther.

While Matt and Josh pitched the tents Gerald set up the stove and dug a circular pit.

Matt scratched his head when he saw the hole. "So what's this? A scale model of Crater Lake?"

Josh jumped in and sat on a snow bench that ran around the rim. "Looks like a sunken dining room to me."

"We could use it as a dining room," Gerald replied, "But it's actually a tub."

"A tub?" Matt raised his eyebrows. He had felt better after confessing his marital problems, and Gerald obviously did too.

Grinning, Gerald handed Matt a steaming bowl of lentil soup. "Isn't that why you make candlesticks? Because I'm a baker and Josh is a butcher?"

Matt objected, "All you two ever talk about are the damned candlesticks. I also make bowls and pens."

Josh rolled his eyes. "After a hard day of skiing, I'd rather unwind in a hot tub than a cold one, but if it comes with soup, I'm good."

As they ate their soup, cloud streamers overhead flamed from gold to red. Josh watched the spectacle. Then he tilted his head and frowned.

"What's wrong?" Matt asked.

"It's just—do you see the little lookout building on top of The Watchman?"

"Yes."

"It looks like there's smoke coming from it."

"Probably a cloud," Matt said.

Gerald shrugged. "A fire in a lookout? Who ya gonna call?" He gathered the soup bowls. "OK, dinner is couscous with green curry, but I suggest we eat in the party tent. Assuming, of course, that Josh has brought something to spill."

They retreated to the big dome tent, balancing their bowls of couscous as they knocked the snow off their boots and crawled in through the vestibule's nylon flap.

Josh unveiled a plastic bottle of Yukon Jack and poured a finger into each of three coffee mugs.

Matt said, "Cheers."

"To the Survivors," Gerald said.

Josh added, "To say nothing of the dog."

While the others drank, Matt paused. "The dog. What dog? Why do you keep bringing up a dog?"

"I don't," Josh said, chuckling. "I have never once mentioned a dog."

"No, Matt's right," Gerald put in. "Every time we toast you say, 'To say nothing of the dog.' What the hell is that about?"

"Actually," Josh said, refilling the cups, "It has to do with my required annual story."

Matt looked at him steadily. "Spill."

"There's nothing to spill. At least nothing you want to hear.

After twenty years of marriage, Sara and I have reached this happy plateau where we can do whatever we want. Isaac and Kaitlin have gone away to college in Bend and Corvallis. The bison business is doing fine. I butcher one a week. Sara does her watercolors. We're even adding the solarium we've always wanted to brighten up the ranch house in winter. Sara drives three hours into Bend every few days, ordering skylights and flooring and whatnot."

Josh paused, a lump in his throat. "This trip around Crater Lake just caps it off. Sara and I honeymooned at the lodge twenty years ago. It's still my favorite place. And now, coming here with my buddies, skiing hard amid all this beauty, it's more than great. It's perfect."

The three ate couscous for a moment in silence. Then Gerald asked, "But what about the dog?"

"It's like your 'Three Men in a Tub,'" Josh said. "Sara gave me a book to read. It's called, *Three Men in a Boat, To Say Nothing of the Dog.*"

Gerald frowned. "Your wife gave you a book? And you actually read it?"

"Oh, come on. I can read. It was a thin book anyway, a travelogue. I guess it was the first of its kind, written in the 1800s in England by a guy named Jerome K. Jerome. It's a riot, about three guys who row up the Thames from London with a dog."

"And this is like us because—?" Matt asked.

"It isn't. That's my point. There is no dog. No one is dogging our steps, trying to nip our heels. Not you, Matt, with your girlfriend, or you, Gerald, with your wife. Especially not here, at Crater Lake."

Roy put down the binoculars, frowning. Did he smell smoke? He went downstairs and found Tyrone crouched by the stove, blowing on kindling. "What the hell are you doing, building a fire? You're supposed to be packing."

"I was cold," Tyrone said.

"Well, put it out. You'll get warm enough snowshoeing. They've set up camp on the other side of the Devils Backbone."

"Is that far?"

"It's two miles with the avalanche detour. And then we'll still have to get back to the truck. We've got a long night ahead of us."

Tyrone crossed his arms. "I don't want to do it. Not unless you explain more about why."

"I'll explain on the way. Just get going."

Reluctantly Tyrone cinched his pack together. He had always relied on his older brother for guidance. Now he was beginning to wonder if he had trusted him too much.

As soon as they were actually on their snowshoes, tromping down the mountain in the twilight, talking became difficult. Then Roy struck off through the dark forest of the avalanche detour, shining a flashlight at tree trunks to find the blue diamond route markers. Tyrone lagged behind, puffing too hard to talk.

Finally, when the moonlit crag of the Devils Backbone loomed against the stars, Tyrone simply stopped. To one side, the lava ridge plunged a thousand feet along a cliff face into the lake. Stars reflected in the dark water far below.

Roy turned, whispering loudly, "Come on. We're almost at the camp."

"I know," Tyrone said. "And I'm not going a step closer until you explain."

Roy walked back with an exasperated sigh.

"Well?" Tyrone asked. "Is the snoring guy bad?"

"Not exactly bad," Roy admitted. "He's just boring and clueless. His wife wants better."

Tyrone lifted his head. "If you harvest all the boring, clueless people in the world, you'd waste a lot of meat."

"It's hard to explain."

"Try."

Roy held up his hands in frustration. "She's trying to make it easy on the guy."

"Doesn't sound easy to me."

"I'm telling the truth. She doesn't want to hurt him."

"So she wants us to shoot him with his own gun and make it look like suicide?" Tyrone shook his head. "I'm not buying it."

"Tyrone! Trust me on this."

"I've trusted you too much. You can do whatever you want, but I'm out." Tyrone set down his backpack, unzipped a pocket, and took out the antique Colt revolver. He held it out handle first.

"All right." Roy took the pistol and slipped it into a pocket of his parka. "I'll deal with it myself."

Tyrone studied him skeptically. "You're going to shoot him anyway?"

"There are worse things than shooting an idiot."

Suddenly a light flashed through the trees. Boots crunched in the snow beside the lava outcropping. A voice called out, "Hello? Is somebody out here?"

"Jesus Christ," Tyrone said.

"Who?" The headlight swiveled toward them.

"Aw, shit." Roy held up his hand to block the glare.

"Hey, you guys must be really lost." A man in ski boots and a puffy red coat walked closer. "Are you all right?"

"Yeah," Roy said. "We're camped back toward The Watchman. We just came out for a moonlight stroll to see the lake."

"Beautiful, isn't it?" The man's head lamp shone directly into their eyes, making it hard to see much of his face. Which of the three skiers was he?

Roy ventured, "I thought we heard someone snoring. Was that you?"

The man laughed and looked aside. Roy held up his flashlight. The two brothers immediately recognized the man from the photograph. He had a flat nose, smooth cheeks, and wrinkled eyes. He wasn't handsome, but he wasn't ugly either.

"Well, people say I snore, but you must have heard something else. I was just taking a leak before going to bed. Then I heard voices out here by the rock." Josh laughed. "Other than the guys I'm skiing with, you're the first people I've seen in three days."

"Really."

"I just can't get over it, finding somebody out here at this time of night."

Roy reached into his pocket. "We came for you, Josh Durbin."

Tyrone raised a hand to stop him. "Don't!"

But Roy shook his arm free and pulled the gun out by its barrel. Then he held it out to Josh, handle first. "Your wife Sara asked us to bring you this."

Josh stared at them, open mouthed. "My old Colt! What on earth?"

Tyrone was staring too, confused. This had been the perfect opportunity for a harvest. Roy could have shot him, or thrown him over the edge, or both. Wasn't that what Roy wanted?

Josh examined the pistol, turning it over in the glare of his head lamp. "It really is my butchering gun. Sara asked you to bring this thing to me all the way out here? Why?"

"She's left you, Josh," Roy's voice was as cold and dark as the lake. "She left you because you're dull. You're not evil, she admits that, but you're boring and clueless and she couldn't stand being trapped out on a lonely, god-forsaken desert ranch with you anymore."

"But she has her watercolors," Josh objected.

"Which you never understood."

"And she's building us a solarium."

Roy shook his head. "Sara hasn't been driving into Bend to order materials for a solarium. She's been moving in with a cardiologist who likes golf, Baroque music, and travel."

"Baroque music?" Josh repeated, bewildered.

"They've bought a condominium together where she can paint the mountains and bicycle along the Deschutes River."

"I don't believe it," Josh said angrily. "You're lying. What about our children?"

"She'll be closer to them in Bend. What were their names? Anyway, at first they didn't like the idea of you two splitting up. But now they've seen how much happier she is with the new guy, and after all, they're kids. They wound up taking sides. Of course they chose their mother. They've already agreed to spend Christmas with her at the doctor's time-share apartment in Los Cabos."

Josh faltered, "I still don't see—"

"You don't see because you're clueless!" Roy shouted. "That's why she left you. Look at us. Look at your Colt. Why else are we here? Your wife is gone. It's over!"

Roy paused to catch his breath. When he spoke again his voice was low. "That's what we came to say."

Josh stood there, staring at the gun. "But why would she send my Colt?"

Roy shook his head. "Eventually, even an idiot like you will figure it out." Then he turned to go, trudging back into the woods the way he had come.

Tyrone hurried after him. When he caught up he clapped his brother on the back. "That was brilliant!"

Roy snowshoed on in silence.

Tyrone lowered his voice. "For a minute I thought you were actually going to harvest him. But now we don't have to shoot anybody. When he realizes why his wife sent the gun, he'll do it himself. You're a genius!"

Roy stopped, his eyes narrowed with anger. "She paid extra to have this job done right."

"We're doing it even better! She wanted everyone to think the guy committed suicide. This way he really does, and we still get ten grand apiece."

Roy shook his head. "He was boring and clueless, but he wasn't supposed to know. You were supposed to turn out his lights—*bang!*—here in his happy place. She said it should be as quick and bittersweet as putting down an old family dog."

A gunshot boomed from the woods behind them. The report began echoing off the lake's cliffs, a cadence of smaller pops.

"Damn." Roy spat. "We made the poor bastard die worse than a dog. Damn it all. This is the last job I do for a woman who wants out."

But Tyrone had cocked his head. "That didn't sound right."

"What?" Roy said. "I'm telling you, twenty thousand dollars is shit."

"Not that. Shh! Come on," Tyrone set off at a run, following their old tracks back toward The Watchman. "This story isn't over."

Mystified, Roy watched his brother disappear into the woods.

Then the gun boomed again.

Josh's second gunshot came closer, chipping bark from a hemlock as it zinged past.

It had been a long time since Roy had run so fast.

Quodlibet:
About the Variations

Oregon is its own inspiration, but in writing this book I was also inspired by the symmetry of Bach's *Goldberg Variations* and the loneliness of Franz Kafka's short stories. I decided to attempt a fugue, using the structure of Bach's music and the theme of loneliness to tell the story of a place and its people.

For my Oregon guidebooks I hiked every trail I could find in the state. I suppose I also spent that time plotting these tales.

Bach's variations begin with a lonely aria. Then he inverts and shifts the aria's seven-note theme in two cycles of fifteen variations. Along the way Bach uses all manner of musical styles, from dances to dirges. To match that structure, the *Oregon Variations* open with an "Aria for Tenderfeet" that states the theme in the second sentence. After that, the stories shift voice, point of view, genre, and setting in two cycles of fifteen.

I've even included a couple of modern fairy tales. "The Vortex" can be read as an updated version of Jack in the Beanstalk, with Amazon as the giant. On the opposite side of the variations' cycle, "Beaver Clan" has an echo of Hamelin's pied piper. But in this version Beaverton is beset by an infestation of mall rats, rather than actual rodents. Either way, you have to pay the piper.

The first variation, the "Eastbank Elegies," is actually a found poem. I simply wrote down the conversational fragments I overheard while strolling Portland's riverfront path one sunny spring day. In musical terms it's an overture, a medley of snippets from the tunes you'll be hearing later.

Some of the stories contain elements of magical realism. In "Aria for Tenderfeet," for example, Jake Dobson is astonished to find that his missing toes have regrown. But were they perhaps there all the time? The disability that trapped him on his ranch may have been psychological. Jake's transformation recalls Kafka's "Metamorphosis," where the narrator awakes from uneasy dreams to find himself transformed into a giant cockroach. Likewise, in "The Starter," is Gabby really an alien who reproduces by means of bread dough? Or is she a metaphor for the narrator's recurring cancer?

The fifteenth story in this collection, halfway through the book, has no words at all. I simply offer two photographs of Crater Lake. I think that's worth a few thousand words. And consider that the pictures are in opposite seasons, on opposite sides of the lake, at the opposite end of the variation cycle from a story about circling the lake in opposite directions.

If you'd like to delve deeper into *The Oregon Variations*, I've posted additional discussion points at *www.oregonhiking.com* under "Short Stories."

Although each of the stories can stand alone, together they might well seem an illusive batch — a hall of mirrors.

Perhaps mirrors are why our country is so lonely: Oregon's stories can be as confounding as inside-out trees, houses with airy crowns trapped in heartwood walls. All the more reason for us to go back through the front door together.

Solution to puzzle on page 134

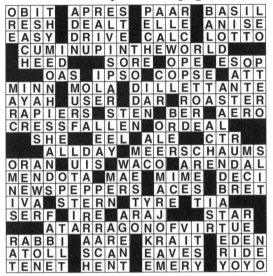

Solution to puzzle on page 304

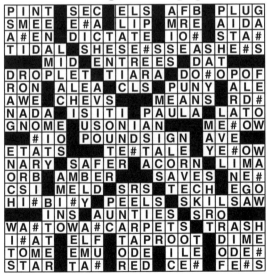

ALSO BY
WILLIAM L. SULLIVAN

Novels

The Case of D.B. Cooper's Parachute
The Ship in the Hill
The Case of Einstein's Violin
A Deeper Wild

Adventure Memoirs

Listening for Coyote
Cabin Fever

History

Oregon's Greatest Natural Disasters
Hiking Oregon's History

Guides

Oregon Trips & Trails
Oregon Favorites
The Atlas of Oregon Wilderness
100 Hikes in Northwest Oregon & Southwest Washington
100 Hikes in the Central Oregon Cascades
100 Hikes in Southern Oregon
100 Hikes / Travel Guide: Oregon Coast & Coast Range
100 Hikes / Travel Guide: Eastern Oregon

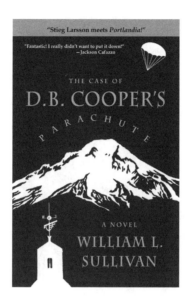

THE CASE OF
D.B. COOPER'S PARACHUTE

What became of D.B. Cooper, the hijacker who parachuted with $200,000 in 1971? In Sullivan's novel a Portland police detective discovers there now appear to be two Coopers, one of them a blackmailing murderer. Voodoo doughnuts and Shanghai tunnels come into play before the real Cooper is unmasked.

THE SHIP IN THE HILL

Based on the actual excavation of a Viking burial ship, this carefully researched historical novel tells the story of two women struggling with power and love—an American archeologist unearthing the ship in southern Norway in 1904 and Asa of Agthir, the queen who sailed it a thousand years earlier in a quest to unify Norway against the Vikings.